Large Print v. 2
Le Carre
The honourable schoolboy

DATE DUE			
DEC 1 1986	FEB 2 0 '92		
APR 1 8 1987	DEC 3 0 1992		
NOV 13 1989	Brevich '93		
NOV 13 1990			
DEC 1 0 1989	JUN 1 4 199		
MAY 2 6 1990	MAY 2 5 1994		
JUL 2 8 '90			
FEB 2 1 '91			
MAR 1 1 '91			
JUN 1 5 199			
Harsh 6/2			
10-13-18			

THE
HONOURABLE
SCHOOLBOY

Also Available in Large Print
by John le Carré

Tinker, Tailor, Soldier, Spy

THE
HONOURABLE
SCHOOLBOY

John le Carré

VOLUME TWO

G.K.HALL &CO.

 Boston, Massachusetts

1977

Library of Congress Cataloging in Publication Data

Le Carré, John, 1931 -
  The honourable schoolboy.

  "Published in large print."
  1. Large type books. I. Title.
[PZ4.L4526Ho 1977b] [PR6062.E33] 823'.9'14 77-51484
ISBN 0-8161-6539-4

Grateful acknowledgment is made to Random House, Inc., and to Faber & Faber Ltd. for permission to reprint four lines of "September 1, 1939" from *The Collected Poetry of W. H. Auden* by W. H. Auden. Copyright 1940 by W. H. Auden.

Published in Large Print by arrangement with Alfred A. Knopf, Inc.

Set in Photon 18 pt Crown

PART II

Shaking the Tree

13
Liese

Star Heights was the newest and tallest apartment block in the Midlevels, built on the round, and by night jammed like a huge lighted pencil into the soft darkness of the Peak. A winding causeway led to it, but the only pavement was a line of curbstone six inches wide between the causeway and the cliff. At Star Heights, pedestrians were in bad taste. It was early evening and the social rush hour was nearing its height.

As Jerry edged his way along the curb, the Mercedes and Rolls-Royces brushed against him in their haste to deliver and collect. He carried a bunch of orchids wrapped in tissue: larger than the bunch Craw had presented to Phoebe Wayfarer, smaller than the one Drake Ko had given the dead boy Nelson. These orchids were for nobody. "When you're my size, sport, you have to have a hell of a good reason for whatever you do."

He felt tense but also relieved that the long, long wait was over.

A straight foot-in-the-door operation, Your Grace, Craw had advised him at yesterday's protracted briefing. *Shove your way in there and start pitching and don't stop till you're out the other side.*

A striped awning led to the entrance hall and a perfume of women hung in the air, like a foretaste of his errand. *And just remember Ko owns the building,* Craw had added sourly, as a parting gift. The interior decoration was not quite finished. Plates of marble were missing round the mail-boxes. A fibreglass fish should have been spewing water into a terrazzo fountain, but the pipes had not yet been connected and bags of cement were heaped in the basin.

He headed for the lifts. A glass booth was marked "Reception" and the Chinese porter was watching him from inside it.

Jerry only saw the blur of him. He had been reading when Jerry arrived, but now he was staring at Jerry, undecided whether to challenge him, but half reassured by the orchids. A couple of American matrons in full war-paint arrived and took up a position near him.

"Great flowers," they said, poking in the tissue.

"Super, aren't they? Here, have them. Present! Come on! Beautiful woman. Naked without them!"

Laughter. The English are a race apart. The porter returned to his reading and Jerry was authenticated. A lift arrived. A herd of diplomats, businessmen, and their squaws shuffled into the lobby, sullen and bejewelled. Jerry ushered the American matrons ahead of him. Cigar smoke mingled with the scent. Slovenly canned music hummed forgotten melodies. The matrons pressed the button for twelve.

"You visiting with the Hammersteins too?" they asked, still looking at the orchids.

At the fifteenth, Jerry made for the fire

stairs. They stank of cat, and rubbish from the chute. Descending, he met an amah carrying a nappy bucket. She scowled at him till he greeted her, then laughed uproariously. He kept going till he reached the eighth floor where he stepped back into the plush of the residents' landing. He was at the end of a corridor. A small rotunda gave on to two gold lift doors. There were four flats, each a quadrant of the circular building, and each with its own corridor. He took up a position in the B corridor with only the flowers to protect him. He was watching the rotunda, his attention on the mouth of the corridor marked C. The tissue round the orchids was damp where he'd been clutching it too tight.

"It's a firm weekly date," Craw had assured him. "Every Monday, flower arrangement at the American Club. Regular as clockwork. She meets a girl-friend there, Nellie Tan, works for Airsea. They take in the flower arrangement and stay for dinner afterwards."

"So where's Ko meanwhile?"

"In Bangkok. Trading."

"Well, let's bloody well hope he stays there."

"Amen, sir. Amen."

With a shriek of new hinges unoiled, the door at his ear was yanked open and a slim young American in a dinner-jacket stepped into the corridor, stopped dead, and stared at Jerry and the orchids. He had blue, steady eyes and he carried a brief-case.

"You looking for me with those things?" he enquired, with a Boston society drawl. He looked rich and assured. Jerry guessed diplomacy or Ivy League banking.

"Well, I don't think so, actually," Jerry confessed, playing the English bloody fool. "Cavendish," he said. Over the American's shoulder Jerry saw the door quietly close on a packed book shelf. "Friend of mine asked me to give these to a Miss Cavendish at 9D. Waltzed off to Manila, left me holding the orchids, sort of thing."

"Wrong floor," said the American, strolling toward the lift. "You want one up. Wrong corridor, too. D's over on the other side. Thattaway.''

Jerry stood beside him, pretending to wait for an up lift. The down lift came first, the young American stepped easily into it, and Jerry resumed his post. The door marked C opened; he saw her come out, and turn to double-lock it. Her clothes were everyday. Her hair was long and ash blond but she had tied it in a pony-tail at the nape. She wore a plain halter-neck dress and sandals, and though he couldn't see her face he knew already she was beautiful. She walked to the lift, still not seeing him, and Jerry had the illusion of looking in on her through a window from the street.

There were women in Jerry's world who carried their bodies as if they were citadels to be stormed only by the bravest, and Jerry had married several; or perhaps they grew that way under his influence. There were women who seemed determined to hate themselves, hunching their backs and locking up their hips. And there were women who had only to walk toward him to bring him a gift. They were the rare ones, and for Jerry at that moment she led the pack.

She had stopped at the gold doors and was watching the lighted numbers. He reached her side as the lift arrived and she still hadn't noticed him. It was packed, as he had hoped it would be. He entered crabwise, intent on the orchids, apologising, grinning, and making a show of holding them high. She had her back to him, and he was standing at her shoulder. It was a strong shoulder, and bare either side of the halter, and Jerry could see small freckles and a down of tiny gold hairs disappearing down her spine. Her face was in profile below him. He peered down at it.

"Lizzie?" he said uncertainly. "Hey, *Lizzie*. It's me, Jerry."

She turned sharply and stared up at him. He wished he could have backed away from her, because he knew her first response would be physical fear of his size, and he was right. He saw it momentarily in her grey eyes, which flickered before holding him in their stare.

"Lizzie *Worthington!*" he declared

more confidently. "How's the whisky, remember me? One of your proud investors. Jerry. Chum of Tiny Ricardo's. One fifty-gallon keg with my name on the label. All paid and above-board."

He had kept it quiet on the assumption that he might be raking up a past she was keen to disown. He had kept it so quiet that their fellow passengers heard either "Raindrops Keep Fallin' on My Head" over the Muzak or the grumbling of an elderly Greek who thought he was boxed in.

"Why, of course," she said, and gave a bright, air-hostess smile. "Jerry!" Her voice faded as she pretended to have it on the tip of her tongue: "Jerry — er —" She frowned and looked upward like a repertory actress doing forgetfulness. The lift stopped at the sixth floor.

"Westerby," he said promptly, getting her off the hook. "Newshound. You put the bite on me in the Constellation bar. I wanted a spot of loving comfort and all I got was a keg of whisky."

Somebody next to him laughed.

"Of *course!* Jerry *darling!* How could

I possibly . . . So, I mean, what are you doing in Hong Kong? My *God!*''

''Usual beat. Fire and pestilence, famine. How about you? Retired, I should think, with your sales methods. Never had my arm twisted so thoroughly in my life.''

She laughed delightedly. The doors had opened at the third floor. An old woman shuffled in on two walking-sticks.

Lizzie Worthington sold in all a cool fifty-five kegs of the blushful Hippocrene, Your Grace, old Craw had said. *Every one of them to a male buyer and a fair number of them, according to my advisers, with service thrown in. Gives a new meaning to the term ''good measure,'' I venture to suggest.*

They had reached the ground floor. She got out first and he walked beside her. Through the main doors he saw her red sports car, with its roof up, waiting in the bay, jammed among the glistening limousines. She must have phoned down and ordered them to have it ready, he thought; if Ko owns the building, he'll make damn sure she gets the treatment.

She was heading for the porter's window. As they crossed the hall, she went on chattering, pivoting to talk to him, one arm held wide of her body, palm upward, like a fashion model. He must have asked her how she liked Hong Kong, though he couldn't remember doing so.

"I adore it, Jerry, I simply *adore* it. Vientiane seems — oh, centuries away. You know Ric died?" She threw this is heroically, as if she and death weren't strangers to each other. "After Ric, I thought I'd never care for anywhere again. I was completely wrong, Jerry. Hong Kong *has* to be the most fun city in the world. Lawrence, darling, I'm sailing my red submarine. It's hen night at the club."

Lawrence was the porter, and the key to her car dangled from a large silver horseshoe which reminded Jerry of Happy Valley races.

"Thank you, Lawrence," she said sweetly, and gave him a smile that would last him all night. "The *people* here are so marvellous, Jerry," she confided to him in a stage whisper as they moved toward the main entrance. "To *think* what we used to say about the Chinese in Laos! Yet here they're just the most marvellous and outgoing and inventive people ever." She had slipped into a stateless foreign accent, he noticed. Must have picked it up from Ricardo and stuck to it for chic. "People think to themselves: Hong Kong — fabulous shopping — tax-free cameras — restaurants. But honestly, Jerry, when you get under the surface, and meet the *true* Hong Kong, and the *people* — it's got everything you could possibly want from life. Don't you adore my new car?"

"So that's how you spend the whisky profits."

He held out his open palm, and she dropped the keys into it so that he could unlock the door for her. Still in dumb show, he gave her the orchids to hold. Behind the black Peak a full moon, not yet risen, glowed like a forest fire. She climbed in, he handed her the keys, and this time he felt the contact of her hand and remembered Happy Valley again, and Ko's kiss as they drove away.

"Mind if I ride on the back?" he asked.

She laughed and pushed open the passenger door for him. "Where are you going with those gorgeous orchids, anyway?"

She started the engine, but Jerry gently switched it off again, so that she stared at him in surprise.

"Sport," he said quietly. "I cannot tell a lie. I'm a viper in your nest, and before you drive me anywhere, you'd better fasten your seat-belt and hear the grisly truth."

He had chosen this moment carefully, because he didn't want her to feel threatened. She was in the driving seat of her own car, under the lighted awning of her own apartment block, within sixty feet of Lawrence, the porter, and he was playing the humble sinner in order to increase her sense of security.

"Our chance reunion was not entire chance. That's point one. Point two, not to put too fine an edge on it, my paper told me to run you to earth and besiege you with many searching questions regarding your late chum Ricardo."

She was still watching him, still waiting. On the point of her chin she had two small parallel scars like claw marks, quite deep. He wondered who had made them, and what with.

"But Ricardo's dead," she said, much too early.

"Sure," said Jerry consolingly. "No question. However, the comic is in possession of what they're pleased to call a hot tip that he's alive after all, and it's my job to humour them."

"But that's absolutely absurd!"

"Agreed. Totally. They're out of their minds. The consolation prize is two dozen well-thumbed orchids and the best dinner in town."

Turning away from him, she gazed through the windscreen, her face in the full glare of the overhead lamp, and Jerry wondered what it must be like to inhabit such a beautiful body, living up to it twenty-four hours a day. Her grey eyes opened a little wider, and he had a shrewd suspicion that he was supposed to notice the tears brimming and the way her hands grasped the steering-wheel for support.

"Forgive me," she murmured. "It's just — when you love a man — give everything up for him — and he dies — then one evening, out of the blue —"

"Sure," said Jerry. "I'm sorry."

She started the engine. "Why should you be sorry? If he's alive, that's bonus. If he's dead, nothing's changed. We're on a pound to nothing." She laughed. "Ric always said he was indestructible."

It's like stealing from a blind beggar, he thought. She shouldn't be let loose.

She drove well but stiffly, and he guessed — because she inspired guesswork — that she had only recently passed her test and that the car was her prize for doing so. It was the calmest night in the world. As they sank into the city, the harbour lay like a perfect mirror at the centre of the jewel box. They talked places. Jerry suggested the Peninsula, but she shook her head.

"Okay. Let's go get a drink first," he said. "Come on, let's blow the walls out!"

To his surprise, she reached across and gave his hand a squeeze. Then he remembered Craw: she did that to everyone, he'd said.

She was off the leash for a night: he had that overwhelming sensation. He remembered taking his daughter out from school when she was young, and how they had to do lots of different things in order to make the afternoon longer.

At a dark disco on Kowloon-side, they drank Rémy Martin with ice and soda. He guessed it was Ko's drink and she had picked up the habit to keep him company. It was early and there were maybe a dozen people, no more. The music was loud and they had to yell to hear each other, but she didn't mention Ricardo. She preferred the music, and listening with her head back. Sometimes she held his hand, and once put her head on his shoulder, and once she blew him a distracted kiss and drifted onto the floor to perform a slow, solitary dance, eyes closed, slightly smiling. The men ignored their own girls and undressed her with their eyes, and the Chinese waiters brought fresh ashtrays every three minutes so that they could look down her dress.

After two drinks and half an hour, she announced a passion for the Duke and the big-band sound, so they raced back to the Island to a place Jerry knew where a live Filipino band gave a fair rendering of Ellington. Cat Anderson was the best thing since sliced bread, she said. Had he heard Armstrong and Ellington together? Weren't they just the greatest? More Rémy Martin while she sang "Mood Indigo" to him.

"Did Ricardo dance?" Jerry asked.

"Did he dance?" she replied softly as she tapped her foot and lightly clicked her fingers to the rhythm.

"Thought Ricardo had a limp," Jerry objected.

"*That* never stopped him," she said, still absorbed by the music. "I'll never go back to him, you understand. Never. That chapter's closed. And how."

"How'd he pick it up?"

"Dancing?"

"The limp."

With her finger curled round an

imaginary trigger, she fired a shot into the air.

"It was either the war or an angry husband," she said. He made her repeat it, her lips close to his ear.

She knew a new Japanese restaurant where they served fabulous Kobe beef.

"Tell me how you got those scars," he asked as they were driving there. He touched his own chin. "The left and the right. What did it?"

"Oh, hunting poor innocent foxes," she said with a light smile. "My dear papa was horse mad. He still is, I'm afraid."

"Where does he live?"

"Daddy? Oh, the usual tumbledown schloss in Shropshire. *Miles* too big but they won't move. No staff, no money, ice cold three-quarters of the year. Mummy can't even boil an egg."

He was still reeling when she remembered a bar where they gave heavenly curry canapés, so they drove around until they found it and she kissed the barman. There was no music, but for some reason he heard himself telling her all about the orphan, till he came to the reasons for their breakup, which he deliberately fogged over.

"Ah, but Jerry, darling," she said sagely. "With twenty-five years between you and her, what else can you expect?"

And with nineteen years and a Chinese wife between you and Drake Ko, what can *you* expect? he thought.

They left — more kisses for the barman — and Jerry was not so intoxicated by her company, or by the brandy-sodas, to miss the point that she made a phone call, allegedly to cancel her date, that the call took a long time, and that when she returned from it she looked rather solemn. In the car again, he caught her eye and thought he read a shadow of mistrust.

"Jerry?"

"Yes?"

She shook her head, laughed, ran her palm along his face, then kissed him. "It's fun," she said.

He guessed she was wondering whether, if she had really sold him that keg of unbranded whisky, she would so thoroughly have forgotten him. He guessed she was also wondering whether, in order to sell him the keg, she had thrown in any fringe benefits of the sort Craw had so coarsely referred to. But that was her problem, he reckoned. Had been from the start.

In the Japanese restaurant they were given the corner table, thanks to Lizzie's smile and other attributes. She sat looking into the room, and he sat looking at Lizzie, which was fine with Jerry but would have given Sarratt the bends. By the candle-light he saw her face very clearly and was conscious for the first time of the signs of wear: not just the claw marks on her chin, but her lines of travel, and of strain, which to Jerry had a determined quality about them, like honourable scars from all the battles against her bad luck and her bad judgment. She wore a gold bracelet, new, and a bashed tin watch with a Walt Disney dial on it and scratched gloved hands pointing to the numerals. Her loyalty to the old watch impressed him and he wanted to know who gave it to her.

"Daddy," she said distractedly.

A mirror was let into the ceiling above them, and he could see her gold hair and the swell of her breasts among the scalps of other diners, and the gold-dust of the hairs on her back. When he tried to hit her with Ricardo, she turned guarded. It should have occurred to Jerry, but it didn't, that her attitude had changed since she made the phone call.

"What guarantee do I have that you will keep my name out of your paper?" she asked.

"Just my promise."

"But if your editor knows I was Ricardo's girl, what's to stop him putting it in for himself?"

"Ricardo had lots of girls. You know that. They came in all shapes and sizes and ran concurrently."

"There was only one of *me*," she said firmly, and he saw her glance toward the door; but then she had that habit anyway, wherever she was, of looking round the room all the time for someone who wasn't there. He let her keep the initiative.

"You said your paper had a hot tip,"

she said. "What do they mean by that?"

He had boned up his answer to this with Craw. It was one they had actually rehearsed. He delivered it therefore with force if not conviction.

"Ric's crash was eighteen months ago in the hills near Pailin on the Thai-Cambodian border. That's the official line. No one found a body, no one found wreckage, and there's talk he was doing an opium run. The insurance company never paid up and Indocharter never sued them. Why not? Ricardo had an exclusive contract to fly for them. For that matter, why doesn't someone sue Indocharter? You, for instance. You were his woman. Why not go for damages?"

"That is a *very* vulgar suggestion," she said, in her duchess voice.

"Beyond that, there's rumours he's been seen recently around the haunts a little. He's grown a beard but he can't cure the limp, they say, nor his habit of sinking a bottle of Scotch a day, nor — saving your presence — chasing after everything that wears a skirt within a five-mile radius of wherever he happens to be standing."

She was forming up to argue, but he gave her the rest while he was about it. "Head porter at the Rincome Hotel, Chiang Mai, confirmed the identification from a photograph, beard notwithstanding. All right, us round-eyes all look the same to them. Nevertheless he was pretty sure. Then only last month a fifteen-year-old girl in Bangkok, particulars to hand, took her little bundle to the Mexican Consulate and named Ricardo as the lucky father. I don't believe in eighteen-month pregnancies and I assume you don't. And don't look at *me* like that, sport. It's not my idea, is it?"

It's London's, he might have added: as neat a blend of fact and fiction as ever shook a tree. But she was actually looking past him, at the door again.

"Another thing I'm to ask you about is the whisky racket," he said.

"It was *not* a racket, Jerry. It was a perfectly valid business enterprise!"

"Sport. *You* were straight as a die. No breath of scandal attaches. Etcetera. But if *Ric* cut a few too many corners, now, that *would* be a reason for doing the old disappearing act, wouldn't it?''

He seriously regretted her discomfort. It ran quite contrary to the feelings he would have wished for her in other circumstances. He watched her and he knew that argument was something she always lost; it planted a hopelessness in her, a resignation to defeat.

''That wasn't Ric's way,'' she said finally, without any conviction at all. ''He liked to be the big man around town. It wasn't his way to run.''

''For example,'' Jerry continued — as her head fell forward in submission — ''were we to prove that your Ric, in flogging *his* kegs, had stuck to the cash and instead of passing it back to the distillery — pure hypothesis, no shred of evidence — then in that case —''

''By the time our partnership was wound up, *every* investor had a certificated contract with interest from the date of purchase. Every penny we borrowed was duly accounted for.''

Till now, it all had been footwork. Now

he saw his goal looming, and he made for it fast.

"Not *duly,* sport," he corrected her, while she continued to stare down at her uneaten food. "Not duly at all. Those settlements were made six months *after* the due date. *Un*duly. That's a very eloquent point, in my view. Question: who bailed Ric out? According to *our* information, the whole world was going for him. The distillers, the creditors, the law, the local community — every one of them had the knife sharpened for him. Till one day — *bingo!* Writs withdrawn, shades of the prison bars recede. How? Ric was on his knees. Who's the mystery angel? Who bought his debts?"

She had lifted her head while he was speaking and now to his astonishment a radiant smile suddenly lit her face, and the next thing he knew, she was waving over his shoulder at someone he couldn't see till he looked into the ceiling mirror and caught the glitter of an electric-blue suit and a full head of black hair well greased; and between the two, a foreshortened chubby Chinese face set on a pair of powerful shoulders, and two curled hands held out in a fighter's greeting while Lizzie piped him aboard.

"Mr. Tiu! What a marvellous coincidence. Come on over! Try the beef. It's *gorgeous*. Mr. Tiu, this is Jerry, from Fleet Street. Jerry, this is a very good friend of mine who helps look after me. He's interviewing me, Mr. Tiu! Me! It's most exciting. All about Vientiane and a poor pilot I tried to help a hundred years ago. Jerry knows everything about me. He's a miracle!"

"We met," said Jerry, with a broad grin.

"Sure," said Tiu, equally happy, and as he spoke, Jerry once more caught the familiar smell of almonds and rose-water mixed, the one his early wife had so much liked. "Sure," Tiu repeated. "You the horse-writer, okay?"

"Okay," Jerry agreed, stretching his smile to breaking-point.

Then of course Jerry's vision of the world turned several somersaults, and he had a whole lot of business to worry about: such as appearing to be as tickled as everybody else by the amazing good luck of Tiu's appearance; such as shaking hands, which was like a mutual promise of future settlement; such as drawing up a chair and calling for drinks, beef and chopsticks, and all the rest. But the thing that stuck in his mind even while he did all this — the memory that lodged there as permanently as later events allowed — had little to do with Tiu or his hasty arrival; or not directly. It was the expression on Lizzie's face as she first caught sight of him, for the fraction of a second before the lines of courage drew the gay smile out of her. It explained to him as nothing else could have done the paradoxes that comprised her: her prisoner's dreams, her borrowed personalities which were like disguises in which she could momentarily escape her destiny. Of course she had summoned Tiu: she had no choice. It amazed him that neither the Circus nor he himself had predicted it. The Ricardo story, whatever the truth of it, was far too hot for her to handle by herself. But the expression in her grey eyes as Tiu entered the restaurant was not relief, but resignation: the doors had slammed on her again; the fun was over. "We're like those bloody glow-worms," the orphan had whispered to him once, raging about her childhood, "carting the bloody fire round on our backs."

Operationally of course, as Jerry recognised immediately, Tiu's appearance was a gift from the gods. If information was to be fed back to Ko, then Tiu was an infinitely more impressive channel for it than Lizzie Worthington could ever hope to be.

She had finished kissing Tiu, so she handed him to Jerry.

"Mr. Tiu, you're my witness," she declared, making a great conspiracy of it. "You must remember every word I say. Jerry, go straight on *just* as if he wasn't here. I mean Mr. Tiu's as silent as the *grave*, aren't you? *Darling*," she said, and kissed him again. "It's *so* exciting," she repeated, and they all settled down for a friendly chat.

"So what you looking for, Mr. Wessby?" Tiu enquired, perfectly affably, while he tucked into his beef. "You a horse-writer, why you bother pretty girls, okay?"

"Good point, sport! Good point! Horses much safer, right?"

They all laughed richly, avoiding one another's eyes.

The waiter put a half-bottle of Black Label Scotch in front of Tiu. He unscrewed it and sniffed at it critically before pouring.

"He's looking for *Ricardo*, Mr. Tiu. Don't you understand? He thinks Ricardo is *alive*. Isn't that wonderful? I mean I have no vestige of feeling for him now, naturally, but it would be lovely to have him back with us. Think of the party we could give!"

"Liese tell you that?" Tiu asked, pouring himself two inches of Scotch. "She tell you Ricardo still around?"

"Who, old boy? Didn't get you. Didn't get the first name."

Tiu jabbed a chopstick at Lizzie. "She tell you he's alive? This pilot guy? This Ricardo? Liese tell you that?"

"I never reveal my sources, Mr. Tiu," said Jerry, just as archly. "That's a journalist's way of saying he's made something up," he explained.

"A horse-writer's way, okay?"

"That's it, that's it!"

Again Tiu laughed, and this time Lizzie laughed even louder. She was slipping out of control again. Maybe it's the drink, thought Jerry, or maybe she goes for the stronger stuff and the drink has stoked the fire. And if he calls me horse-writer again, maybe I'll take defensive action.

Lizzie again, a party-piece: "Oh, Mr. Tiu, Ricardo was so *lucky!* Think who he had. Indocharter — me — everyone. There I was, working for this little airline — some dear Chinese people Daddy knew — and Ricardo, like all the pilots, was a shocking businessman — got into the most *frightful* debt." With a wave of her hand, she brought Jerry into the act. "My God, he even tried to involve *me* in one of his schemes, can you imagine! — selling whisky, if you please — and suddenly my lovely, dotty Chinese friends decided they needed another charter pilot. They settled his debts, put him on a salary, they gave him an old banger to fly —''

Jerry now took the first of several irrevocable steps. ''When Ricardo went missing, he wasn't flying an old banger, sport. He was flying a brand-new Beechcraft,'' he corrected her deliberately. ''Indocharter never had a Beechcraft to their name. They haven't now. My editor's checked it right through — don't ask me how. Indocharter never hired one, never leased one, never crashed one.''

Tiu gave another jolly whoop of laughter.

Tiu is a very cool bishop, Your Eminence, Craw had warned. *Ran Monsignor Ko's San Francisco diocese with exemplary efficiency for five years, and the worst the narcotics artists could hang on him was washing his Rolls-Royce on a saint's day.*

''Hey, Mr. Wessby, maybe Liese stole them one!'' Tiu cried in his half-American accent. ''Maybe she go out nights steal aircraft from other airlines!''

"Mr. Tiu, that's very naughty of you!" Lizzie declared.

"How you like that, horse-writer? How you like?"

The merriment at their table was by now so loud for three people that several heads turned to peer at them. Jerry saw them in the mirrors, where he half expected to spot Ko himself, with his crooked boat people's walk, swaying toward them through the wicker doorway. Lizzie plunged wildly on.

"Oh, it was a complete fairy tale! One moment Ric can scarcely eat, *and* owed all of us money — Charlie's savings, my allowance from Daddy — Ric practically ruined us all. Of course everyone's money just naturally belonged to him — and the next thing we knew, Ric had work, he was in the clear, life was a ball again. All those other poor pilots grounded, and Ric and Charlie flying all over the place like —"

"Like blue-arsed flies," Jerry suggested, at which Tiu was so doubled with hilarity that he was obliged to hold on to Jerry's shoulder to keep himself afloat — while Jerry had the uncomfortable feeling of being physically measured for the knife.

"Hey listen, that pretty good! Blue-arse fly! I like that! You pretty funny fellow, horse-writer!"

It was at this point, under the pressure of Tiu's cheerful insults, that Jerry used very good footwork indeed. Afterwards, Craw said the best. He ignored Tiu entirely and picked up that other name which Lizzie had let slip:

"Yeah, whatever happened to old Charlie, by the way?" he asked, not having the least idea who Charlie was. "What became of him after Ric did his disappearing number? Don't tell me he went down with his ship as well?"

Once more she floated away on a fresh wave of narrative, and Tiu patently enjoyed everything he heard, chuckling and nodding while he ate.

He's here to find out the score, Jerry thought. He's much too sharp to put the brakes on Lizzie. It's me he's worried about, not her.

"Oh, Charlie's indestructible,

completely immortal," Lizzie declared, and once more selected Tiu as her foil: "Charlie *Marshall,* Mr. Tiu," she explained. "Oh, you should meet him, a fantastic half-Chinese, all skin and bones and opium and a completely brilliant pilot. His father's old Kuomintang, a terrific brigand, and lives up in the Shans. His mother was some poor Corsican girl — you know how the Corsicans flocked into Indo-China — but really he is an utterly fantastic character. Do you know why he calls himself Marshall? His father wouldn't give him his own name. So what does Charlie do? Gives himself the highest rank in the army instead. 'My dad's a general but I'm a marshal,' he'd say. Isn't that cute? And *far* better than *admiral,* I mean."

"Super," Jerry agreed. "Marvellous. Charlie's a prince."

"Liese some pretty utterly fantastic character herself, Mr. Wessby," Tiu remarked handsomely, so on Jerry's insistence they drank to that — to her fantastic character.

"Hey, what's all this 'Liese' thing,

actually?'' Jerry asked as he put down his glass. ''You're *Lizzie*. Who's this Liese? Mr. Tiu, I don't know the lady. Why am I left out of the joke?''

Here Lizzie did definitely turn to Tiu for guidance, but Tiu had ordered himself some raw fish and was eating it rapidly and with total devotion.

''Some horse-writer ask pretty damn questions,'' he remarked, through a full mouth.

''New town, new leaf, new name,'' Lizzie said finally, with an unconvincing smile. ''I wanted a change, so I chose a new name. Some girls get a new hair-do, I get a new name.''

''Got a new fellow to go with it?'' Jerry asked.

She shook her head, eyes down, while Tiu let out a whoop of laughter.

''What's happened to this town, Mr. Tiu?'' Jerry demanded, instinctively covering for her. ''Chaps all gone blind or something? Crikey, I'd cross continents for her, wouldn't you? Whatever she calls herself, right?''

''Me, I go from Kowloon-side to Hong

Kong-side, no further!'' said Tiu, hugely entertained by his own wit. ''Or maybe I stay Kowloon-side and call her up, tell her come over see me one hour!'' At which Lizzie's eyes stayed down and Jerry thought it would be quite fun, on another occasion when they all had more time, to break Tiu's fat neck in several places.

Unfortunately, however, breaking Tiu's neck was not at present on Craw's shopping list.

The money, Craw had said. *When the moment's right, open up one end of the gold seam and that's your grand finale.*

So he started her off about Indocharter. Who were they, what was it like to work for them? She rose to it so fast he began to wonder whether she enjoyed this knife-edge existence more than he had realised.

''Oh, it was a fabulous adventure, Jerry! You can't begin to imagine it, I assure you.'' Ric's multinational accent again. '' 'Airline' — just the word is so absurd. I mean don't for a minute think of your bright new planes and your glamorous hostesses and champagne and caviar or anything like that *at all*. This was work. This was pioneering, which is what drew me in the first place. I could *perfectly* well have simply lived off Daddy, or my aunts. I mean mercifully I'm totally independent, but *who* can resist challenge? All we started out with was a couple of dreadful old DC-3s *literally* stuck together with string and chewing-gum. We even had to *buy* the safety certificates. Nobody would issue them. After that we flew literally anything. Hondas, vegetables, pigs — oh, the boys had such a story about those poor pigs. They broke loose, Jerry. They came into the first class, even into the cabin, imagine!''

"Like passengers," Tiu explained, with his mouth full. "She fly first-class pigs, okay, Mr. Wessby?"

"What routes?" Jerry asked when they had recovered from their laughter.

"You can see how he interrogates me, Mr. Tiu? I never knew I was so glamorous! So mysterious! We flew everywhere, Jerry. Bangkok, Cambodia sometimes. Battambang, Phnom Penh, Kampong Cham when it was open. Everywhere. Awful places.''

''And who were your customers? Traders, taxi jobs — who were the regulars?''

''Absolutely anyone we could get. Anyone who could pay. Preferably in advance, naturally.''

Pausing from his Kobe beef, Tiu felt inspired to offer social chit-chat.

''Your father some big lord, okay, Mr. Wessby?''

''More or less,'' said Jerry.

''Lords some pretty rich fellows. Why you gotta be a horse-writer, okay?''

Ignoring Tiu entirely, Jerry played his trump card and waited for the ceiling mirror to crash on to their table.

''There's a story that you people had some local Russian Embassy link,'' he said easily, straight at Lizzie. ''That ring a bell at all, sport? Any Reds under your bed at all, if I may ask?''

Having resumed his eating, Tiu was taking care of his rice, holding the bowl under his chin and shovelling it non-stop;

but this time, significantly, Lizzie didn't give him half a glance.

"*Russians?*" she repeated, puzzled. "Why on earth should Russians come to *us?* They had regular Aeroflot flights in and out of Vientiane every week."

Though he would have sworn, then or later, that she was telling the truth, Jerry acted not quite satisfied. "Not even *local* runs?" he insisted. "Fetching and carrying, courier service, or whatever?"

"Never. How could we? Besides, the Chinese simply *loathe* the Russians, don't they, Mr. Tiu?"

"Russians pretty bad people, Mr. Wessby," Tiu agreed. "They stink pretty bad."

So do you, thought Jerry, catching a fresh waft of that early wife's body-water.

Jerry laughed at his own absurdity. "I've got editors like other people have stomach-ache," he protested. "He's *convinced* we can do a Red-under-the-bed job. 'Ricardo's Soviet paymasters' . . . 'Did Ricardo take a dive for the Kremlin?' "

"Paymaster?" Lizzie repeated, utterly

mystified. "Ric never received a penny from the Russians. What *are* they talking about?"

Jerry again: "But Indocharter did, didn't they? Unless my lords and masters have been sold a total pup, which I suspect they have been, as usual. They drew money from the local Russian Embassy and piped it down to Hong Kong in U.S. dollars. That's *London's* story and they're sticking to it."

"They're mad," she said confidently. "I've never heard such nonsense."

To Jerry she seemed even relieved that the conversation had taken this improbable course. Ricardo alive — there she was drifting through a minefield. Ko as her lover — that secret was Ko's or Tiu's to dispense, not hers. But Russian money — Jerry was as certain as he dared be that she knew nothing and feared nothing about it.

He offered to ride back with her to Star Heights, but Mr. Tiu lived that way, she said.

"See you again pretty soon, Mr. Wessby," Tiu promised.

"Look forward to it, sport," said Jerry.

"You wanna stick to horse-writing, hear that? In my opinion, you get more money that way, Mr. Wessby, okay?" There was no menace in his voice or in the friendly way he patted Jerry's upper arm. Tiu did not even speak as if he expected his advice to be taken as any more than a confidence between friends.

Then suddenly it was over. Lizzie kissed the headwaiter, but not Jerry. She sent Jerry, not Tiu, for her coat, so that she wouldn't be alone with him. She scarcely looked at him as she said goodbye.

Dealing with beautiful women, Your Grace, Craw had warned, *is like dealing with known criminals, and the lady you are about to solicit undoubtedly falls within that category.*

Wandering home through the moonlit streets — the long trek, beggars, eyes in doorways notwithstanding — Jerry subjected Craw's dictim to closer scrutiny. On "criminal" he really couldn't rule at all: "criminal" seemed a pretty variable sort of standard at the best of times, and neither the Circus nor its agents existed to uphold some parochial concept of the law. Craw had told him that in slump periods Ricardo had made her carry little parcels for him over frontiers. Big deal. Leave it to the owls. "Known" criminal, however, was quite a different matter. "Known" he would go along with absolutely. Remembering Elizabeth Worthington's caged stare at Tiu, he reckoned he had known that face, that look, and that dependence in one guise or another for the bulk of his waking life.

It has been whispered once or twice by certain trivial critics of George Smiley that at this juncture he should somehow have seen which way the wind was blowing with Jerry, and hauled him out of the field. Effectively, Smiley was Jerry's case officer, after all. Smiley alone kept Jerry's file, welfared and briefed him. Had George been at his peak, they say, instead of half-way down the other side, he would have read the warning signals between the lines of Craw's reports and headed Jerry off in time. They might just as well have complained that he was a second-rate fortune-teller. The facts, as they came to Smiley, are these.

On the morning following his "pass" at Lizzie Worth or Worthington — the jargon has no sexual connotation — Craw debriefed Jerry for more than three hours on a car pick-up, and his report describes Jerry as being, quite reasonably, in a state of "anti-climactic gloom." He appeared, said Craw, to be afraid that Tiu, or even Ko, might blame the girl for her "guilty knowledge" and even lay hands on her. Jerry referred more than once to Tiu's patent contempt for the girl — and for himself, and, he suspected, for all Europeans — and repeated his comment about travelling from Kowloon-side to Hong Kong-side for her and no further. Craw countered by pointing out that Tiu could at any time have shut her up; and that her knowledge, on Jerry's own testimony, did not extend even as far as the Russian gold seam, let alone to brother Nelson.

Jerry, in short, was producing the

standard post-operational manifestations of a fieldman. A sense of guilt, coupled with forboding, an involuntary movement of affiliation toward the target person — these are as predictable as a burst of tears in an athlete after the big race.

At their next contact — an extended limbo call on the second day, at which, to buoy him up, Craw passed on Smiley's warm personal congratulations somewhat ahead of receiving them from the Circus — Jerry sounded in altogether better case, but he was worried about his daughter Cat. He had forgotten her birthday — he said it was tomororw — and wished the Circus to send her at once a Japanese cassette player with a bunch of cassettes to start off her collection. Craw's telegram to Smiley named the cassettes, asked for immediate action by housekeepers, and requested that Shoemaker Section — the Circus forgers, in other words — run up an accompanying card in Jerry's handwriting, text given: "Darling Cat. Asked a friend of mine to post this in London. Look after yourself, my dearest, love to you now and ever, Pa."

Smiley authorised the purchase, instructing housekeepers to dock the cost from Jerry's pay at source. He personally checked the parcel before it was sent, and approved the forged card. He also verified what he and Craw already suspected: that it was not Cat's birthday, or anywhere near. Jerry simply had a strong urge to make a gesture of affection: once more, a normal symptom of temporary field fatigue. Smiley cabled Craw to stay close to him but the initiative was with Jerry, and Jerry made no further contact till the night of the fifth day, when he demanded — and got — a crash meeting within the hour. This took place at their standing after-dark emergency rendezvous, an all-night roadside café in the New Territories, under the guise of a casual encounter between old colleagues. Craw's letter, marked "Personal to Smiley only," was a follow-up to his telegram. It arrived at the Circus by hand of the Cousin's courier two days after the episode it describes: on day seven therefore. Writing on the assumption that the Cousins would contrive to read the text despite the seal and other devices, Craw crammed it with evasions, work names, and cryptograph, which are here restored to their real meaning:

Westerby was very angry. He demanded to know what the hell Sam Collins was doing in Hong Kong and in what way Collins was involved in the Ko case. I have not seen him so disturbed before. I asked him what made him think Collins was around. He replied that he had seen him that very night — eleven-fifteen exactly — sitting in a parked car in the Midlevels, on a terrace just below Star Heights, under a streetlamp, reading a newspaper. The position Collins had taken up, said Westerby, gave him a clear view to Lizzie Worthington's windows on the eighth floor, and it was Westerby's assumption that he was engaged in some sort of surveillance. Westerby, who was on foot at the time, insists that he "damn nearly went up to Sam and asked him outright." But Sarratt discipline held firm, and he kept going down the hill on his own side of the road. But he does claim that as soon as Collins saw him, he started the car and drove up the hill at speed. Westerby has the licence number, and of course it is the correct one. Collins confirms the rest.

In accordance with our agreed position in this contingency (your signal of Feb. 15th), I gave Westerby the following answers:

1. Even if it *was* Collins, the Circus had no control over his movements. Collins had left the Circus under a cloud, before the fall, he was a known gambler, drifter, wheeler-dealer, etc., and the East was his natural stomping-ground. I told Westerby he was being a fat-headed idiot to assume that Collins was still on the payroll, or, worse, had any part in the Ko case.

2. Collins is facially a *type,* I said: regular-featured, moustached, etc., looked like half the pimps in London.

I doubted whether from across a road at eleven-fifteen at night, Westerby could be certain of his identification. Westerby retorted that he had A-1 vision and that Sam had his newspaper open at the racing page.

3. Anyway, what was Westerby himself doing, I enquired, round Star Heights at eleven-fifteen at night? Answer, returning from drinking with the U.P.I. mob and hoping for a cab. At this I pretended to explode, and said that nobody who had been on a U.P.I. thrash could see an elephant at five yards, let alone Sam Collins at twenty-five, in a car, at dead of night. Over and out — I hope.

That Smiley was seriously concerned about this incident goes without saying. Only four people knew of the Collins ploy: Smiley, Connie Sachs, Craw, and Sam himself. That Jerry should have stumbled on him provided an added anxiety in an operation already loaded with imponderables.

But Craw was deft, and Craw believed

he had talked Jerry down, and Craw was the man on the spot. Just possibly in a perfect world, Craw might have made it his business to find out whether there had really been a U.P.I. party in the Midlevels that night — and on learning that there had not, he might have challenged Jerry again to explain his presence in the region of Star Heights, and in that case Jerry would probably have thrown a tantrum and produced some other story that was not checkable: that he had been with a woman, for instance, and Craw could mind his bloody business. Of which the net result would have been needless bad blood and the same take-it-or-leave-it situation as before.

It is also tempting, but unreasonable, to expect of Smiley that with so many other pressures upon him — the continued and unabating quest for Nelson, daily sessions with the Cousins, rear-guard actions round the Whitehall corridors — he should have drawn the inference closest to his own lonely experience: namely, that Jerry, having no taste for sleep or company that evening, had wandered the night pavements till he found himself standing outside the building where Lizzie lived, and hung about, as Smiley did, without exactly knowing what he wanted, beyond the off chance of a sight of her. The rush of events which carried Smiley along was far too powerful to permit of such fanciful abstractions. Not only did the eighth day, when it came, put the Circus effectively on a war footing; it is also the pardonable vanity of lonely people everywhere to assume that they have no counterparts.

14
The Eighth Day

The jolly mood of the fifth floor was a great relief after the depression of the previous gathering. "A burrowers' honeymoon," Guillam called it, and tonight was its highest point, its attenuated star-burst of a consummation, and it came exactly eight days, in the chronology which historians afterwards impose on things, after Jerry and Lizzie and Tiu had had their full and frank exchange of views on the subject of Tiny Ricardo and the Russian gold seam — to the great delight of the Circus planners. Guillam had wangled Molly along specially.

They had run in all directions, these shady night animals, down old paths and new paths and old paths grown over till they were rediscovered; and now at last, behind their twin leaders — Connie Sachs alias Mother Russia, and di Salis alias the Doc — they crammed themselves, all twelve of them, into the very throne-room itself, under Karla's portrait, in an obedient half-circle round their chief, Bolshies and yellow perils together. A plenary session, then: for people unused to such drama, a monument of history indeed. And Molly primly at Giullam's side, her hair brushed long to hide the bite marks on her neck.

Di Salis does most of the talking. The other ranks feel this to be appropriate. After all, Nelson Ko is the Doc's patch entirely: Chinese to the sleeve-ends of his tunic. Reining himself right in — his spiky wet hair, his knees and feet and fussing fingers all but still for once — he keeps things in a low and almost deprecating key of which the inexorable climax is accordingly more thrilling. The climax even has a name. It is Ko Sheng-hsiu — alias Ko, Nelson — later known also as Yao Kai-sheng, under which name he was still later disgraced in the Cultural Revolution.

"But within these walls, gentlemen," pipes the Doc, whose awareness of the female sex is inconsistent, "we shall continue to call him Nelson." Born 1928 of humble proletarian stock, in Swatow — to quote the official sources, says the Doc — and soon afterwards removed to Shanghai. No mention, in either official or unofficial handouts, of Mr. Hibbert's Lord's Life Mission school, but a sad reference to "exploitation at the hands of Western Imperialists in childhood," who poisoned him with religion. When the Japanese reached Shanghai, Nelson joined the refugee trail to Chungking, all as Mr. Hibbert has described.

From an early age, the Doc continues, once more according to official records, Nelson secretly devoted himself to seminal revolutionary reading and took an active part in clandestine Communist groups, despite the oppression of the loathsome Chiang Kai-shek rabble. On the refugee trail he also attempted "on many occasions" to escape to Mao, but his extreme youth held him back. Returning to Shanghai, he became, already as a student, a leading cadre member of the outlawed Communist movement and undertook special assignments in and around the Kiangnan shipyards to subvert the pernicious influence of K.M.T. Fascist elements. At the University of Communications he appealed publicly for a united front of students and peasants. Graduated with conspicuous excellence in 1951. . . .

Di Salis interrupts himself, and in a sharp release of tension throws up one arm and clenches the hair at the back of his head.

"The usual unctuous portrait, Chief, of a student hero who sees the light before his time," he sings.

"What about Leningrad?" Smiley asks, from his desk, while he jots the occasional note.

"Nineteen fifty-three to six."

"Yes, Connie?"

Connie is in her wheelchair again. She blames the freezing month and that toad Karla, jointly.

"We have a Brother Bretlev, darling. Bretlev, Ivan Ivanovitch, Academician, Leningrad faculty of shipbuilding, old-time China hand, devilled in Shanghai for Centre's China hounds. Revolutionary war-horse, latter-day Karla-trained university talent-spotter trawling the overseas students for likely lads and lasses."

For the burrowers on the Chinese side — the yellow perils — this intelligence is new and thrilling, and produces an excited crackle of chairs and papers till at a sign from Smiley, di Salis lets go his head and takes up his narrative once more.

"Nineteen fifty-seven returned to Shanghai and was put in charge of a railway workshop —"

Smiley again: "But his dates at Leningrad were 'fifty-three to 'fifty-six?"

"Correct," says di Salis.

"Then there seems to be a missing year."

Now no papers crackle and no chairs, either.

"A tour of Soviet shipyards is the official explanation," says di Salis, with a smirk at Connie and a mysterious, knowing writhe of the neck.

"Thank you," says Smiley and makes another note. " 'Fifty-seven," he repeats. "Was that before or after the Sino-Soviet split, Doc?"

"Before. The split started in earnest in 'fifty-nine."

Smiley asks here whether Nelson's brother receives a mention anywhere; or is Drake as much disowned in Nelson's China as Nelson is in Drake's?

"In one of the earliest biographies, Drake is referred to, but not by name. In the later ones, a brother is said to have died during the Communist take-over of 'forty-nine."

Smiley makes a rare joke, which is followed by dense, relieved laughter. "This case is littered with people pretending to be dead," he complains. "It will be a positive relief to me to find a real corpse somewhere."

Only hours later, this *mot* was remembered with a shudder.

"We also have a note that Nelson was a model student at Leningrad," di Salis goes on. "At least in Russian eyes. They sent him back with the highest references."

Connie from her iron chair allows herself another interjection. She has brought Trot, her mangy mongrel, with her. He lies misshapenly across her vast lap, stinking and occasionally sighing, but not even Guillam, who is a dog-hater, has the nerve to banish him.

"Oh, and so they would, dear, wouldn't they?" she cries. "The Russians would praise Nelson's talents to the skies, 'course they would, specially if Brother Ivan Ivanovitch Bretlev has snapped him up at university, and Karla's lovelies have spirited him off to training school and all! Bright little mole like Nelson, give him a decent start in life for when he gets home to China! Didn't do him much good later though, did it, Doc? Not when the Great Beastly Cultural Revolution got him in the neck! The generous admiration of Soviet imperialist running dogs wasn't at all the thing to be wearing in your cap *then,* was it?"

Of Nelson's fall, few details are

available, the Doc proclaims, speaking louder in response to Connie's outburst. "One must assume that it was violent, and as Connie has pointed out, those who were highest in Russian favour fell the hardest."

He glances at the sheet of paper which he holds crookedly before his blotched face. "I won't give you all his appointments at the time of his disgrace, Chief, because he lost them anyway. But there is no doubt that he did indeed have effective management of most of the shipbuilding in Kiangnan, and consequently of a large part of China's naval tonnage."

"I see," says Smiley quietly. Jotting, he purses his lips as if in disapproval, while his eyebrows lift very high.

"His post at Kiangnan also procured him a string of seats on the naval planning committees and in the field of communications and strategic policy. By 'sixty-three his name is beginning to pop up regularly in the Cousins' Peking watch reports."

"Well done, Karla," Guillam says

quietly from his place at Smiley's side, and Smiley, still writing, actually echoes this sentiment with a "Yes."

"The only one, Peter dear!" Connie yells, suddenly unable to contain herself. "The only one of all those toads to see it coming! A voice in the wilderness, wasn't he, Trot? 'Look out for the yellow peril,' he told 'em. 'One day they're going to turn round and bite the hand that's feeding 'em, sure as eggs. And when that happens you'll have eight hundred million new enemies banging on your own back door. *And* your guns will all be pointing the wrong way. Mark my words.'

"Told 'em," she repeats, hauling at the mongrel's ear in her emotion. "Put it all in a paper, 'Threat of Deviation by Emerging Socialist Partner.' Circulated every little brute in Moscow Centre's Collegium. Drafted it word for word in his clever little mind while he was doing a spot of time in Siberia for Uncle Joe Stalin, bless him. 'Spy on your friends today, they're certain to be your enemies tomorrow,' he told them. Oldest maxim of the trade, Karla's favourite. When he was given his job back, he practically nailed it on the door in Dzerzhinski Square. No one paid a blind bit of notice. Not a scrap. Fell on barren ground, my dear. Five years later, he was proved right, and the Collegium didn't thank him for that, either, *I* can tell you! He's been right a sight too often for their liking, the boobies — hasn't he, Trot! *You* know, don't you, darling, *you* know what the old fool-woman's on about!'' At which she lifts the pulling dog a few inches in the air by its forepaws and lets it flop back onto her lap again.

Connie can't bear old Doc hogging the limelight, they secretly agree. She sees the logic of it, but the woman in her can't abide the reality.

''Very well, he was purged, Doc,'' Smiley says quietly, restoring calm. ''Let's go back to 'sixty-seven, shall we?'' And puts his chin back in his hand.

In the gloom, Karla's portrait peers stodgily down as di Salis resumes. ''Well, the usual grim story, one supposes, Chief,'' he chants. ''The dunce's cap, no doubt. Spat on in the street. Wife

669

and children kicked and beaten up. Indoctrination camps, labour education 'on a scale commensurate with the crime.' Urged to reconsider the peasant virtues. One report has him sent to a rural commune to test himself. And when he came crawling back to Shanghai they'd have made him start at the bottom again, driving bolts into a railway line or whatever. As far as the *Russians* were concerned — if that's what we're talking about" — he hurries on before Connie can interrupt again — "he was a wash-out. No access, no influence, no friends."

"How long did it take him to climb back?" Smiley enquires, with a characteristic lowering of the eyelids.

"About three years ago he started to be functional again. In the long run he has what they need most: brains, technical know-how, experience. But his *formal* rehabilitation didn't really occur till the beginning of 'seventy-three."

While di Salis goes on to describe the stages of Nelson's ritual reinstatement, Smiley quietly draws a folder to him and refers to certain other dates which, for reasons as yet unexplained, are suddenly acutely relevant to him.

"The payments to Drake have their beginnings in January 'seventy-three," he murmurs. "They rise steeply in mid-'seventy-three."

"With Nelson's *access,* darling," Connie whispers after him, like a prompter from the wings. "The more he knows, the more he tells, and the more he tells, the more he gets. Karla only pays for goodies, and even then it hurts like blazes."

"By 'seventy-three," says di Salis, "Nelson, having made all the proper confessions, has been embraced into the Shanghai municipal revolutionary committee, and appointed responsible person in a naval unit of the People's Liberation Army. Six months later —"

"Date?" Smiley interrupts.

"July."

Six months later, di Salis continues, Nelson is seen to be acting in an unknown capacity with the Central Committee of the Chinese Communist Party.

"Holy *smoke,*" says Guillam softly,

and Molly Meakin gives his hand a hidden squeeze.

"And a report from the Cousins," says di Salis, "undated as usual but well attested, has Nelson down as an informal adviser to the Munitions and Ordnance Committee of the Ministry of Defence."

Rather than orchestrate this revelation with his customary range of mannerisms, di Salis again contrives to keep rock-still to great effect.

"In terms of *eligibility,* Chief," he goes on quietly, "from an *operational* standpoint, we on the China side of your house would regard this as one of the key positions in the whole of the Chinese administration. If we could pick ourselves one slot for an agent inside the mainland, Nelson's might well be the one."

"Reasons?" Smiley enquires, still alternating between his jottings and the open folder before him.

"The Chinese navy is still in the Stone Age. We do have a formal interest in Chinese technical intelligence, naturally, but our real priorities — like those of Moscow, no doubt — are strategic and political. Beyond that, Nelson could supply us with the total capacity of all Chinese shipyards. Beyond that again, he could tell us the Chinese submarine potential, which has been frightening the daylights out of the Cousins for years. And of ourselves too, I may add, off and on."

"So think what it's doing for Moscow," an old burrower murmurs out of turn.

"The Chinese are supposedly developing their own version of the Russian G-2 class submarine," di Salis explains. "No one knows a lot about it. Have they their own design? Have they two or four tubes? Are they armed with sea-to-air missiles or sea-to-sea? What is the financial appropriation for them? There's talk of a Han class. We had word they laid one down in 'seventy-one. We've never had confirmation. In Dairen in 'sixty-four, they allegedly built a G class armed with ballistic missiles but it still hasn't been officially sighted. And so forth and so on," he says deprecatingly, for, like most of the Circus, he has a rooted dislike of military matters and would prefer the more artistic targets.

"For hard and fast detail on those subjects the Cousins would pay a fortune," di Salis says. "In a couple of years, Langley could spend hundreds of millions in research, over-flights, satellites, listening devices, and God knows what — and still not come up with an answer half as good as one photograph. So if Nelson —" He lets the sentence hang, which is somehow a lot more effective than making it finite.

Connie whispers, "Well *done, Doc,*" but still for a while nobody else speaks; they are held back by Smiley's jotting, and his continued examination of the folder.

"Good as Haydon," Guillam mutters. "Better. China's the last frontier. Toughest nut in the trade."

Smiley sits back, his calculations apparently finished.

"Ricardo made his trip a few months after Nelson's formal rehabilitation," he says.

Nobody sees fit to question this.

"Tiu travels to Shanghai, and six weeks later Ricardo —"

In the far background, Guillam hears the bark of the Cousins' telephone switched through to his room, and it is a thing he afterwards avers most strongly — whether in truth or with hindsight — that the unloveable image of Sam Collins was at this point conjured out of his subconscious memory like a djinni out of a lamp, and that he wondered yet again how he could ever have been so unthinking as to let Sam Collins deliver that vital letter to Martello.

"Nelson has one more string to his bow, Chief," di Salis continues, just as everyone is assuming he is done. "I hesitate to offer it with any confidence, but in the circumstances I dare not omit it altogether. A barter report from the West Germans, dated a few weeks ago. According to *their* sources, Nelson is lately a member of what we have for want of information dubbed the Peking Tea Club, an embryonic body which we believe has been set up to co-ordinate the Chinese intelligence effort. He came in first as an adviser on electronic surveillance, and was then co-opted as a full member. It functions, so far as we can fathom, somewhat as our own Intelligence Steering Group. But I must emphasise that this is a shot in the dark. We know absolutely nothing about the Chinese services, and nor do the Cousins."

For once at a loss for words, Smiley stares at di Salis, opens his mouth, closes it, then pulls off his glasses and polishes them.

"And Nelson's *motive?*" he asks, still oblivious to the steady bark of the Cousins' bell. "A shot in the dark, Doc? How would you see that?"

Di Salis gives an enormous shrug, so that his tallow hair bucks like a floor-mop. "Oh, anybody's guess," he says waspishly. "Who believes in *motive* these days? It would have been perfectly natural for him to respond to Centre's recruitment overtures while a student in Leningrad, of course, provided they were made in the right way. Not a disloyal thing at all. Not doctrinally, anyway. Russia was China's big elder brother. Nelson needed merely to be told he had been chosen as one of a special vanguard of vigilantes. I see no great art to that."

Outside the room, the green phone just goes on ringing, which is remarkable. Martello is not usually so persistent. Only Guillam and Smiley are allowed to pick it up. But Smiley has not heard it, and Guillam is damned if he will budge while di Salis is extemporising on Nelson's possible reasons for becoming Karla's mole.

"When the Cultural Revolution came, many people in Nelson's position believed that Mao had gone mad," di Salis explains, still reluctant to theorise. "Even some of his own generals thought so. The humiliations Nelson suffered made him conform outwardly — while inwardly, perhaps, he remained bitter — who knows? — and vengeful."

"The alimony payments to Drake started at a time when Nelson's rehabilitation was barely complete," Smiley objects mildly. "What is the presumption there, Doc?"

All this is just too much for Connie, and once again she brims over. "Oh, George, how can you be so naïve? *You* can find the line, dear, *course* you can! Those poor Chinese can't afford to hang a top technician in the cupboard half his life and not use him! Karla saw the drift, didn't he, Doc? He read the wind and went with it. He kept his poor little Nelson on a string and as soon as he started to come out of the wilderness again he had his legmen get alongside him: "It's *us,* remember? Your friends! *We* don't let you down! *We* don't spit on you in the street! Let's get back to business!' You'd play it just the same way yourself, you know you would!''

"And the money?" Smiley asks. "The half million?"

"Stick and carrot! Blackmail implicit, rewards enormous. Nelson's hooked both ways."

But it is di Salis, Connie's outburst notwithstanding, who has the last word: "He's Chinese. He's pragmatic. He's Drake's brother. He can't get out of China —"

"Not yet," says Smiley softly, glancing at the folder again.

"— and he knows very well his market value to the Russian service. 'You can't eat politics, you can't sell them, and you can't sleep with them,' Drake liked to say. So you might as well make money out of them."

"Against the day when you *can* leave China and spend it," Smiley concludes and, as Guillam tiptoes from the room, silently closes the folder and takes up his sheet of jottings. "Drake tried to get him out and failed, so he took the Russians' money till . . . till what? Till Drake has better luck, perhaps."

In the background, the insistent snarling of the green telephone has finally ceased.

"Nelson is Karla's mole," Smiley remarks at last, once more almost himself. "He's sitting on a priceless crock of Chinese intelligence. That alone we could do with. He's acting on Karla's orders. The orders themselves are of inestimable value to us. They would show us precisely how much the Russians know about their Chinese enemy, and even what they intend toward him. We could take back-bearings galore. Yes, Peter?"

In the breaking of tragic news there is no transition. One minute a concept stands, the next it lies smashed, and for those affected the world has altered irrevocably. As a cushion, however, Guillam had used official Circus stationery and the written word. By writing his message to Smiley in signal form, he hoped that the sight of it would prepare him in advance. Walking quietly to the desk, the form in his hand, he laid it on the glass sheet and waited.

"About *Charlie Marshall,* the other pilot, by the way," Smiley asked of the gathering, still oblivious. "Have the Cousins run him to earth yet, Molly?"

"His record is much the same as Ricardo's," Molly Meakin replied, glancing queerly at Guillam. Still at Smiley's side, he looked suddenly grey and middle-aged and ill. "Like Ricardo, he flew for the Cousins in the Laos war, Mr. Smiley. They were contemporaries at Langley's secret aviation school in Oklahoma. They dumped him when Laos ended and have no further word on him.

Enforcement say he has ferried opium, but they say that of all of the Cousins' pilots."

"I think you should read that," Guillam said, pointing firmly at the message.

"Marshall must be our next step," Smiley said. "We have to maintain the pressure."

Picking up the signal form at last, he held it critically to his left side, where the reading-light was brightest. He read with his eyebrows raised and his lids lowered. As always, he read twice. His expression did not change, but those nearest him said the movement went out of his face.

"Thank you, Peter," he said quietly, laying the paper down again. "And thank you everyone else. Connie and the Doc, perhaps you'd stay behind. I trust the rest of you will get a good night's sleep."

Among the younger sparks this hope was greeted with cheerful laughter, for it was well past midnight already.

The girl from upstairs slept, a neat brown doll along the length of one of Jerry's legs, plump and immaculate by the orange night-light of the rain-soaked Hong Kong sky. She was snoring her head off, and Jerry was staring through the window thinking of Lizzie Worthington. He thought of the twin claw marks on her chin and wondered again who had put them there. He thought of Tiu, imagining him as her jailer, and he rehearsed the name horse-writer until it really annoyed him. He wondered how much more waiting there was, and whether at the end of it he might have a chance with her, which was all he asked: a chance. The girl stirred, but only to scratch her rump. From next door, Jerry heard a ritual clicking as the habitual mah-jong party washed the pieces before distributing them.

The girl had not been unduly responsive to Jerry's courtship at first — a gush of impassioned notes jammed through her letter-box at all hours of the previous few days — but she did need to pay her gas bill. Officially, she was the property of a businessman, but recently his visits had become fewer and most recently had ceased altogether, with the result that she could afford neither the fortune-teller nor mah-jong, nor the stylish clothes she had set her heart on for the day she broke into Kung Fu films. So she succumbed, but on a clear financial understanding.

Her main fear was of being known to consort with the hideous *kwailo,* and for this reason she had put on her entire outdoor equipment to descend the one floor: a brown raincoat with transatlantic brass buckles on the epaulettes, plastic yellow boots, and a plastic umbrella with red roses. Now this equipment lay around the parquet floor like armour after the battle, and she slept with the same noble exhaustion. So that when the phone rang her only response was a drowsy Cantonese oath.

Lifting the receiver, Jerry nursed the idiotic hope it might be Lizzie, but it wasn't.

"Get your ass down here fast," Luke said. "And Stubbsie will *love* you. *Move* it. I'm doing you the favour of our career."

"Where's here?" Jerry asked.

"Downstairs, you ape."

He rolled the girl off him but she still didn't wake.

The roads glittered with unexpected rain and a thick halo ringed the moon. Luke drove as if they were in a jeep: in high gear with hammer changes on the corners. Fumes of whisky filled the car.

"What have you got, for Christ's sake?" Jerry demanded. "What's going on?"

"Great meat. Now shut up."

"I don't want meat. I'm suited."

"You'll want this one. *Man,* you'll want this one."

They were heading for the harbour tunnel. A flock of cyclists without lights lurched out of a side turning, and Luke had to mount the central reservation to avoid them.

"Look for a damn great building site," Luke said. A patrol car overtook them, all lights flashing. Thinking he was going to be stopped, Luke lowered his window.

"We're *press,* you idiots!" he screamed. "We're *stars,* hear me?"

Inside the patrol car as it passed they had a glimpse of a Chinese sergeant and his driver, and an august-looking European perched in the back like a judge. Ahead of them, to the right of the carriage-way, the promised building site sprang into view: a cage of yellow girders and bamboo scaffolding alive with sweating coolies. Cranes, glistening in the wet, dangled over them like whips. The floodlighting came from the ground and poured wastefully into the mist.

"Look for a low place just near," Luke ordered, slowing down to sixty. "White. Look for a white place."

Jerry pointed to it: a two-storey complex of weeping stucco, neither new nor old, with a twenty-foot stand of bamboos by the entrance, and an ambulance. The ambulance stood open and the three attendants lounged in it, smoking, watching the police who milled around the forecourt as if it were a riot they were handling.

"He's giving us an hour's start over the field."

"Who?"

"Rocker. Rocker is. Who do you think?"

"Why?"

"Because he hit me, I guess. He loves me. He loves you, too. He said to bring you specially."

"Why?"

The rain fell steadily.

"Why? Why? Why?" Luke echoed, furious. "Just hurry!"

The bamboos were out of scale, higher than the wall. A couple of orange-clad priests were sheltering against them, clapping cymbals. A third held an umbrella. There were flower stalls and hearses and from somewhere out of sight the sounds of leisurely incantation. The entrance lobby was a jungle swamp reeking of formaldehyde.

"Big Moo's special envoy," said Luke.

"Press," said Jerry.

The police nodded them through, not looking at their cards.

"Where's the Superintendent?" said Luke.

The smell of formaldehyde was awful. A young sergeant led them. They pushed through a glass door to a room where old men and women, maybe thirty of them, mostly in pyjama suits, waited phlegmatically as if for a late train, under shadowless neon lights and an electric fan. One old man was clearing out his throat, snorting onto the green tiled floor. Seeing the giant *kwailos,* they stared in polite amazement. The pathologist's office was yellow. Yellow walls; yellow blinds, closed; an air-conditioner that wasn't working. The same green tiles, easily washed down.

"Great *smell,*" said Luke.

"Like home," Jerry agreed.

Jerry wished it was battle. Battle was easier. The sergeant told them to wait while he went ahead. They heard the squeak of trolleys, low voices, the clamp of a freezer door, the low hiss of rubber soles. A volume of *Gray's Anatomy* lay next to the telephone. Jerry turned the pages, staring at the illustrations. Luke perched on a chair. An assistant in short rubber boots and overalls brought tea. White cups, green rims, and the Hong Kong monogram with a crown.

"Can you tell the sergeant to hurry, please?" said Luke. "You'll have the whole damn town here in a minute."

"Why us?" said Jerry again.

Luke poured some tea onto the tiled floor, and while it ran into the gutter he topped up the cup from his whisky flask. The sergeant returned, beckoning quickly with his slender hand. They followed him back through the waiting-room. This way there was no door, just a corridor, and a turn like a public lavatory, and they were there.

The first thing Jerry saw was the trolley chipped to hell; there's nothing older or more derelict than worn-out hospital equipment, he thought. The walls were covered in green mould, green stalactites hung from the ceiling, a battered spittoon was filled with used tissues. They clean out the noses, he remembered, before they pull down the sheet to show you. It's a courtesy, so that you aren't shocked. The fumes of formaldehyde made his eyes run. A Chinese pathologist was sitting at the window, making notes on a pad. A couple of attendants were hovering, and more police. There seemed to a general sense of apology around; Jerry couldn't make it out.

The Rocker was ignoring them. He was in a corner, murmuring to the august-looking gentleman from the back of the patrol car, but the corner wasn't far away and Jerry heard "slur on our reputation" spoken twice, in an indignant, nervous tone. Over the body lay a white sheet with a blue cross on it, made in two equal lengths. So that they can use it either way round, Jerry thought. It was the only trolley in the room. The only sheet. The rest of the exhibition was inside the two big freezers with the wooden doors, walk-in size, big as a butcher's shop. Luke was going out of his mind with impatience.

"Jesus, Rocker!" he called across the room. "How much longer you going to keep the lid on this? We got work to do."

No one bothered with him. Tired of waiting, Luke yanked back the sheet. Jerry looked, and looked away. The autopsy room was next door, and he could hear the sound of sawing, like the snarling of a dog.

No wonder they're all so apologetic,

Jerry thought stupidly. Bringing a round-eye corpse to a place like this.

"Jesus *Christ*," Luke was saying. "Holy *Christ*. Who did it to him? How do you *make* those marks? That's a triad thing. *Jesus*."

The dampened window gave on to the courtyard. Jerry could see the bamboos rocking in the rain and the liquid shadows of an ambulance delivering another customer, but he doubted whether any of them looked like this. A police photographer had appeared and there were flashes. A telephone extension hung on the wall. The Rocker was talking into it. He still hadn't looked at Luke, or at Jerry.

"I want him out of here," the august gentleman said.

"Soon as you like," said the Rocker. He returned to the telephone. "In the Walled City, sir. . . . Yes, sir. . . . In an alley, sir. Stripped. Lot of alcohol. . . . The forensic pathologist recognized him immediately, sir. . . . Yes, sir, the bank's here already, sir." He rang off. "Yes, sir, no, sir, three bags full, sir." He dialled a number.

Luke was making notes. "Jesus," he kept saying in awe. "Jesus. They must have taken *weeks* to kill him. Months."

He had died twice, Jerry decided. Once to make him talk and once to shut him up. The things they had done to him first were all over his body, in big and small patches, the way fire hits a carpet, eats holes, then suddenly gives up. Then there was the thing round his neck, a different, faster death altogether. They had done that last, when they didn't want him any more.

Luke called to the pathologist. "Turn him over, will you? Would you mind please turning him over, *sir?*"

The Superintendent had put down the phone.

"What's the story?" said Jerry, straight at him. "Who is he?"

"Name of Frost," the Rocker said, staring back with one eyelid drooping. "Senior official of the South Asian & China. Trustee Department."

"Who killed him?" Jerry asked.

"Yeah, who did it? That's the point,"

said Luke, writing hard.

"Mice," said the Rocker.

"Hong Kong has no triads, no Communists, and no Kuomintang. Right, Rocker?"

"And no whores," the Rocker said.

The august gentleman spared the Rocker further reply. "A vicious case of mugging," he declared over the policeman's shoulder. "A filthy, vicious mugging, exemplifying the need for public vigilance at all times. He was a loyal servant of the bank."

"That's not a mugging," said Luke, looking at Frost again. "That's a *party.*"

"He certainly had some damned odd friends," the Rocker said, still staring at Jerry.

"What's that supposed to mean?" said Jerry.

"What's the story so far?" said Luke.

"He was on the town till midnight. In the company of a couple of Chinese males. One cathouse after another. Then we lose him. Till tonight."

"The bank's offering a reward of fifty thousand dollars," said the august man.

"Hong Kong or U.S.? said Luke, writing.

The august man said, "Hong Kong," very tartly.

"Now, you boys go easy," the Rocker warned. "There's a sick wife in Stanley Hospital, and there's kids —"

"And there's the reputation of the bank," said the august man.

"That will be our first concern," said Luke.

They left half an hour later, still ahead of the field.

"Thanks," said Luke to the Superintendent.

"For nothing," said the Rocker. His drooping eyelid, Jerry noticed, leaked when he was tired.

We've shaken the tree, thought Jerry as they drove away. Boy, oh, boy, have we shaken the tree!

They sat in the same attitudes, Smiley at his desk, Connie in her wheelchair, di Salis gazing into the languid smoke-coil of his pipe. Guillam stood at Smiley's side, the grate of Martello's voice still in his

693

ears. Smiley, with a slight circular movement of his thumb, was polishing his spectacles with the fat end of his tie.

Di Salis, the Jesuit, spoke first. Perhaps he had the most to disown. "There is nothing in logic to link us with this incident. Frost was a libertine. He kept Chinese women, he was manifestly corrupt. He took our bribe without demur. Heaven knows what bribes he has not taken in the past. I will not have it laid at my door."

"Oh, *stuff*," Connie muttered. She sat expressionless and the dog lay sleeping on her lap. Her crippled hands lay over his brown back for warmth. In the background Fawn was pouring tea. Smiley took neither milk nor sugar.

Smiley spoke to the signal form. Nobody had seen his face since he had first looked down to read it.

"Connie, I want the arithmetic," he said.

"Yes, dear."

"Outside these four walls, who is conscious that we leaned on Frost?"

"Craw. Westerby. Craw's policeman.

And if they've any mind, the Cousins will have guessed."

"Not Lacon, not Whitehall."

"And *not* Karla, dear," Connie declared, with a sharp look at the murky portrait.

"No. Not Karla. I believe that." From his voice, they could feel the intensity of the conflict as his intellect forced its will upon his emotions. "For Karla, it would be a most exaggerated response. If a bank account is blown, all he need do is open another elsewhere. He doesn't need *this*." With the tips of his fingers, he precisely moved the signal form an inch up the glass. "The ploy went as planned. The response was simply —" He began again. "The response was more than we expected. Operationally nothing is amiss. Operationally we have advanced the case."

"We've *drawn* them, dear," Connie said firmly.

Di Salis blew up completely. "I insist you do not speak as if we were all of us accomplices here. There is no proven link and I consider it invidious that you should suggest there is.''

Smiley remained remote in his response: *''I* would consider it invidious if I suggested anything else. I ordered this initiative. I refuse not to look at the consequences merely because they are ugly. Put it on my head. But don't let's deceive ourselves.''

''Poor devil didn't know enough, did he?'' Connie mused, seemingly to herself. At first nobody took her up. Then Guillam did: what did she mean by that?

''Frost had nothing to betray, darling,'' she explained. ''That's the worst that can happen to anyone. What could he give them? One zealous journalist, name of Westerby. They had that already, little dears. So of course, they went on. And on.'' She turned to Smiley's direction. He was the only one who shared so much history with her. ''We used to make it a *rule* — remember, George — when the boys went in? We always gave them something they could confess.''

With loving care, Fawn set down a paper cup on Smiley's desk, a slice of lemon floating on the tea. His skull-like grin moved Guillam to repressed fury.

"When you've handed that round, get out," he snapped in his ear. Still smirking, Fawn left.

"Where is Ko, in his mind, at this moment?" Smiley asked, still talking to the signal form. He had locked his fingers under his chin and might have been praying.

"Funk and fuzzy-headedness," Connie declared with confidence. "Fleet street on the prowl, Frost dead and he's still no further forward."

"Yes. Yes, he'll dither. 'Can he hold the dam? Can he plug the leaks? Where *are* the leaks, anyway?' . . . That's what we wanted. We've got it." He made the smallest movement of his bowed head, and it pointed toward Guillam. "Peter, you will please ask the Cousins the step up their surveillance on Tiu. Static posts only, tell them. No street-work, no frightening the game, no nonsense of that kind. Telephone, mail, the easy things only. Doc, when did Tiu last visit the mainland?"

Di Salis grudgingly gave a date.

"Find out the route he travelled and where he bought his ticket. In case he does it again."

"It's on record already," di Salis retorted sulkily and made a most unpleasing sneer, looking to heaven and writhing with his lips and shoulders.

"Then kindly be so good as to make me a separate note of it," Smiley replied with unshakeable forbearance. "Westerby," he went on in the same flat voice, and for a second Guillam had the sickening feeling that Smiley was suffering from some kind of hallucination, and thought that Jerry was in the room with him, to receive his orders like the rest of them. "I pull him out — I can do that. His paper recalls him, why shouldn't it? Then what? Ko waits. He listens. He hears nothing. And he relaxes."

"And enter the narcotics heroes," Guillam said, glancing at the calendar.

"Or I pull him out and I replace him, and another fieldman takes up the trail. Is he any less at risk than Westerby is now?"

"It never works," Connie muttered.

"Changing horses. Never. You know that. Briefing, training, re-gearing, new relationships. Never."

"I don't see that he *is* at risk!" di Salis asserted shrilly.

Swinging angrily round, Guillam started to slap him down, but Smiley spoke ahead of him: "Why not, Doc?"

"Accepting your hypothesis — which I don't — Ko is not a man of violence. He's a successful businessman and his maxims are face, and expediency, and merit, and hard work. I won't have him spoken of as if he were some kind of thug. I grant you he has people, and perhaps his people are less nice than he when it comes to method. Much as we are Whitehall's people. That doesn't make blackguards of Whitehall, I trust."

For Christ's sake, out with it! thought Guillam.

"Westerby is not a Frost," di Salis persisted, in the same didactic, nasal whine. "Westerby is not a dishonest servant. Westerby has not betrayed Ko's confidence, or Ko's money, or Ko's brother. In Ko's eyes, Westerby represents a large newspaper. And Westerby has let it be known — both to Frost and to Tiu, I understand — that his paper possesses a greater degree of knowledge in the matter than he himself. Ko understands the world. By removing one journalist, he will not remove the risk. To the contrary, he will bring out the whole pack.''

''Then what is in his mind?'' said Smiley.

''Uncertainty. Much as Connie said. He cannot gauge the threat. The Chinese have little place for abstracts, less still for abstract situations. He would like the threat to blow over, and if nothing concrete occurs, he will assume it has done so. That is not a habit confined to the Occident. I am extending your hypothesis.'' He stood up. ''I am not endorsing it. I refuse to. I dissociate myself from it absolutely.''

He stalked out. On Smiley's nod, Guillam followed him. Only Connie stayed behind.

Smiley had closed his eyes and his brow was drawn into a rigid knot above the bridge of his nose. For a long while Connie said nothing at all. Trot lay as dead across her lap, and she gazed down at him, fondling his belly.

"Karla wouldn't give two pins, would he, dearie?" she murmured. "Not for one dead Frost, nor for ten. That's the difference, really. We can't write it much larger than that, can we, not these days? Who was it who used to say, 'We're fighting for the survival of Reasonable Man'? Steed-Asprey? Or was it Control? I loved that. It covered it all. Hitler. The new thing. That's who we are: reasonable. Aren't we, Trot? We're not just English. We're reasonable."

Her voice fell a little. "Darling, what about Sam? Have you had *thoughts?*"

It was still a long while before Smiley spoke, and when he did so, his voice was harsh, like a voice to keep her at a distance.

"He's to stand by. Do nothing till he has the green light. He knows that. He's to wait till the green light." He drew in a deep breath and let it out again. "He may not even be needed. We may quite well manage without him. It all depends how Ko jumps.''

"George, darling, *dear* George."

In silent ritual, she pushed herself to the grate, took up the poker, and with a huge effort stirred the coals, clinging to the dog with her free hand.

Jerry stood at the kitchen window, watching the yellow dawn cut up the harbour mist. Last night there had been a storm, he remembered. Must have hit an hour before Luke telephoned. He had watched it from the mattress while the girl lay snoring along his leg. First the smell of vegetation, then the wind rustling guiltily in the palm trees, dry hands rubbed together. Then the hiss of rain like tons of molten shot being shaken into the sea. Finally the sheet lightning rocking the harbour in long slow breaths while salvos of thunder cracked over the dancing roof-tops. I killed him, he thought. Give or take a little, it was me who gave him the shove. "It's not just the generals, it's every man who carries a gun." Quote source and context.

The phone was ringing. Let it ring, he thought. Probably Craw, wetting his pants. He picked up the receiver. Luke, sounding even more than usually American.

"Hey, man! Big drama! Stubbsie just came through on the wire. Personal for Westerby. Eat before reading. Want to hear it?"

"No."

"A swing through the war zones. Cambodia's airlines and the siege economy. Our man amid shot and shell! You're in luck, sailor! They want you to get your ass shot off!"

And leave Lizzie to Tiu, he thought, ringing off.

And for all I know, to that bastard Collins too, lurking in her shadow like a white slaver. Jerry had worked to Sam a couple of times while Sam was plain Mr. Mellon of Vientiane, an uncannily successful trader, headman of the local round-eye crooks. He reckoned him one of the most unappetising operators in the game.

He returned to his place at the window

thinking of Lizzie again, up there on her own giddy roof-top. Thinking of little Frost, and of his fondness for being alive. Thinking of the smell that had greeted him when he returned here, to his flat. It was everywhere. It overrode the reek of the girl's deodorant, the stale cigarette smoke, the smell of gas, and the smell of cooking oil from the mah-jong players next door. It even overrode the memory of Frost's formaldehyde. Catching it, Jerry had actually charted in his imagination the route Tiu had taken as he foraged: where he had lingered, and where he had skimped on his journey through Jerry's clothes, Jerry's pantry, and Jerry's few possessions. A smell of rose-water and almonds mixed, favoured by an early wife.

15
Siege Town

When you leave Hong Kong, it ceases to exist. When you have passed the last Chinese policeman in British ammunition boots and puttees, and held your breath as you race sixty feet above the roofs of the grey slums, when the out-islands have dwindled into the blue mist, you know that the curtain has been rung down, the props cleared away, and the life you lived there was all illusion. But this time for once, Jerry couldn't rise to that feeling: he carried the memory of the dead Frost and the live girl with him, and they were still beside him as he reached Bangkok.

As usual it took him all day to find what he was looking for; as usual he was about to give up. In Bangkok, in Jerry's view, that happened to everyone: a tourist looking for a *wat,* a journalist for a story — or Jerry for Ricardo's friend and partner Charlie Marshall — your prize sits down the far end of some damned alley, jammed between a silted *klong* and a pile of concrete trash, and it costs you five dollars U.S. more than you expected. Also, though this was theoretically Bangkok's dry season, Jerry could not remember ever being here except in rain, which cascaded in unheralded bursts from the polluted, burning sky. Afterwards people always told him he got the one wet day. He started at the airport, because he was already there and because he reasoned that in the South East no one can fly for long without flying through Bangkok. Charlie wasn't around any more, they said; someone even assured him Charlie had stopped being a pilot after Ric died. Someone else said he was in jail, someone else again that he was most likely in "one of the dens." A ravishing Air Vietnam hostess said with a giggle that he was making freight hops to Saigon; she only ever saw him in Saigon.

"Out of where?" Jerry asked.

"Maybe Phnom Penh, maybe Vientiane," she said — but Charlie's destination, she insisted, was always Saigon and he never hit Bangkok. Jerry checked the telephone directory and there was no Indocharter listed. On an off chance he looked up Marshall too, discovered one — even a Marshall, C. — called him, but found himself talking not to the son of a Kuomintang war-lord who had christened himself with high military rank but to a puzzled Scottish trader who kept saying, "Listen, but *do* come round."

He went to the jail where the *farangs* are locked up when they can't pay or have been rude to a general, and checked the record. He walked along the balconies and peered through the cage doors and spoke to a couple of crazed hippies. But while they had a good deal to say about being locked up, they hadn't seen Charlie Marshall and they hadn't heard of him, and to put it delicately they didn't care about him either. In a black mood he drove to the so-called sanatorium where addicts enjoy their cold turkey, and there was great excitement because a man in a strait-jacket had succeeded in putting his own eyes out with his fingers, but it wasn't Charlie Marshall, and no, they had no pilots, no Corsicans, no Corsican Chinese, and *certainly* no son of a Kuomintang general.

So Jerry started on the hotels where pilots might hang out in transit. He didn't like the work, because it was deadening and, more particularly, he knew that Ko had a big outfit here. He had no serious doubt that Frost had blown him; he knew that most rich overseas Chinese legitimately run several passports and the Swatownese more than several; he knew that Ko had a Thai passport in his pocket and probably a couple of Thai generals as well. And he knew that when they were cross the Thais killed a great deal sooner and more thoroughly than almost everyone else, even though when they condemned a man to the firing-squad, they shot him through a stretched bed sheet in order not to offend the laws of the Lord Buddha. For that reason among a good few others, Jerry felt less than comfortable shouting Charlie Marshall's name all over the big hotels.

He tried the Erawan, the Hyatt, the Miramar, and the Oriental and about thirty others, and at the Erawan he trod specially lightly, remembering that China Airsea had a suite there and Craw said Ko used it often. He formed a picture of Lizzie with her blond hair, playing hostess for him or stretched out at the poolside sunning her long body while the tycoons sipped their Scotches and wondered how much would buy an hour of her time.

While he rode round, a sudden rainstorm pelted fat drops so foul with soot that they blackened the gold of the street temples. The taxi-driver aquaplaned on the flooded roads, missing the water-buffaloes by inches, the garish buses jingled and charged at them, blood-stained Kung Fu posters screamed at them; but Marshall — Charlie Marshall — *Captain* Marshall — was not a name to anyone, though Jerry dispensed coffee money liberally. Charlie's got a girl, thought Jerry. He's got a girl and uses her place, just as I would.

At the Oriental he tipped the porter and arranged to collect messages and use the telephone, and best of all he obtained a receipt for two nights' lodging with which to taunt Stubbs. But his trail round the hotels had scared him, he felt exposed and at risk, so to sleep, for a dollar a night, he took a prepaid room in a nameless back-street doss-house where the formalities of registration were dispensed with: a place like a row of beach huts, with all the room doors opening straight on to the pavement in order to make fornication easier, and open garages with plastic curtains that screened the number of your car.

By the evening he was reduced to stomping the air-freight agencies, asking about a firm called Indocharter, though he wasn't too keen to do that either, and he was seriously wondering whether to believe the Air Vietnam hostess and take up the trail in Saigon, when a Chinese girl in one of the agencies said, "Indocharter? That's Captain Marshall's line."

She directed him to a bookshop where Charlie Marshall bought his literature and collected his mail whenever he was in town. The shop was also run by Chinese, and when Jerry mentioned Marshall the old proprietor burst out laughing and said Charlie hadn't been in for months. The old man was very small, with false teeth that grimaced.

"He owe you money? Charlie Marshall owe you money, clash a plane for you?" He once more hooted with laughter and Jerry joined in.

"Super. Great. Listen, what do you do with all the mail when he doesn't come here? Do you send it on?"

Charlie Marshall, he didn't get no mail, the old man said.

"Ah, but, sport, if a letter comes tomorrow, where will you send it?"

To Phnom Penh, the old man said, pocketing his five dollars, and fished a scrap of paper fom his desk so that Jerry could copy down the address.

"Maybe I should buy him a book," said Jerry, looking round. "What does he like?"

"Flench," the old man said automatically and, taking Jerry upstairs, showed him his sanctum for round-eye culture: for the English, pornography printed in Brussels; for the French, row after row of tattered classics — Voltaire, Montesquieu, Hugo. Jerry bought a copy of *Candide* and slipped it into his pocket. Visitors to this room were *ex officio* celebrities apparently, for the old man produced a visitor's book and Jerry signed it: "J. Westerby, newshound." The comments column was played for laughs, so he wrote, "A most distinguished emporium."

Then he looked back through the pages and asked, "Charlie Marshall sign here too, sport?"

The old man showed him Charlie Marshall's signature a couple of times — "Address: here," he had written.

"How about his friend?"

"Flend?"

"Captain Ricardo."

At this the old man grew very solemn and gently took away the book.

He went round to the Foreign Correspondents' Club at the Oriental, and it was empty except for a troop of Japanese who had just returned from

Cambodia. They told him the state of play there as of yesterday, and he got a little drunk. And as he was leaving, to his momentary horror, the dwarf appeared, in town for consultation with the local bureau. He had a Thai boy in tow, which made him particularly pert. "Why, *Westerby!* But *how's* the Secret Service today?" He played this joke on pretty well everyone, but it didn't improve Jerry's peace of mind.

At the doss-house he drank a lot more Scotch but the exertions of his fellow guests kept him awake. Finally, in self-defence he went out and found himself a girl, a soft little creature from a bar up the road, but when he lay alone his thoughts once more homed on Lizzie: like it or not, she was his bed companion.

How much was she consciously involved with them? he wondered. Did she know what she was playing with when she set Jerry up for Tiu? Did she know what Drake's boys had done to Frost? Did she know they might do it to Jerry? It even entered his mind that she had been there while they did it, and that thought appalled him. No question: Frost's body was still very fresh in his memory. It was one of the worst.

By two in the morning he decided he was going to have a bout of fever, he was sweating and turning so much. Once, he heard sounds of soft footsteps inside the room and flung himself into a corner, clutching a teak table-lamp ripped from its socket. At four he was woken by that amazing Asian hubbub: pig-like hawking sounds, bells, cries of old men *in extremis,* the crowing of a thousand roosters echoing in the tile and concrete corridors. He fought with the broken plumbing and began the laborious business of getting clean from a thin trickle of cold water. At five the radio was turned on full blast to get him out of bed, and a whine of Asian music announced that the day had begun in earnest. By then he had shaved as if it were his wedding day, and at eight he cabled his plans to the comic for the Circus to intercept.

At eleven he caught the plane to Phnom Penh. As he climbed aboard the Air

Cambodge Caravelle, the ground hostess turned her lovely face to him and, in her best lilting English, melodiously wished him a "nice fright."

"Thanks. Yes. Super," he said, and chose the seat over the wing where you stood the best chance. As they slowly took off, he saw a group of fat Thais playing lousy golf on perfect links just beside the runway.

There were eight names on the flight manifest when Jerry read it at the check-in, but only one other passenger boarded the plane, a black-clad American boy with a brief-case. The rest was cargo, stacked aft in brown gunny bags and rush boxes. A siege plane, Jerry thought automatically. You fly in with the goods, you fly out with the lucky. The stewardess offered him an old *Jours de France* and a barley sugar. He read the *Jours de France* to put some French back into his mind, then remembered *Candide* and read that. He had brought the book-bag, and in the book-bag he had Conrad. In Phnom Penh he always read Conrad; it tickled him to remind himself he was sitting in the last of the true Conrad river ports.

To land, they flew in high, then pancaked in a tight uneasy spiral to avoid random small-arms fire from the jungle. There was no ground control, but Jerry hadn't expected any. The stewardess didn't know how close the Khmer Rouge were to the town, but the Japanese had said fifteen kilometres on all fronts and less where there were no roads. The Japanese had said the airport was under fire but only from rockets and sporadically. No 105s. Not yet, but there's always a beginning, thought Jerry.

Then olive earth leapt at them and Jerry saw bomb craters spattered like egg-spots, and the yellow lines from the tyre tracks of the convoys. As they landed feather-light on the pitted runway, the inevitable naked brown children splashed contentedly in a mud-filled crater.

He stepped on to the tarmac and as the heat hit him with a slap, so did the roar of transport planes taking off and landing. Yet for all that, he had the illusion of arriving on a calm summer's day: for in

Phnom Penh, like nowhere else Jerry had ever been, war took place in an atmosphere of peace. He remembered the last time he was here, before the bombing halt. A group of Air France passengers bound for Tokyo had been dawdling curiously on the apron, not realising they had landed in a battle. No one told them to take cover, no one was with them. F-4s and 111s were screaming over the airfield, there was shooting from the perimeter, Air America choppers were landing the dead in nets like frightful catches from some red sea, and a Boeing 707, in order to take off, had to crawl across the entire airfield, running the gauntlet in slow motion. Spellbound, Jerry had watched her lollop out of range of the ground fire, and all the way he had waited for the thump that would tell him she had been hit in the tail. But she had kept going as if the innocent were immune, and disappeared into the untroubled horizon.

Now ironically, with the end so close, he noticed that the accent was on the cargo of survival. On the farther side of the airfield huge chartered all-silver American transport planes, 707s and four-engined turbo-prop C-130s marked "Trans World," "Bird Airways," or not marked at all, were landing and taking off in a clumsy, dangerous shuttle as they brought the ammunition and rice in from Thailand and Saigon. On his hasty walk to the terminal Jerry saw two landings, and each time held his breath waiting for the late back-charge of the jets as they fought and shivered to a halt inside the *revêtement* of earth-filled ammunition boxes at the soft end of the landing-strip. Even before they stopped, flight handlers in flack-jackets and helmets had converged like unarmed platoons to wrest their precious sacks from the holds.

Yet even these bad omens could not destroy his pleasure at being back.

"Vous restez combien de temps, Monsieur?" the immigration officer enquired.

"Toujours, sport," said Jerry. "Long as you'll have me. Longer." He thought of asking after Charlie Marshall then and there, but the airport was stiff with police and spooks of every sort, and as long as he

718

didn't know what he was up against it seemed wise not to advertise his interest. There was a colourful array of old aircraft with new insignia, but he couldn't see any belonging to Indocharter, whose registered markings, Craw had told him at the valedictory briefing just before he left Hong Kong, were believed to be Ko's racing colours: sea grey and sky blue.

He took a taxi and rode in front, gently declining the driver's courteous offers of girls, shows, clubs, boys. The *flamboyants* made a luscious arcade of orange against the slate monsoon sky. He stopped at a haberdasher to change money *au cours flexible,* a term he loved. The money-changers used to be Chinese, Jerry remembered. This one was Indian: the Chinese get out early, but the Indians stay to pick the carcass. Shanty towns lay left and right of the road. Refugees crouched everywhere, cooking, dozing in silent groups. A ring of small children sat passing round a cigarette.

"Nous sommes un village avec une population des millions," said the driver in his schoolroom French.

An army convoy drove at them, headlights on, sticking to the centre of the road. The taxi-driver obediently pulled into the dirt. An ambulance brought up the rear, both doors open. The bodies were stacked feet outward, legs like pigs' trotters, marbled and bruised. Dead or alive, it scarcely mattered. They passed a cluster of stilt houses smashed by rockets, and entered a provincial French square: a restaurant, an *épicerie,* a *charcuterie,* advertisements for Byrrh and Coca-Cola. On the curb, children squatted, watching over litre winebottles filled with stolen petrol. Jerry remembered that too: that was what had happened in the shellings. The shells touched off the petrol and the result was a blood-bath. It would happen again this time. Nobody learned anything, nothing changed, the offal was cleared away by morning.

"Stop!" said Jerry and on the spur of the moment handed the driver the piece of paper on which he had written down the Bangkok bookshop's address for Charlie Marshall. He had imagined he should creep up on the place at dead of night, but in the sunlight there seemed no point any more.

"*Y aller?*" the driver asked, turning to look at him in surprise.

"That's it, sport."

"*Vous connaissez cette maison?*"

"Chum of mine."

"*A vous? Un ami à vous?*"

"Press," said Jerry, which explains any lunacy.

The driver shrugged and pointed the car down a long boulevard, past the French cathedral, into a mud road lined with courtyard villas which became quickly dingier as they approached the edge of town. Twice Jerry asked the driver what was special about the address, but the driver had lost his charm and shrugged away the questions. When they stopped, he insisted on being paid off, and drove away racing the gear changes in rebuke.

It was just another villa, the lower half hidden behind a wall pierced with a wrought-iron gate. Jerry pushed the bell and heard nothing. When he tried to force the gate, it wouldn't move. He heard a window slam and thought, as he looked quickly up, that he saw a brown face slip away behind the mosquito wire. Then the gate buzzed and yielded, and he walked up a few steps to a tiled verandah and another door, this one of solid teak with a tiny shaded grille for looking out but not in. He waited, then hammered heavily on the knocker, and heard the echoes bounding all over the house. The door was double, with a join at the centre. Pressing his face to the gap, he saw a strip of tiled floor and two steps, presumably the last two steps of a staircase. On the lower of these stood two smooth brown feet, naked, and two bare shins, but he saw no farther than the knees.

"Hullo!" he yelled, still at the gap. "*Bonjour!* Hullo!" And when the legs still did not move: "*Je suis un ami de Charlie Marshall! Madame, Monsieur, je suis un ami anglais de Charlie Marshall! Je veux lui parler.*"

He took out a five-dollar bill and shoved it through the gap but nothing happened, so he took it back and instead tore a piece of paper from his notebook. He headed his message "To Captain C. Marshall" and introduced himself by name as "a British journalist with a proposal to our mutual interest," and gave the address of his hotel. Threading this note also through the gap, he looked for the brown legs again but they had vanished, so he walked till he found a *cyclo,* then rode in the *cyclo* till he found a cab: and no, thank you, no, thank you, he didn't want a girl — except that, as usual, he did.

The hotel used to be the Royal. Now it was *Le Phnom.* A flag was flying from the mast-head, but its grandeur already looked desperate. Signing himself in, he saw living flesh basking round the courtyard pool and once more thought of Lizzie. For the girls, this was the hard school, and if she'd carried little packets for Ricardo, then ten to one she'd been through it. The prettiest belonged to the richest, and the richest were Phnom Penh's Rotarian crooks: the gold and rubber smugglers, the police chiefs, the big-fisted Corsicans who made neat deals with the Khmer Rouge in mid-battle.

There was a letter waiting for him, the flap not sealed. The receptionist, having read it himself, politely watched Jerry do the same. A gilt-edged invitation card with an Embassy crest invited him to dinner. His host was someone he had never heard of. Mystified, he turned the card over. A scrawl on the back read "Knew your friend George of the *Guardian*," and "guardian" was the word that introduced. Dinner and dead-letter boxes, he thought: what Sarratt scathingly called the great Foreign Office disconnection.

"*Téléphone?*" Jerry enquired.

"*Il est foutu, Monsieur.*"

"*Electricité?*"

"*Aussi foutue, Monsieur, mais nous - avons beaucoup de l'eau.*"

"Keller!" said Jerry with a grin.

"*Dans la cour, Monsieur.*"

He walked into the gardens. Among the flesh sat a bunch of warries from the Fleet Street Heavies, drinking Scotch and exchanging hard stories. They looked like boy pilots in the Battle of Britain fighting a borrowed war, and they watched him in collective contempt for his upper-class origins. One wore a white kerchief, and lank hair bravely tossed back.

"Christ, it's the Duke," he said. "How'd you get here? Walk on the Mekong?"

But Jerry didn't want them, he wanted Keller. Keller was permanent. He was a wireman and he was American and Jerry knew him from other wars. More particularly, no *uitlander* newsman came to town without putting his cause at Keller's feet, and if Jerry was to have credibility, then Keller's chop would supply it, and credibility was increasingly dear to him. He found Keller in the car-park. Broad shoulders, grey-headed, one sleeve rolled down. He was standing with his sleeved arm stuffed into his pocket, watching a driver hose out the inside of a Mercedes.

"Max. Super."

"Ripping," said Keller after glancing at him, then went back to his watching. Beside him stood a pair of slim Khmer boys looking like fashion photographers, in high-heeled boots and bell-bottoms and cameras dangling over their glittering, unbuttoned shirts. As Jerry looked on, the driver stopped hosing and began scrubbing the upholstery with an army pack of lint which turned brown the more he rubbed. Another American joined the group and Jerry guessed he was Keller's newest stringer. Keller went through stringers fairly fast.

"What happened?" said Jerry as the driver began hosing again.

"Two-dollar hero caught very expensive bullet," said the stringer. "That's what happened." He was a pale Southerner with an air of being amused, and Jerry was prepared to dislike him.

"Right, Keller?" Jerry asked.

"Photographer," Keller said.

"One of Keller's native picture-warriors," said the Southerner, still grinning.

Keller's wire service ran a stable of them. All the big services did: Cambodian boys, like the couple standing here. They paid them two U.S. to go to the front and twenty for every photo printed. Jerry had heard that Keller was losing them at the rate of one a week.

"Took it clean through the shoulder while he was running and stooping," said the stringer. "Lost it through the lower back. Went through him like grass through a goose." He seemed impressed.

"Where is he?" said Jerry for something to say, while the driver continued to mop and hose and scrub.

"Dying right up the road there. What happened, see, couple of weeks back those bastards in the New York bureau dug their toes in about medication. We used to ship them to Bangkok. Not now. Man, not now. Know something? Up the road they lie on the floor and have to bribe the nurses to take them water. Right, boys?"

The two Cambodians smiled politely.

"Want something, Westerby?" Keller asked.

Keller's face was grey and pitted. Jerry knew him best from the sixties in the Congo, where Keller had burned his hand pulling a kid out of a lorry. Now the fingers were welded like a webbed claw, but otherwise he looked the same. Jerry remembered that incident best because he had been holding the other end of the kid.

"Comic wants me to take a look round," Jerry said.

"Can you still do that?"

Jerry laughed and Keller laughed, and they drank Scotch in the bar till the car was ready, chatting about old times. At the main entrance, they picked up a girl who had been waiting all day, just for Keller, a tall Californian with too much camera and long, restless legs. As the phones weren't working, Jerry insisted on stopping off at the British Embassy so that he could reply to his invitation.

Keller wasn't very polite: "You some kinda spook or something these days, Westerby, slanting your stories, arse-licking for deep background and a pension on the side or something?" There were people who said that was roughly Keller's position, but there are always people.

"Sure," said Jerry amiably. "Been at it for years."

The sandbags at the entrance were new and new anti-grenade wires glistened in the teeming sunlight. In the lobby, with the spine-breaking irrevelance which only diplomats can quite achieve, a big

728

partioned poster recommended "British High Performance Cars" to a city parched of fuel, and supplied cheerful photographs of several unavailable models.

"I will tell the Counsellor you have accepted," said the receptionist solemnly.

The Mercedes still smelt a little warm from the blood, but the driver had turned up the air-conditioning.

"What do they do in there, Westerby?" Keller asked. "Knit or something?"

"Or something." Jerry smiled, mainly to the Californian girl.

Jerry sat in front, Keller and the girl in the back.

"Okay. So hear this," said Keller.

"Sure," said Jerry.

Jerry had his notebook open and scribbled while Keller talked. The girl wore a short skirt and Jerry and the driver could see her thighs in the mirror. Keller had his good hand on her knee. Her name of all things was Lorraine and, like Jerry, she was formally taking a swing through the war zones for her group of Midwest dailies. Soon they were the only car. Soon even the *cyclos* stopped, leaving them peasants, and bicycles, and buffaloes, and the flowered bushes of the approaching countryside.

"Heavy fighting on all the main highways," Keller intoned at near dictation speed. "Rocket attacks at night, *plastics* during the day, Lon Nol still thinks he's God, and the U.S. Embassy has hot flushes supporting him then trying to throw him out." He gave statistics, ordnance, casualties, the scale of U.S. aid. He named generals known to be selling American arms to the Khmer Rouge, and generals who ran phantom armies in order to claim the troops' pay, and generals who did both.

"The usual snafu," he went on. "Bad guys are too weak to take the towns, good guys are too crapped out to take the countryside, and nobody wants to fight except the Coms. Students ready to set fire to the place soon as they're no longer exempt from the war, food riots any day now, corruption like there was no tomorrow, no one can live on his salary, fortunes being made, and the place bleeding to death. Palace is unreal and the Embassy is a nut-house, more spooks than straight guys and all pretending they've got a secret. Want more?''

''How long do you give it?''

''A week. Ten years.''

''How about the airlines?''

''Airlines is all we have. Mekong's good as dead, so's the roads. Airlines have the whole ballpark. We did a story on that. You see it? They ripped it to pieces. Jesus,'' he said to the girl. ''Why do I have to give a rerun for the poms?''

''More,'' said Jerry, writing.

''Six months ago this town had five registered airlines. Last three months we got thirty-four new licences issued and there's like another dozen in the pipeline. Going rate is three million riels to the Minister personally and two million spread around his people. Less if you pay gold, less still if you pay abroad. We're working route thirteen,'' he said to the girl. ''Thought you'd like to take a look.''

''Great,'' said the girl and pressed her knees together, entrapping Keller's good hand.

They passed a statue with its arm shot off and after that the road followed the river bend.

"That's if Westerby here can handle it," Keller added as an afterthought.

"Oh, I think I'm in pretty good shape," said Jerry, and the girl laughed, changing sides a moment.

"K.R. got themselves a new position out on the far bank there, hon," Keller explained, talking to the girl in preference. Across the brown, fast water, Jerry saw a couple of T-28s, poking around looking for something to bomb. There was a fire, quite a big one, and the smoke column rose straight into the sky like a virtuous offering.

"Where do the overseas Chinese come in?" Jerry asked. "In Hong Kong no one's heard of this place."

"Chinese control eighty percent of our commerce and that includes airlines. Old or new. Cambodian's lazy, see, hon? Your Cambodian's content to take his profit out of American aid. Your Chinese aren't like that. Oh, no, siree. Chinese like to work, Chinese like to turn their cash over. They fixed our money market, our transport monopoly, our rate of inflation, our siege economy. War's getting to be a wholly owned Hong Kong subsidiary. Hey, Westerby, you still got that wife you told me about, the cute one with the eyes?''

"Took the other road," Jerry said.

"Too bad. She sounded real great. He had this great wife," said Keller to the girl.

"How about you?" asked Jerry.

Keller shook his head and smiled at the girl. "Care if I smoke, hon?" he asked confidingly.

There was a gap in Keller's welded claw which could have been drilled specially to hold a cigarette, and the rim of it was brown with nicotine. Keller put his good hand back on her thigh. The road turned to track, and deep ruts appeared where the convoys had passed. They entered a short tunnel of trees, and as they did so a thunder of shell-fire opened to their right and the trees arched like trees in a typhoon.

"*Wow!*" the girl yelled. "Can we slow down a little?" And she began hauling at the straps of her camera.

"Be my guest. Medium artillery," said Keller. "Ours," he added as a joke. The girl lowered the window and shot off some film. The barrage continued, the trees danced, but the peasants in the paddy didn't even lift their heads. When it died, the bells of the water-buffaloes went on ringing like an echo. They drove on. On the near river-bank, two kids had an old bike and were swapping rides. In the water, a shoal of them were diving in and out of an inner tube, brown bodies glistening. The girl photographed them too.

"You still speak French, Westerby? Me and Westerby did a thing together in the Congo awhile back," he explained to the girl.

"I heard," she said knowingly.

"Poms get education," Keller explained. Jerry hadn't remembered him so talkative. "They get *raised*. That right, Westerby? Specially lords, right? Westerby's some kind of lord."

"That's us, sport. Scholars to a man. Not like you hayseeds."

"Well, you speak to the driver, right? We got instructions for him, you do the saying. He hasn't had time to learn English yet. Go left."

"*A gauche,*" said Jerry.

The driver was a boy, but he already had the guide's boredom.

In the mirror Jerry noticed that Keller's white claw was shaking as he drew on the cigarette. He wondered if it always did. They passed through a couple of villages. It was very quiet. He thought of Lizzie and the claw marks on her chin. He longed to do something plain with her, like taking a walk over English fields. Craw said she was a suburban drag-up. It touched him that she had a fantasy about horses.

"Westerby."

"Yes, sport?"

"That thing you have with your fingers. Drumming them. Mind not doing that? Bugs me. It's repressive, somehow." He turned to the girl. "They been pounding this place for years, hon," he said expansively. "Years." He blew out a gust of cigarette smoke.

"About the airline thing," Jerry suggested, pencil ready to write again. "What's the arithmetic?"

"Most of the companies take dry-wing leases out of Vientiane. That includes maintenance, pilot, depreciation, but not fuel. Maybe you knew that. Best is own your own plane. That way you have the two things. You milk the siege and you get your ass out when the end comes. Watch for the kids, hon," he told the girl as he drew again on his cigarette. "While there's kids around there won't be trouble. When the kids disappear it's bad news. Means they've hidden them. Always watch for kids."

The girl Lorraine was fiddling with her camera again. They had reached a rudimentary check-point. A couple of sentries peered in as they passed, but the driver didn't even slow down. They approached a fork and the driver stopped.

"The river," Keller ordered. "Tell him to stay on the river-bank."

Jerry told him. The boy seemed surprised; seemed even about to object, then changed his mind.

736

"Kids in the villages," Keller was saying, "kids at the front. No difference. Either way, kids are a weather-vane. Khmer soldiers take their families with them to war as a matter of course. If the father dies, there'll be nothing for the family anyway, so they might as well come along with the military where there's food. Another thing, hon, another thing is, the widows must be right on hand to claim evidence of the father's death, right? That's a human-interest thing for you — right, Westerby? If they don't claim, the commanding officer will deny it and steal the man's pay for himself. Be my guest," he said as she wrote. "But don't think anyone will print it. This war's over. Right, Westerby?"

"Finito," Jerry agreed.

She would be funny, he decided. If Lizzie were here, she would definitely see a funny side and laugh at it. Somewhere among all her imitations, he reckoned, there was a lost original, and he definitely intended to find it. The driver drew up beside an old woman and asked her something in Khmer, but she put her face in her hands and turned her head away.

"Why'd she do *that,* for God's sakes?" the girl cried angrily. "We didn't want anything bad. Jesus!"

"Shy," said Keller in a flattening voice.

Behind them the artillery barrage fired another salvo and it was like a door slamming, barring the way back. They passed a *wat* and entered a market square made of wooden houses. Saffron-clad monks stared at them, but the girls tending the stalls ignored them and the babies went on playing with the bantams.

"So what was the check-point for?" the girl asked as she photographed. "Are we somewhere dangerous now?"

"Getting there, hon, getting there. Now shut up."

Ahead of them Jerry could hear the sound of automatic fire, M-16s and AK-47s mixed. A jeep raced at them out of the trees and at the last second veered, banging and tripping over the ruts. At the same moment the sunshine went out. Till now they had accepted it as their right, a liquid, vivid light washed clean by the rainstorms. This was March and the dry season; this was Cambodia, where war, like cricket, was played in decent weather. But now black clouds collected, the trees closed round them like winter, and the wooden houses pulled into the dark.

"What do the Khmer Rouge dress like?" the girl asked in a quieter voice. "Do they have *uniforms?*"

"Feathers and a G-string," Keller roared. "Some are even bottomless." As he laughed, Jerry heard the taut strain in his voice, and glimpsed the trembling claw as he drew on his cigarette. "Hell, hon, they dress like farmers, for Christ's sake. They just have these black pyjamas."

"Is it always so empty?"

"Varies," said Keller.

"And Ho Chi Minh sandals," Jerry put in distractedly.

A pair of green water birds lifted across the track. The sound of firing was no louder.

"Didn't you have a daughter or something? What happened there?" Keller said.

"She's fine. Great."

"Called what?"

"Catherine," said Jerry.

"Sounds like we're going away from it," Lorraine said, disappointed. They passed an old corpse with no arms. The flies had settled on the face wounds in a black lava.

"Do they always do that?" the girl asked, curious.

"Do what, hon?"

"Take off the boots?"

"Sometimes they take the boots off, sometimes they're the wrong damn size," said Keller in another queer snap of anger. "Some cows got horns, some cows don't, and some cows is horses. Now shut up, will you? Where you from?"

"Santa Barbara," said the girl.

Abruptly the trees ended. They turned a bend and were in the open again, with the brown river right beside them. Unbidden, the driver stopped, then gently backed into the trees.

"Where's he going?" the girl asked. "Who told him to do that?"

"I think he's worried about his tyres,

sport," said Jerry, making a joke of it.

"At thirty bucks a day?" said Keller, also as a joke.

They had found a little battle. Ahead of them, dominating the river bend, stood a smashed village on high waste ground without a living tree near it. The ruined walls were white and the torn edges yellow. With so little vegetation the place looked like the remnants of a Foreign Legion fort, and perhaps it was just that. Inside the walls brown lorries clustered, like lorries at a building site. They heard a few shots, a light rattle. It could have been huntsmen shooting at the evening flight. Tracer flashed, a trio of mortar bombs struck, the ground shook, the car vibrated, and the driver quietly unwound his window while Jerry did the same. But the girl had opened her door and was getting out, one classic leg after the other. Rummaging in a black air-bag, she produced a telefoto lens, screwed it into her camera, and studied the enlarged image.

"That's all there is?" she asked doubtfully. "Shouldn't we see the enemy as well? I don't see anything but our guys and a lot of dirty smoke.''

"Oh, they're out on the other side there, hon," Keller said.

"Can't we see?'' There was a small silence while the two men conferred without speaking.

"Look," said Keller. "This was just a tour, okay, hon? The detail of the thing gets very varied. Okay?''

"I just think it would be great to see the enemy. I want confrontation, Max. I really do. I like it.''

They started walking.

Sometimes you do it to save face, thought Jerry, other times you just do it because you haven't done your job unless you've scared yourself to death. Other times again, you go in order to remind yourself that survival is a fluke. But mostly you go because the others go — for machismo — and because in order to belong you must share.

In the old days perhaps, Jerry had gone for more select reasons. In order to know himself: the Hemingway game. In order to raise his threshold of fear. Because in battle, as in love, desire escalates. When you have been machine-gunned, single rounds seem trivial. When you've been shelled to pieces, the machine-gunning's child's play, if only because the impact of plain shot leaves your brain in place, where the clump of a shell blows it through your ears. And there is a peace: he remembered that too. At bad times in his life — money, children, women all adrift — there had been a sense of peace that came from realising that staying alive was his only responsibility. But this time, he thought, this time it's the most damn-fool reason of all, and that's because I'm looking for a drugged-out pilot who knows a man who used to have Lizzie Worthington for his mistress.

They were walking slowly because the girl in her short skirt had difficulty picking her way over the slippery ruts.

"Great chick," Keller murmured.

"Made for it," Jerry agreed dutifully.

With embarrassment Jerry remembered how in the Congo they used to be confidants, confessing their loves and weaknesses. To steady herself on the rutted ground, the girl was swinging her arms about.

Don't point, thought Jerry; for Christ's sake, don't point. That's how photographers get theirs.

"Keep walking, hon," Keller said shrilly. "Don't think of anything. Walk. Want to go back, Westerby?"

They stepped round a little boy playing privately with stones in the dust. Jerry wondered whether he was gun-deaf. He glanced back. The Mercedes was still parked in the trees. Ahead he could pick out men in low firing positions among the rubble, more men than he had realised.

The noise rose suddenly. On the far bank a couple of bombs exploded in the middle of the fire: the T-28s were trying to spread the flames. A ricochet tore into the bank below them, flinging up wet mud and dust. A peasant rode past them on his bicycle, serenely. He rose into the village, through it, and out again, slowly past the ruins and into the trees beyond. No one shot at him, no one challenged him. He could be theirs or ours, thought Jerry. He came into town last night, tossed a *plastic* into a cinema, and now he's returning to his kind.

"Jesus," cried the girl, with a laugh, "why didn't *we* think of bicycles?"

With a clatter of bricks falling, a volley of machine-gun bullets slapped all round them. Below them in the river-bank, by the grace of God, ran a line of empty leopard spots, shallow firing positions dug into the mud. Jerry had picked them out already. Grabbing the girl, he threw her down. Keller was already flat. Lying beside her, Jerry discerned a deep lack of interest. Better a bullet or two here than getting what Frostie got.

The bullets threw up screens of mud and whined off the road. They lay low, waiting for the firing to tire. The girl was looking excitedly across the river, smiling. She was blue-eyed and flaxen and Aryan. A mortar bomb landed behind them on the verge, and for the second time Jerry shoved her flat. The blast swept over them, and when it was past feathers of earth drifted down like a propitiation. But she came up smiling. When the Pentagon thinks of civilization, thought Jerry, it thinks of you.

In the fort the battle had suddenly thickened. The lorries had disappeared, a dense pall had gathered, the flash and din of mortar was incessant, light machine-gun fire challenged and answered itself with increasing swiftness. Keller's pocked face appeared white as death over the edge of his leopard spot.

"K.R.'s got them by the balls!" he yelled. "Across the river, ahead, and now from the other flank. We should have taken the other lane!"

Christ, Jerry thought, as the rest of the memories came back to him, Keller and I once fought over a girl too. He tried to remember who she was and who had won.

They waited, the firing died. They walked back to the car and gained the fork in time to meet the retreating convoy. Dead and wounded were littered along the roadside, and women crouched among them, fanning the stunned faces with palm leaves.

They got out of the car again. Refugees trundled buffaloes and handcarts and one another, while they screamed at their pigs and children. One old woman screamed at the girl's camera, thinking the lens was a gun barrel. There were sounds Jerry couldn't place, like the ringing of bicycle bells and wailing, and sounds he could, like the drenched sobs of the dying and the clump of approaching mortar fire. Keller was running beside a lorry, trying to find an English-speaking officer; Jerry loped beside him yelling the same questions in French.

"Ah, to hell," said Keller, suddenly bored. "Let's go home." His English lordling's voice: "The *people* and the *noise*," he explained. They returned to the Mercedes.

For a while they were stuck in the column, with the lorries cutting them to the side and the refugees politely tapping at the window asking for a ride. Once Jerry thought he saw Deathwish the Hun riding pillion on an army motor-bike. At the next fork Keller ordered the driver to turn left.

"More private," he said, and put his good hand back on the girl's knee. But Jerry was thinking of Frost in the mortuary, and the whiteness of his screaming jaw.

"My old mother *always* told me," Keller declared in a folksy drawl, "Son, don't never go back through the jungle the same way as you came. Hon?"

"Yes?"

"Hon, you just lost your cherry. My humble congratulations." The hand slipped a little higher.

From all round them came the sound of pouring water like so many burst pipes as a sudden torrent of rain fell. They passed a settlement full of chickens running in a flurry. A barber's chair stood empty in the rain. Jerry turned to Keller.

"This siege economy thing," he resumed as they settled to one another again. "Market forces and so forth. You reckon that story will go?"

"Could do," said Keller airily. "It's been done a few times. But it travels."

"Who are the main operators?"

Keller named a few.

"Indocharter?"

"Indocharter's one," said Keller.

Jerry took a long shot: "There's a

clown called Charlie Marshall flies for them, half Chinese. Somebody said he'd talk. Met him?"

"Nope."

He reckoned that was far enough: "What do most of them use for machines?"

"Whatever they can get. DC-4s, you name it. One's not enough. You need two at least — fly one, cannibalise the second for parts. Cheaper to ground a plane and strip it than bribe the customs to release the spares."

"What's the profit?"

"Unprintable."

"Much opium around?"

"There's a whole damn refinery out on the Bassac, for Christ's sakes. Looks like something out of Prohibition times. I can arrange a tour if that's what you're after."

The girl Lorraine was at the window, staring at the rain. "I don't see any kids, Max," she announced. "You said to look out for no kids, that's all. Well, I've been watching and they've disappeared." The driver stopped the car. "It's raining, and I read somewhere that when it rains Asian kids like to come out and play. So, you know, where's the kids?'' she said, but Jerry wasn't listening to what she'd read. Ducking and peering through the windscreen all at once, he saw what the driver saw, and it made his throat dry.

''You're the boss, sport,'' he said to Keller quietly. ''Your car, your war, and your girl.''

In the mirror, to his pain, Jerry watched Keller's pumice-stone face torn between experience and incapacity.

''Drive at them slowly,'' Jerry said, when he could wait no longer. *''Lentement.''*

''That's right,'' Keller said. ''Do that.''

Fifty yards ahead of them, shrouded by the teeming rain, a grey lorry had pulled broadside across the track, blocking it. In the mirror, a second had pulled out behind them, blocking their retreat.

''Better show our hands,'' said Keller in a hoarse rush. With his good one he wound down his window. The girl and Jerry did the same. Jerry wiped the windscreen clear of mist and put his hands on the console. The driver held the wheel at the top.

"Don't smile at them, don't speak to them," Jerry ordered.

"Jesus Christ," said Keller. "Holy God."

All over Asia, thought Jerry, pressman had their favourite stories of what the Khmer Rouge did to you, and most of them were true. Even Frost at this moment would have been grateful for · his relatively peaceful end. He knew newsmen who carried poison, or a concealed gun, to save themselves from just this moment. If you're caught, the first night is the only night to get out, he remembered: before they take your shoes, and your health, and God knows what other parts of you. The first night is your only chance, said the folklore. He wondered whether he should repeat it for the girl, but he didn't want to hurt Keller's feelings.

The Mercedes was ploughing forward in first gear, engine whining. The rain was flying all over the car, thundering on the roof, smacking the bonnet, and darting

751

through the open windows. If we bog down, we're finished, Jerry thought. Still the lorry ahead had not moved and it was no more than fifteen yards away, a glistening monster in the downpour. In the dark of the lorry's cab they saw thin faces watching them. At the last minute it lurched backward into the foliage, leaving just enough room to pass. The Mercedes tilted. Jerry had to hold the door pillar to stop himself rolling onto the driver. The two offside wheels skidded and whined, the bonnet swung and all but lurched onto the fender of the lorry.

"No licence plates," Keller breathed. "Holy Christ."

"Don't hurry," Jerry warned the driver. *"Toujours lentement.* Don't put on your lights." He was watching in the mirror.

"And those were the black pyjamas?" the girl said excitedly. "And you wouldn't even let me take a picture?"

No one spoke.

"What did they want? Who are they trying to ambush?" she insisted.

"Somebody else," said Jerry. "Not us."

"Some bum following us," said Keller. "Who cares?"

"Shouldn't we warn someone?"

"There isn't the apparatus," said Keller.

They heard shooting behind them but they kept going.

"Fucking rain," Keller breathed, half to himself. "Why the hell do we get rain suddenly?"

It had all but stopped.

"But Christ, Max," the girl protested, "if they've got us pinned out on the floor like this, why don't they just finish us off?"

Before Keller could reply, the driver did it for him in French, softly and politely, though only Jerry understood.

"When they want to come, they will come," he said, smiling at her in the mirror. "In the bad weather. While the Americans are adding another five metres of concrete to the Embassy roof, and the soldiers are crouching in capes under their trees, and the journalists are drinking whisky, and the generals are at the opium houses, the Khmer Rouge will come out of the jungle and cut our throats.''

''What did he say?'' Keller demanded. ''Translate that, Westerby.''

''Yeah, what *was* all that?'' said the girl. ''It sounded really great. Like a proposition or something.''

''Didn't quite get it actually, sport. Sort of outgunned me.''

They all broke out laughing, too loud, the driver as well.

And all through it, Jerry realised, he had thought of nobody but Lizzie. Not to the exclusion of danger — quite the contrary. Like the new, glorious sunshine which suddenly engulfed them, she was the prize of his survival.

At *Le Phnom,* the same sun was beating gaily on the poolside. There had been no rain in the town, but a bad rocket near the girls' school had killed eight or nine children. The Southern stringer had that moment returned from counting them.

''So how did Maxie make out at the bang-bangs?'' he asked Jerry as they met in the hall. "Seems to me like his nerve is creaking at the joints a little these days."

"Take your grinning little face out of my sight," Jerry advised. "Otherwise actually I'll smack it." Still grinning, the Southerner departed.

"We could meet tomorrow," the girl said to Jerry. "Tomorrow's free all day."

Behind her, Keller was making his way slowly up the stairs, a hunched figure in a one-sleeved shirt, pulling himself by the bannister rail.

"We could even meet tonight, if you wanted," Lorraine said.

For a while, Jerry sat alone in his room writing postcards for Cat. Then he set course for Max's bureau. He had a few more questions about Charlie Marshall; and besides, he had a notion old Max would appreciate his company.

His duty done, he took a *cyclo* and rode up to Charlie Marshall's house again, and though he pummelled on the door and yelled, all he could see was the same bare brown legs motionless at the bottom of the stairs, this time by candle-light. But the page torn from his notebook had disappeared.

He returned to the town and, still with an hour to kill, settled at a pavement café in one of a hundred empty chairs and drank a long Pernod, remembering how once the girls of the town had ticked past him here on their little wicker carriages, whispering clichés of love in singsong French. Tonight the darkness trembled to nothing more lovely than the thud of occasional gun-fire, while the town huddled, waiting for the blow.

Yet it was not the shelling but the silence that held the greatest fear. Like the jungle itself, silence, not gunfire, was the natural element of the approaching enemy.

When a diplomat wants to talk, the first thing he thinks of is food, and in diplomatic circles one dined early because of the curfew. Not that diplomats were subject to such rigours, but it is a charming arrogance of diplomats the world over to suppose they set an example — to whom, or of what, the devil himself will never know. The Counsellor's house was in a flat, leafy enclave bordering Lon Nol's palace. In the driveway as Jerry arrived, an official limousine was emptying its occupants, watched over by a jeep stiff with militia. It's either royalty or religion, Jerry thought as he got out; but it was no more than a senior American diplomat and his wife arriving for a meal.

"Ah. You must be Mr. Westerby," said his hostess.

She was tall and Harrods and amused by the idea of a journalist, as she was amused by anyone who was not a diplomat, and of counsellor rank at that. "John has been *dying* to meet you," she declared brightly, and Jerry supposed she was putting him at his ease. He followed the trail upstairs. His host stood at the top, a wiry man with a moustache and a stoop and a boyishness which Jerry more usually associated with the clergy.

"Oh, well done! Smashing. You're the cricketer. Well done. Mutual friends, right? We're not allowed to use the balcony tonight, I'm afraid," he said, with a naughty glance toward the American corner. "Good men are too scarce, apparently. Got to stay under cover. Seen where you are?" He stabbed a commanding finger at a leather-framed placement chart showing the seating arrangement. "Come and meet some people. Just a minute." He drew him slightly aside, but only slightly. "It all goes through me, right? I've made that absolutely clear. Don't let them get you into a corner, right? Quite a little *squall* running, if you follow me. Local thing. Not your problem."

The senior American appeared at first sight small, being dark and tidy, but when he stood to shake Jerry's hand, he was nearly Jerry's height. He wore a tartan jacket of raw silk and he held a walkie-talkie radio in a black plastic case. His brown eyes were intelligent but over-respectful, and as they shook hands, a voice inside Jerry said "Cousin."

"Glad to know you, Mr. Westerby. I understand you're from Hong Kong. Your Governor there is a very good friend of mine. Beckie, this is Mr. Westerby, a friend of the Governor of Hong Kong and a good friend of John, our host."

He indicated a large woman bridled in dull hand-beaten silver from the market. Her bright clothes flowed in an Asian medley.

"Oh, *Mr. Westerby,*" she said. "From Hong Kong. *Hello.*"

The remaining guests were a mixed bag of local traders. Their womenfolk were Eurasian, French, and Corsican. A houseboy hit a silver gong. The dining-room ceiling was concrete, but as they trooped in Jerry saw several eyes lift to make sure. A silver card holder told him he was "The Honourable G. Westerby," a silver menu holder promised him *le roast beef à l'anglaise,* silver candlesticks held long candles of a devotional kind, Cambodian boys flitted and backed at the half-crouch with trays of food cooked this morning while the electricity was on. A much travelled French beauty sat to Jerry's right with a lace handkerchief between her breasts. She held another in her hand, and each time she ate or drank she dusted her little mouth. Her name card called her Countess Sylvia.

"*Je suis très, très diplomée,*" she whispered to Jerry as she pecked and dabbed. "*J'ai fait la science politique, mécanique, et l'électricité générale.* In January I have a bad heart. Now I recover."

"Ah, well now, me, I'm not qualified at *anything,*" Jerry insisted, making far too much of a joke of it. "Jack of all trades, master of none, that's us." To put this into French took him quite some while, and he was still labouring at it when from somewhere fairly close a burst of machine-gun fire sounded, far too long for the health of the gun. There were no answering shots. The conversation hung.

"Some bloody idiot shooting at the geckos, I should think," said the Counsellor, and his wife laughed at him fondly down the table, as if the war were a little side-show they had laid on between them for their guests. The silence returned, more pregnant than before. The little Countess put her fork on her plate and it clanged like a tram in the night.

"*Dieu,*" she said.

At once, everyone started talking. The

American wife asked Jerry where he was *raised,* and when they had been through that she asked him where his *home* was, so Jerry gave Thurloe Square, old Pet's place, because he didn't feel like talking about Tuscany.

"We own land in Vermont," she said firmly. "But we haven't built on it yet."

Two rockets fell at the same time. Jerry reckoned they were east about half a mile. Glancing round to see whether the windows were closed, Jerry caught the brown gaze of the American husband fixed on him with mysterious urgency.

"You have plans for tomorrow, Mr. Westerby?" he asked.

"Not particularly."

"If there's anything we can do, let me know."

"Thanks," said Jerry, but he had the feeling that wasn't the point of the question.

A Swiss trader with a wise face had a funny story. He used Jerry's presence to repeat it.

"Some time back, the whole town was alight with shooting, Mr. Westerby," he said. "We were all going to die. Oh, *definitely*. Tonight we die! Everything — shells, tracer — poured into the sky, one million dollars' worth of ammunition, we heard afterwards. Hours on end. Some of my friends went round shaking hands with one another." An army of black ants emerged from under the table and began marching in single column across the perfectly laundered damask cloth, making a careful detour round the silver candlesticks and the silver flower bowl brimming with hibiscus. "The Americans radioed around, hopped up and down, we all considered very carefully our position on the evacuation list, but a funny thing, you know: the telephones were working and we even had electricity. What did the target turn out to be?" The others were already laughing hysterically. "Frogs! Some very greedy *frogs!*"

"Toads," somebody corrected him, but it didn't stop the laughter.

The American diplomat, a model of courteous self-criticism, supplied the amusing epilogue.

"The Cambodians have an old

superstition, Mr. Westerby,'' he said. ''When there's an eclipse of the moon, you must make a lot of noise. You must shoot off fireworks, you must bang tin cans, or, best still, fire off a million dollars' worth of ordnance. Because if you don't — why, the frogs will gobble up the moon. We *should* have known, but we *didn't* know, and in consequence we were made to look very, very silly indeed,'' he said proudly.

''Yes, I'm afraid you boobed there, old boy,'' the Counsellor said with satisfaction.

But though the American's smile remained frank and open his eyes continued to impart something far more pressing — such as a message between professionals.

Someone talked about servants and their amazing fatalism. An isolated detonation, loud and seemingly quite near, ended the performance. As the Countess Sylvia reached for Jerry's hand, their hostess smiled interrogatively at her husband down the table.

''John, darling,'' she asked in her most

hospitable voice, "was that incoming or outgoing?"

"Outgoing," he replied, with a laugh. "Oh, outgoing definitely. Ask our journalist friend if you don't believe me. He's been through a few wars, haven't you, Westerby?"

At which the silence, yet again, joined them like a forbidden topic. The American lady clung to that piece of land in Vermont: perhaps, after all, they *should* build on it. Perhaps, after all, it was time.

"Maybe we should just *write* to that architect," she said.

"Maybe we should," her husband agreed, and at that moment they were flung into a pitched battle. From very close a prolonged burst of pom-poms lit the washing in the courtyard and a cluster of machine-guns — as many as twenty — crackled in a sustained and desperate fire. By the flashes they saw the servants scurry into the house, and over the firing they heard orders given and replied to, scream for scream, and the crazy ringing of hand-gongs.

Inside the room, nobody moved except the American diplomat, who lifted his walkie-talkie to his lips, drew out the aerial, and murmured something before putting it to his ear. Jerry glanced downward and saw the Countess's hand battened trustingly to his own. Her cheek brushed his shoulder. The firing faltered. He heard the clump of a small bomb close. No vibration, but the flames of the candles tilted in salute and on the mantelshelf a couple of heavy invitation cards flopped over with a slap and lay still, the only recognisable casualties. Then as a last and separate sound, they heard the grizzle of a departing single-engined plane like the distant grousing of a child.

It was capped by the Counsellor's easy laughter as he addressed his wife. "Ah, well now, that *wasn't* the eclipse, I'm afraid, was it, Hills? That was the advantage of having Lon Nol as our neighbour. One of his pilots gets fed up with not being paid now and then, so he takes up a plane and has a pot-shot at the palace. Darling, are you going to take the gels off to powder their noses and do whatever you all do?''

It's anger, Jerry decided, catching the senior American's eye again. He's like a man with a mission to the poor who has to waste his time with the rich.

Downstairs Jerry, the Counsellor, and the American stood alone in the ground-floor study. The Counsellor had acquired a wolfish shyness.

"Yes, well," he said. "Now I've put you both on the map, perhaps I should leave you to it. Whisky in the decanter, right, Westerby?"

"Right, John," said the American, but the Counsellor didn't seem to hear.

"Just remember, Westerby: the mandate's *ours,* right? We're keeping the bed warm. Right?" With a knowing wag of the finger, he disappeared.

The study was candle-lit, a small masculine room with no mirrors or pictures, just a ribbed teak ceiling and a green metal desk. The geckos and the bullfrogs would have baffled the most sophisticated microphone.

"Hey, let me get that," said the

American, arresting Jerry's progress to the sideboard, and made a show of getting the mix just right for him: water or soda, don't let me drown it.

"Seems kind of a long way round to bring two friends together," the American said, in a taut, chatty tone, from the sideboard as he poured.

"Does rather."

"John's a great guy, but he's kind of a stickler for protocol. Your people have no resources here right now but they have certain rights, so John likes to make sure that the ball doesn't slip out of his court for good. I can understand his point of view. Just that things take a little longer sometimes."

He handed Jerry a long brown envelope from inside the tartan jacket, and with the same pregnant intensity as before watched while he broke the seal. The paper had a smeared and photographic quality.

Somewhere a child moaned, and was silenced. The garage, Jerry thought: the servants have filled the garage with refugees and the Counsellor is not to know.

ENFORCEMENT SAIGON reports Charlie MARSHALL rpt MARSHALL scheduled hit Battambang ETA 1930 tomorrow via Pailin . . . converted DC-4 Carvair, Indocharter markings manifest quotes miscellaneous cargo . . . scheduled continue Phnom Penh.

Then he read the time and date of transmission and anger hit him like a wind storm. He remembered yesterday's foot-slogging in Bangkok and today's hairbrained taxi ride with Keller and the girl, and with a "Jesus *Christ*" he slammed the message back on the table between them: "How long have you been sitting on this? That's not tomorrow. That's tonight!"

"Unfortunately our host could not arrange the wedding any earlier. He has an extremely crowded social programme. Good luck."

Just as angry as Jerry, he quietly took back the signal, slipped it into the pocket of his jacket, and disappeared upstairs to his wife, who was busy admiring her hostess's indifferent collection of pilfered Buddhas.

He stood alone. A rocket fell and this time it was close. The candles went out and the night sky seemed finally to be splitting with the strain of this illusory, Gilbertian war. Mindlessly the machine-guns joined the clatter. The little bare room with its tiled floor rattled and sang like a sound machine.

Only as suddenly to stop again, leaving the town to the silence.

"Something wrong, old boy?" the Counsellor enquired genially from the doorway. "Yank rub you up the wrong way, did he? They seem to want to run the world single-handed these days."

"I'll need six-hour options," Jerry said. The Counsellor didn't quite follow. Having explained to him how they worked, Jerry stepped quickly into the night.

"Got transport, have you, old boy? That's the way. They'll shoot you, otherwise. Mind how you go."

He strode quickly, driven by his irritation and disgust. It was long after curfew. There were no streetlamps, no stars. The moon had vanished, and the squeak of his crêpe soles ran with him like an unwanted companion. The only light came from the perimeter of the palace across the road, but none spilled onto Jerry's side of the street. High walls blocked off the inner building, high wires crowned the walls, and barrels of the light anti-aircraft guns gleamed bronze against the black and soundless sky. Young soldiers dozed in groups and as Jerry strode past them a fresh roll of gong-beats sounded: the master of the guard was keeping the sentries awake. There was no traffic, but between the sentry posts the refugees had made up their own night villages in a long column down the pavement. Some had draped themselves with strips of brown tarpaulin, some had plank bunks, and some were cooking by tiny flames, though God alone knew what they had found to eat. Some sat in neat social groups, facing in upon each other. On an ox-cart a girl lay with a boy, children Cat's age when he last had seen her in the flesh. But from the hundreds of them not one sound came, and after he had gone a distance he actually turned and peered to make sure they were there. If they were, the darkness and the silence hid them. He thought of the dinner party. It had taken place in another land, another universe entirely. He was irrelevant here, yet somehow he had contributed to the disaster.

For no reason that he knew of, the sweat began running off him and the night air made no cooling impact. The dark was as hot as the day. Ahead of him in the town a stray rocket struck carelessly. They creep into the paddies until they're within range, he thought. They lie up, hugging their bits of drain-pipe and their little bomb, then fire and run like hell for the jungle. The palace was behind him. A battery fired a salvo and for a few seconds he was able to see his way by the flashes. The road was broad, a boulevard, and as best he could he kept to the crown. Occasionally he made out the gaps of the side-streets passing him in geometric regularity. If he stooped, he could even see the tree-tops retreating into the paler sky. Once a *cyclo* pattered by, toppling nervously out of the turning, hitting the curb, then steadying. He thought of shouting to it but he preferred to keep on striding.

A male voice greeted him doubtfully out of the darkness — a whisper, nothing indiscreet: *"Bon soir? Monsieur? Bon soir?"*

The sentries stood every hundred metres in ones or twos, holding their carbines in both hands. Their murmurs came to him like invitations, but Jerry was always careful and kept his hands wide of his pockets where they could watch them. Some, seeing the enormous sweating round-eye, laughed and waved him on. Others stopped him at pistol point and gazed up at him earnestly by the light of bicycle lamps while they asked him questions in order to practise their French. Some requested cigarettes and these he gave. He tugged off his drenched jacket and opened his shirt to the waist, but still the air wouldn't cool him and he wondered again whether he had a fever and whether, like last night in Bangkok, he would wake up in his bedroom crouching in the darkness waiting to brain someone with a table-lamp.

The moon appeared, lapped by the foam of the rain clouds. By its light his hotel resembled a locked fortress. He reached the garden wall and followed it leftwards along the trees until it turned again. He threw his jacket over the wall and with difficulty climbed after it. He crossed the lawn to the steps, pushed open the door to the lobby, and stepped back with a surge of disgust. The lobby was in pitch blackness except for a single moonbeam, which shone like a spotlight on a huge luminous chrysalis spun around the naked brown larva of a human body.

It was the night watchman in his hammock, asleep under a mosquito net.

"*Vous désirez, Monsieur?*" a voice asked softly.

The boy handed him a key and a note, and silently accepted his tip. Jerry struck his lighter and read the note: "Darling, I'm in room 28 and lonely. Come and see me. L."

What the hell? he thought; maybe it'll

put the bits back together again. He climbed the stairs to the second floor, forgetting her terrible banality, thinking only of her long legs and her tilting rump as she negotiated the ruts along the riverbank; her cornflower eyes and her regular all-American gravity as she lay in the leopard spot; thinking only of his own yearning for human touch. Who gives a damn about Keller? he thought. To hold someone is to exist. Perhaps she's frightened too. He knocked on the door, waited, gave it a shove.

"Lorraine? It's me. Westerby."

Nothing happened. He lurched toward the bed, conscious of the absence of any female smell, even face powder or deodorant. On his way there he saw by the same moonlight the dreadfully familiar sight of blue jeans, heavy bean-boots, and a tattered Olivetti portable not unlike his own.

"Come one step nearer and it's statutory rape," said Luke, uncapping the whisky bottle on his bedside table.

16
Friends of Charlie Marshall

He crept out before light, having slept on Luke's floor. He took his typewriter and shoulder-bag, though he expected to use neither. He left a note for Keller asking him to wire Stubbs that he was following the siege story out to the provinces. His back ached from the floor and his head from the bottle.

Luke had come for the bang-bangs, he said; bureau was giving him a rest from Big Moo. Also Jake Chiu, his irate landlord, had finally thrown him out of his apartment.

"I'm destitute, Westerby!" he had cried, and began wailing round the room, *"Destitute,"* till Jerry, to buy himself some sleep and stop the neighbour's banging, slipped his spare flat-key off its ring and flung it at him.

"Until I get back," he warned. "Then *out*. Understood?"

Jerry asked about the Frost thing. Luke had forgotten all about it and had to be reminded. Ah, *him,* he said. *Him*. Yeah, well there were stories he'd been cheeky to the triads, and maybe in a hundred years they would all come true, but meanwhile who gave a damn?

But sleep hadn't come so easy even then. They discussed today's arrangements. Luke had proposed to do whatever Jerry was doing. Dying alone was a bore, he had insisted. Better they got drunk and found some whores. Jerry had replied that Luke would have to wait awhile before the two of them went into the sunset together, because he was going fishing for the day and he was going alone.

"Fishing for what, for hell's sakes? If there's a story, share it. Where can you go that is not more beautiful for Brother Lukie's presence?"

Pretty well anywhere, Jerry had said unkindly, and managed to leave without waking him.

He made first for the market and sipped a *soupe chinoise,* studying the stalls and shop fronts. He selected a young Indian who was offering nothing but plastic buckets, water-bottles, and brooms, yet looking very prosperous on the profits.

"What else do you sell, sport?"

"Sir, I sell all things to all gentlemen."

They foxed around. No, said Jerry, it was nothing to smoke that he wanted, and nothing to swallow, nothing to sniff and nothing for the wrists, either. And no, thank you, with all respect to the many beautiful sisters, cousins, and young men of his circle, Jerry's other needs were also taken care of.

"Then, oh, gladness, sir, you are a most happy man."

"I was *really* looking for something for a friend," said Jerry.

The Indian boy looked sharply up and down the street and he wasn't foxing any more.

"A *friendly* friend, sir?"

"Not very."

They shared a *cyclo.* The Indian had an uncle who sold Buddhas in the silver market, and the uncle had a back room with locks and bolts on the door. For thirty American dollars Jerry bought a neat brown Walther automatic with twenty rounds of ammunition. The Sarratt bearleaders, he reckoned as he climbed back into the *cyclo,* would have fallen into a deep swoon. First for what they called improper dressing, a crime of crimes. Second because they preached the hardy nonsense that small guns gave more trouble than use. But they'd have had a bigger fit still if he'd carted his Hong Kong Webley through customs to Bangkok and thence to Phnom Penh, so in Jerry's view they could count themselves lucky, because he wasn't walking into this one naked whatever their doctrine of the week.

At the airport there was no plane to Battambang, but there was never a plane to anywhere. There were the silver rice jets howling on and off the landing-strip, and there were new *revêtements* being built after a fresh fall of rockets in the night. Jerry watched the earth arriving in lorry-loads, and the coolies filling ammunition boxes frantically. In another life, he decided, I'll go into the sand business and flog it to besieged cities.

In the waiting-room Jerry found a group of stewardesses drinking coffee and laughing, and in his breezy way he joined them. A tall girl who spoke English made a doubtful face and disappeared with his passport and five dollars.

"C'est impossible," they all assured him while they waited for her. *"C'est tout occupé."*

The girl returned smiling. "The pilot is *very* susceptible," she said. "If he don't like you, he don't take you. But I show him your photograph and he has agreed to *surcharger*. He is allowed to take only thirty-one *personnes* but he take you, he don't care, he do it for friendship if you give him one thousand five hundred riels."

The plane was two-thirds empty, and the bullet-holes in the wings wept dew like undressed wounds.

At that time, Battambang was the safest town left in Lon Nol's dwindling

779

archipelago, and Phnom Penh's last farm. For an hour they lumbered over supposedly Khmer Rouge-infested territory without a soul in sight. As they circled, someone shot lazily from the paddies and the pilot pulled a couple of token turns to avoid being hit, but Jerry was more concerned to mark the ground layout before they landed: the park-bays; which runways were civil and which were military; the wired-off enclave which contained the freight huts. They landed in an air of pastoral affluence. Flowers grew round the gun emplacements, fat brown chickens scurried in the shell-holes, water and electricity abounded, though a telegram to Phnom Penh already took a week.

Jerry trod very carefully now. His instinct for cover was stronger than ever. *The Honourable Gerald Westerby, the distinguished hack, reports on the siege economy.* When you're my size, sport, you have to have a hell of a good reason for whatever you're doing. So he put out smoke, as the jargon goes.

At the enquiry desk, watched by several

quiet men, he asked for the names of the best hotels in town and wrote down a couple while he continued to study the groupings of planes and buildings. Meandering from one office to another, he asked what facilities existed to air-freight news copy to Phnom Penh and no one had the least idea. Continuing his discreet reconnaissance, he waved his cable card around and enquired how to get to the governor's palace, implying that he might have business with the great man personally. By now he was the most distinguished reporter who had ever been to Batambang. Meanwhile he noted the doors marked "Crew" and the doors marked "Private," and the position of the men's rooms, so that later, when he was clear, he could make himself a sketch plan of the entire concourse, with emphasis on the exits to the wired-off part of the airfield.

Finally he asked who was in town just now among the pilots. He was friendly with several, he said, so his simplest plan — should it become necessary — was probably to ask one of them to take his copy in his flight-bag. A stewardess gave names from a list, and while she did this Jerry gently turned the list round and read off the rest. The Indocharter flight was listed but no pilot was mentioned.

"Captain Andreas still flying for Indocharter?" he enquired.

"Le capitaine qui, Monsieur?"

"Andreas. We used to call him André. Little fellow, always wore dark glasses. Did the Kampong Cham run."

She shook her head. Only Captain Marshall and Captain Ricardo, she said, flew for Indocharter, but Captain Ric had immolated himself in an accident. Jerry affected no interest but established in passing that Captain Marshall's Carvair was due to take off in the afternoon, as forecast in last night's signal, but there was no freight space available; everything was taken, Indocharter was always fully contracted.

"Know where I can reach him?"

"Captain Marshall never flies in the mornings, Monsieur."

He took a cab into town. The best hotel was a flea-bitten dug-out in the main street. The street itself was narrow, stinking, and deafening: an Asian boom town in the making, pounded by the din of Hondas and crammed with the frustrated Mercedes of the quick rich. Keeping his cover going, he took a room and paid for it in advance, to include *service spécial,* which meant nothing more exotic than clean sheets as opposed to those which still bore the marks of other bodies. He told his driver to return in an hour. By force of habit he secured an inflated receipt. He showered, changed, and listened courteously while the houseboy showed him where to climb in after curfew; then he went out to find breakfast because it was still only nine in the morning.

He carried his typewriter and shoulder-bag with him. He saw no other round-eyes. He saw basket-makers, skin-sellers, and fruit-sellers, and once again the inevitable bottles of stolen petrol laid along the pavement waiting for an attack to touch them off. In a mirror hung in a tree he watched a dentist extract teeth from a patient tied in a high chair, and he watched the red-tipped tooth being solemnly added to the thread that displayed the day's catch.

All of thse things Jerry recorded in his notebook, as became a zealous reporter of the social scene. And from a pavement café, as he consumed cold beer and fresh fish, he watched the dingy half-glazed offices marked "Indocharter" across the road and waited for someone to come and unlock the door. No one did. *Captain Marshall never flies in the mornings, Monsieur.*

At a chemist's shop that specialised in children's bicycles, he bought a roll of sticking-plaster and back in his room taped the Walther to his ribs rather than have it waving around in his waistband. Thus equipped, the intrepid journalist set forth to live some more cover, which sometimes, in the psychology of a fieldman, is no more than a gratituous act of self-legitimisation as the heat begins to gather.

The governor lived on the edge of town, behind a verandah and French colonial portals, and a secretariat seventy strong.

The vast concrete hall led to a waiting-room never finished, and to much smaller offices behind, and in one of these, after a fifty-minute wait, Jerry was admitted to the presence of a tiny, very senior black-suited Cambodian sent by Phnom Penh to handle noisome correspondents. Word said he was the son of a general and managed the Battambang end of the family opium business. His desk was much too big for him. Several attendants lounged about and they all looked very severe. One wore a uniform with a lot of medal ribbons.

Jerry asked for deep background and made a list of several charming dreams: that the Communist enemy was all but beaten; that there was serious discussion about reopening the entire national road system; that tourism was the growth industry of the province. The general's son spoke slow and beautiful French, and it clearly gave him great pleasure to hear himself, for he kept his eyes half closed and smiled as he spoke, as if listening to beloved music.

"I may conclude, Monsieur, with a word

of warning to your country. You are American?''

"English."

"It is the same. Tell your government, sir. If you do not help us to continue the fight against the Communists, we shall go to the Russians and ask them to replace you in our struggle."

Oh, Mother, thought Jerry. Oh, boy. Oh, God.

"I will give them that message," he promised, and made to go.

"Un instant, Monsieur," said the senior officer sharply, and there was a stirring among his dozing courtiers. He opened a drawer and pulled out an imposing folder. Frost's will, Jerry thought. My death warrant. Stamps for Cat.

"You are a writer?"

"Yes."

Ko's putting the arm on me. Prison tonight, and wake up with my throat cut tomorrow.

"You were at the Sorbonne, Monsieur?" the official enquired.

"Oxford."

"Oxford in London?"

"Yes."

"Then you have read the great French poets, Monsieur?"

"With intense pleasure," Jerry replied fervently. The courtiers were looking extremely grave.

"Then perhaps Monsieur will favour me with his opinion of the following few verses." In his dignified French, the little official began to read aloud, slowly conducting with his palm.

> *"Deux amants assis sur la terre*
> *Regardaient la mer,"*

he began and continued for perhaps twenty excruciating lines while Jerry listened in mystification.

"Voilà," said the official finally and put the file aside. *"Vous l'aimez?"* he enquired, severely fixing his eye upon a neutral part of the room.

"Superbe," said Jerry with a gush of enthusiasm. *"Merveilleux.* The sensitivity."

"They are by whom, would you think?"

Jerry grabbed a name at random: "By Lamartine?"

The senior official shook his head. The courtiers were observing Jerry even more closely.

"Victor Hugo?" Jerry ventured.

"They are by me," said the official, and with a sigh returned his poems to the drawer. The courtiers relaxed. "See that this literary person has every facility," he ordered.

Jerry returned to the airport to find it a milling, dangerous chaos. Mercedes raced up and down the approach as if someone had invaded their nest, the forecourt was a turmoil of beacons, motorcycles, and sirens; and the hall, when he argued his way through the cordon, was jammed with scared people fighting to read noticeboards, yell at each other, and hear the blaring loudspeakers all at the same time.

Forcing a path to the information desk, Jerry found it closed. He leapt on the counter and saw the airfield through a hole in the antiblast board. A squad of armed soldiers was jog-trotting down the empty runway toward a group of white poles where the national flags drooped in the windless air. They lowered two of the flags to half-mast, and inside the hall the loudspeakers interrupted themselves to blare a few bars of the national anthem. Over the seething heads Jerry searched for someone he might talk to. He selected a lank missionary with cropped yellow hair and glasses and a six-inch silver cross pinned to the pocket of his brown shirt. A pair of Cambodians in dog-collars stood miserably beside him.

"Vous parlez français?"

"Yes, but I also speak English!"

A lilting, corrective tone. Jerry guessed he was a Dane.

"I'm press. What's the fuss?" He was shouting at the top of his voice.

"Phnom Penh is closed," the missionary bellowed in reply. "No planes may leave or land."

"Why?"

"Khmer Rouge have hit the ammunition dump in the airport. The town is closed till morning at the least!"

The loudspeaker began chattering again. The two priests listened. The missionary stooped nearly double to catch their murmured translation.

"They have made a great damage and devastated half a dozen planes already. They have laid them waste entirely. The authority is also suspecting sabotage. Maybe she also takes some prisoners. Why are they putting an ammunition house inside the airport in the first case? That was most dangerous. What is the reason here?"

"Good question," Jerry agreed.

He ploughed across the hall. His master plan was already dead, as his master plans usually were. The "Crew Only" door was guarded by a pair of very serious crushers, and in the tension he saw no chance of brazening his way through. The thrust of the crowd was toward the passenger exit, where harassed ground staff were refusing to accept boarding tickets, and harassed police were being besieged with letters of *laissez-passer* designed to put the prominent outside their reach. He let it carry him. At the edges, a team of French traders was screaming for a refund, and the elderly were preparing to settle for the night. But the centre pushed and peered and exchanged fresh rumours, and the momentum carried him steadily to the front. Reaching it, Jerry discreetly took out his cable card and climbed over the improvised barrier. The senior policeman was sleek and well covered and he watched Jerry disdainfully while his subordinates toiled. Jerry strode straight up to him, his shoulder-bag dangling from his hand, and pressed the cable card under his nose.

"*Sécurité américaine,*" he roared in awful French and, with a snarl at the two men on the swing-doors, barged his way onto the tarmac and kept going, while his back waited all the time for a challenge or a warning shot or, in the trigger-happy atmosphere, a shot that was not even a warning. He walked angrily, with rough authority, swinging his shoulder-bag Sarratt-style to distract. Ahead of him — sixty yards, soon fifty — stood a row of single-engined military trainers without insignia. Beyond lay the caged enclosure and the freight huts, numbered nine to eighteen, and beyond the freight huts Jerry saw a cluster of hangars and park-bays marked "Prohibited" in just about every language except Chinese.

Reaching the trainers, Jerry strode imperiously along the line of them as if he were carrying out an inspection. They were anchored with bricks on wires. Pausing but not stopping, he stabbed irritably at a brick with his buckskin boot, yanked at an aileron, and shook his head. From their sandbagged emplacement, to his left, an anti-aircraft gun crew watched him indolently.

"Qu'est-ce que vous faites?"

Half turning, Jerry cupped his hands to his mouth. "Watch the damn sky, for Christ's sakes," he yelled in good American, pointing angrily to heaven, and kept going till he reached the high cage. It was open and the huts lay ahead of him. Once past them he would be out of sight of both the terminal and the control tower. He was walking on smashed concrete with couch-grass in the cracks. There was nobody in sight. The huts were weather-board, thirty feet long, ten high, with palm roofs. He reached the first. The boarding on the windows read "Bomb Cluster Fragmentation Without Fuses." A trodden dust path led to the hangars on the other side. Through the gap Jerry glimpsed the parrot colours of parked cargo planes.

"Got you," Jerry muttered aloud as he emerged on the safe side of the huts, because there ahead of him, clear as day, like a first sight of the enemy after months of lonely marching, a battered blue-grey DC-4 Carvair, fat as a frog, squatted on the crumbling tarmac with her nose-cone open. Diesel oil was dripping in a fast black rain from both her starboard engines, and a spindly Chinese in a sailing cap laden with military insignia stood smoking under the loading bay while he marked an inventory. Two coolies scurried back and forth with sacks, and a third worked the ancient loading lift. At his feet, chickens scrabbled petulantly. And on the fuselage, in flaming crimson against Drake Ko's faded racing colours, ran the letters "OCHART." The others had been lost in a repair job.

Oh, Charlie's indestructible, completely immortal! Charlie Marshall, *Mr. Tiu, a fantastic half-Chinese, all skin and bones and opium and a completely brilliant pilot. . . .*

He'd bloody well better be, sport, thought Jerry with a shudder, as the coolies loaded sack after sack through the open nose and into the battered belly of the plane.

The Reverend Ricardo's lifelong Sancho Panza, Your Grace, Craw had said, in extension of Lizzie's description. *Half Chow, as the good lady advised us, and the proud veteran of many futile wars.*

Jerry remained standing, making no attempt to conceal himself, dangling the bag from his fist, and wearing the apologetic grin of an English stray. Coolies now seemed to be converging on the plane from several points at once: there were many more than two. Turning his back on them, Jerry repeated his routine of strolling along the line of huts, much as he had walked along the line of trainers, or along the corridor toward Frost's room, peering through cracks in the weather-board and seeing nothing but the occasional broken packing-case. *The concession to operate out of Battambang costs half a million U.S. renewable,* Keller had said. At that price, who pays for redecoration?

The line of huts broke and he came on four army lorries loaded high with fruit, vegetables, and unmarked gunny bags. Their tailboards faced the plane and they sported artillery insignia. Two soldiers stood in each lorry, handing the gunny bags down to the coolies. The sensible thing would have been to drive the lorries onto the tarmac, but a mood of discretion prevailed. *The army likes to be in on things,* Keller had said. *The navy can make millions out of one convoy down the Mekong, the air force is sitting pretty. Bombers fly fruit and the choppers can airlift the rich Chinese instead of the wounded out of the siege towns. Only the fighter boys go hungry, because they have to land where they take off. But the army really has to scratch around to make a living.*

Jerry was closer to the plane now and could hear the squawking as Charlie Marshall fired commands at the coolies.

The huts began again. Number 18 had double doors and the name "Indocharter" daubed in green down the woodwork so that from any distance the letters looked like Chinese characters. In the gloomy interior a Chinese peasant couple squatted on the dust floor. A tethered pig lay with its head on the old man's slippered foot. Their other possession was a long rush parcel meticulously bound with string. It could have been a corpse. A water jar stood in one corner with two rice-bowls at its base. There was nothing else in the hut. Welcome to the Indocharter transit lounge, Jerry thought. With the sweat running down his ribs he tagged himself to the line of coolies till he drew alongside Charlie Marshall, who went on squawking in Khmer at the top of his voice while his shaking pen checked each load on the inventory.

He wore an oily white short-sleeved shirt with enough gold stripes on the epaulettes to make a full general in anybody's air force. Two American combat patches were stitched to his shirt front, amid an amazing collection of medal ribbons and Communist red stars. One patch read "Kill a Commie for Christ," and the other "Christ Was a Capitalist at Heart." His head was turned down and his face was in the shadow of his huge sailing cap, which slopped freely over his ears.

Jerry waited for him to look up. The coolies were already yelling for Jerry to move on, but Charlie Marshall kept his head turned stubbornly down while he added and wrote on the inventory and squawked furiously back at them.

"Captain Marshall, I'm doing a story on Ricardo for a London newspaper," said Jerry quietly. "I want to ride with you as far as Phnom Penh and ask you some questions."

As he spoke, he gently laid the volume

of *Candide* on top of the inventory, with three one-hundred-dollar bills poking outward in a discreet fan. When you want a man to look one way, says the Sarratt school of illusionists, always point him in the other.

"They tell me you like Voltaire," he said.

"I don't like anybody," Charlie Marshall retorted in a scratchy falsetto at the inventory, while the cap slipped still lower over his face. "I hate the whole human race, hear me?" His vituperation, despite its Chinese cadence, was unmistakeably French-American. "Jesus Christ, I hate mankind so damn much that if it don't hurry and blow itself to pieces, I'm personally going to buy some bombs and go out there *myself!*"

He had lost his audience. Jerry was half-way up the steel ladder before Charlie Marshall had completed his thesis.

"Voltaire didn't know a damn bloody thing!" he screamed at the next coolie. "He fought the wrong damn war, hear me? Put it over there, you lazy coon, and grab another handful! *Dépêche-toi, crétin, oui?"*

But all the same he jammed Voltaire into the back pocket of his baggy trousers.

The inside of the plane was dark and roomy and as cool as a cathedral. The seats had been removed, and perforated green shelves like meccano had been fitted to the walls. Carcasses of pig and guinea-fowl hung from the roof. The rest of the cargo was stowed in the gangway, starting from the tail-end, which gave Jerry no good feeling about taking off, and consisted of fruit and vegetables and the gunny bags Jerry had spotted in the army trucks, marked "GRAIN," "RICE," "FLOUR," in letters large enough for the most illiterate narcotics agent to read. But the sticky smell of yeast and molasses that already filled the hold required no labels at all.

Some of the bags had been arranged in a ring, to make a sitting area for Jerry's fellow passengers. Chief of these were two austere Chinese men, dressed very poorly in grey, and from their sameness and their demure superiority Jerry at once inferred an expertise of some kind; he remembered explosives-wallahs and pianists he had occasionally ferried thanklessly in and out of badland. Next to them, but respectfully apart, four hillsmen armed to the teeth sat smoking and cropping from their rice-bowls. Jerry guessed Meo or one of the Shan tribes from the northern borders where Charlie Marshall's father had his army, and he guessed from their ease that they were part of the permanent help.

In a separate class altogether sat the quality: the colonel of artillery himself, who had thoughtfully supplied the transport and the troop escort, and his companion, a senior officer of customs, without whom nothing could have been achieved. They reclined regally in the gangway on chairs specially provided, watching proudly while the loading continued, and they wore their best uniforms, as the ceremony demanded.

There was one other member of the party and he lurked alone on top of the cases in the tail, head almost against the roof, and it was not possible to make him out in any detail. He sat with a bottle of whisky to himself, and even a glass to himself. He wore a Fidel Castro hat and a full beard. Gold links glittered on his dark arms, known in those days (to all but those who wore them) as C.I.A. bracelets, on the happy assumption that a man ditched in hostile country could buy his way to safety by doing out a link at a time. But his eyes, as they watched Jerry along the well-oiled barrel of an AK-47 automatic rifle, had a fixed brightness.

He was covering me through the nose-cone, Jerry thought. He had a bead on me from the moment I left the hut.

The two Chinese were cooks, he decided in a moment of inspiration — ''cooks'' being the underworld nickname for chemists. Keller had said that the Air Opium lines had taken to bringing in the raw base and refining it in Phnom Penh, but were having hell's own job persuading the cooks to come and work in siege conditions.

''Hey, you! Voltaire!''

Jerry hurried forward to the edge of the

hold. Looking down, he saw the old peasant couple standing at the bottom of the ladder and Charlie Marshall trying to wrench the pig from them while he shoved the old woman up the steel ladder.

"When she come up, you gotta reach out and grab her, hear me?" he called, holding the pig in his arms. "She fall down and break her arse, we gotta whole lot more trouble with the coons. You some crazy narcotics hero, Voltaire?"

"No."

"Well, you grab hold of her completely, hear me?"

She started up the ladder. When she had gone a few rungs, she began croaking and Charlie Marshall contrived to get the pig under his arm while he gave her a sharp crack on the rump and screamed at her in Chinese. The husband scurried up after her, and Jerry hauled them both to safety.

Finally Charlie Marshall's own clown's head appeared through the cone, and though it was swamped by the hat, Jerry had his first glimpse of the face beneath: skeletal and brown, with sleepy Chinese eyes and a big French mouth which twisted all ways when he squawked. He shoved the pig through, Jerry grabbed it and carted it, screaming and wriggling, to the old peasants. Then Charlie hauled his own fleshless frame aboard, like a spider climbing out of a drain. At once the officer of customs, and the colonel of artillery stood up, brushed the seats of their uniforms, and progressed swiftly along the gangway to the shadowed man in the Castro hat squatting on the packing-cases. Reaching him, they waited respectfully, like sidemen taking the offertory to the altar.

The link bracelets flashed, an arm reached down, once, twice, and a devout silence descended while the two men carefully counted a lot of banknotes and everybody watched. In rough unison, they returned to the top of the ladder where Charlie Marshall waited with the manifest. The officer of customs signed it, the colonel of artillery looked on approvingly; then they both saluted and disappeared down the ladder. The nose-cone juddered to an almost closed position, Charlie Marshall gave it a kick, flung some matting across the gap, and clambered quickly over the packing-cases to an inside stairway leading to the cabin.

Jerry clambered after him and, having settled himself into the co-pilot's seat, silently totted up his blessings: We're above five hundred tons overweight. We're leaking oil. We're carrying an armed bodyguard. We're forbidden to take off. We're forbidden to land, and Phnom Penh airport's probably got a hole in it the size of Buckinghamshire. We have an hour and a half of Khmer Rouge between us and salvation, and if anybody turns sour on us at the other end, ace operator Westerby is caught with his knickers round his ankles and about two hundred gunny bags of opium base in his arms.

"You know how to fly this thing?" Charlie Marshall yelled as he struck at a row of mildewed switches. "You some kinda great flying hero, Voltaire?"

"I hate it all."

"Me too."

Seizing a swatter, Charlie Marshall

flung himself upon a huge bottle-fly that was buzzing the windscreen, then started the engines one by one, until the whole dreadful plane was heaving and rattling like a London bus on its last journey home up Clapham Hill. The radio crackled and Charlie Marshall took time off to give an obscene instruction to the control tower, first in Khmer and afterwards, in the best aviation tradition, in English. Heading for the far end of the runway, they passed a couple of gun emplacements and for a moment Jerry expected an over-zealous crew to loose off at the fuselage, till in gratitude he remembered the army colonel and his lorries and his pay-off.

Another bottle-fly appeared and this time Jerry took possession of the fly-swatter. The plane seemed to be gathering no speed at all, but half the instruments read zero, so he couldn't be sure. The din of the wheels on the runway seemed louder than the engines. Jerry remembered old Sambo's chauffeur driving him back to school: the slow, inevitable progress down the Western bypass toward Slough and finally Eton.

A couple of the hillsmen had come forward to see the fun and were laughing their heads off. A clump of palm trees came hopping toward them, but the plane kept its feet firmly on the ground. Charlie Marshall absently pulled back the stick and retracted the landing-gear. Uncertain whether the nose had really lifted, Jerry thought of school again, and competing in the long jump, and recalled the same sensation of not rising, yet ceasing to be on the earth.

He felt the jolt and heard the swish of leaves as the underbelly cropped the trees. Charlie Marshall was screaming at the plane to pull itself into the damn air, and for an age they made no height at all but hung and wheezed a few feet above a winding road which climbed inexorably toward a ridge of hills. Charlie Marshall was lighting a cigarette, so Jerry held the wheel in front of him and felt the live kick of the rudder. Taking back the controls, Charlie Marshall put the plane into a slow bank toward the lowest point of the range. He held the turn, crested the range, and went on to make a complete circle. As they looked down on the brown roof-tops and the river and the airport, Jerry reckoned they had an altitude of a thousand feet. As far as Charlie Marshall was concerned, that was a comfortable cruising height, for now at last he took his hat off and, with the air of a man who had done a good job well, treated himself to a large glass of Scotch from the bottle at his feet. Below them dusk was gathering, and the brown earth was fading softly into mauve.

"Thanks," said Jerry, accepting the bottle. "Yes, I think I might."

Jerry kicked off with a little small talk — if it is possible to talk small while you are shouting at the top of your voice.

"Khmer Rouge just blew up the airport ammunition dump!" he bellowed. "It's closed for landing and take-off."

"They did?" For the first time since Jerry had met him, Charlie Marshall seemed both pleased and impressed.

"They say you and Ricardo were great buddies."

"We bomb everything. We killed half

the human race already. We see more dead people than alive people. Plain of Jars, Danang — we're such big damn heroes that when we die Jesus Christ going to come down personally with a chopper and fish us out the jungle.''

''They tell me Ric was a great guy for business!''

''Sure! He the greatest! Know how many offshore companies we got, me and Ricardo? Six. We got foundations in Liechtenstein, corporations in Geneva, we got a bank manager in the Dutch Antilles, lawyers, Jesus. Know how much money I got?'' He slapped his back pocket. ''Three hundred U.S. exactly. Charlie Marshall and Ricardo killed half the whole damn human race together. Nobody gives us no money. My father killed the other half and he got plenty *plenty* money. Ricardo, he always got these crazy schemes always. Shell cases. Jesus. We're going to pay the coons to collect up all the shell cases in Asia, sell 'em for the next war!''

The nose dropped and he hauled it up again with a foul French oath. ''Latex! We gotta steal all the latex out of

Kampong Cham! We fly to Kampong Cham, we got big choppers, red crosses. So what do we do? We bring out the damn wounded. Hold still, you crazy bastard, hear me?'' He was talking to the plane again. In the nose-cone, Jerry noticed a long line of bullet-holes which had not been very well patched. Tear here, he thought absurdly.

"Human hair. We were gonna be millionaires out of hair. All the coon girls in the villages got to grow long hair and we're going to cut it off and fly it to Bangkok for wigs."

"Who was it paid Ricardo's debts so that he could fly for Indocharter?"

"Nobody!"

"Somebody told me it was Drake Ko."

"I never heard of Drake Ko. On my deathbed, I tell my mother, my father: bastard Charlie, the General's boy, he never heard of Drake Ko in his life."

"What did Ricardo do for Ko that was so special that Ko paid all his debts?"

Charlie Marshall drank some whisky straight from the bottle, then handed it to Jerry. His fleshless hands shook wildly whenever he took them off the stick, and his nose ran all the while. Jerry wondered how many pipes a day he was up to. He had once known a *pied-noir* hotelier in Luang Prabang who needed sixty to do a good day's work. *Captain Marshall never flies in the mornings,* he thought.

"American always in a hurry," Charlie Marshall complained, shaking his head. "Know why we gotta take this stuff to Phnom Penh now? Everybody impatient. Everybody want quick-shot these days. Nobody got time to smoke. Everybody got to turn on quick. You wanta kill the human race, you gotta take time, hear me?"

Jerry tried again. One of the four engines had given up, but another had developed a howl as if from a broken silencer, so that he had to yell even louder than before.

"What did Ricardo do for all that money?" he repeated.

"Listen, Voltaire, okay? I don't like politics, I'm just a simple opium smuggler, okay? You like politics you go back below and talk to those crazy Shans.

'You can't eat politics. You can't screw politics. You can't smoke politics.' He tell my father.''

"Who did?''

"Drake Ko tell my father, my father tell me, and me — I tell the whole damn human race! Drake Ko some philosopher, hear me?''

For its own reasons, the plane had begun falling steadily till it was a couple of hundred feet above the paddies. They saw a village, and cooking fires burning, and figures running wildly toward the trees, and Jerry wondered seriously whether Charlie Marshall had noticed. But at the last minute, like a patient jockey, he hauled and leaned and finally got the horse's head up, and they both had some more Scotch.

"You know him well?''

"Who?''

"Ko.''

"I never met him in my life, Voltaire. You wanna talk about Drake Ko, you go ask my father. He cut your throat.''

"How about Tiu? Tell me, who's the couple with the pig?'' Jerry yelled, to keep the conversation going while Charlie took back the bottle for another pull.

"Haw people, down from Chiang Mai. They worried about their lousy son in Phnom Penh. They think he too damn hungry, so they take him a pig."

"So how about Tiu?"

"I never heard of Mr. Tiu, hear me?"

"Ricardo was seen up in Chiang Mai three months ago," Jerry yelled.

"Yeah — well, Ric's a damn fool," said Charlie Marshall with feeling. "Ric's gotta keep his ass out of Chiang Mai or somebody shoot it right off. Anybody lying dead they gotta keep their damn mouth shut, hear me? I say to him, 'Ric, you my partner. Keep your damn mouth shut and your ass out of sight or certain people get personally pretty mad with you.' "

The plane entered a rain cloud and at once began losing height fast. Rain raced over the iron deck and down the insides of the windows. Charlie Marshall flicked some switches up and down; there was a bleeping from the controls panel and a couple of pin-lights came on, which no amount of swearing could put out. To

Jerry's anazement they began climbing again, though in the racing cloud he doubted his judgment of the angle. Glancing behind him in order to check, he was in time to glimpse the bearded figure of the dark-skinned paymaster in the Fidel Castro cap retreating down the cabin ladder, holding his AK-47 by the barrel.

They continued climbing, the rain ended, and the night surrounded them like another country. The stars broke suddenly above them, they jolted over the moonlit crevasses of the cloud-tops, they lifted again, the cloud vanished for good, and Charlie Marshall put on his hat and announced that both starboard engines had now ceased to play any part in the festivities. In this moment of respite, Jerry asked his maddest question.

"So where's Ricardo now, sport? Got to find him, see. Promised my paper I'd have a word with him. Can't disappoint them, can we?"

Charlie Marshall's sleepy eyes had all but closed. He was sitting in a half-trance with his head against the seat and the brim of his hat over his nose.

"What's that, Voltaire? You speak at all?"

"Where is Ricardo now?"

"Ric?" Charlie Marshall repeated, glancing at Jerry in a sort of wonder. "Where Ricardo is, Voltaire?"

"That's it, sport. Where is he? I'd like to have an exchange of views with him. That's what the three hundred bucks were about. There's another five hundred if you could find the time to arrange an introduction."

Springing suddenly to life, Charlie Marshall delved for the *Candide* and slammed it into Jerry's lap while he delivered himself of a furious outburst.

"I don't know where Ricardo is *ever,* hear me? I never don't want a friend in my life. If I see that crazy Ricardo, I shoot his balls right off in the street, hear me? He dead. So he can stay dead till he dies. He tell everyone he got killed. So maybe for once in my life I'm going to believe that bastard!"

Pointing the plane angrily into the cloud, he let it fall toward the slow flashes of Phnom Penh's artillery batteries to make a perfect three-point landing in what to Jerry was pitch darkness. He waited for the burst of machine-gun fire from the ground defences, he waited for the sickening free fall as they nosedived into a mammoth crater, but all he saw, quite suddenly, was a newly assembled *revêtement* of the familiar mud-filled ammunition boxes, arms open and palely lit, waiting to receive them. As they taxied toward it, a brown jeep pulled in front of them with a green light winking on the back, like a flashlight being turned on and off by hand. The plane was humping over grass. Hard beside the *revêtement* Jerry could see a pair of green lorries and a tight knot of waiting figures looking anxiously toward them, and behind them the dark shadow of a twin-engined sports plane. They parked, and Jerry heard at once from the hold beneath their penthouse the creak of the nose-cone opening, followed by the clatter of feet on the iron ladder and the quick call and answer of voices. The speed of their departure took him by surprise. But he heard something else that turned his blood cold and made him charge down the steps to the belly of the plane.

"Ricardo!" he yelled. "Stop! Ricardo!"

But the only passengers left were the old couple clutching their pig and their parcel. Seizing the steel ladder, he let himself fall, jolting his spine as he hit the tarmac with his heels. The jeep had already left with the Chinese cooks and their Shan bodyguard. As he ran forward, Jerry could see the jeep racing for an open gateway at the perimeter of the airfield. It passed through, and two sentries slammed the gates and took up their position as before. Behind him the helmeted flight-handlers were swarming toward the Carvair. A couple of lorry-loads of police looked on, and for a moment the Western fool in Jerry was seduced into thinking they might be playing some restraining rôle, till he realised they were Phnom Penh's guard of honour for a three-ton load of opium. But his eye was for one figure only, and that was the tall bearded man with the

Fidel Castro hat and the AK-47 and the heavy limp that sounded like a hard-soft drum-beat as the rubber-soled flying boots hobbled down the steel ladder.

Jerry saw him just. The door of the little Beechcraft waited open for him, and there were two ground crew poised to help him in. As he reached them, they held out their hands for the rifle but Ricardo waved them aside. He had turned and was looking for Jerry. For a second they saw each other. Jerry was falling and Ricardo was lifting the gun, and for twenty seconds Jerry reviewed his life from birth till now while a few more bullets ripped and whined round the battle-torn airfield. By the time Jerry looked up again, the firing had stopped, Ricardo was inside the plane, and his helpers were pulling away the chocks. As the little plane lifted into the flashes, Jerry ran like the devil for the darkest part of the perimeter before anybody else decided that his presence was obstructive to good trading.

Just a lovers' tiff, he told himself, sitting in a taxi-cab, and he held his hands over his head and tried to damp down the wild shaking of his chest. That's what you get for trying to play footsie-footsie with an old flame of Lizzie Worthington's. Somewhere a rocket fell and he didn't gave a damn.

He allowed Charlie Marshall two hours, though he reckoned one was generous. It was past curfew but the day's crisis had not ended with the dark; there were traffic checks all the way to *Le Phnom,* and the sentries held their machine-pistols at the ready. In the square two men were screaming at each other by torchlight before a gathering crowd. Farther down the boulevard, troops had surrounded a floodlit house and were leaning against the wall of it, fingering their guns. The driver said the secret police had made an arrest there. A colonel and his people were still inside with a suspected agitator. In the hotel forecourt tanks were parked, and in his bedroom Jerry found Luke lying on the bed drinking contentedly.

"Any water?" Jerry asked.
"Yip."

He turned on the bath and started to undress until he remembered the Walther.

"Filed?" he asked.

"Yip," said Luke again. "And so have you."

"Ha ha."

"I had Keller cable Stubbsie under your byline."

"The airport story?"

Luke handed him a tear-sheet. "Added some true Westerby colour. How the buds are bursting in the cemeteries. Stubbsie loves you."

"Well, thanks."

In the bathroom, Jerry unstuck the Walther from the plaster and slipped it in the pocket of his jacket where he would be able to get at it.

"Where we going tonight?" Luke called through the closed door.

"Nowhere."

"What the hell's that mean?"

"I've got a date."

"A woman?"

"Yes."

"Take Lukie. Three in a bed."

Jerry sank gratefully into the tepid water. "No."

"Call her. Tell her to whip in a whore for Lukie. Listen, there's that hooker from Santa Barbara downstairs. I'm not proud. I'll bring her."

"No."

"For Christ's sakes!" Luke shouted, now serious. "Why the hell not?" He had come right to the locked door to make his protest.

"Sport, you've got to get off my back," Jerry advised. "Honest. I love you, but you're not everything to me, right? So stay off."

"Thorn in your breeches, huh?" Long silence. "Well don't get your ass shot off, pardner, it's a stormy night out there."

When Jerry returned to the bedroom, Luke was back on the bed staring at the wall and drinking methodically.

"You know, you're worse than a bloody woman," Jerry told him, pausing at the door to look back at him.

The whole childish exchange would not have caused him another moment's thought had it not been for the way things turned out afterwards.

This time Jerry didn't bother with the bell on the gate, but climbed the wall and grazed his hands on the broken glass that ran along the top of it. He didn't make for the front door either, or go through the formality of watching the brown legs waiting on the bottom stair. Instead he stood in the garden waiting for the thump of his heavy landing to fade and for his eyes and ears to catch a sign of habitation from the big villa which loomed darkly above him with the moon behind it.

A car drew up without lights and two figures got out, by their size and quietness Cambodian. They pressed the gate bell and at the front door murmured the magic password through the crack, and were instantly, silently admitted. Jerry tried to fathom the layout. It puzzled him that no telltale smell escaped either from the front of the house or into the garden where he stood. There was no wind. He knew that for a large *divan* secrecy was vital, not because the law was punitive, but because the bribes were. The villa possessed a chimney and a courtyard and two floors: a place to live comfortably as a French *colon,* with a little family of concubines and half-caste children. The kitchen, he guessed, would be given over to preparation. The safest place to smoke would undoubtedly be upstairs in rooms which faced the courtyard. And since there was no smell from the front door, Jerry reckoned that they were using the rear of the courtyard rather than the wings or the front.

He trod soundlessly till he came to the paling that marked the rear boundary. It was lush with flowers and creeper. A barred window gave a first foothold to his bucksin boot, an overflow pipe a second, a high extractor fan a third, and as he climbed past it to the upper balcony he caught the smell he expected: warm and sweet and beckoning. On the balcony there was still no light, though the two Cambodian girls who squatted there were easily visible in the moonlight and he could see their scared eyes fixing him as he appeared out of the sky. Beckoning them to their feet, he walked them ahead of him, led by the smell.

The shelling had stopped, leaving the night to the geckos. Jerry remembered that Cambodians liked to gamble on the number of times they cheeped: tomorrow will be a lucky day; tomorrow won't; tomorrow I will take a bride; no, the day after. The girls were very young and they must have been waiting for the customers to send for them. At the rush door they hesitated and stared unhappily back at him. Jerry signalled and they began pulling aside layers of matting until a pale light gleamed onto the balcony, no stronger than a candle. He stepped inside, keeping the girls ahead of him.

The room must once have been the master bedroom, with a second, smaller room connecting. He had his hand on the shoulder of one girl. The other followed submissively. Twelve customers lay in the first room, all men. A few girls lay between them, whispering. Barefooted coolies ministered, moving with great deliberation from one recumbent body to the next, threading a pellet onto the needle, lighting it and holding it across the bowl of the pipe while the customer took a long steady draught and the pellet burned itself out. The conversation was slow and murmured and intimate, broken by soft ripples of grateful laughter. Jerry recognised the wise Swiss from the Counsellor's dinner party. He was chatting to a fat Cambodian. No one was interested in Jerry; like the orchids he carried at Lizzie Worthington's apartment block, the girls authenticated him.

"Charlie Marshall," Jerry said quietly. A coolie pointed to the next room. Jerry dismissed the two girls and they slipped away. The second room was smaller and Charlie Marshall lay in the corner, while a Chinese girl in an elaborate cheongsam crouched over him preparing his pipe. Jerry supposed she was the daughter of the house and that Charlie Marshall was getting the grand treatment because he was both an habitué and a supplier. He knelt the other side of him. An old man was watching from the doorway. The girl watched also, the pipe still in her hands.

"What you want, Voltaire? Why don't you leave me be?"

"Just a little stroll, sport. Then you can come back."

Taking his arm, Jerry lifted him gently to his feet, while the girl helped.

"How much has he had?" he asked the girl. She held up three fingers.

"And how much does he like?" he asked.

She lowered her head, smiling. A whole lot more, she was saying.

Charlie Marshall walked shakily at first, but by the time they reached the balcony he was prepared to argue, so Jerry lifted him up and carried him across his body like a fire victim, down the wooden steps and across the courtyard. The old man bowed them obligingly through the front door, a grinning coolie held the gate onto the street, and both were clearly very thankful to Jerry for showing so much tact. They had gone perhaps fifty yards when a pair of Chinese boys came rushing down the road at them, yelling and waving sticks like small paddles. Setting Charlie Marshall upright but holding him firmly with his left hand, Jerry let the first boy strike, deflected the paddle, then hit him at half strength with a two-knuckle punch just below the eye. The boy ran away, his friend after him. Still clutching Charlie Marshall, Jerry walked him till they came to the river and a heavy patch of darkness. Then he sat him down on the bank like a puppet in the sloped, dry grass.

"You gonna blow my brains out, Voltaire?"

"We're going to have to leave that to the opium, sport," said Jerry.

Jerry liked Charlie Marshall, and in a perfect world he would have been glad to spend an evening with him at the *fumerie* and hear the story of his wretched but extraordinary life. But now his fist grasped Charlie Marshall's tiny arm remorselessly lest he took it into his hollow head to bolt; for he had a feeling Charlie could run very fast when he became desperate. He half lay therefore, much as he had lounged among the magic mountain of possessions in old Pet's place, on his left haunch and his left elbow, holding Charlie Marshall's wrist into the mud, while Charlie Marshall lay flat on his back. From the river thirty feet below them came the murmured chant of the sampans as they drifted like long leaves across the golden moon path. From the sky — now in front of them, now behind — came the occasional ragged flashes of outgoing gun-fire as some bored battery commander decided to justify his existence. And sometimes from much nearer came the lighter, sharper snap as the Khmer Rouge replied, but only as tiny interludes between the racket of the geckos and the greater silence just beyond. By the moonlight Jerry looked at his watch, then at the crazed face, trying to calculate the strength of Charlie Marshall's cravings. If Charlie was a night smoker and slept in the mornings, then his needs must come on fast. The wet on his face was already unearthly. It flowed from the heavy pores and from the stretched eyes, and from the sniffing, weeping nose. It channelled itself meticulously along the engraved creases, making neat reservoirs in the caverns.

"Jesus, Voltaire. Ricardo's my friend. He got a lot of philosophy, that guy. You want to hear him talk, Voltaire. You wanna hear his ideas."

"Yes," Jerry agreed. "I do."

Charlie Marshall grabbed hold of Jerry's hand.

"Voltaire, these are good guys, hear me? Mr. Tiu . . . Drake Ko. They don't want to hurt nobody. They wanna do business. They got something to sell, they got people buying it! It's a service! Nobody gets his rice-bowl broken. Why you want to screw that up? You're a nice guy yourself. I saw. You carry the old boy's pig, okay? Whoever saw a round-eye carry a slant-eye pig before? But Jesus, Voltaire, you screw it out of me, they will kill you very completely, because that Mr. Tiu, he's a business-like and very philosophical gentleman, hear me? They kill *me,* they kill *Ricardo,* they kill *you,* they kill the whole damn human race!"

The artillery fired a barrage, and this time the jungle replied with a small salvo of missiles, perhaps six, which hissed over their heads like whirring boulders from a catapult. Moments later they heard the detonations somewhere in the centre of the town. After them, nothing. Not the wail of a fire engine, not the siren of an ambulance.

"Why would they kill *Ricardo?*" Jerry asked. "What's *Ricardo* done wrong?"

"Voltaire! Ricardo's my friend! Drake Ko my father's friend! Those old men big brothers. They fight some lousy war together in Shanghai about two hundred and fifty years ago, okay? I go see my father. I tell him, 'Father you gotta love me once. You gotta quit calling me your spider bastard, and you gotta tell your good friend Drake Ko to take the heat off Ricardo. You gotta say, "Drake Ko, that Ricardo and my Charlie, they are like you and me. They brothers, same as us. They learn fly together in Oklahoma, they kill the human race together. And they some pretty good friends. And that's a fact." ' My father hate me very bad, okay?"

"Okay."

"But he send Drake Ko a damn long personal message all the same."

Charlie Marshall breathed in, on and on,

as if his little breast could scarcely hold enough air to feed him. "That Lizzie. She some woman. Lizzie, she go personally to Drake Ko herself. Also on a very private basis. And she say to him, 'Mr. Ko, you gotta take the heat off Ric.' That's a very delicate situation there, Voltaire. We all got to hold on to each other tight or we fall off the crazy mountain-top, hear me? Voltaire, let me go. I beg! I completely beg, for Christ's sake, *je m'abîme,* hear me? That's all I know!"

Watching him, listening to his wracked outbursts, how he collapsed and rallied and broke again and rallied less, Jerry felt he was witnessing the last martyred writhing of a friend. His instinct was to lead Charlie slowly and let him ramble. His dilemma was that he didn't know how much time he had before whatever happens to an addict happened. He asked questions, but often Charlie didn't seem to hear them. At other times he appeared to answer questions Jerry hadn't put. And sometimes a delayed-action mechanism threw out an answer to a question which Jerry had long abandoned. At Sarratt the inquisitors said a broken man was dangerous because he paid you money he didn't have in order to buy your love. But for whole precious minutes Charlie could pay nothing at all.

"Drake Ko never went to Vientiane in his life!" Charlie yelled suddenly. "You crazy, Voltaire! A big guy like Ko bothering with a dirty little Asian town? Drake Ko some philosopher, Voltaire! You wanna watch that guy pretty careful!" Everyone, it seemed, was some philosopher — or everyone but Charlie Marshall. "In Vientiane nobody even heard Ko's name! Hear me, Voltaire?"

At another point, Charlie Marshall wept and seized Jerry's hands and enquired between sobs whether Jerry also had a father.

"Yes, sport, I did," said Jerry patiently. "And in his way he was a general too."

Over the river two white flares shed an amazing daylight, inspiring Charlie to reminisce on the hardships of their early days together in Vientiane. Sitting bolt upright, he drew a house in diagram in the mud. That's where Lizzie and Ric and Charlie Marshall lived, he said proudly: in a stinking flea-hut on the edge of town, a place so lousy even the geckos got sick from it. Ric and Lizzie had the royal suite, which was the only room this flea-hut contained, and Charlie's job was to keep out of the way and pay the rent and fetch the booze. But the memory of their dreadful economic plight moved Charlie to a fresh storm of tears.

"So what did you live on, sport?" Jerry asked, expecting nothing from the question. "Come on. It's over now. What did you live on?"

More tears while Charlie confessed to a monthly allowance from his father, whom he loved and revered.

"That crazy Lizzie," said Charlie through his grief, "that crazy Lizzie, she make trips to Hong Kong for Mellon."

Somehow Jerry contrived to keep himself steady in order not to shake Charlie from his course: "Mellon? Who's this Mellon?" he asked. But the soft tone made Charlie sleepy, and he started playing with the mud house, adding a chimney and smoke.

"Come on, damn you! *Mellon! Mellon!*" Jerry shouted straight into Charlie's face, trying to shock him into replying. "*Mellon,* you hashed-out wreck! Trips to Hong Kong!" Lifting Charlie to his feet, he shook him like a rag doll, but it took a lot more shaking to produce the answer, and in the course of it Charlie Marshall implored Jerry to understand what it was like to love, really to love, a crazy round-eye hooker and know you could never have her, even for a night.

Mellon was a creepy English trader, nobody knew what he did. A little of this, a little of that, Charlie said. People were scared of him. Mellon said he could get Lizzie into the big-time heroin trail. "With your passport and your body," Mellon had told her, "you can go in and out of Hong Kong like a princess."

Exhausted, Charlie sank to the ground and crouched before his mud house. Squatting beside him, Jerry fastened his fist to the back of Charlie's collar, careful not to hurt him.

"So she did that for him, did she, Charlie? Lizzie carried for Mellon." With his palm, he gently tipped Charlie's head round till his lost eyes were staring straight at him.

"Lizzie don't carry for *Mellon*, Voltaire," Charlie corrected him. "Lizzie carry for *Ricardo*. Lizzie don't love Mellon. She love *Ric* and *me*."

Staring glumly at the mud house, Charlie burst suddenly into raucous dirty laughter, which then petered out with no explanation.

"You louse it up, Lizzie!" Charlie called teasingly, poking a finger into the mud door. "You louse it up as usual, honey! You talk too much. Why you tell everyone you Queen of England? Why you tell everyone you some great spook-lady? Mellon get very very mad with you, Lizzie. Mellon throw you out, right out on your ass. Ric got pretty mad too, remember? Ric smash you up real bad and Charlie have to take you to the doctor in the middle of the damn night, remember? You got one hell of a big mouth, Lizzie, hear me? You my sister, but you got the biggest damn mouth *ever!*"

Till Ricardo closed it for her, Jerry thought, remembering the grooves on her chin. Because she spoiled the deal with Mellon.

Still crouching at Charlie's side and clutching him by the scruff, Jerry watched the world around him vanish, and in place of it he saw Sam Collins sitting in his car below Star Heights, with a clear view of the eighth floor, while he studied the racing page of the newspaper at eleven o'clock at night. Not even the clump of a rocket falling quite close could distract him from that freezing vision. And he heard Craw's voice above the mortar fire, intoning on the subject of Lizzie's criminality. When funds were low, Craw had said, Ricardo had made her carry little parcels across frontiers for him.

And how did London town learn *that,* Your Grace — Jerry would have liked to ask old Craw — if not from Sam Collins alias Mellon himself?

A three-second rainstorm had washed away Charlie's mud house and he was furious about it. He was splashing around on all fours looking for it, weeping and cursing frantically. The fit passed and he started talking about his father again, and how the old man had found employment for his natural son with a certain distinguished Vientiane airline — though Charlie till then had been quite keen to get out of flying for good on account of losing his nerve.

One day, it seemed, the General just lost patience with Charlie. He called together his bodyguard and came down from his hilltop in the Shans to a little opium town called Fang, not far inside the Thai border. There, after the fashion of patriarchs the world over, the General rebuked Charlie for his spendthrift ways.

Charlie had a special squawk for his father and a special way of puffing out his wasted cheeks in military disapproval.

" 'So you better do some proper damn work, for a change — hear me, you *kwailo* spider bastard? You better stay away from horse gambling, hear me, and strong liquor, and opium. And you better take those Commie stars off your tits and sack that stink friend Ricardo of yours. And you better cease financing his woman, hear me? Because I don't gonna keep you one day more, not one *hour,* you spider bastard, and I hate you so much one day I kill you because you remind me of that Corsican whore your mother!' "

Then to the job itself — Charlie's father, the General, still speaking: " 'Certain very fine Chiu Chow gentlemen who are pretty good friends of pretty good friends of mine, hear me, happen to have a controlling interest in a certain aviation company. Also I got certain shares in that company. Also this company happens to bear the distinguished title of Indocharter Aviation. So these good friends, they do me a favour to assist me in my disgrace for my three-legged spider-bastard son and I pray sincerely you may fall out of the sky and break your *kwailo* neck.' "

So Charlie flew his father's opium for Indocharter — one, two flights a week at first, but regular, honest work and he liked it. His nerve came back, he steadied down, and he felt real gratitude toward his old man. He tried, of course, to get the Chiu Chow boys to take Ricardo too, but they wouldn't. After a few months they did agree to pay Lizzie twenty bucks a week to sit in the front office and sweet-mouth the clients. These were the golden days, Charlie implied. Charlie and Lizzie earned the money, Ricardo wasted it on ever crazier enterprises, everybody was happy, everybody was employed.

Till one evening, like a nemesis, Tiu appeared and screwed the whole thing up. He appeared just as they were locking up the company's offices, straight off the pavement without an appointment, asking for Charlie Marshall by name and describing himself as part of the company's Bangkok management. The Chiu Chow boys came out of the back office, took one look at Tiu, vouched for his good faith, and made themselves scarce.

Charlie broke off in order to weep on Jerry's shoulder.

"Now listen to me carefully, sport,"

Jerry urged. "Listen. This is the bit I like, okay? You tell me this bit carefully and I'll take you home. Promise. *Please.*"

But Jerry had it wrong. It was no longer a matter of making Charlie talk. Jerry was now the drug on which Charlie Marshall depended. It was no longer a matter of holding him down, either. Charlie Marshall clutched Jerry's breast as if it were the last raft on his lonely sea, and their conversation had become a desperate monologue from which Jerry stole his facts while Charlie Marshall cringed and begged and howled for his tormentor's attention, making jokes and laughing at them through his tears. Downriver one of Lon Nol's machine-guns which had not yet been sold to the Khmer Rouge was firing tracer into the jungle by the light of another flare. Long golden bolts flowed in streams above and below the water, and lit a small cave where they disappeared into the trees.

Charlie's sweat-soaked hair was pricking Jerry's chin and Charlie was gabbling and dribbling all at the same time.

"Mr. Tiu don't wanna talk in no office, Voltaire. Oh, no! Mr. Tiu don't dress too good, either. Tiu very Chiu Chow person, he use Thai passport like Drake Ko, he use crazy name and keep very very low appearance when he come to Vientiane. 'Captain Marshall,' he say to me, 'how you like earn a lot of extra cash by performing certain interesting and varied work outside the company's hours, tell me? How you like fly a certain unconventional journey for me once? They tell me you some pretty damn fine pilot these days, very steady. How you like earn yourself not less than maybe four to five thousand U.S. for one day's work, not even a whole day? How would that personally attract you, Captain Marshall?' 'Mr. Tiu,' I tell him" — Charlie is shouting hysterically now — " 'without in any way prejudicing my negotiating position, Mr. Tiu, for five thousand bucks U.S. in my present serene mood I go down to hell for you and I bring you the devil's balls back!' Tiu say he come back one day and I gotta keep my damn mouth shut."

Suddenly Charlie had changed to his father's voice, and he was calling himself a spider bastard and the son of a Corsican whore — till gradually it dawned on Jerry that Charlie was describing the next episode in the story.

Amazingly, it turned out, Charlie had kept to himself the secret of Tiu's offer until he next saw his father, this time in Chiang Mai for a celebration of the Chinese New Year. He had not told Ric and he had not even told Lizzie — maybe because at this point they weren't getting on too well any more, and Ric was having himself a lot of women on the side.

The General's counsel was not encouraging: " 'Don't you touch that horse! That Tiu, he got some pretty highly big connections, and they all a bit too special for a crazy little spider bastard like you, hear me! Jesus Christ, who ever heard of a Swatownese give five thousand dollar to a lousy half-*kwailo* to improve his mind with travel!' "

"So you passed the deal to Ric, right?" said Jerry quickly. "Right, Charlie? You told Tiu, 'Sorry, but try Ricardo.' Is that how it went?''

But Charlie Marshall was missing — believed dead. He had fallen straight off Jerry's chest and lay flat in the mud with his eyes closed, and only his occasional gulps for breath — greedy, rasping draughts of it — and the crazy beating of his pulse where Jerry held his wrist testified to the life inside the frame.

"Voltaire," Charlie whispered. "On the Bible, Voltaire. You're a good man. Take me home. Jesus, take me home, Voltaire."

Stunned, Jerry stared at the prone and broken figure and knew that he had to ask one more question, even if it was the last in both their lives. Reaching down, he dragged Charlie to his feet for the last time. And there for an hour in the black road, struggling on his arm, while more aimless barrages stabbed the darkness, Charlie Marshall screamed, and begged, and swore he would love Jerry always if only he didn't have to reveal what arrangements his friend Ricardo had made for his survival. But Jerry explained that without that, the mystery was not even half revealed. And perhaps Charlie Marshall, in his ruin and despair, as he sobbed out the forbidden secrets, understood Jerry's reasoning: that in a city about to be given back to the jungle, there was no destruction unless it was complete.

As gently as he could, Jerry carried Charlie Marshall down the road, back to the villa and up the steps, where the same silent faces gratefully received him. I should have got more, he thought. I should have told him more as well; I didn't tend the two-way traffic in the way they ordered. I stayed too long with the business of Lizzie and Sam Collins. I did it upside down, I foozled my shopping list, I loused it up like Lizzie. He tried to feel sorry about that but he couldn't, and the things he remembered best were the things that weren't on the list at all, and they were the same things that stood up in his mind like monuments while he typed his message to dear old George.

He typed with the door locked and the

gun in his belt. There was no sign of Luke, so Jerry assumed he had gone off to a whore-house, still in his drunken sulk. It was a long signal, the longest of his career: "Know this much in case you don't hear from me again." He reported his contact with the Counsellor, he gave his next port of call and gave Ricardo's address, and a portrait of Charlie Marshall and of the three-sided household in the flea-hut, but only in the most formal terms, and he left out entirely his new-found knowledge regarding the rôle played by the unsavoury Sam Collins. After all, if they knew it already what was the point of telling it to them again? He left out the place-names and the proper names and made a separate key of them, then spent another hour putting the two messages into a first-base code that wouldn't fool a cryptographer for five minutes, but was beyond the ken of ordinary mortals, and of mortals like his host the British Counsellor. He ended with a reminder to housekeepers to check whether Blatt & Rodney had made that latest money draft to Cat. He burned the *en clair* texts, rolled the encoded versions into a newspaper, then lay on the newspaper and dozed, the gun awkwardly at his side.

At six he shaved, transferred his signals to a paperback novel which he felt able to part with, and took himself for a walk in the morning quiet. In the *place,* the Counsellor's car was parked conspicuously. The Counsellor himself was parked equally conspicuously on the terrace of a pretty bistro, wearing a Riviera straw hat reminiscent of Craw's, and treating himself to hot croissants and *café au lait.* Seeing Jerry, he gave an elaborate wave.

Jerry wandered over to him: "Morning," he said.

"Ah, you've got it! Good man!" the Counsellor cried, bounding to his feet. "Been *longing* to read it ever since it came out."

Parting with the signal, conscious only of its omissions, Jerry had a feeling of end-of-term. He might come back, he might not, but things would never be quite the same again.

The exact circumstances of Jerry's departure from Phnom Penh are relevant because of Luke, later.

For the first part of the morning that remained, Jerry pursued his obsessional search for cover, which was the natural antidote, perhaps, to his increasing sense of nakedness. Diligently he went on the stomp for refugee and orphan stories, which he filed through Keller at midday, together with a quite decent atmosphere piece on his visit to Battambang, which, though never used, has at least a place in his dossier. There were two refugee camps at that time, both blossoming, one in an enormous hotel on the Bassac, Sihanouk's personal and unfinished dream of paradise; one in the railway-yards near the airport, two or three families packed into each carriage. He visited both and they were the same: young Australian heroes struggling with the impossible, the only water filthy, a rice hand-out twice a week, and the children chirruping "Hi" and "Bye-bye" after him while he trailed his Cambodian interpreter up and down their lines, besieging everyone with questions, acting large, and looking for that extra something that would melt Stubbsie's heart.

At a travel office he noisily booked a passage to Bangkok. Making for the airport, he had a sudden sense of *déjà vu*. Last time I was here, I went water-skiing, he thought. The round-eye traders kept houseboats moored along the Mekong. And for a moment he saw himself — and the city — in the days when the Cambodian war still had a certain ghastly innocence: ace operator Westerby, risking mono, bouncing boyishly over the brown water of the Mekong, towed by a jolly Dutchman in a speed launch that burned enough petrol to feed a family for a week. The greatest hazard was the two-foot wave, he remembered, which rolled down the river every time the guards on the bridge let off a depth-charge to prevent the Khmer Rouge divers from blowing it up. But now the river was theirs, so was the jungle. And so, tomorrow or the next day, was the town.

At the airport, he ditched the Walther in a rubbish bin and at the last minute bribed his way aboard a plane to Saigon, which was his destination. Taking off, he wondered who had the longer expectation of survival, himself or the city.

Luke, on the other hand, with the key to Deathwish the Hun's flat nestling in his pocket, flew to Bangkok, and as luck had it he flew under Jerry's name, since Jerry was on the flight list and Luke was not, and the remaining places were all taken. In Bangkok he attended a hasty bureau conference at which the magazine's local manpower was carved up between various bits of the crumbling Vietnam front. Luke got Hué and Danang and accordingly left for Saigon next day, thence north by connecting midday plane.

Contrary to later rumour, the two men did not meet in Saigon.

Nor did they meet in the course of the northern roll-back.

The last they saw of each other, in any mutual sense, was on that final evening in Phnom Penh, when Jerry had bawled

Luke out and Luke had sulked: and that's a fact — a commodity which was afterwards notoriously hard to come by.

17
Ricardo

At no time in the entire case did George Smiley hold the ring with such tenacity as now. In the Circus, nerves were stretched to snapping-point. The bloody inertia and the bouts of frenzy which Sarratt habitually warned against becme one and the same. Each day that brought no hard news from Hong Kong was another day of disaster. Jerry's long signal was put under the microscope and held to be ambiguous, then neurotic.

Why had he not pressed Marshall harder? Why had he not raised the Russian spectre again? He should have grilled Charlie about the gold seam; he should have carried on where he left off with Tiu. Had he forgotten that his main job was to sow alarm and only afterwards to obtain information? As to his obsession with that wretched daughter of his — God Almighty, doesn't the fellow *know* what signals cost? (They seemed to forget it was the Cousins who were footing the bill.) And what was all this about having no more to do with British Embassy officials standing proxy for the absent Circus resident? All right, there had been a delay in the pipeline in getting the signal across from the Cousins' side of the house. Jerry had still run Charlie Marshall to earth, hadn't he? It was absolutely no part of a fieldman's job to dictate the "do"s and "don't"s to London. Housekeeping Section, who had arranged the contact, wanted him rebuked by return.

Pressure from outside the Circus was even fiercer. Colonial Wilbraham's faction had not been idle, and the Steering Group, in a startling about-turn, decided that the Governor of Hong Kong should after all be informed of the case, and soon. There was high talk of calling him back to London on a pretext. The panic had arisen because Ko had once more been received at Government House, this time at one of the Governor's talk-in suppers, at which influential Chinese were invited to air their opinions off the record.

By contrast Saul Enderby and his fellow hard-liners pulled the opposite way: "To hell with the Governor. What we want is full partnership with the Cousins immediately!" George should go to Martello *today,* said Enderby, and make a clean breast of the whole case and invite them to take over the last stage of development. He should stop playing hide-and-seek about Nelson, he should admit that he had no resources, he should let the Cousins compute the possible intelligence dividend for themselves, and if they brought the job off, so much the better: let them claim the credit on Capitol Hill, to the confusion of their enemies. The result of this generous and timely gesture, Enderby argued — coming bang in the middle of the Vietnam fiasco — would be an indissoluble intelligence partnership for years to come, a view which in his shifty way Lacon seemed to support. Caught in the cross-fire, Smiley suddenly found himself saddled with a double reputation. The Wilbraham set branded him as anti-Colonial and pro-American, while Enderby's men accused him of ultra-conservatism in the handling of the special relationship.

Much more serious however was Smiley's impression that some hint of the row had reached Martello by other routes, and that he would be able to exploit it. For example, Molly Meakin's sources spoke of a burgeoning relationship between Enderby and Martello at the personal level, and not just because their children were all being educated at the Lycée in South Kensington. It seemed that the two men had taken to fishing together at weekends in Scotland, where Enderby had a bit of water. Martello supplied the plane, said the joke later, and Enderby supplied the fish. Smiley also learned around this time, in his unworldly way, what everyone else had known from the beginning and assumed he knew too. Enderby's third and newest wife was American and rich. Before their marriage she had been a considerable hostess of the

Washington establishment, a rôle she was now repeating with some success in London.

But the underlying cause of everybody's agitation was finally the same. On the Ko front, nothing ultimately was happening. Worse still, there was an agonising shortage of operational intelligence. Every day now, at ten o'clock, Smiley and Guillam presented themselves at the Annexe and every day came away less satisfied. Tiu's domestic telephone line was tapped, so was Lizzie Worthington's. The tapes were locally monitored, then flown back to London for detailed processing. Jerry had sweated Charlie Marshall on a Wednesday. On the Friday, Charlie was sufficiently recovered from his ordeal to ring Tiu from Bangkok and pour out his heart to him. But after listening for less than thirty seconds, Tiu cut him short with an instruction to "get in touch with Harry right away," which left everybody mystified: nobody had a Harry anywhere.

On the Saturday there was drama because the watch on Ko's home number had him cancelling his regular Sunday-morning golf date with Mr. Arpego. Ko pleaded a pressing business engagement. This was it! This was the breakthrough! Next day, with Smiley's consent, the Hong Kong Cousins locked a surveillance van, two cars, and a Honda on to Ko's Rolls-Royce as it entered town. What secret mission at five-thirty on a Sunday morning was so important to Ko that he would abandon his weekly golf? The answer turned out to be his fortune-teller, a venerable old Swatownese who operated from a speedy spirit temple in a side-street off the Hollywood Road. Ko spent more than an hour with him before returning home, and though some zealous child inside the Cousins' van trained a concealed directional microphone on the temple window for the entire session, the only sounds he recorded apart from the traffic turned out to be cluckings from the old man's hen-house. Back at the Circus, di Salis was called in. What on earth would anyone be going to the fortune-teller at six in the morning for, least of all a millionaire?

Greatly amused by their perplexity, di Salis twirled his hair in delight. A man of Ko's standing would insist on being the first client in a fortune-teller's day, he said, while the great man's mind was still clear to receive the intimations of the spirits.

Then nothing happened for five weeks. Nothing. The mail and phone checks spewed out wads of indigestible raw material which, when refined, produced not a single intelligence lead. Meanwhile the artificial deadline imposed by the Enforcement Agency drew steadily nearer, on which day Ko should become open game for whoever could pin something on him soonest.

Yet Smiley kept his head. He resisted all recriminations, both of his own handling of the case and of Jerry's. The tree had been shaken, he maintained, Drake Ko was running scared, and time would show they were right. He refused to be hustled into some dramatic gesture to Martello, and he held resolutely to the terms of the deal that he had outlined in his letter, and of which a copy now lodged with Lacon. He also refused, as his charter allowed him, to enter into any discussion of operational detail, either with the Steering Group or with Enderby personally, except where issues of protocol or local mandate were concerned. To give way on this, he knew very well, would only have meant providing the doubters with fresh ammunition with which to shoot him down.

He held this line for five weeks, and on the thirty-sixth day, either God or the forces of logic — or better, the forces of Ko's human chemistry — delivered to Smiley a substantial if mysterious consolation. Ko took to the water. Accompanied by Tiu and an unknown Chinese later identified as the lead captain of Ko's junk-fleet, he spent the better part of three days touring the Hong Kong out-islands, returning each evening at dusk. Where they went, there was as yet no telling. Martello proposed a series of helicopter overflights to observe their course, but Smiley turned down the suggestion flat. Static surveillance from the quayside confirmed that they apparently left and returned by a different route each day, and that was all. And on the last day, the fourth, the boat did not return at all.

Panic. Where had it gone? Martello's masters in Langley, Virginia, flew into a complete spin and decided that Ko and the *Admiral Nelson* had deliberately strayed into China waters. Even that they had been abducted. Ko would never be seen again, and Enderby, going downhill fast, actually telephoned Smiley and told him it would be "your damn fault if Ko pops up in Peking yelling the odds about Secret Service persecution." Even Smiley, for one agonising day, secretly wondered whether, against all reason, Ko had indeed gone to join his brother.

Then of course, next morning early, the launch sailed back into the main harbour looking as if it had just returned from a regatta, and Ko gaily disembarked, following his beautiful Liese down the gangway.

It was this intelligence which, after very long thought and a renewed and detailed reading of Ko's file — not to mention much tense debate with Connie and di Salis — determined Smiley to take two decisions at once or, in gambler's terms, to play the only two cards that were left to him.

One: Jerry should advance to the "last stage," by which Smiley meant Ricardo. He hoped by this step to maintain the pressure on Ko, and provide Ko, if he needed it, with the final proof that he must act.

Two: Sam Collins should "go in."

This second decision was reached in consultation with Connie Sachs alone. It finds no mention in Jerry's main dossier, but only in a secret appendix later released, wth deletions, for wider scrutiny.

The fragmenting effect upon Jerry of these delays and hesitations was something not the greatest intelligence chief on earth could have included in his calculations. To be aware of it was one thing — and Smiley undoubtedly was, and even took one or two steps to forestall it. To be guided by it, to set it on the same plane as the factors of high policy which he was having daily fired at him, would have been downright irresponsible. A general is nothing without priorities.

The fact remains that Saigon was the worst place on earth for Jerry to be kicking his heels. Periodically, as the delays dragged on, there was talk at the Circus of sending him somewhere more salubrious — for instance, to Singapore or Kuala Lumpur — but the arguments of expediency and cover always kept him where he was; besides, tomorrow everything might change. There was also the matter of his personal safety. Hong Kong was not to be considered, and in both Singapore and Bangkok, Ko's influence was sure to be strong. Then, cover again: with the collapse approaching, where more natural than Saigon?

Yet it was a half-life Jerry lived, and in a half-town. For forty years, give or take, war had been Saigon's staple industry, but the American pull-out of '73 had produced a slump from which, to the end, the city never properly recovered, so that even this long-awaited final act, with its cast of millions, was playing to quite poor audiences. Even when he took his obligatory rides to the sharp end of the fighting, Jerry had a sense of watching a rained-off cricket match where the contestants wanted only to go back to the pavilion. The Circus forbade him to leave Saigon on the grounds that he might be needed elsewhere at any moment, but the injunction, literally observed, would have made him look ridiculous, and he ignored it. Xuan Loc was a boring French rubber town fifty miles out, on what was now the city's tactical perimeter. For this was a different war entirely from Phnom Penh's, more technical and more European in inspiration. Where the Khmer Rouge had no armour, the North Vietnamese had Russian tanks and 130 millimetre artillery, which they drew up on the classic Russian pattern, wheel to wheel, as if they were about to storm Berlin under Marshal Zhukov, and nothing would move till the last gun was laid and primed. He found the town half deserted, and the Catholic church empty except for one French priest.

"C'est terminé," the priest explained to him simply. The South Vietnamese would do what they always did, he said. They would stop the advance, then turn and run.

They drank wine together staring at the empty square.

Jerry filed a story saying the rot this time was irreversible, and Stubbsie shoved it on the spike with a laconic "PREFER PEOPLE TO PROPHECIES STUBBS."

Back in Saigon, on the steps of the Hotel Caravelle, begging children peddled useless garlands of flowers. Jerry gave them money and to save them face took their flowers, then dumped them in the waste-paper basket in his room. When he sat downstairs, they tapped on the window and sold him *Stars & Stripes.* In the almost empty bars where he drank, the girls collected to him desperately as if he were their last chance before the end. Only the police were in their element. They stood at every corner in white helmets and fresh white gloves, as if already waiting to direct the victorious enemy traffic when it arrived. They rode like monarchs past the refugees in their bird-coops on the pavement.

Jerry returned to his hotel room and Hercule rang, his favourite Vietnamese, whom he had been avoiding for all he was worth. Hercule, as he called himself, was anti-establishment and anti-Thieu and had made a quiet living supplying British journalists with information on the Vietcong, on the questionable grounds that the British were not involved in the war. "The British are my friends!" he begged into the phone. "Get me out! I need papers, I need money!"

Jerry said, "Try the Americans," and rang off hopelessly.

The Reuters office, when Jerry filed his stillborn copy, was a monument to forgotten heroes and the romance of failure. Under the glass desk-tops lay the photographed heads of tousled boys, on the walls famous rejection slips and samples of editorial fury; in the air a stink of old newsprint, and the

Somewhere-in-England sense of makeshift habitation which enshrines the secret nostalgia of every exiled correspondent. There was a travel agent just round the corner, and later it turned out that Jerry had twice in that period booked himself passages to Hong Kong, then not appeared at the airport. He was serviced by an earnest young Cousin named Pike, who had Information cover and occasionally came to the hotel with signals in yellow envelopes marked "RUSH PRESS" for authenticity. But the message inside was the same: no decision, stand by, no decision. He read Ford Madox Ford and a truly terrible novel about old Hong Kong. He read Greene and Conrad and T. E. Lawrence, and still no word came. The shellings sounded worst at night, and the panic was everywhere, like a spreading plague. In search of Stubbsie's people not prophecies, he went down to the American Embassy where ten thousand-odd Vietnamese were beating at the doors in an effort to prove their American citizenship. As he watched, a South

864

Vietnamese officer rode up in a jeep, leapt out, and began yelling at the women, calling them whores and traitors — picking, as it happened, a group of bona-fide U.S. wives to bear the brunt.

Again Jerry filed and again Stubbs threw his story out, which no doubt added to his depression. A few days later the Circus planners lost their nerve. As the rout continued, and worsened, they signalled Jerry to fly at once to Vientiane and keep his head down till ordered otherwise by a Cousins' postman. So he took a room at the Constellation, where Lizzie had liked to hang out, and he drank at the bar where Lizzie had liked to drink, and he occasionally chatted to Maurice the proprietor, and he waited. The bar was of concrete, two feet deep, so that if the need arose it could do duty as a bomb shelter or firing position. Each night in the gloomy dining room attached to it, one old *colon* ate and drank fastidiously, a napkin tucked into his collar. Jerry sat reading at another table. They were the only diners ever, and they never spoke. In the streets, the Pathet Lao — not long down from the hills — walked righteously in pairs and in great number, wearing Maoist caps and tunics and avoiding the glances of the girls. They had commandeered the corner villas and the villas along the road to the airport. They had camped in immaculate tents which peeked over the walls of overgrown gardens.

"Will the coalition hold?" Jerry asked Maurice once.

Maurice was not a political man. He gave a huge shrug. "It's the way it is," he replied in a stage French accent, and in silence handed Jerry a ballpoint pen as a consolation. It had "Löwenbräu" written on it: Maurice owned the concession for the whole of Laos, selling — it was said — several bottles a year. Jerry avoided absolutely the street that housed the Indocharter offices, just as he restrained himself from taking a look, out of curiosity, at the flea-hut on the edge of town which, on Charlie Marshall's testimony, had housed their *ménage à trois*. When asked, Maurice said there were very few Chinese left in town these days: "Chinese do not like," he said with another smile, tilting his head at the Pathet Lao on the pavement outside.

There remains the mystery of the telephone transcripts. Did Jerry ring Lizzie from the Constellation, or not? And if he did ring her, did he mean to talk to her, or only to listen to her voice? And if he intended to talk to her, then what did he propose to say? Or was the very act of making the phone call — like the act of booking airline passages in Saigon — in itself sufficient catharsis to hold him back from the reality?

What is certain is that nobody — neither Smiley nor Connie nor anyone else who read the crucial transcripts — can be seriously accused of failing in their duty, for the entry was at best ambivalent:

0055 hrs HK time. Incoming overseas call, personal for subject. Operator on the line. Subject accepts call, says "hullo" several times.

Operator: "Speak up, please, caller!" (repeated in French and ? Lao)

Subject: "Hullo? Hullo?"
Operator: "Can you hear me, caller? Speak up, please!"
(repeated in French and ? Lao)
Subject: "Hullo? Liese Worth here. Who's calling, please?" Call disconnected from caller's end.

The transcript nowhere mentions Vientiane as the place of origin and it is even doubtful whether Smiley saw it, since his cryptonym does not appear in the signing panel.

Anyway, whether it was Jerry who made that call or someone else, the next day a pair of Cousins, not one, brought him his marching orders and at long long last the welcome relief of action. The bloody inertia, however many interminable weeks of it, had ended — as it happened for good.

Jerry spent the afternoon fixing himself visas and transport, and next morning at dawn he crossed the Mekong into North East Thailand, carrying his shoulder-bag and his typewriter. The long wooden ferry boat was crammed with peasants and shrieking pigs. At the shack that controlled the crossing point, he pledged himself to return to Laos by the same route. Documentation would otherwise be impossible, the officials warned him severely. If I return at all, he thought. Looking back to the receding shores of Laos, he saw an American car parked on the tow-path, and beside it two slender, stationary figures watching. The Cousins we have always with us.

On the Thai bank everything was immediately impossible. Jerry's visa was not enough, his photographs bore no likeness, the whole area was forbidden to *farangs*. Ten dollars secured a revised opinion. After the visa, the car. Jerry had insisted on an English-speaking driver and the rate had been fixed accordingly, but the old man who waited for him spoke nothing but Thai, and little of that. By bawling English phrases into the nearby rice shop, Jerry finally hooked a fat supine boy who had some English and said he could drive.

A laborious contract was drawn up. The

old man's insurance did not cover another driver, and anyway it was out of date. An exhausted travel clerk issued a new policy while the boy went home to make his arrangements. The car was a clapped-out red Ford with bald tyres. Of all the ways Jerry didn't intend to die in the next day or two, this was one of them. They haggled, Jerry put up another twenty dollars. At a garage full of chickens he watched every move of the mechanics till the new tyres were in place.

Having thus wasted an hour, they set out at a breakneck speed south-eastwards over flat farm country. The boy played ''The lights are always out in Massachusetts'' five times before Jerry asked for silence.

The road was tarmac but deserted. Occasionally a yellow bus came side-winding down the hill toward them, and at once the driver accelerated and stayed on the crown till the bus had yielded a foot and thundered past. Once while he was dozing, Jerry was startled by the crunch of bamboo fencing and woke in time to see a foundation of splinters lift into the sunlight just ahead of him, and a pick-up truck rolling into the ditch in slow motion. He saw the door float upward like a leaf and the flailing driver follow it through the fence and into the high grass. The boy hadn't even slowed down, though his laughter made them swerve all over the road. Jerry shouted "Stop!" but the boy would have none of it.

"You want to get blood on your suit? You leave that to the doctors," he advised sternly. "I look after you, okay? This very bad country here. Lot of Commies."

"What's your name?" said Jerry resignedly.

It was unpronounceable, so they settled on Mickey.

It was two more hours before they hit the first barrier. Jerry dozed again, rehearsing his lines. There's always one more door you have to put your foot in, he thought. He wondered whether a day would come — for the Circus — for the comic — when the old entertainer would not be able to pull the gags any more; when just the sheer energy of bare-arsing his way over the threshold would defeat him, and he would stand there flaccid, sporting his friendly salesman's grin while the words died in his throat. Not this time, he thought hastily. Dear God, not this time please.

They stopped, and a young monk scurried out of the trees with a *wat* bowl and Jerry dropped a few *baht* into it. Mickey opened the boot. A police sentry peered inside, then ordered Jerry out and led him and Mickey over to a captain, who sat in a shaded hut all his own. The captain took a long while to notice Jerry at all.

"He ask you American?" said Mickey.

Jerry produced his papers.

On the other side of the barrier the perfect tarmac road ran straight as a pencil over the flat scrub land.

"He says what you want here?" Mickey said.

"Business with the colonel."

Driving on, they passed a village and a cinema. Even the latest films up here are silents, Jerry recalled. He had once done a story about them. Local actors made the voices and invented whatever plots came into their heads. He remembered John Wayne with a squeaky Thai voice, and the audience ecstatic, and the interpreter explaining to him that they were hearing an imitation of the local mayor, who was a famous queen.

They were passing forest, but the shoulders of the road had been cleared fifty yards on either side to cut the risk of ambush. Occasionally they came on sharp white lines which had nothing to do with earth-bound traffic. The road had been laid by the Americans with an eye to auxiliary landing-strips.

"You know this colonel guy?" Mickey asked.

"No," said Jerry.

Mickey laughed in delight. "Why you want?"

Jerry didn't bother to answer.

The second road-block came twenty miles later, in the centre of a small village given over to police. A cluster of grey trucks stood in the courtyard of the *wat;* four jeeps were parked beside the roadblock. The village lay at a junction.

At right angles to their road a yellow dust path crossed the plain and snaked into the hills on either side.

This time Jerry took the initiative, leaping from the car immediately with a merry cry of "Take me to your leader!" Their leader turned out to be a nervous young captain with the anxious frown of a man trying to keep abreast of matters beyond his learning. He sat in the police station with his pistol on the desk. The police station was temporary, Jerry noticed. Out of the window he saw the bombed ruins of what he took to be the last one.

"My colonel is a busy man," the captain said, through Mickey the driver.

"He is also a very brave man," Jerry said.

There was dumb show till they had established "brave."

"He has shot many Communists," Jerry said. "My paper wishes to write about this brave Thai colonel."

The captain spoke for quite a while, and suddenly Mickey began hooting with laughter: "The captain say we don't got no Commies. We only got Bangkok! Poor people up here don't know nothing, because Bangkok don't give them no schools, so the Commies come talk to them in the night and the Commies tell them all their sons go Moscow, learn be big doctors, so they blow up the police station."

"Where can I find the colonel?"

"Captain say we stay here."

"Will he ask the colonel to come to us?"

"Colonel very busy man."

"Where is the colonel?"

"He next village."

"What is the name of the next village?"

The driver once more collapsed with laughter. "It don't got no name. That village all dead."

"What was the village called before it died?"

Mickey said a name.

"Is the road open as far as this dead village?"

"Captain say military secret. That mean he don't know."

"Will the captain let us through to take a look?"

A long exchange followed. "Sure," said Mickey finally. "He say we go. Okay."

"Will the captain radio the colonel and tell him we are coming?"

"Colonel very busy man."

"Will he radio him?"

"Sure," said the driver, as if only a hideous *farang* could have made a meal of such a patently obvious detail.

They climbed back into the car. The boom lifted and they continued along the perfect tarmac road with its cleared shoulders and occasional landing marks. For twenty minutes they drove without seeing another living thing, but Jerry wasn't consoled by the emptiness. He had heard that for every Communist guerrilla fighting with a gun in the hills, it took five in the plains to produce the rice, the ammunition, and the infrastructure, and these were the plains. They came to a dust path on their right, and the dust of it was smeared across the tarmac from recent use. Mickey swung down it, following the heavy tyre tracks, playing "The lights are always out in Massachusetts" again, and singing the words very loud, Jerry notwithstanding.

"This way the Commies think we plenty people," he explained amid more laughter, thus making it impossible for him to object. To Jerry's surprise he also produced a huge, long-barrelled .45 target pistol from the bag beneath his seat. Jerry ordered him sharply to shove it back where it came from. Minutes later they smelt burning, then they drove through wood-smoke, then they reached what was left of the village: clusters of cowed people, a couple of acres of burnt teak trees like a petrified forest, three jeeps, twenty-odd police, and a stocky lieutenant-colonel at their centre. Villagers and police alike were gazing at a patch of smouldering ash sixty yards across, in which a few charred beams sketched the outline of the burned houses.

The colonel watched them park and he watched them walk over. He was a fighting man. Jerry saw it immediately. He was squat and strong, and he neither smiled nor scowled. He was swarthy and greying, and he could have been Malay, except that he was thicker in the trunk.

He wore parachute wings and flying wings and a couple of rows of medal ribbons. He wore battle-drill and a regulation automatic in a leather holster on his right thigh, and the restraining straps hung open.

''You the newsman?'' he asked Jerry in flat, military American.

''That's right.''

The colonel turned to the driver. He said something, and Mickey walked hastily back to the car, got into it, and stayed there.

''What do you want?''

''Anybody die here?''

''Three people. I just shot them. We got thirty-eight million.'' His functional American-English, all but perfect, came as a growing surprise.

''Why did you shoot them?''

''At night the C.T.s held classes here. People come from all around to hear the C.T.s.''

Communist terrorists, thought Jerry. He had an inkling it was originally a British phrase. A string of lorries was nosing down the dust path. Seeing them, the villagers began picking up their bedrolls and children. The colonel gave an order, and his men formed them into a rough file while the lorries turned round.

"We find them a better place," the colonel said. "They start again."

"Who did you shoot?"

"Last week two of my men got bombed. The C.T.'s operated from this village." He picked out a sullen woman at that moment clambering on the lorry and called her back so that Jerry could take a look at her. She stood with her head bowed.

"They stay in her house," he said. "This time I shoot her husband. Next time I shoot her."

"And the other two?" Jerry asked.

He asked because to keep asking is to stay punching, but it was Jerry, not the colonel, who was under interrogation. The colonel's eyes were hard and appraising and held a lot in reserve. They looked at Jerry enquiringly but without anxiety.

"One of the C.T.s sleep with a girl here," he said simply. "We're not only the police. We're the judge and courts as well.

There's no one else. Bangkok don't care for a lot of public trials up here. That's the way it is."

The villagers had boarded the lorries. They drove away without looking back. Only the children waved over the tailboards. The jeeps followed, leaving the three of them, and the two cars, and a boy, perhaps fifteen.

"Who's he?" said Jerry.

"He comes with us. Next year — year after, maybe — I shoot him too."

Jerry rode in the jeep beside the colonel, who drove. The boy sat impassively in the back, murmuring yes and no while the colonel lectured him in a firm, mechanical tone. Mickey followed in the car. On the floor of the jeep, between the seat and the pedals, the colonel kept four grenades in a cardboard carton. A small machine-gun lay along the rear seat, and the colonel didn't bother to move it for the boy. Above the driving mirror beside the votive pictures hung a postcard portrait of John Kennedy, with the legend "Ask not what your country can do for you. Ask rather what you can do for your country." Jerry had taken his notebook out. The lecture to the boy continued.

"What are you saying to him?"

"I am explaining the principles of democracy."

"What are they?

"No Communism and no generals," he replied, and laughed.

At the main road they turned right, farther into the interior, Mickey following in the red Ford.

"Dealing with Bangkok is like climbing that big tree," the colonel said to Jerry, pointing at the forest. "You climb one branch, go up a bit, change branches, the branch breaks, you go up again. Maybe one day you get to the top general. Maybe never."

Two small kids flagged them down, and the colonel stopped to let them squeeze in beside the boy.

"I don't do that too often," he said with a smile. "I do that to show you I'm a nice guy. The C.T.s get to know you stop for kids, they put out kids to stop you. You got to vary yourself. That way you stay alive.''

He had turned in to forest again. They drove a few miles and let the small children out, but not the sullen boy. The trees stopped and gave way to desolate scrub land. The sky grew white, with the shadows of the hills just breaking through the mist.

''What's he done?'' Jerry asked.

''Him? He's a C.T.,'' the colonel said. ''We catch him.'' In the forest Jerry saw a flash of gold, but it was only a *wat*. ''Last week one of my police turns informer to C.T. I send him on patrol, shoot him, make him a big hero. I fix the wife a pension, I buy a big flag for the body, I make a great funeral, and the village gets a bit richer. That guy's not an informer any more. He's a folk hero. You got to win the hearts and minds of the people.''

''No question,'' Jerry agreed.

They had reached a wide dry paddy-field with two women hoeing at the centre and otherwise nothing in sight but a far hedge and rocky dune land fading into the white sky. Leaving Mickey in the Ford,

Jerry and the colonel began walking across the field, the sullen boy trailing behind him.

"You British?"

"Yes."

"I was at Washington International Police Academy," said the colonel. "Very nice place. I studied law enforcement at Michigan State. They showed us a good time. You want to keep clear of me a little?" he asked politely as they trod meticulously over the plough. "They shoot me, not you. They shoot a *farang*, they get too much trouble here. They don't want that. Nobody shoots a *farang* in my territory."

They had reached the women. The colonel spoke to them, walked a distance, stopped, looked back at the sullen boy, and returned to the women and spoke to them a second time.

"What's that about?" said Jerry.

"I ask them if there's any C.T.s around. They tell me no. Then I think, Maybe the C.T.s want this boy back. So I go back and tell them, 'If anything goes wrong, we shoot you women first.'" They had reached the hedge. The dunes lay ahead of them, overgrown with high bushes and palms like sword blades. The colonel cupped his hands and yelled until an answering call came.

"I learned that in the jungle," he explained with another smile. "When you're in the jungle, always call first."

"What jungle was that?" said Jerry.

"Stand near to me now please. Smile when you speak to me. They like to see you very clear."

They had reached a small river. Around it, a hundred or more males, some even younger than the boy, picked indifferently at the rocks with axes and spades, or humped bags of cement from one vast pile to another. A handful of armed police looked negligently on. The colonel called up the boy and spoke to him, and the boy bowed his head and the colonel boxed him sharply on the ears. The boy muttered something and the colonel hit him again, then patted him on the shoulder, whereupon like a freed but crippled bird the boy scuffled away to join the labour force.

"You write about C.T.s, you write about my dam, too," the colonel ordered as they started their return talk. "We're going to make this fine pasture here. They will name it after me."

"What jungle did you fight in?" Jerry repeated.

"Laos. Very hard fighting."

"You volunteered?"

"Sure. I got kids, need the money. I joined PARU. Heard of PARU? Police Aerial Reinforcement Unit. The Americans ran it. They got it made. I write a letter resigning from the Thai police. They put it in a drawer. If I get killed, they pull out the letter to prove I resigned before I joined PARU."

"That where you met Ricardo?"

"Sure. Ricardo's my friend. We fought together, shoot a lot of bad guys."

"I want to see him," said Jerry. "I met a girl of his in Saigon. She told me he had a place up here. I want to make him a business proposition."

They passed the women again. The colonel waved at them but they ignored him. Jerry was watching his face but he could as soon have watched a boulder back on the dunes. The colonel climbed into the jeep. Jerry got in after him.

"I thought maybe you could take me to him. I could even make him rich for a few days."

"This for your paper?"

"It's private."

"A private business proposition?" the colonel asked.

"That's right."

As they drove back to the road, two cement-mixer lorries came toward them and the colonel had to back to let them pass. Automatically Jerry noticed the name painted on the yellow sides. As he did so, he caught the colonel's eye watching him. They continued toward the interior, driving as fast as the jeep would go, in order to beat anybody's bad intentions along the way. Faithfully Mickey followed behind.

"Ricardo is my friend and this is my territory," the colonel repeated. The statement, though familiar, was this time an entirely explicit warning. "He lives here under my protection, according to an arrangement we have made. Everybody around here knows that. The villagers know it, C.T. knows it. Nobody hurts Ricardo or I'll shoot every C.T. on the dam."

As they turned off the main road into the dust path again, Jerry saw the light skid marks of a small plane written on the tarmac.

"This where he lands?"

"Only in the rainy season." The colonel continued outlining his ethical position in the matter: "If Ricardo kills you, that's his business. One *farang* shoots another on my territory, that's natural." He could have been explaining basic arithmetic to a child. "Ricardo is my friend," he repeated without embarrassment. "My comrade."

"He expecting me?"

"Please pay attention to him. Captain Ricardo is sometimes a sick man."

Tiu make a special place for him, Charlie Marshall had said, *a place where only crazy people go. Tiu say to him, "You stay alive, you keep the plane, you ride shot-gun for Charlie*

Marshall any time you like, carry money for him, if that's the way Charlie wants it. That's the deal and Drake Ko don't never break a deal," he say. *But if Ric make trouble, or if Ric louses up, or if Ric shoot his big mouth off about certain matters, Tiu and his people kill that crazy bastard so completely he don't never know who he is.*

"Why doesn't Ric just take the plane and run for it?" Jerry had asked.

Tiu got Ric's passport, Voltaire. Tiu buy Ric's debts and his business enterprises and his police record. Tiu pinned about fifty tons of opium on him and Tiu got the proof all ready for the narcs for if ever he need it. Ric, he's free to walk out any damn time he wants. They got prisons waiting for him everywhere.

The house stood on stilts at the centre of a wide dust path, with a balcony all round it and a small stream beside it and a couple of Thai girls under it, and one of them was feeding her baby while the other stirred a cook pot. Behind the house lay a flat brown field with a shed at one end big enough to house a small plane — say, a Beechcraft — and there was a silvered track of pressed grass down the field where one might recently have landed. There were no trees near the house and it stood on a small rise. It had all-round vision and broad windows not very high, which Jerry guessed had been altered to provide a wide angle of fire from inside.

Short of the house the colonel told Jerry to get out, and walked back with him to Mickey's car. He spoke to Mickey and Mickey leapt out and unlocked the boot. The colonel reached under the car seat and pulled out the target pistol and tossed it contemptuously into the jeep. He frisked Jerry, then he frisked Mickey; then he searched the car for himself. Then he told them both to wait and climbed the steps to the first floor. The girls ignored him.

"He fine colonel," said Mickey.

They waited.

"England rich country," said Mickey.

"England a very *poor* country," Jerry retorted as they continued to watch the house.

"Poor country, rich people," said Mickey. He was still shaking with laughter at his own good joke as the colonel came out of the house, climbed into the jeep, and drove away.

"Wait here," said Jerry. He walked slowly to the foot of the steps, cupped his hands to his mouth, and called upwards.

"My name's Westerby. You may remember shooting at me in Phnom Penh a few weeks ago. I'm a poor journalist with expensive ideas."

"What do you want, Voltaire? Somebody told me you were dead already."

A Latin-American voice, deep and feathered, from the darkness above.

"I want to blackmail Drake Ko. I reckon that between us we could sting him for a couple of million bucks and you could buy your freedom."

In the darkness of the trap above him Jerry saw a single gun barrel, like a Cyclopean eye, wink, then settle its gaze on him again.

"*Each,*" Jerry called. "Two for you, two for me. I've got it all worked out. With my brains and your information and Lizzie Worthington's figure, I reckon it's a dead cert."

He started walking slowly up the steps. Voltaire, he thought; when it came to spreading the word, Charlie Marshall didn't hang around. As to being dead already — give it a little time, he thought.

As Jerry climbed through the trap he moved from the dark into the light, and the Latin-American voice said, "Stay right there." Doing as he was told, Jerry was able to look round the room, which was a mix between a small armaments museum and an American P.X. On the centre table on a tripod stood an AK-47 similar to the one Ricardo had already fired at him, and as Jerry had suspected, it covered all four approaches through the windows. But in case it didn't, there were a couple of spares and beside each gun a decent pile of ammunition clips. Grenades lay about like fruit, in clusters of three and four, and on the hideous walnut cocktail cabinet under a plastic effigy of the Madonna lay a selection of pistols and automatics for all occasions.

There was only one room but it was large, with a low bed with japanned and lacquered ends, and Jerry had a silly moment wondering how the devil Ricardo had ever got it into his Beechcraft. There were two refrigerators and an ice-maker, and there were painfully worked oil paintings of nude Thai girls, drawn with the sort of erotic inaccuracy that usually comes with too little access to the subject. There was a filing cabinet with a Luger on it and there was a book shelf with works on company law, international taxation, and sexual technique. On the walls hung several locally carved icons of saints, the Virgin, and the Christ-child. On the floor lay a steel scaffold of a rowing-boat, with a sliding seat for improving the figure.

At the centre of all this, in much the same pose in which Jerry had first set eyes on him, sat Ricardo in a senior executive's swivel chair, wearing his

C.I.A. bracelets and a sarong and a gold cross on his handsome bare chest. His beard was a lot less full than when Jerry had seen it last, and he guessed the girls had clipped it for him. He wore no cap, and his crinkly black hair was threaded into a small gold ring at the back of his neck. He was broad-shouldered and muscular and his skin was tanned and oily and his chest was matted with hair.

He also had a bottle of Scotch at his elbow, and a jug of water, but no ice because there was no electricity for the refrigerators.

"Take off your jacket please, Voltaire," Ricardo ordered, so Jerry did, and with a sigh Ricardo stood up, and picked an automatic from the table, and walked slowly round Jerry, studying his body while he gently probed it for weapons.

"You play tennis?" he enquired from behind him, running one hand very lightly down Jerry's back. "Charlie said you got muscles like a gorilla." But Ricardo did not really ask questions of anyone but himself. "I like very much tennis. I am an extremely good player. I win always.

Here unfortunately I have little opportunity."

He sat down again. "Sometimes you got to hide with the enemy to get away from your friends. I ride horses, box, shoot, I got degrees, I fly an aeroplane, I know a lot of things about life, I'm very intelligent, but, owing to unforeseen circumstances, I live in the jungle like a monkey." The automatic lay casually in his left hand. "That what you call a paranoid, Voltaire? Somebody who think everybody his enemy?"

"I rather think it is."

To produce the well-trodden witticism, Ricardo laid a finger to his bronzed and oiled breast: "Well, this paranoid got real enemies," he said.

"With two million bucks," said Jerry, still standing where Ricardo had left him, "I'm sure most of them could be eliminated."

"Voltaire, I must tell you honestly that I regard your business proposition as crap."

Ricardo laughed. That was to say he made a fine display of his white teeth against his newly clipped beard, and flexed his stomach muscles a little, and kept his eyes fixed dead level on Jerry's face while he sipped his glass of whisky. He's got a brief, thought Jerry, same as I have. *If he shows up, you hear him out,* Tiu had no doubt said to him. And when Ricardo had heard him out — then what?

"I definitely understood you had had an accident, Voltaire," said Ricardo sadly and shook his head as if complaining about the poor quality of his information. "You want a drink?"

"Thanks, I'll pour it for myself," said Jerry. The glasses were in a cabinet, all different colours and sizes. Deliberately Jerry walked over to it and helped himself to a long pink tumbler with a dressed girl outside and a naked girl inside. He poured a couple of fingers of Scotch into it, added a little water, and sat down opposite Ricardo at the table, while Ricardo studied him with interest.

"You do exercises, weight-lifting, something?" Ricardo enquired confidingly.

"Just the odd bottle," said Jerry.

Ricardo laughed inordinately, still examining him very closely with his flickering bedroom eyes.

"That was a very bad thing you did to little Charlie, you know that? I don't like you to sit on my friend's head in the darkness while he catch cold turkey. Charlie going to take a long while to recover. That's no way to make friends with Charlie's friends, Voltaire. They say you even been rude to Mr. Ko. Took my little Lizzie out to dinner. That true?"

"I took her out to dinner."

"You screw her?"

Jerry didn't answer. Ricardo gave another burst of laughter, which stopped as suddenly as it had started. He took a long draught of whisky and sighed.

"Well, I hope she's grateful, that's all." Ricardo was at once a much misunderstood man. "I forgive her. Okay? You see Lizzie again, tell her I, Ricardo, forgive her. I train her. I put her on the right road. I tell her a lot of things — art, culture, politics, business, religion — I teach her how to make love, and I send her into the world. Where would she be without my connections? Where? Living in the jungle with Ricardo like a monkey. She owes me everything.

"*Pygmalion* — know that movie? Well, I'm the professor. I tell her some things — know what I mean? — I tell her things no man can tell her but Ricardo. Seven years in Vietnam. Two years in Laos. Four thousand dollars a month from C.I.A., and me a Catholic. You think I can't tell her some things, a girl like that from nowhere, an English scrubber? She got a kid, you know that? Little boy in London. She walk out on him, imagine. Such a mother, huh? Worse than a whore."

Jerry found nothing useful to say. He was looking at the two large rings side by side on the middle fingers of Ricardo's heavy right hand, and in his memory measuring them against the twin scars on Lizzie's chin. It was a downward blow, he decided, a right cross while she was below him. It seemed strange he hadn't broken her jaw. Perhaps he had, and she'd had a lucky mend.

"You gone deaf, Voltaire? I said outline to me your business proposition. Without prejudice, you understand. Except I don't believe a word of it."

Jerry helped himself to some more whisky: "I thought maybe if you told me what it was Drake Ko wanted you to do that time you flew for him, and if Lizzie could get me alongside Ko, and we all kept our hands on the table, we'd have a good chance of taking him to the cleaners."

Now he said it, it sounded even lamer than when he had rehearsed it, but he didn't particularly care.

"You crazy, Voltaire. Crazy. You're making pictures in the air."

"Not if Ko was asking you to fly into the China mainland for him, I'm not. Ko can own the whole of Hong Kong for all I care, but if the Governor ever got to hear of that little adventure, I reckon he and Ko would stop kissing overnight. That's for openers. There's more."

"What are you talking about, Voltaire? China? What nonsense is this you are telling me about the China *mainland?*"

He shrugged his glistening shoulders and drank, smirking into his glass. "I do not read you, Voltaire. You talk through your ass. What makes you think I fly to China for Ko? Ridiculous. Laughable."

As a liar, Jerry reckoned, Ricardo was about three leagues lower down the chart than Lizzie, which was saying quite a lot.

"My editor makes me think it, sport. My editor is a very sharp fellow. Lot of influential and knowledgeable friends. They tell him things. Now, for instance, my editor has a very good hunch that not long after you died so tragically in that air crash of yours you sold a damn great load of raw opium to a friendly American purchaser engaged in the suppression of dangerous drugs. Another hunch of his tells him it was Ko's opium, not yours to sell at all, and that it was addressed to the China mainland. Only you decided to play the angles instead."

He went straight on, while Ricardo's eyes watched him over the top of his whisky glass. "Now, if that were so, and Ko's ambition were, let us say, to reintroduce the opium habit to the mainland — slowly, but gradually creating new markets, you follow me — well, I reckon he would go a very long distance to prevent that information making the front pages of the world's press. That's not all either. There are other aspects altogether, for us even more lucrative.''

"What's that, Voltaire?" Ricardo asked and continued watching him as fixedly as if he had him in the sights of his rifle. "What are these other aspects you refer to? Kindly tell me, please."

"Well, I think I'll hold back on that," said Jerry with a frank smile. "I think I'll keep it warm while you give me a little something in return."

A girl came silently up the stairs carrying bowls of rice and lemon grass and boiled chicken. She was trim and entirely beautiful. They could hear voices from underneath the house, including Mickey's, and the sound of the baby laughing.

"Who you got down there, Voltaire?" Ricardo asked vaguely, half waking from his reverie. "You got some damn bodyguard or something?''

"Just the driver."

"He got guns?"

Receiving no reply, Ricardo shook his head in wonder. "You're some crazy fellow," he remarked, as he waved at the girl to get out. "You're some really crazy fellow." He handed Jerry a bowl and chopsticks. "Holy Maria. That Tiu, he's a pretty rough guy. I'm a pretty rough guy myself. But those Chinese can be very hard people, Voltaire. You mess with a guy like Tiu, you get pretty big trouble."

"We'll beat them at their own game," said Jerry. "We'll use English lawyers. We'll stack it so high a board of bishops couldn't knock it down. We'll collect witnesses. You, Charlie Marhsall, whoever else knows. Give dates and times of what he said and did. We'll show him a copy and we'll bank the others and we'll make a contract with him. Signed, sealed, and delivered. Legal as hell. That's what he likes. Ko's a very legal-minded man. I've been into his business affairs. I've seen his bank statements, his assets. The story's pretty good as it stands. But with the other aspects I'm talking about, I reckon it's cheap at five million. Two for you. Two for me. One for Lizzie."

"For her, nothing."

Ricardo was stooping over the filing cabinet. Pulling open a drawer, he began picking through the contents, studying brochures and correspondence.

"You ever been to Bali, Voltaire?"

Solemnly pulling on a pair of reading glasses, Ricardo sat at the table again and began studying the file. "I bought some land there a few years back. A deal I made. I make many deals. Walk, ride, I got a Honda seven fifty there, a girl. In Laos we kill everybody, in Vietnam we burn the whole damn countryside, so I buy this land in Bali, bit of land we don't burn for once and a girl we don't kill, know what I mean? Fifty acres of scrub. Here, come here."

Peering over his shoulder, Jerry saw a planner's mimeographed diagram of an isthmus broken into numbered building plots, and in the bottom left corner the words "Ricardo & Worthington Ltd., Dutch Antilles."

"You come into business with me, Voltaire. We develop this thing together, okay? Build fifty houses, have one each, nice people, put Charlie Marshall out there as manager, get some girls, make a colony maybe — artists, concerts sometimes — you like music, Voltaire?"

"I need hard facts," Jerry insisted firmly. "Dates, times, places, witnesses' statements. When you've told me, I'll trade you. I'll explain those other aspects to you — the lucrative ones. I'll explain the whole deal."

"Sure," said Ricardo distractedly, still studying the map. "We screw him. Sure we do."

This is how they lived together, Jerry thought: with one foot in fairyland and the other in jail, bolstering each other's fantasies, a beggars' opera with a cast of three.

For a while now Ricardo fell in love with his sins and there was nothing Jerry could do to stop him. In Ricardo's simple world, to talk about himself was to get to know the other person better.

So he talked about his big soul, about his

great sexual potency and his concern for its continuation, but most of all he talked about the horrors of war, a subject on which he considered himself uniquely well informed.

"In Vietnam I fall in love with a girl, Voltaire. I, Ricardo, I fall in love. This is very rare and holy to me. Black hair, straight back, face like a Madonna, little tits. Each morning I stop the jeep as she walks to school, each morning she says 'No.' 'Listen,' I tell her. 'Ricardo is not American. He is Mexican.' She never even heard of Mexico. I go crazy, Voltaire. For weeks I, Ricardo, live like a monk. The other girls, I don't touch them any more. Every morning. Then one day I'm in first gear already and she throws up her hand — stop! She gets in beside me. She leaves school, goes out to live in a kampong, I tell you one day the name.

"The B-52s go in and flatten the village. Some hero doesn't read the map. Little villages, they're like stones on the beach, each one the same. I'm in the chopper behind. Nothing's stopping me. Charlie Marshall's beside me and he's screaming me I'm crazy. I don't care. I go down, land, I find her. The whole village dead. I find her. She's dead too, but I find her. I get back to base, the military police beat me up, I get seven weeks in solitary, lose my service stripes. Me. Ricardo.''

"You poor thing," said Jerry, who had played these games before and hated them — disbelieved or believed them, but always hated them.

"You are right," said Ricardo, acknowledging Jerry's homage with a bow. " 'Poor' is the correct word. They treat us like peasants. Me and Charlie, we fly everything. We were never properly rewarded. Wounded, dead, bits of bodies, dope. For nothing. Jesus, that was shooting, that war. Twice I fly into Yunnan Province. I am fearless. Totally. Even my good looks do not make me afraid for myself."

"Counting Drake Ko's trip," Jerry reminded him, "you would have been there three times, wouldn't you?"

"I train pilots for the Cambodian air force. For nothing. The Cambodian air force, Voltaire! Eighteen generals, fifty-four planes — and Ricardo. End of your time, you get the life insurance — that's the deal. A hundred thousand U.S. Only you. Ricardo die, his next of kin get nothing — that's the deal. Ricardo make it, he get it all. I talk to some friends from the French Foreign Legion once. They know the racket, they warn me. 'Take care, Ricardo. Soon they send you to bad spots you can't get out of. That way they don't have to pay you.' Cambodians want me to fly on half fuel. I got wing tanks and refuse. Another time they fix my hydraulics. I engineer the plane myself. That way they don't kill me. Listen, I snap my fingers, Lizzie come back to me. Okay?''

Lunch was over.

''So how did it go with Tiu and Drake?'' said Jerry. With confession, they say at Sarratt, all you have to do is tilt the stream a little.

For the first time, it seemed to Jerry, Ricardo stared at him with the full intensity of his animal stupidity.

''You confuse me, Voltaire. If I tell you too much, I have to shoot you. I'm a very talkative person, you follow me? I get lonely up here, it is my disposition always to be lonely. I like a guy, I talk to him, then I regret myself. I remember my business commitments, follow me?"

An inner stillness came over Jerry now, as Sarratt man became Sarratt recording angel with no part to play but to receive and to remember. Operationally, he knew, he stood close to journey's end: even if the journey back was, at best, imponderable. Operationally, by any precedents he understood, muted bells of triumph should have been sounding in his awe-struck ear. But that didn't happen. And the fact that it didn't was an early warning to him even then, that his quest was no longer, in every respect, on all fours with that of the Sarratt bearleaders.

At first — with allowances for Ricardo's vaunting ego — the story went much as Charlie Marshall had said it went. Tiu came to Vientiane dressed like a coolie and smelling of cat scent and asked around for the finest pilot in town, and naturally he was at once referred to

Ricardo, who as it happened was resting between business commitments and available for certain specialised and highly rewarded work in the aviation field.

Unlike Charlie Marshall, Ricardo told his story with a studious directness, as if he expected to be dealing with intellects inferior to his own. Tiu introduced himself as a person with wide contacts in the aviation industry, mentioned his undefined link with Indocharter, and went over the ground he had already covered with Charlie Marshall. Finally he came to the project in hand — which is to say that, in fine Sarratt style, Tiu fed Ricardo the cover story. A certain major Bangkok trading company, with which Tiu was proud to be associated, was in the throes of an extremely legitimate deal with certain officials in a neighbouring friendly foreign country.

"I ask him, Voltaire, very seriously, 'Mr. Tiu, maybe you just discovered the moon. I never heard yet an Asian country with a friendly foreign neighbour.' Tiu laughed at my joke. He naturally considered it a witty contribution," said Ricardo very seriously, in one of his strange outbreaks of business-school English.

Before consummating their profitable and legitimate deal, however, Tiu explained, in Ricardo's language, his business associates were faced with the problem of paying off certain officials and other parties inside that friendly foreign country who had cleared away tiresome bureaucratic obstacles.

"Why was this a problem?" Ricardo had asked, not unnaturally.

Suppose, said Tiu, the country was Burma. Just suppose. In modern Burma officials were not allowed to enrich themselves, nor could they easily bank money. In such a case some other means of payment would have to be found.

Richardo suggested gold. Tiu, said Ricardo, regretted himself: in the country he had in mind, even gold was difficult to negotiate. The currency selected in this case was therefore to be opium, he said: four hundred kilos of it. The distance was not great, the inside of a day would see

Ricardo there and back; the fee was five thousand dollars, and the remaining details would be vouchsafed to him just before departure in order to avoid "a needless erosion of the memory," as Ricardo put it, in another of those bizarre linguistic flourishes which must have formed a major part of Lizzie's education at his hands. Upon Ricardo's return from what Tiu was certain would be a painless and instructive flight, five thousand U.S. dollars in convenient denominations would at once be his — subject, of course, to Ricardo producing, in whatever form should prove convenient, confirmation that the consignment had reached its destination.

A receipt, for example.

Ricardo, as he described his own footwork, now showed a crude cunning in his dealings with Tiu. He told him he would think about this offer. He spoke of other pressing commitments and his ambitions to open his own airline. Then he set to work to find out who the hell Tiu was. He discovered at once that, following their interview, Tiu had returned not to

Bangkok but to Hong Kong on the direct flight. He made Lizzie pump the Chiu Chow boys at Indocharter, and one of them let slip that Tiu was a big cat in China Airsea, because when he was in Bangkok he stayed in the China Airsea suite at the Erawan Hotel. By the time Tiu returned to Vientiane to hear Ricardo's answer, Ricardo therefore knew a lot more about him — even, though he made little of it, that Tiu was right-hand man to Drake Ko.

Five thousand U.S. dollars for a one-day trip, he now told Tiu at this second interview, was either too little or too much. If the job was as soft as Tiu insisted, it was too much. If it was as totally crazy as Ricardo suspected, it was too little. Ricardo suggested a different arrangement: a "business compromise," he said. He was suffering, he explained — in a phrase he had no doubt used often — from "a temporary problem of liquidity." In other words (Jerry interpreting) he was broke as usual, and the creditors were at his throat. What he required immediately was a regular income, and this was best obtained by Tiu arranging for him to be taken on by Indocharter as a pilot-consultant for a year at an agreed salary of twenty-five thousand U.S. dollars.

Tiu did not seem too shocked by the idea, said Ricardo. Upstairs in the stilt-house, the room grew very quiet.

Secondly, instead of being paid five thousand dollars on delivery of the consignment, Ricardo wanted an advance of twenty thousand U.S. dollars now, with which to settle his outstanding commitments. Ten thousand would be considered earned as soon as he had delivered the opium, and the other ten thousand would be deductible "at source" — another Ricardo *nom de guerre* — from his Indocharter salary over the remaining months of his employment. If Tiu and his associates couldn't manage this, Ricardo explained, then unfortunately he would have to leave town before he could make the opium delivery.

Next day, with variations, Tiu agreed to the terms. Rather than advance Ricardo twenty thousand dollars, Tiu and his associates proposed to buy Ricardo's debts directly from his creditors. That way, he explained, they would feel more comfortable. The same day, the arrangement was *sanctified* — Ricardo's religious convictions were never far away — by a formidable contract, drawn in English and signed by both parties. Ricardo — Jerry silently recorded — had just sold his soul.

"What did Lizzie think of the deal?" Jerry asked.

He shrugged his smooth shoulders. "Women," Ricardo said.

"Sure," said Jerry, returning his knowing smile.

Ricardo's future thus secured, he resumed a "suitable professional life-style," as he called it. A scheme to float an all-Asian football pool claimed his attention, so did a fourteen-year-old girl in Bangkok named Rosie, whom on the strength of his Indocharter salary he periodically visited for the purpose of training her for life's great stage.

Occasionally but not often, he flew the odd run for Indocharter, but nothing demanding: "Chiang Mai couple of times. Saigon. Couple of times into the Shans, visit Charlie Marshall's old man, collect a little mud maybe, take him a few guns, rice, gold. Battambang maybe."

"Where's Lizzie meanwhile?" Jerry asked in the same easy, man-to-man tone as before.

The same contemptuous shrug: "Sitting in Vientiane. Does her knitting. Scrubs a little at the Constellation. That's an old woman already, Voltaire. I need youth. Optimism. Energy. People who respect me. It is my nature to give. How can I give to an old woman?"

"Until?" Jerry repeated.

"Huh?"

"So when did the kissing stop?"

Misunderstanding the phrase, Ricardo looked suddenly very dangerous, and his voice dropped to a low warning: "What the hell you mean?"

Jerry soothed him with the friendliest of smiles. "How long did you draw your pay and kick around before Tiu collected on the contract?"

Six weeks, said Ricardo, recovering his

composure. Maybe eight. Twice the trip was on, then cancelled. Once, it seemed, he was ordered to Chiang Mai and loafed for a couple of days till Tiu called to say the people at the other end weren't ready. Increasingly Ricardo had the feeling he was mixed up in something deep, he said, but history, he implied, had always cast him for the great rôles of life and at least the creditors were off his back.

Ricardo broke off and once more studied Jerry closely, scratching his beard in contemplation. Finally he sighed and, pouring them both a whisky, pushed a glass across the table. Below them the perfect day was preparing its own slow death. The green trees had grown heavy; the wood-smoke from the girls' cook pot smelt damp.

"Where you go from here, Voltaire?"

"Home," said Jerry.

Ricardo let out a fresh burst of laughter. "You stay the night, I send you one of my girls."

"I'll make my own damn way, actually, sport," Jerry said. Like fighting animals, the two men surveyed each other, and for a moment the spark of battle was very close indeed.

"You some crazy fellow, Voltaire," Ricardo muttered.

But Sarratt man prevailed. "Then one day the trip was on, right?" Jerry said. "And nobody cancelled. Then what? Come on sport, let's have the story."

"Sure," said Ricardo. "Sure, Voltaire," and drank, still watching him. "How it happened," he said. "Listen, I tell you how it happened, Voltaire."

And then I'll kill you, said his eyes.

Ricardo was in Bangkok. Rosie was being demanding. Tiu had insisted Ricardo should always be within reach, and one morning early, maybe five o'clock, a messenger arrived at their love-nest summoning him to the Erawan immediately. Ricardo was impressed by the suite. He would have wished it for himself.

"Ever seen Versailles, Voltaire? A desk so big as a B-52. This Tiu is a very different human individual to the cat-scent coolie who came to Vientiane, okay?

916

This is a very influential person. 'Ricardo,' he tell me. 'This time is for certain. This time we deliver.' "

Tiu's orders were simple. In a few hours there was a commercial flight to Chiang Mai. Ricardo should take it. Rooms had been booked for him at the Hotel Rincome. He should stay the night there. Alone. No drink, no women, no society.

" 'You better take plenty to read, Mr. Ricardo,' he tell me. 'Mr. Tiu,' I tell him. 'You tell me where to fly. You don't tell me where to read. Okay?' This guy is very arrogant behind his big desk — understand me, Voltaire? I am obliged to teach him manners."

Next morning, someone would call for Ricardo at six o'clock at his hotel announcing himself as a friend of Mr. Johnny. Ricardo should go with him.

Things went as planned. Ricardo flew to Chiang Mai, spent an abstemious night at the Rincome, and at six o'clock two Chinese, not one, called for him and drove him north for some hours till they came to a Hakka village. Leaving the car, they walked for half an hour till they reached an empty field with a hut at one end of it. Inside the hut stood "a dandy little Beechcraft," brand new, and inside the Beechcraft sat Tiu, with a lot of maps and documents on his lap, in the seat beside the pilot's. The rear seats had been removed to make space for the gunny bags. A couple of Chinese crushers stood off watching, and the over-all mood, Ricardo implied, was not all he would have liked.

"First I got to empty my pockets. My pockets are very personal to me, Voltaire. They are like a lady's handbag. Mementoes. Letters. Photographs. My Madonna. They retain everything. My passport, my pilot's licence, my money . . . even my bracelets," he said and lifted his brown arms so that the gold links jingled.

After that, he said with a frown of disapproval, there were yet more documents to sign. Such as a power of attorney, signing over whatever bits of Ricardo's life were left to him after his Indocharter contract. Such as various confessions to "previous technically illegal undertakings," several of them — Ricardo asserted in considerable outrage — performed on behalf of Indocharter. One of the Chinese crushers even turned out to be a lawyer. Ricardo considered this particularly unsporting.

Only then did Tiu unveil the maps, and the instructions, which Ricardo now reproduced in a blend of his own style and Tiu's: " 'You head north, Mr. Ricardo, and you keep heading north. Maybe you clip the edges off Laos, maybe you stay over the Shans, I don't give a damn. Flying is your business, not mine. Fifty miles inside the China border you pick up the Mekong and follow it. Then you keep going north till you find a little hill town called Tienpao stuck on a tributary of that very famous river. Head due east twenty miles, you find a landing-strip — one white flare, one green — you do me a favour please. You land there. A man will be waiting for you. He speaks very lousy English, but he speaks it. Here is half one-dollar bill. This man will have the other half. Unload the opium. This man will give you a package, and certain particular instructions. The package is your receipt, Mr. Ricardo. When you return, bring it with you and obey all instructions most absolutely, including especially your place of landing. Do you understand me entirely, Mr. Ricardo?' "

"What kind of package?" Jerry asked.

"He don't say and I don't care. 'You do that,' he tell me, 'and keep your big mouth shut, Mr. Ricardo, and my associates will look after you all your life like you are their son. Your children, they look after — your girls. Your girl in Bali. All your life they will be grateful men. But you screw them, or you go big-mouthing round town, they definitely kill you, Mr. Ricardo, believe me. Not tomorrow maybe, not the next day, but they definitely kill you. We got a contract, Mr. Ricardo. My associates don't never break a contract. They are very legal men.' I got sweat on me, Voltaire. I am in perfect condition, a fine athlete, but I sweat. 'Don't you worry, Mr. Tiu,' I tell him. 'Mr. Tiu, sir. Any time you want to fly opium into Red China, Ricardo's your man.' Voltaire, believe me, I was very concerned."

Ricardo squeezed his nose as if it were smarting with sea water.

"Hear this, Voltaire. Listen most attentively. When I was young and crazy, I flew twice into Yunnan Province for the Americans. To be a hero, one must do certain crazy things, and if you crash, maybe one day they get you out. But each time I flew, I look down at the lousy brown earth and I see Ricardo in a wood cage. No women, extremely lousy food, no place to sit, no place to stand or sleep, chains on my arms, no status or position assured to me. 'See the imperialist spy and running dog.' Voltaire, I do not like this vision. To be locked all my life in China for running opium? I am not enthusiastic. 'Sure, Mr. Tiu! Bye-bye! See you this afternoon!' I have to consider most seriously."

The brown haze of the sinking sun suddenly filled the room. On Ricardo's chest, despite the perfection of his condition, the same sweat had gathered. It lay in beads over the matted black hair and on his oiled shoulders.

"Where was Lizzie in all this?" Jerry asked again.

Ricardo's answer was nervous and already angry. "In Vientiane! On the moon! In bed with Charlie! What the hell do I care?"

"Did she know of the deal with Tiu?"

Ricardo gave only a scowl of contempt.

Time to go, Jerry thought. Time to light the last fuse and run. Below, Mickey was making a great hit with Ricardo's women. Jerry could hear his singsong chattering, broken by their high-pitched laughter, like the laughter of a whole class at girls' school.

"So away you flew," he said. He waited, but Ricardo remained lost in thought.

"You took off and headed north," Jerry said.

Lifting his eyes a little, Ricardo held Jerry in a bullish, furious stare, till the invitation to describe his own heroic feat finally got the better of him.

"I never flew so good in my life. Never. I was magnificent. That little black Beechcraft. North a hundred miles because I don't trust nobody. Maybe those clowns have got me locked on a radar screen somewhere? I don't take no chances. Then east, but very slowly, very low over the mountains, Voltaire. I fly between the cow's legs, okay? In the war we have little landing-strips up there, crazy listening places in the middle of badland. I flew those places, Voltaire. I know them. I find one right at the top of a mountain, you can reach it only from the air. I take a look, I see the fuel dump, I land, I refuel, I take a sleep, it's crazy. But Jesus, Voltaire, it's not Yunnan Province, okay? It's not China — and Ricardo, the American war criminal and opium smuggler, is not going to spend the rest of his life hanging from a hen-hook in Peking, okay? Listen, I brought that plane back south again. I know places, I know places I could lose a whole air force, believe me."

Ricardo became suddenly very vague about the next few months of his life. He had heard of the Flying Dutchman, and he said that was what he became; he flew, hid again, flew, resprayed the Beechcraft, changed the registration once a month, sold the opium in small lots in order not to be conspicuous, a kilo here, fifty there, bought a Spanish passport from an Indian but had no faith in it, kept away from everyone he knew, including Rosie in Bangkok, and even Charlie Marshall. It was also the time, Jerry remembered from his briefing by old Craw, when Ricardo sold Ko's opium to the Enforcement heroes but got the cold shoulder on his story. On Tiu's orders, said Ricardo, the Indocharter boys had been quick to post him dead, and changed his flight route southwards to distract attention. Ricardo heard of this and did not object to being dead.

"What did you do about Lizzie?" Jerry asked.

Again Ricardo flared. "Lizzie, Lizzie! You got some fixation about that scrubber, Voltaire, that you throw *Lizzie* in my face all the time? I never knew a woman so irrelevant. Listen, I give her to Drake Ko, okay? I make her fortune."

Seizing his whisky glass, he drank from it, still glowering.

She was lobbying for him, Jerry thought. She and Charlie Marshall. Plodding the pavements trying to buy Ricardo's neck for him.

"You referred boastingly to other lucrative aspects of the case," Ricardo said in a peremptory resumption of his business-school English. "Kindly advise me what they are, Voltaire."

Sarratt man had this part off pat. "Number one: Ko was being paid large sums by the Russian Embassy in Vientiane. The money was syphoned through Indocharter and ended up in a slush account in Hong Kong. We've got the proof. We've got photostats of the bank statements."

Ricardo pulled a face as if his whisky didn't taste right, then went on drinking.

"Whether the money was for reviving the opium habit in Red China or for some other service, we don't yet know," said Jerry. "But we will. Point two. Do you want to hear it or am I keeping you awake?"

Ricardo had yawned.

"Point two," Jerry continued. "Ko has

a younger brother in Red China. Used to be called Nelson. Ko pretends he's dead but he's a big beef with the Peking administration. Ko's been trying to get him out for years. Your job was to take in opium and bring out a package. The package was brother Nelson. That's why Ko was going to love you like his own son if you brought him back. And that's why he was going to kill you if you didn't. If that's not a five-million-dollar touch, what is?''

Nothing much happened to Ricardo as Jerry watched him in the failing light, except that the slumbering animal in him visibly woke. To set down his glass, he leaned forward slowly, but he couldn't conceal the tautness of his shoulders or the knotting of the muscles of his stomach. To flash a smile of exceptional good will at Jerry, he turned quite languidly, but his eyes had a brightness that was like a signal to attack. So that when he reached out and patted Jerry's cheek affectionately with his right hand, Jerry was quite ready to fall straight back with it if necessary, on the off chance he would manage to throw Ricardo across the room.

"Five million bucks, Voltaire!" Ricardo exclaimed with steely-bright excitement. "Five million! Listen — we got to do something for poor old Charlie Marshall, okay? For love. Charlie's always broke. Maybe we put him in charge of the football pool once. Wait a minute. I get some more Scotch, we celebrate." He stood up, his head tilted to one side; he held out his naked arms. "Voltaire," he said softly. *"Voltaire!"* Affectionately, he took Jerry by the cheeks and kissed him. "Listen, that's some research you guys did! That's some pretty smart editor you work for. You be my business partner. Like you say. Okay? I need an Englishman in my life. I got to be like Lizzie once, marry a schoolmaster. You do that for Ricardo, Voltaire? You hold me down a little?"

"No problem," said Jerry, smiling back.

"You play with the guns a minute, okay?"

"Sure."

"I got to tell those girls some little thing."

"Sure."

"Personal family thing."

"I'll be here."

From the top of the trap Jerry looked urgently down after him. Mickey, the driver, was dandling the baby on his arm, chucking it under the ear. In a mad world you keep the fiction going, he thought; stick to it till the bitter end and leave the first bite to him. Returning to the table, Jerry took Ricardo's pencil and his pad of paper and wrote out a non-existent address in Hong Kong where he could be reached at any time. Ricardo had still not returned, but when Jerry stood he saw him coming out of the trees behind the car. He likes contracts, he thought; give him something to sign. He took a fresh sheet of paper. "I, Jerry Westerby, do solemnly swear to share with my friend Captain Tiny Ricardo all proceeds relating to our joint exploitation of his life story," he wrote, and signed his name.

Ricardo was coming up the steps. Jerry thought of helping himself from the private armoury, but he guessed Ricardo was waiting for him to do just that. While Ricardo poured more whisky, Jerry handed him the two sheets of paper.

"I'll draft a legal deposition," he said, looking straight into Ricardo's burning eyes. "I have an English lawyer in Bangkok whom I trust entirely. I'll have him check it over and bring it back to you to sign. After that we'll plan the march route and I'll talk to Lizzie. Okay?"

"Sure. Listen, it's dark out there. They got a lot of bad guys in that forest. You stay the night. I talk to the girls. They like you. They say you very strong man. Not so strong as me, but strong."

Jerry said something about not wasting time. He'd like to make Bangkok by tomorrow, he said. To himself he sounded as lame as a three-legged mule — good enough to get in maybe, but never to get out. But Ricardo seemed content to the point of serenity. Maybe it's the ambush deal, thought Jerry, something the colonel is arranging.

"Go well, horse-writer. Go well, my friend."

Ricardo put both hands on the back of Jerry's neck and let his thumb-prints settle into Jerry's jaw, then drew Jerry's head forward for another kiss, and Jerry let it happen. Though his heart thumped and his wet spine felt sore against his shirt, Jerry let it happen.

Outside it was half dark. Ricardo did not see them to the car but watched them indulgently from under the stilts, the girls sitting at his feet, while he waved with both naked arms.

From the car Jerry turned and waved back. The last sun lay dying in the teak trees. My last ever, he thought.

"Don't start the engine," he told Mickey quietly. "I want to check the oil."

Perhaps it's just me who's mad. Perhaps I really got myself a deal, he thought.

Sitting in the driver's seat, Mickey released the catch and Jerry pulled up the bonnet but there was no little *plastic,* no leaving-present from his new friend and partner. He pulled up the dip-stick and pretended to read it.

"You want oil, horse-writer?" Ricardo

yelled down the dust path.

"No, we're all right. So long!"

"So long."

He had no torch, but when he crouched and groped under the chassis in the gloom, he again found nothing.

"You lost something, horse-writer?" Ricardo called again, cupping his hands to his mouth.

"Start the engine," Jerry said and got into the car.

"Lights on, Mister?"

"Yes, Mickey. Lights on."

"Why he call you horse-writer?"

"Mutual friends."

If Ricardo has tipped off the C.T.s, thought Jerry, it won't make any damn difference either way. Mickey put on the lights, and inside the car the American dashboard lit up like a small city.

"Let's go," said Jerry.

"Quick-quick?"

"Yes, quick-quick."

They drove five miles, seven, nine. Jerry was watching them on the indicator, reckoning twenty to the first check-point and forty-five to the second.

Mickey had hit seventy and Jerry was in no mood to complain. They were on the crown of the road and the road was straight, and beyond the ambush strips the tall teaks slid past them like orange ghosts.

"Fine man," Mickey said. "He's plenty fine lover. Those girls say he some pretty fine lover."

"Watch for wires," Jerry said.

On the right the trees broke and a red dust track disappeared into the cleft.

"He get pretty good time in there," said Mickey. "Girls, he get kids, he get whisky. He get real good time."

"Pull in, Mickey. Stop the car. Here in the middle of the road where it's level. Just do it, Mickey."

Mickey began laughing.

"Girls get good time, too," Mickey said. "Girls get candy, little baby get candy, everybody get candy!"

"Stop the damn car!"

At his leisurely pace, Mickey brought the car to a halt, still giggling about the girls.

"Is that thing accurate?" Jerry asked.

his finger pressed to the petrol gauge.

"Accurate?" Mickey echoed, puzzled by the English.

"Petrol. Gas. Full? Or half full? Or three-quarters? Has it been reading right on the journey?"

"Sure. He right."

"When we arrived at the burnt village, Mickey, you had half-full gas. You still have half-full gas."

"Sure."

"You put any in? From a can? You fill car?"

"No."

"Get out."

Mickey began protesting, but Jerry leaned across him, opened his door, shoved Mickey straight through it onto the tarmac, and followed him. Seizing Mickey's arm, he jammed it into his back and frog-marched him at a gallop across the road to the edge of the wide soft shoulder and twenty yards into it, then threw him into the scrub and fell half beside him, half onto him, so that the wind went out of Mickey's stomach in a single astonished hiccup, and it took him all of half a minute before he was able to give vent to an indignant "Why for?"

But Jerry by that time was pushing his face into the earth to keep it out of the blast.

The old Ford seemed to burn first and explode afterwards, finally lifting into the air in one last assertion of life, before collapsing dead and flaming on its side. While Mickey gasped in admiration, Jerry looked at his watch. Eighteen minutes since they had left the stilt house. Maybe twenty. Should have happened sooner, he thought. Not surprising Ricardo was keen for us to go. At Sarratt they wouldn't even have seen it coming; this was an Eastern treat, and Sarratt's natural soul was with Europe and the good old days of the cold war — Czecho, Berlin, and the old fronts. Jerry wondered which brand of grenade it was. The Vietcong preferred the American type; they loved its double action. All you needed, they said, was a wide throat to the petrol tank. You took out the pin, you put an elastic band over the spring, you slipped the grenade into the petrol tank, and you waited patiently for the petrol to eat its way through the rubber. The result was one of those Western inventions it took the Vietcong to discover. Ricardo must have used fat elastic bands, he decided.

They made the first check-point in four hours, walking on the road. Mickey was extremely happy about the insurance situation, assuming that since Jerry had paid the premium, the money was automatically theirs to squander. Jerry could not deter him from this view. But Mickey was also scared: first of C.T.s, then of ghosts, then of the colonel. So Jerry explained to him that neither the ghosts nor the C.T.s would venture near the road after that little episode. As for the colonel — though Jerry didn't mention this to Mickey — well, he was a father and a soldier and he had a dam to build. Not for nothing was he building it with Drake Ko's cement and China Airsea's transport.

At the check-point they eventually found a truck to take Mickey home. Riding with him a distance, Jerry promised the comic's support in any insurance haggle, but Mickey in his euphoria was deaf to doubts. Amid much laughter they exchanged addresses and many hearty handshakes; then Jerry dropped off at a roadside café to wait half a day for the bus that would carry him eastwards toward a fresh field of war.

Need Jerry have ever gone to Ricardo in the first place? Would the outcome, for himself, have been different if he had not? Or did Jerry, as Smiley's defenders to this day insist, by his pass at Ricardo, supply the last crucial heave which shook the tree and caused the coveted fruit to fall?

For the George Smiley Supporters' Club there is no question: the visit to Ricardo was the final straw, and Ko's back broke under it. Without it he might have gone on dithering until the open season started, by which time Ko himself, and the intelligence on him, would be up for grabs. End of argument. And on the face of it, the facts demonstrate a wonderful causality. For this is what happened.

A mere six hours after Jerry and his driver Mickey had picked themselves out of the dust of that roadside in North East Thailand, the whole of the Circus fifth floor exploded into a blaze of ecstatic jubilation which could have outshone the pyre of Mickey's borrowed Ford car any night. In the rumpus room, where Smiley announced the news, Doc di Salis actually danced a stiff little jig, and Connie would unquestionably have joined him if her arthritis had not held her to that wretched chair. Trot howled, Guillam and Molly embraced, and only Smiley amid so much revelry preserved his usual slightly startled air, though Molly swore she saw him redden as he blinked around the company.

He had just had word, he said. A flash communication from the Cousins. At seven this morning, Hong Kong time, Tiu had telephoned Ko at Star Heights, where he had been spending the night relaxing with Lizzie Worth. Lizzie herself took the call in the first instance, but Ko came in on the extension and sharply ordered Lizzie to ring off, which she did. Tiu had proposed breakfast in town at once: "At George's place," said Tiu, to the great entertainment of the transcribers. Three hours later Tiu was on the phone to his travel agent making hasty plans for a business trip to mainland China. His first stop would be Canton, where China Airsea kept a representative, but his ultimate destination was Shanghai.

So how did Ricardo get through to Tiu so fast without the telephone? The most likely theory is the colonel's police link to Bangkok. And from Bangkok? Heaven knows. Trade telex, the exchange-rate network — anything is possible. The Chinese have their own ways of doing these things.

On the other hand, it may just be that Ko's patience chose this moment to snap of its own accord, and that the breakfast at George's place was about something entirely different. Either way, it was the breakthrough they had all been dreaming of, the triumphant vindication of Smiley's footwork. By lunch-time Lacon had called in person to offer his congratulations, and by early evening Saul Enderby had made a gesture nobody from the wrong side of Trafalgar Square had ever made before.

He had sent round a crate of champagne from Berry Brothers & Rudd, a vintage Krug, a real beauty. Attached to it was a note to George saying "To the first day of summer." And indeed, though late April, it seemed to be just that. Through the thick net curtains of the lower floors, the plane trees were already in leaf. Higher up a cluster of hyacinths had bloomed in Connie's window box. "Red," she said as she drank Saul Enderby's health. "Karla's favourite colour, bless him."

18

The River Bend

The air base was neither beautiful nor victorious. Technically — since it was in North East Thailand — it was under Thai command, and in practice the Thais were allowed to collect the garbage and occupy the stockade close to the perimeter. The check-point was a separate town. Amid smells of charcoal, urine, pickled fish, and Calor gas, chains of collapsing tin hovels plied the historic trades of military occupation. The brothels were manned by crippled pimps, the tailor shops offered wedding tuxedos, the bookshops offered pornography and travel, the bars were called Sunset Strip, Hawaii, and Lucky Time. At the M.P. hut, Jerry asked for Captain Urquhart of public relations, and the black sergeant squared to throw him out when he said he was press. On the base telephone Jerry heard a lot of clicking and popping before a slow Southern voice said, "Urquhart isn't around just now. My name is Masters. Who's this again?"

"We met last summer at General Crosse's briefing," Jerry said.

A long silence followed, presumably while the code words "Urquhart" and "Crosse" were hunted down in the contingency book.

"Well now, so we did, man," said the same amazingly slow voice, reminding him of Deathwish. "Pay off your cab. Be right down. Blue jeep. Wait for the whites of its eyes."

A flow of air-force personnel was drifting in and out of the camp, blacks and whites, in scowling segregated groups. A white officer passed. The blacks gave him the black-power salute. The officer warily returned it. The enlisted men wore Charlie Marshall-style patches on their uniforms, mostly in praise of drugs. The mood was sullen, defeated, and innately violent. The Thai troops greeted nobody.

Nobody greeted the Thais.

A blue jeep with lights flashing and siren wailing pulled up with a ferocious skid on the other side of the boom. The sergeant waved Jerry through. A moment later he was careering over the runway at breakneck speed toward a long string of low white huts at the centre of the airfield. His driver was a lanky boy with all the signs of a probationer.

"You Masters?" Jerry asked.

"No, sir. Sir, I just carry the Major's bags," he said.

They passed a ragged baseball game, siren wailing all the time, lights still flashing.

"Great cover," said Jerry.

"What's that, sir?" the boy yelled above the din.

"Forget it."

It was not the biggest base. Jerry had seen larger. They passed lines of Phantoms and helicopters, and as they approached the white huts he realised that they comprised a separate spook encampment, with their own compound and aerial masts and their own cluster of little black-painted small planes — "weirdos," they used to be called — which before the pull-out had dropped and collected God knew whom in God knew where.

They entered by a side door which the boy unlocked. The short corridor was empty and soundless. A door stood ajar at the end of it, made of traditional fake rosewood. Masters wore a short-sleeved air-force uniform with few insignia. He had medals and the rank of major and Jerry guessed he was the paramilitary type of Cousin, maybe not even career. He was sallow and wiry, with resentful tight lips and hollow cheeks. He stood before a fake fireplace, under an Andrew Wyeth reproduction, and there was something strangely still about him, and disconnected. He was like a man being deliberately slow when everyone else was in a hurry. The boy made the introductions and hesitated. Masters stared at him until he left, then turned his colourless gaze to the table where the coffee was.

"Look like you need breakfast,"

Masters said. He poured coffee and proffered a plate of doughnuts, all in slow motion.

"Facilities," he said.

"Facilities," Jerry agreed.

An electric typewriter lay on the desk, and plain paper beside it. Masters walked stiffly to a chair and perched on the arm. Taking up a copy of *Stars & Stripes,* he held it in front of him while Jerry settled at the desk.

"Hear you're going to win it all back for us single-handed," said Masters to his *Stars & Stripes*. "Well now."

Jerry set up his portable in preference to the electric, and stabbed out his report in a series of quick smacks, which to his own ear grew louder as he laboured. Perhaps to Master's ear also, for he looked up frequently, though only as far as Jerry's hands and the toy-town portable.

Jerry handed him his copy.

"Your orders are to remain here," Masters said, articulating each word with great deliberation. "Your orders are to remain here while we dispatch your signal. Man, will we dispatch that signal.

Your orders are to stand by for confirmation and further instructions. That figure? Does that figure, *sir?*"

"Sure," said Jerry.

"Heard the glad news by any chance?" Master enquired. They were facing each other. Not three feet lay between them. Masters was staring at Jerry's signal, but his eyes did not appear to be scanning the lines.

"What news is that, sport?"

"We just lost the war, Mr. Westerby. Yes, sir. Last of the brave just had themselves scraped off the roof of the Saigon Embassy by chopper, like a bunch of rookies caught with their pants down in a whore-house. Maybe that doesn't affect you. Ambassador's dog survived, you'll be relieved to hear. Newsman took it out on his damn lap. Maybe that doesn't affect you either. Maybe you're not a dog-lover. Maybe you feel about dogs the same way I personally feel about newsmen, Mr. Westerby, sir."

Jerry had caught the smell of brandy on Master's breath, which no amount of coffee could conceal, and he guessed he had been drinking for a long time without succeeding in getting drunk.

"Mr. Westerby, sir?"

"Yes, old boy."

Masters held out his hand. *"Old boy,* I want you to shake me by the hand."

The hand stuck between them, thumb upward.

"What for?" said Jerry.

"I want you to extend to me the hand of welcome, sir. The United States of America has just applied to join the club of second-class powers, of which I understand your own fine nation to be chairman, president, and oldest member. *Shake it!"*

"Proud to have you aboard," said Jerry and obligingly shook the Major's hand.

He was at once rewarded by a brilliant smile of false gratitude.

"Why, sir, I call that *real* handsome of you, Mr. Westerby. Anything we can do to make your stay with us more comfortable, I invite you to let me know. If you want to rent the place, no reasonable offer refused, we say."

"You could shove a little Scotch through

946

the bars," Jerry said, pulling a dead grin.

"*Mah pleasure,*" said Masters, in a drawl so long it was like a slow punch. "Man after my own heart. Yes, sir."

Masters left him with a half-bottle of J & B from the cupboard, and some back numbers of *Playboy*.

"We keep these handy for English gentlemen who didn't see fit to lift a damn finger to help us," he explained confidingly.

"Very thoughtful of you," said Jerry.

"I'll go send your letter home to Mummy. How *is* the Queen, by the way?"

Masters didn't turn a key, but when Jerry tested the door handle it was locked. The windows overlooking the airfield were smoked and double glazed. On the runway aircraft landed and took off without making a sound. This is how they tried to win, Jerry thought: from inside sound-proof rooms, through smoked glass, using machines at arm's length. This is how they lost. He drank, feeling nothing. . . . Waiting. So it's over, he thought, and that was all. So what was his next stop? Charlie Marshall's old man?

Little swing through the Shans, heart-to-heart chat with the General's bodyguard? He waited, his thoughts crowding formlessly. He sat down, then lay on the sofa and for a while slept. He woke abruptly to the sound of canned music occasionally interrupted by an announcement of homely-wise assurance. Would Captain somebody do so and so? Once the speaker offered higher education. Once cut-price washing-machines. Once prayer. Jerry prowled the room, made nervous by the crematorium quiet and the music.

He crossed to the other window, and in his mind Lizzie's face bobbed along at his shoulder, the way the orphan's once had, but no longer. He drank more whisky. I should have slept in the truck, he thought. Altogether I should sleep more. So they've lost the war at last. It seemed a long time since he'd slept the way he'd like to. Old Frostie had rather put an end to that. His hand was shaking: Christ, look at that. He thought of Luke. Time we went on a bender together. He must be back by now, if he hasn't had his arse shot off. Got to stop the old brain a bit, he thought. But sometimes the old brain hunted on its own these days. Bit too much, actually. Got to tie it down, he told himself sternly. *Man.*

He thought of Ricardo's grenades. Hurry up, he thought. Come on, let's have a decision. *Where* next? *Who* now? No whys. His face was dry and hot, and his hands moist. He had a headache just above the eyes. Bloody music, he thought. Bloody, bloody end-of-world music. He was casting round urgently for somewhere to switch it off when he saw Masters standing in the doorway, an envelope in his hand and nothing in his eyes. Jerry read the signal. Masters settled on the chair arm again.

" 'Son, come home,' " Masters intoned, mocking his own Southern drawl. " 'Come directly home. Do not pass *go.* Do not collect two hundred dollars.' The Cousins will fly you to Bangkok. From Bangkok you will pro-ceed immediately to London, England, *not* repeat not London, Ontario, by a flight of *your* own choosing. You will on no account return to Hong Kong. You will not! No *sir!* Mission accomplished, *son.* Thank you and well done. Her Majesty is so *thrilled.* So hurry home to dinner, we got hominy grits and turkey, and blueberry pie. Sounds like a bunch of fairies you're working for, man."

Jerry read the signal a second time.

"Plane leaves for Bangkok one one hundred," Masters said. He wore his watch on the inside of his wrist, so that its information was private to himself. "Hear me?"

Jerry grinned. "Sorry, sport. Slow reader. Thanks. Too many big words. Lot to get the old mind round. Look, left my things at the hotel."

"My houseboys are at your royal command."

"Thanks, but if you don't mind, I'd prefer to avoid the official connection."

"Please yourself, sir, please yourself."

"I'll find a cab at the gates. There and back in an hour. Thanks," he repeated.

"Thank *you.*"

Sarratt man provided a smart piece of tradecraft for the kiss-off. "Mind if I leave that there?" he asked, nodding to his scruffy portable where it lay beside

Masters's golf-ball I.B.M.

"Sir, it shall be our most treasured possession."

If Masters had bothered to look at him at that moment, he might have hesitated when he saw the purposeful brightness in Jerry's eye. If he had known Jerry's voice better perhaps, or noticed its particularly friendly huskiness, he might also have hesitated. If he had seen the way Jerry clawed at his forelock, arm across his body in an attitude of instinctive self-concealment, or responded to Jerry's sheepish grin of thanks as the probationer returned to drive him to the gates in the blue jeep — well, again he might have had his doubts. But Major Masters was not only an embittered professional with a lot of disillusionment to his credit. He was a Southern gentleman suffering the stab of defeat at the hands of unintelligible savages; and he hadn't too much time just then for the contortions of a bone-weary overdue Brit using his expiring spookhouse as a post office.

A mood of festivity attending the

leavetaking of the Circus's Hong Kong operations party, and it was only enriched by the secrecy of the arrangements. The news of Jerry's reappearance triggered it. The content of his signal intensified it and coincided with word from the Cousins that Drake Ko had cancelled all his social and business engagements and withdrawn to the seclusion of his house, Seven Gates, in Headland Road. A photograph of Ko, taken in long shot from the Cousins' surveillance van, showed him in quarter-profile, standing in his own large garden, at the end of an arbour of rose-trees, staring out to sea. The concrete junk was not visible, but he was wearing his floppy beret.

"Like a latter-day Jay Gatsby, my dear!" Connie Sachs cried in delight as they all pored over it. "Mooning at the blasted light at the end of the pier, or whatever the ninny did!"

When the van returned that way two hours later, Ko was in the identical pose, so they didn't bother to re-shoot. More significant was the fact that Ko had ceased to use the telephone altogether —

or at least those lines on which the Cousins ran a tap.

Sam Collins also sent a report, the third in a stream, but by far his longest to date. As usual it arrived in a special cover addressed to Smiley personally, and as usual he discussed its contents with nobody but Connie Sachs. And at the very moment when the party was leaving for London Airport, a last-minute message from Martello advised them that Tiu had returned from China and was at present closeted with Ko in Headland Road.

But the most important ceremony, then and later in Guillam's recollection, and the most disturbing, was a small war party held in Martello's rooms in the Annexe, which, exceptionally, was attended not only by the usual quintet of Martello, his two quiet men, Smiley, and Guillam, but also by Lacon and Saul Enderby as well, who significantly arrived in the same official car. The purpose of the ceremony — called by Smiley — was the formal handing over of the keys. Martello was now to receive a complete portrait of the Dolphin case, including the all-important link with Nelson. He was to be indoctrinated, with certain minor omissions which only showed up later, as a full partner in the enterprise.

How Lacon and Enderby muscled in on the occasion, Guillam never quite knew and Smiley was afterwards understandably reticent about it. Enderby declared in a fat voice that he had come along in the "interest of good order and military discipline." Lacon looked more than usually wan and disdainful. Guillam had the strongest impression they were up to something, and this was further strengthened by his observation of the interplay between Enderby and Martello: in short, these buddies cut each other so dead they put Guillam in mind of two secret lovers meeting at communal breakfast in a country house, a situation in which he often found himself.

It was the *scale* of the thing, Enderby explained at one point. Case was blowing up so big he really thought there ought to be a few official flies on the wall. It was the Colonial lobby, he explained at another. Wilbraham was raising a stink with Treasury.

"All right, so we've heard the dirt," said Enderby, when Smiley had finished his lengthy summary and Martello's praises had all but brought the roof down. "Now whose finger's on the trigger, George, point one?" he demanded to know, and after that the meeting became very much Enderby's show, as meetings with Enderby usually did. "Who calls the shots when it gets hot? You, George? Still? I mean you've done a good planning job, I grant you, but it's old Marty here who's providing the artillery, isn't it?"

At which Martello had another bout of deafness, while he beamed upon all the great and lovely British people he was privileged to be associated with, and let Enderby go on doing his hatchet-work for him.

"Marty, how do *you* see this one?" Enderby pressed, as if he really had no idea; as if he never went fishing with Martello, or gave lavish dinners for him, or discussed top-secret matters out of school.

A strange insight came to Guillam at this moment, though he kicked himself afterwards for making too little of it. *Martello knew.* The revelations about Nelson, which Martello had affected to be dazzled by, were not revelations at all, but restatements of information that he and his quiet men already possessed. Guillam read it in their pale, wooden faces and their watchful eyes. He read it in Martello's fulsomeness. *Martello knew.*

"Ah, technically this is George's show, Saul," Martello reminded Enderby loyally, in answer to his question, but with just enough spin on the "technically" to put the rest in doubt. "George is on the bridge, Saul. We're just there to stoke the engines."

Enderby staged an unhappy frown and shoved a matchstick between his teeth. "George, how does that grab *you?* You content to let that happen, are you? Let Marty chuck in the cover, the accommodation out there, communications, all the cloak-and-dagger stuff, surveillance, charging round Hong Kong and whatnot? While you call the shots? Bit like wearing someone else's dinner-jacket, I'd have thought."

Smiley was firm enough but, to Guillam's eye, a deal too concerned with the question and not nearly concerned enough with the thinly veiled collusion.

"Not at all," said Smiley. "Martello and I have a clear understanding. The spearhead of the operation will be shared by ourselves. If supportive action is required, Martello will supply it. The product is then halved. If one is thinking in terms of a dividend for the American investment, it comes with the partition of the product. The responsibility for obtaining it remains ours." He ended strongly: "The letter of agreement setting all this out has of course long been on file."

Enderby glanced at Lacon. "Oliver, you said you'd send me that. Where is it?"

Lacon put his long head on one side and pulled a dreary smile at nothing in particular. "Kicking around your Third Room, I should think, Saul."

Enderby tried another tack: "And you two guys can see the deal holding up in all contingencies, can you? I mean, who's handling the safe houses, all that? Burying the body sort of thing?"

Smiley again: "Housekeeping Section has already rented a cottage in the country, and is preparing it for occupation," he said stolidly.

Enderby took the wet matchstick from his mouth and broke it into the ashtray. "Could have had my place if you'd asked," he muttered absently. "Bags of room. Nobody ever there. Staff. Everything." But he went on worrying at his theme. "Look here. Answer me this one. Your man panics. He cuts and runs through the back streets of Hong Kong. Who plays cops-and-robbers to get him back?" -

Don't answer it. Guillam prayed. He has absolutely no business to plumb around like this! Tell him to get lost!

Smiley's answer, though effective, lacked the fire Guillam longed for. "Oh, I suppose one can always invent a *hypothesis,*" he objected mildly. "I think the best one can say is that Martello and I would at that stage pool our thoughts and act for the best."

"George and I have a fine working relationship, Saul," Martello declared handsomely. "Just fine."

"Much *tidier,* you see, George," Enderby resumed, through a fresh matchstick. "Much *safer* if it's an all-Yank do. Marty's people make a hash and all they do is apologise to the Governor, post a couple of blokes to Walla Walla, and promise not to do it again. That's it. What everyone expects of 'em anyway. Advantage of a disgraceful reputation — right, Marty? Nobody's surprised if you screw the housemaid."

"Why, *Saul,*" said Martello, and laughed richly at the great British sense of humour.

"Much more tricky if *we're* the naughty boys, George," Enderby went on. "Or *you* are, rather. Governor could blow you down with one puff, the way it's set up at the moment. Wilbraham's crying all over his desk already."

Against Smiley's distracted obduracy, there was however no progress to be made, so for the while Enderby bowed out and they resumed their discussion of the "meat and potatoes," which was Martello's amusing phrase for modalities. But before they finished, Enderby had one last shot at dislodging Smiley from his primacy, choosing again the issue of the efficient handling and after-care of the catch.

"George, who's going to manage all the grilling and stuff? You using that funny little Jesuit of yours, the one with the smart name?"

"Di Salis will be responsible for the Chinese aspects of the debriefing and our Soviet research section the Russian."

"That the crippled don woman, is it, George? The one Bill shoved out to grass for drinking?"

"It is they, between them, who have brought the case this far," said Smiley.

Inevitably Martello sprang into the breach: "Ah, now, George, I won't have that! Sir, I will not! Saul, Oliver, I wish you to know that I regard the Dolphin case, in all its aspects, Saul, as a personal triumph for George here and for George *alone!*"

With a big hand all round for dear old George, they made their way back to Cambridge Circus.

"Gunpowder, treason, and plot!" Guillam expostulated. "Why's Enderby selling you down the river? What's all that tripe about losing the letter?"

"Yes," said Smiley at last, but from far away. "Yes, that's very careless of them. I thought I'd send them a copy, actually. Blind, by hand, for information only. Enderby seemed so *woolly,* didn't he? Will you attend to that, Peter, ask the mothers?"

The mention of the letter of agreement — *heads* of agreement, as Lacon called it — revived Guillam's worst misgivings. He remembered how he had foolishly allowed Sam Collins to be the bearer of it, and how, according to Fawn, he had spent more than an hour cloistered with Martello under the pretext of delivering it. He remembered Sam Collins also as he had glimpsed him in Lacon's anteroom, the mysterious confidant of Lacon and Enderby, lazing around Whitehall like a blasted Cheshire cat. He remembered

Enderby's taste for backgammon, which he played for very high stakes, and it even passed through his head, as he tried to sniff out the conspiracy, that Enderby might be a client of Sam Collins's club. From that notion he soon pulled back, discounting it as too absurd. But ironically it later turned out to be true. And he remembered his fleeting conviction — based on little but the physiognomy of the three Americans, and therefore soon also to be dismissed — that they knew already what Smiley had come to tell them.

But Guillam did not pull back from the notion of Sam Collins as the ghost at that morning's feast, and as he boarded the plane at London Airport, exhausted by his long and energetic farewell from Molly, the same ghost grinned at him through the smoke of his infernal brown cigarette.

The flight was uneventful except in one respect. They were three strong, and in the seating arrangements Guillam had won a small battle in his running war with Fawn. Over Housekeeping Section's dead body, Guillam and Smiley flew first class, while Fawn, the baby-sitter, took an aisle seat at the front of the tourist compartment, cheek by jowl with the airline security guards, who slept innocently for most of the journey while Fawn sulked. There had never been any suggestion, fortunately, that Martello and his quiet men would fly with them, for Smiley was determined that that should not happen on any account. As it was, Martello flew west, staging in Langley for instructions and continuing through Honolulu and Tokyo in order to be on hand in Hong Kong for their arrival.

As an unconsciously ironic footnote to their departure, Smiley left a long handwritten note to Jerry, to be presented to him on his arrival at the Circus, congratulating him on his first-rate performance. The carbon copy is still in Jerry's dossier. Nobody has thought to remove it. Smiley speaks of Jerry's ''unswerving loyalty'' and of ''setting the crown on more than twenty years of service.'' He includes an apocryphal message from Ann, ''who joins me in wishing you an equally distinguished career in letters." And he winds up rather awkwardly with the sentiment that "one of the privileges of our work is that it provides us with such wonderful colleagues. I must tell you that we all think of you in those terms."

Certain people do still ask why no anxious word about Jerry's whereabouts had reached the Circus before take-off. He was, after all, several days overdue. Once more they look for ways of blaming Smiley, but there is no evidence of a lapse on the Circus's side. For the transmission of Jerry's report from the air base in North East Thailand — his last — the Cousins had cleared a line through Bangkok direct to the Annexe in London. But the arrangement was valid for one signal and one answer-back only, and a follow-up was not envisaged.

Accordingly, the grizzle, when it came, was routed first to Bangkok on the military network, thence to the Cousins in Hong Kong on *their* network — since Hong Kong was held to have a total lien on all Dolphin-starred material — and only then, marked "Routine," repeated by Hong Kong to London, where it kicked around in several rosewood in-trays before anybody noted its significance. And it must be admitted that the languid Major Masters had attached very little significance to the no-show, as he later called it, of some travelling English fairy. "ASSUME EXPLANATION YOUR END," his message ends. Major Masters now lives in Norman, Oklahoma, where he runs a small automobile repair business.

Nor did Housekeeping Section have any reason to panic — or so they still plead. Jerry's instructions on reaching Bangkok were to find himself a plane, any plane, using his air-travel card, and get himself to London. No date was mentioned and no airline. The whole purpose was to leave things fluid. Most likely he had stopped over somewhere for a bit of relaxation. Many homing fieldmen do, and Jerry was on record as sexually oriented. So they kept their usual watch on flight lists and made a provisional booking at Sarratt for the two weeks' drying-out and recycling ceremony, then returned their attention to the far more urgent business of setting up the Dolphin safe house.

This was a charming mill-house, quite remote, though situated in the commuter town of Maresfield, Sussex, and on most days they found a reason for going down there. As well as di Salis and a sizeable part of his Chinese archive, a small army of interpreters and transcribers had to be accommodated, not to mention technicians, baby-sitters, and a Chinese-speaking doctor. In no time at all the residents were complaining noisily to the police about the influx of Japanese. The local paper carried a story that they were a visiting dance troupe. Housekeeping Section had inspired the leak.

Jerry had nothing to collect at the hotel — and, as it happened, no hotel — but he reckoned he had an hour to get clear, perhaps two. He had no doubt the Americans had the whole town wired, and he knew there would be nothing easier, if London asked for it, than for Major Masters to have Jerry's name and description broadcast as an American deserter travelling on a false-flag passport. Once his taxi was clear of the gates, therefore, he took it to the southern edge of town, waited, then took a second taxi and pointed it due north.

A wet haze lay over the paddies and the straight road ran into it endlessly. The radio pumped out female Thai voices like a slow-motion nursery rhyme. They passed an American electronics base, a circular grid a quarter of a mile wide floating in the haze and known locally as the Elephant Cage. Giant bodkins marked the perimeter, and at the middle, surrounded by webs of strung wire, burned a single infernal light like the promise of a future war. He had heard there were twelve hundred language students inside the place, but not one soul was to be seen.

He needed time, and in the event he helped himself to more than a week. Even now, he needed that long to bring himself to the point, because Jerry at heart was a soldier and voted with his feet. *In the beginning was the deed,* Smiley liked to say to him, in his failed-priest mood, quoting from Goethe. For Jerry that simple statement had become a pillar of his uncomplicated philosophy. What a man thinks is his own business. What matters is what he does.

Reaching the Mekong by early evening, he selected a village and for a couple of days strolled idly up and down the river-bank, trailing his shoulder-bag and kicking at an empty Coca-Cola tin with the toe of his buckskin boot. Across the river, behind the brown anthill mountains, lay the Ho Chi Minh trail. He had once watched a B-52 strike from this very point, three miles away in central Laos. He remembered how the ground shook under his feet and the sky emptied and burned, and he had known — he had really for a moment known — what it was like to be in the middle of it.

In this same spot, to use Frost's jolly phrase, Jerry Westerby blew the walls out, much along the lines the housekeepers expected of him, if not in quite the circumstances. In a river-side bar where they played old tunes on a nickelodeon, he drank black-market P.X. Scotch and night after night drove himself into oblivion, leading one laughing girl after another up the unlit staircase to a tattered bedroom, till finally he stayed there sleeping and didn't come down.

Waking with a jolt, clear-headed at dawn, to the screaming of roosters and the clatter of river traffic, Jerry would force himself to think long and generously of his chum and mentor, George Smiley. It was an act of will that made him do this, almost an act of obedience. He wished, quite simply, to rehearse the articles of his creed, and his creed till now had been old George. At Sarratt they have a very wordly and relaxed attitude to the motives of a fieldman, and no patience at all for the fiery-eyed zealot who grinds his teeth and says, "I hate Communism." If he hates it that much, they argue, he's most likely half-way in love with it already. What they really like — and what Jerry possessed, what he *was*, in effect — was the fellow who hadn't a lot of time for flannel but loved the service and knew — though God forbid he should make a fuss of it — that *we* were right. *We* being a necessarily flexible notion, but to Jerry it meant George and that was that.

Old George. Super. Good morning.

He saw him as he liked to remember him best, the first time they met, at Sarratt soon after the war. Jerry was still an army subaltern, his time nearly up and Oxford looming, and he was bored stiff. The course was for London Occasionals: people who, having done the odd bit of skulduggery without going formally onto the Circus payroll, were being groomed as an auxiliary reserve. Jerry had already volunteered for full-time employment, but Circus personnel had turned him down, which scarcely helped his mood.

So when Smiley waddled into the paraffin-heated lecture hut in his heavy overcoat and spectacles, Jerry inwardly groaned and prepared himself for another creaking fifty minutes of boredom — on good places to look for dead-letter boxes, most likely, followed by a sort of clandestine nature ramble through Rickmansworth, trying to spot hollow trees in graveyards. There was comedy while the Directing Staff cranked the lectern lower so that George could see over the top. In the end he stood himself a little fussily at the side of it and declared that his subject this afternoon was "Problems of Maintaining Courier Lines Inside Enemy Territory." Slowly it dawned on Jerry that he was talking not from the textbook but from experience: that this little pedant with the diffident voice and the blinking, apologetic manner had sweated out three years in some benighted German town, holding the threads of a very respectable network, while he waited for the boot through the door panel or the pistol butt across the face that would introduce him to the pleasures of interrogation.

When the meeting was over, Smiley asked to see him. They met in a corner of an empty bar, under the antlers where the darts board hung.

"I'm so sorry we couldn't have you," Smiley said. "I think our feeling was you needed a little more time *outside* first." Which was their way of saying he was immature. Too late, Jerry remembered

Smiley as one of the non-speaking members of the Selection Board that had failed him. "Perhaps if you could get your degree and make your way a little in a different walk of life, they would change their way of thinking. Don't lose touch, will you?"

After which, somehow, old George had always been there. Never surprised, never out of patience, old George had gently but firmly rejigged Jerry's life till it was Circus property. His father's empire collapsed: George was waiting with his hands out to catch him. His marriages collapsed: George would sit all night for him, hold his head.

"I've always been grateful to this service that it gave me a chance to pay," Smiley had said. "I'm sure one should feel that. I don't think we should be afraid of . . . devoting ourselves. Is that old-fashioned of me?"

"You point me, I'll march," Jerry had replied. "Tell me the shots and I'll play them."

There was still time. He knew that. Train to Bangkok, hop on a plane home, and the worst he would get was a flea in his ear for jumping ship for a few days. "Home," he repeated to himself. Bit of a problem. Home to Tuscany and the yawning emptiness of the hilltop without the orphan? Home to old Pet, sorry about the teacup? Home to dear old Stubbsie, key appointment as desk jockey with special responsibility for the spike? Or home to the Circus: "We think you'd be happiest in Banking Section." Even — great thought — home to Sarratt, training job, winning the hearts and minds of new entrants while he commuted dangerously from a maisonette in Watford.

On the third or fourth morning he woke very early. Dawn was just rising over the river, turning it first red, then orange, now brown. A family of water-buffaloes wallowed in the mud, their bells jingling. In mid-stream three sampans were linked in a long and complicated trawl. He heard a hiss and saw a net curl, then fall like hail on the water.

Yet it's not for want of a future that I'm here, he thought. It's for want of a present.

Home's where you go when you run out of homes, he thought. Which brings me to Lizzie. Vexed issue. Shove it on the back burner. Spot of breakfast.

Sitting on the teak balcony munching eggs and rice, Jerry remembered George breaking the news to him about Haydon: El Vino's bar, Fleet Street, a rainy midday. Jerry had never found it possible to hate anyone for very long, and after the initial shock there had really not been much more to say.

"Well, no point in crying in the old booze, is there, sport? Can't leave the ship to the rats. Soldier on, that's the thing."

To which Smiley agreed; yes, that was the thing, to soldier on, grateful for the chance to pay. Jerry had even found a sort of rum comfort in the fact that Bill was one of the clan. He had never seriously doubted, in his vague way, that his country was in a state of irreversible decline, or that his own class was to blame for the mess. "We *made* Bill," ran his argument, "so it's right we should carry the brunt of his betrayal." Pay, in fact. Pay. What old George was on about.

Pottering beside the river again, breathing the free warm air, Jerry chucked flat stones to make them bounce.

Lizzie, he thought. Lizzie Worthington, suburban bolter. Ricardo's pupil and punch-ball. Charlie Marshall's big sister and earth mother and unattainable whore. Drake Ko's cage-bird. My dinner companion for all of four hours. And to Sam Collins — to repeat the question — what had she been to him? For Mr. Mellon, Charlie's ''creepy English trader'' of eighteen months ago, she was a courier working the Hong Kong heroin trail. But she was more than that. Somewhere along the line, Sam had shown her a bit of ankle and told her she was working for Queen and country. Which glad news Lizzie had promptly shared with her admiring circle of friends. To Sam's fury, and he dropped her like a hot brick. So Sam had set her up as a patsy of some kind. A coat-trailer on probation. In one way this thought amused Jerry very much, for Sam had a reputation as an ace operator, whereas Lizzie Worthington might well star at Sarratt as the archetypal Woman Never to Be Recruited as Long as She Can Speak or Breathe.

Less funny was the question of what she meant to Sam *now*. What kept him skulking in her shadow like a patient murderer, smiling his grim iron smile? That question worried Jerry very much. Not to put too fine a point on it, he was obsessed by it. He definitely did not wish to see Lizzie taking another of her dives. If she went anywhere from Ko's bed, it was going to be into Jerry's. For some while, off and on — ever since he had met her, in fact — he had been thinking how much Lizzie would benefit from the bracing Tuscan air. And while he didn't know how or why Sam Collins came to be in Hong Kong, or even what the Circus at large intended for Drake Ko, he had the strongest possible impression — and here was the nub of the thing — that by pushing off to London at this moment, far from carting Lizzie away on his white charger, Jerry was leaving her sitting on a very large bomb.

Which struck him as unacceptable. In other times, he might have been prepared to leave that problem to the owls, as he had left so many other problems in his day. But these were not other times. This time, as he now realized, it was the Cousins who were paying the piper, and while Jerry had no particular quarrel with the Cousins, their presence made it a much rougher ball game. So that whatever vague notions he had about George's humanity did not apply.

Also he cared about Lizzie. Urgently. There was nothing imprecise in his feelings at all. He ached for her, warts and all. She was his kind of loser, and he loved her. He had worked it out and drawn the line, and that, after several days of counting on beads, was his net unalterable solution. He was a little awed, but very pleased by it.

Gerald Westerby, he told himself. You were present at your birth. You were present at your several marriages and at some of your divorces, and you will certainly be present at your funeral. High time, in our considered view, that you were present at certain other crucial moments in your history.

Taking a bus up-river a few miles, he walked again, rode on *cyclos,* sat in bars, made love to the girls, thinking only of Lizzie. The inn where he stayed was full of children and one morning he woke to find two of them sitting on his bed, marvelling at the enormous length of the *farang's* legs and giggling at the way his bare feet hung over the end. Maybe I'll just stay here, he thought. But by then he was fooling, because he knew that he had to go back and ask her, even if the answer was a custard pie. From the balcony he launched paper aeroplanes for the children, and they clapped and danced, watching them float away.

He found a boatman and, when evening came, crossed the river to Vientiane, avoiding the formalities of immigration. Next morning, also without formality, he wangled himself aboard an unscheduled Royal Air Lao DC-8, and by afternoon he was airborne and in possession of a delicious warm whisky and chatting merrily to a couple of friendly opium dealers. As they landed, black rain was falling and the windows of the airport bus were foul with dust. Jerry didn't mind at all. For the first time in his life, returning to Hong Kong was quite like coming home after all.

Inside the reception area nevertheless, Jerry played a cautious hand. No trumpets, he told himself: definitely. The few days' rest had done wonders for his presence of mind. Having taken a good look round, he made for the men's room instead of the immigration desks and lay up there till a big load of Japanese tourists arrived, then barged over to them and asked who spoke English. Having cut out four of them, he showed them his Hong Kong press card, and while they stood in line waiting for their passport check he besieged them with questions about why they were here and what they proposed to do, and with whom, and wrote wildly on his pad before choosing four more and repeating the process. Meanwhile he waited for the police on duty to change watch. At four o'clock they did, and he at once made for a door marked "No Entry," which he had noted earlier. He banged on it till it was opened, and started to walk through to the other side.

"Where the hell are you going?" asked an outraged Scottish police inspector.

"Home to the comic, sport. Got to file the dirt on our friendly Japanese visitors."

He showed his press card.

"Well go through the damn gates, like everyone else."

"Don't be bloody silly. I haven't got my passport. That's why your distinguished colleague brought me through this way in the first place."

Bulk, a ranking voice, a patently British appearance, an affecting grin, won him a space in a city-bound bus five minutes later. Outside his apartment block he dawdled but saw no one suspicious, but this was China and who could tell?

The lift as usual emptied for him. Riding in it, he hummed Deathwish the Hun's one record in anticipation of a hot bath and change of clothes. At his front door he had a moment's anxiety when he noticed the tiny wedges he had left in place lying on the floor, till he belatedly remembered Luke and smiled at the prospect of their reunion. He unlocked the burglar door, and as he did so he heard the sound of humming from inside, a droning monotone, which could have been an air-conditioner but not Deathwish's. Bloody idiot Luke has left the gramophone on, he thought, and it's about to brew up. Then he thought, I'm doing him an injustice; it's that fridge.

Then he opened the door and saw Luke's dead body strewn across the floor with half his head shot to pieces, and half the flies in Hong Kong swarming over it and round it; and all he could think of to do, as he quickly closed the door behind him and jammed his handkerchief over his mouth, was run into the kitchen in case there was still someone there. Returning to the living-room, he pushed Luke's feet aside and dug up the parquet brick where he had cached his forbidden side-arm and his escape kit, and put them in his pocket before he vomited.

Of course, he thought. That's why Ricardo was so certain the horse-writer was dead.

Join the club, he thought, as he stood out in the street again, with rage and grief pounding in his ears and eyes: Nelson Ko's dead, but he's running China. Ricardo's dead, but Drake Ko says he can stay alive as long as he sticks to the shady side of the street. Jerry Westerby the horse-writer is also completely dead, except that Ko's stupid pagan vicious bastard of a henchman, Mr. Tiu, was so thick he shot the wrong round-eye.

19
Golden Thread

The inside of the American Consulate in
Hong Kong could have been the inside of
the Annexe, right down to the ever-
present fake rosewood and the bland
courtesy and the airport chairs and the
heartening portrait of the President, even
if this time it was Ford. Welcome to your
Howard Johnson spookhouse, Guillam
thought. The section they worked in was
called the isolation ward and had its own
doorway to the street, guarded by two
Marines. They had passes in false names
— Guillam's was Gordon — and for the
duration of their stay there, except on the
telephone, they never spoke to a soul
inside the building except one another.
"We're not just deniable, gentlemen,"
Martello had told them proudly in the

briefing, "we're also invisible." That was how it was going to be played, he said. The U.S. Consul General could put his hand on the Bible and swear to the Governor they weren't there and his staff were not involved, said Martello; "Blind eye right down the line." After that, he handed over to George, because "George, this is your show from soup to nuts."

Downhill they had five minutes' walk to the Hilton, where Martello had booked them rooms. Uphill, though it would have been hard going, they had ten minutes' walk to Lizzie Worth's apartment block. They had been here five days and now it was evening, but they had no way of telling because there were no windows in the operations room; there were maps and sea charts instead, and a couple of telephones manned by Martello's quiet men, Murphy and his friend. Martello and Smiley had a big desk each; Guillam, Murphy, and his friend shared the table with the telephones, and Fawn sat moodily at the centre of an empty row of cinema chairs along the black wall, like a bored critic at a preview, sometimes picking his teeth and sometimes yawning but refusing to take himself off as Guillam repeatedly advised him. Craw had been spoken to but ordered to keep clear of everything — a total duck-dive. Smiley was frightened for him since Frost's death and would have preferred him evacuated, but the old boy wouldn't leave.

It was also for once the hour of the quiet men: "Our final detailed briefing," Martello had called it. "Ah, that's if it's okay by *you,* George." Pale Murphy, wearing a white shirt and blue trousers, was standing on the raised podium before a wall chart, soliloquising from pages of detailed notes. The rest of them sat at his feet and listened mainly in silence, including Smiley and Martello. Murphy could have been describing a vacuum cleaner, and to Guillam that made his monologue the more hypnotic.

The chart showed largely sea, but at the top and to the left hung a lace-fringe of the South China coast. Behind Hong Kong the spattered outskirts of Canton were just visible below the batten which held the chart in place, and due south of Hong Kong at the very mid-point of the chart stretched the green outline of what looked to be a cloud divided into four sections, marked A, B, C, and D. These, said Murphy reverently, were the fishing beds and the cross at the centre was Centre Point, sir. Murphy spoke only to Martello, whether it was George's show from soup to nuts or not.

"Sir, basing on the last occasion Drake exited Red China, sir, and updating our assessment to the situation as of now, we and navy int. between us, sir —"

"Murphy, Murphy," put in Martello quite kindly, "ease off a little, will you, friend? This isn't training school any more, okay? Loosen your girdle, will you, son?"

"Sir. One. Weather," Murphy said, quite untouched by this appeal. "April and May are the transitional months, sir, between the north-east monsoons and the beginning of the south-west monsoons. Forecasts day-to-day are unpredictable, sir, but no extreme conditions are foreseen for the trip." He was using the pointer to show the line from Swatow southward to the fishing beds, then from the fishing beds north-west past Hong Kong up the Pearl River to Canton.

"Fog?" Martello said.

"Fog is traditional for the season, and cloud is anticipated at six to seven oktas, sir."

"What the hell's an okta, Murphy?"

"One okta is one eighth of sky area covered, sir. Oktas have replaced the former tenths. No typhoons have been recorded in April for over fifty years and navy int. calls typhoons unlikely. Wind is easterly, nine to ten knots, but any fleet that runs with it must count on periods of calm — also contrary winds too, sir. Humidity around eighty percent, temperature fifteen to twenty-four centigrade. Sea conditions calm with a small swell. Currents around Swatow tend to run north-east through the Taiwan Strait, at around three sea miles per day. But farther westward — on *this* side, sir —"

"That's one thing I *do* know, Murphy," Martello put in sharply. "I know where west is, dammit." Then he grinned at Smiley as if to say "these young whipper-snappers."

Murphy was again unmoved. "We have to be prepared to calculate the speed factor and consequently the progress of the fleet at any one point in its journey, sir."

"Sure, sure."

"Moon, sir," Murphy continued. "Assuming the fleet to have exited Swatow on the night of Friday, April twenty-fifth, the moon would be three days off of full —"

"Why do we assume that, Murphy?"

"Because that's when the fleet exited Swatow, sir. We had confirmation from navy int. one hour ago. Column of junks sighted at the eastern end of fishing bed C and easing westward with the wind, sir. Positive identification of the lead junk confirmed."

There was a prickly pause. Martello coloured.

"You're a clever boy, Murphy," Martello said in a warning tone. "But you should have given me that information a little earlier."

"Yes, sir. Assuming also that the intention of the junk containing Nelson Ko is to hit Hong Kong waters on the night of May fourth, the moon will be in its last quarter, sir. If we follow precedents right down the line —"

"We do," said Smiley firmly. "The escape is to be an exact repetition of Drake's own journey in 'fifty-one."

Once more, no one doubted him, Guillam noticed. Why not? It was utterly bewildering.

"— then our junk should hit the southernmost out-island of Po Toi at twenty hundred hours tomorrow, and rejoin the fleet up along the Pearl River in time to make Canton harbour between zero ten-thirty and twelve hundred hours the following day, May fifth, sir."

While Murphy droned on, Guillam covertly kept his eye on Smiley, thinking, as he often did, that he knew him no better today than when he first met him back in the dark days of the cold war in Europe. Where did he slip away to at all odd hours? Mooning about Ann? About Karla? What company did he keep that brought him back to the hotel at four in the morning? Don't tell me George is having a second spring, he thought.

Last night at eleven there had been a scream from London, so Guillam had trailed up here to unbutton it. Westerby adrift, they said. They were terrified Ko had had him murdered — or, worse, abducted and tortured — and that the operation would abort in consequence. Guillam thought it more likely Jerry was holed up with a couple of air hostesses somewhere en route to London, but with that priority on the signal he had no option but to wake Smiley and tell him. He rang his room and got no answer, so he dressed and banged on Smiley's door, and finally he was reduced to picking the lock, for now it was Guillam's turn to panic: he thought Smiley might be ill.

But Smiley's room was empty and his bed unslept in, and when Guillam went through his things he was fascinated to see that the old fieldman had gone to the length of sewing false name-tapes in his shirts. That was all he discovered, however. So he settled in Smiley's chair and dozed and didn't wake till four, when he heard a tiny flutter and opened his eyes to see Smiley stooped and peering at him from about six inches away; how he got into the room so silently, God alone knew.

"Gordon?" he asked softly. "What can I do for you?" — for they were on an operational footing of course, and lived with the assumption the rooms were bugged. For the same reason Guillam did not speak but handed Smiley the envelope containing Connie's message, which he read and reread, then burned. Guillam was impressed how seriously he took the news. Even at that hour he insisted on going straight up to the Consulate to attend to it, so Guillam went along to carry his bags.

"Instructive evening?" he asked lightly as they plodded the short way up the hill.

"I? Oh, to a point, thank you, to a point," Smiley replied, doing his disappearing act, and that was all Guillam or anyone could get out of him about his nocturnal or other ambles.

Meanwhile, without the smallest explanation of his source, George was bringing in hard operational data in a manner that brooked no enquiry from anyone.

"Ah, George, we can count on that, can we?" Martello asked in bewilderment, on the first occasion that this happened.

"What? Oh yes, yes, indeed you may."

"Great. Great footwork, George. I admire you," said Martello heartily after a further puzzled silence, and from then on they had gone along with it. They had no choice. For nobody, not even Martello, quite dared to challenge Smiley's authority.

"How many days' fishing is that, Murphy?" Martello was asking.

"Fleet will have had seven days' fishing and hopefully make Canton with full holds, sir."

"That figure, George?"

"Yes, oh yes — nothing to add, thank you."

Martello asked what time the fleet would have to leave the fishing beds in order for Nelson's junk to make tomorrow evening's rendezvous on time.

"I have put it at eleven tomorrow morning," Smiley said without looking up from his notes.

"Me too," said Murphy.

"This rogue junk, Murphy," Martello said, with another deferential glance at Smiley.

"Yes, sir," said Murphy.

"Can it break away from the pack that easy? What would be its cover for entering Hong Kong waters, Murphy?"

"Happens all the time, sir. Red Chinese junk-fleets operate a collective catch system without profit motivation, sir. Consequence of that, you get the single junks that break away at night-time and come in without lights and sell their fish to the out-islanders for money."

"*Literally* moonlighting!" Martello exclaimed, much amused by the felicity of the expression.

Smiley had turned to the map of Po Toi island on the other wall and was tilting his head in order to intensify the magnification of his spectacles.

"What size of junk are we talking about here?" Martello asked.

"Twenty-eight-man long-liners, sir, baited for shark, golden thread, and conger."

"Did Drake use that type also?"

"Yes," said Smiley, still watching the map. "Yes, he did."

"And she can come that close in, can she? Provided the weather allows?"

Again it was Smiley who answered. Till today, Guillam had not heard him so much as speak of a boat in his life.

"The draw of a long-liner is very modest," he remarked. "She can come in pretty well as close as she wishes, provided always that the sea is not too rough."

From the back bench Fawn gave an immoderate laugh. Wheeling round in his chair, Guillam shot him a foul look. Fawn leered and shook his head, marvelling at his master's omniscience.

"How many junks make up a fleet?" Martello asked.

"Twenty to thirty," said Smiley.

"Check," said Murphy meekly.

"So what does Nelson *do,* George? Kind of get out to the edge of the pack there and stray a little?"

"He'll hang back," said Smiley. "The fleets like to move in column astern. Nelson will tell his skipper to take the rear position."

"Will he, by God," Martello muttered under his breath. "Murphy, what identifications are traditional?"

"Very little known in that area, sir. Boat people are notoriously evasive. They have no respect for marine regulations. Out to sea, they show no lights at all, mostly for fear of pirates."

Smiley was lost to them again. He had sunk into a wooden immobility, and though his eyes stayed fixed on the big sea chart, his mind, Guillam knew, was anywhere but with Murphy's dreary recitation of statistics. Not so Martello.

"How much coastal trade do we have over all, Murphy?"

"Sir, there are no controls and no data."

"Any quarantine checks as the junks enter Hong Kong waters, Murphy?"

Martello asked.

"Theoretically all vessels should stop and have themselves checked, sir."

"And in practice, Murphy?"

"Junks are a law to themselves, sir. Technically, Chinese junks are forbidden to sail between Victoria Island and Kowloon point, sir, but the last thing the Brits want is a hassle with the mainland over rights of way. Sorry, sir."

"Not at all," said Smiley politely, still gazing at the chart. "Brits we are and Brits we shall remain."

It's his Karla expression, Guillam decided; the one that comes over him when he looks at the photograph. He catches sight of it, it surprises him, and for a while he seems to study its contours, its blurred and sightless gaze. Then the light slowly goes out of his eyes, and somehow the hope as well, and you feel he's looking inward, in alarm.

"Murphy, did I hear you mention navigation lights?" Smiley enquired, turning his head slightly but still staring toward the chart.

"Yes, sir."

"I expect Nelson's junk to carry three," said Smiley. "Two green lights vertically on the stern mast and one red light to starboard."

"Yes, sir."

Martello tried to catch Guillam's eye but Guillam wouldn't play.

"But it may not," Smiley warned as an afterthought. "It may carry none at all, and simply signal from close in."

Murphy resumed. A new heading: Communications.

"Sir, in the communications area, sir, few junks have their own transmitters but most all have receivers. Once in a while you get a skipper who buys a cheap walkie-talkie with range about one mile to facilitate the trawl, but they've been doing it so long they don't have much call to speak to each other, I guess. Then as to finding their way — well, navy int. says that's near enough a mystery. We have reliable information that many long-liners operate on a primitive compass, a hand lead and line, or even just a rusty alarm clock for finding true north."

"Murphy, how the *hell* do they work

that, for God's sakes?" Martello cried.

"Line with a lead plumb and wax stuck to it, sir. They sound the bed and know where they are from what sticks to the wax."

"Well, they *really* do it the hard way," Martello declared.

A phone rang. Martello's other quiet man took the call, listened, then put his hand over the mouthpiece.

"Quarry Worth's just gotten back, sir," he said to Smiley. "Party drove around for an hour, now she's checked in her car back at the block. Mac says sounds like she's running a bath, so maybe she plans going out again later."

"And she's alone," Smiley said impassively. It was a question.

"She alone there, Mac?" He gave a hard laugh. "I'll bet you would, you dirty bastard. Yes, *sir,* lady's all alone taking a bath, and Mac there says when will we ever get to use video as well. Is the lady *singing* in the bath, Mac?" He rang off. "She's not singing."

"Murphy, get on with the war," Martello snapped.

Smiley would like the interception plans rehearsed once more, he said.

"Why, George! Please! It's your show, remember?"

"Perhaps we could look again at the big map of Po Toi island, could we? And then Murphy could break it down for us, would you mind?"

"*Mind, George, mind?*" Martello cried, so Murphy began again, this time using a pointer. "Navy int. observation posts *here,* sir . . . constant two-way communication with base, sir . . . no presence at all within two sea miles of the landing zone. . . . Navy int. to advise base the moment the Ko launch starts back for Hong Kong, sir. . . . Interception will take place by regular British police vessel as the Ko launch enters harbour. . . . U.S. to supply op. int. and stand off only, for unforeseen supportive situation. . . ."

Smiley monitored every detail with a prim nod of his head.

"After all, Marty," he put in at one point, "once Ko has Nelson aboard, there's nowhere else he *can* go, is there?

Po Toi is right at the edge of China waters. It's us or nothing.''

One day, thought Guillam, as he continued listening, one of two things will happen to George. He'll cease to care or the paradox will kill him. If he ceases to care, he'll be half the operator he is. If he doesn't, that little chest will blow up from the struggle of trying to find the explanation for what we do. Smiley himself, in a disastrous off-the-record chat to senior officers, had put the names to his dilemma, and Guillam with some embarrassment recalled them to this day. To be *inhuman in defence of our humanity,* he had said, *harsh in defence of compassion.* To be *single-minded in defence of our disparity.* They had filed out in a veritable ferment of protest; why didn't George just do the job and shut up instead of taking his faith out and polishing it in public till the flaws showed? Connie had even murmured a Russian aphorism in Guillam's ear, which she insisted on attributing to Karla. "There'll be no war, will there, Peter darling?'' she had said reassuringly, squeezing his hand as he led her along the corridor. "But in the struggle for peace not a single stone will be left standing, bless the old fox. I'll bet they didn't thank him for *that* one in the Collegium, either."

A thud made Guillam swing round. Fawn was changing cinema seats again. Seeing Guillam, he flared his nostrils in an insolent sneer.

He's off his head, thought Guillam with a shiver.

Fawn too, for different reasons, was now causing Guillam serious anxiety. Two days ago, in Guillam's company, he had been the author of a disgusting incident. Smiley as usual had gone out alone. To kill time Guillam had hired a car and driven Fawn up to the China border. Returning, they were waiting at some country traffic-lights when a Chinese boy drew alongside on a Honda. Guillam was driving. Fawn had the passenger seat. Fawn's window was lowered; he had taken his jacket off and was resting his left arm on the door where he could admire a new gilt watch he had bought himself in the Hilton shopping concourse.

As they pulled away, the Chinese boy ill-advisedly made a dive for the watch, but Fawn was much too quick for him. Catching hold of the boy's wrist instead, he held on to it, towing him beside the car while the boy struggled vainly to break free. Guillam had driven fifty yards or so before he realised what had happened, and he at once stopped the car, which was what Fawn was waiting for. He hopped out before Guillam could stop him, lifted the boy straight off his Honda, led him to the side of the road, and broke both his arms for him, then returned smiling to the car. Terrified of a scandal, Guillam drove rapidly from the scene, leaving the boy screaming and staring at his dangling arms. He reached Hong Kong determined to report Fawn to George immediately, but luckily for Fawn it was eight hours before Smiley surfaced, and by then Guillam reckoned George had enough on his plate already.

Another phone was ringing, the red. Martello took the call himself. He listened a moment, then burst into a loud laugh.

"They found him," he told Smiley, holding the phone to him.

"Found whom?"

The phone hovered between them.

"Your *man*, George. Your Weatherby —"

"Westerby," Murphy corrected him, and Martello shot him a venomous look.

"They got him," said Martello.

"Where is he?"

"Where *was* he, you mean! George, he just had himself the time of his life in two cathouses up along the Mekong. If our people are not exaggerating, he's the hottest thing since Barnum's baby elephant left town in 'forty-nine!"

"And where is he now, please?"

Martello handed him the phone. "Why don't you just have 'em read you the signal, okay? They have some story that he crossed the river." He turned to Guillam and winked. "They tell me there's a couple of places in Vientiane where he might find himself a little action too," he said, and went on laughing richly while Smiley sat patiently with the telephone to his ear.

Jerry chose a cab with two wing mirrors and sat in the front. In Kowloon he hired a car from the biggest outfit he could find, using the escape passport and driving licence because marginally he thought the false name was safer if only by an hour. As he headed up the Midlevels, it was dusk and still raining and huge haloes hung from the neon lights that lit the hillside. He passed the American Consulate and drove past Star Heights twice, half expecting to see Sam Collins, and on the second occasion he knew for sure he had found her flat and that her light was burning: an arty Italian affair by the look of it, that hung across the picture window in a gracious droop, three hundred dollars' worth of pretension. Also the frosted glass of a bathroom window was lit. The third time he passed, he saw her pulling a wrap over her shoulders, and instinct or something about the formality of her gesture told him she was once more preparing to go out for the evening but that this time she was dressed to kill.

Every time he allowed himself to remember Luke, a darkness covered his eyes and he imagined himself doing the noble useless things like telephoning Luke's family in California, or the dwarf at the bureau, or even for whatever purpose the Rocker. Later, he thought. Later, he promised himself, he would mourn Luke in fitting style.

He coasted slowly into the driveway that led to the entrance till he came to the slip-road to the car-park. The park was three tiers deep and he idled round it till he found her red Jaguar stowed in a safe corner behind a chain to discourage careless neighbours from approaching its peerless paint-work. She had put a mock leopard-skin cover on the steering-wheel. She just couldn't do enough for the damn car. Get pregnant, he thought, in a burst of fury; buy a dog. Keep mice. For two pins he'd have smashed the front in, but those two pins had held Jerry back more times than he liked to count. If she's not using it, then he's sending a limousine for her, he thought. Maybe with Tiu riding shot-gun, even. Or maybe he'll come himself. Or maybe she's just getting herself dolled up for the evening sacrifice and not going out at all. He wished it was Sunday. He remembered Craw saying that Drake Ko spent Sundays with his family, and that on Sundays Lizzie had to make her own running. But it wasn't Sunday, and neither did he have dear old Craw at his elbow telling him — on what evidence Jerry could only guess — that Ko was away in Bangkok or Timbuctoo conducting his business.

Grateful that the rain was turning to fog, he headed back up the slipway to the drive and at the junction found a narrow piece of shoulder where, if he parked hard against the barrier, the other traffic could complain but squeeze past. He grazed the barrier and didn't care. From where he now sat, he could watch the pedestrians coming in and out under the striped awning of the block, and the cars joining or leaving the main road. He felt no sense of caution at all. He lit a cigarette and the limousines crackled past him both ways, but none belonged to Ko. Occasionally as a car edged by him, the driver paused to hoot or shout a complaint and Jerry ignored him. Every few seconds his eyes took in the mirrors, and once when a plump figure not unlike Tiu padded guiltily up behind him, he actually dropped the safety catch of the pistol in his jacket pocket before admitting to himself that the man lacked Tiu's brawn. Probably been collecting gambling debts from the *pak-pai* drivers, he thought, as the figure went by him.

He remembered being with Luke at Happy Valley. He remembered being with Luke.

He was still looking in the mirror when the red Jaguar hissed up the slipway behind him, just the driver, and the roof closed, no passenger. The one thing he hadn't thought of was that she might take the lift right down to the car-park and collect the car herself rather than have the porter bring it to the door for her as he did before. Pulling out after her, he glanced up and saw the lights still burning in her window. Had she left somebody behind? Or did she propose to come back shortly? Then he thought, Don't be so damn clever. She's just careless about lights.

The last time I spoke to Luke, it was to tell him to get out of my hair, he thought, and the last time he spoke to me was to tell me he'd covered my back with Stubbsie.

She had turned down the hill toward the town. He headed down after her, and for a space nothing followed him, which seemed unnatural, but these were unnatural hours and Sarratt man was dying in him faster than he could handle. She was heading for the brightest part of town. He supposed he still loved her, though just now he was prepared to suspect anybody of anything. He kept close behind her, remembering that she used her mirror seldom. In this dusky fog she would only see his headlights anyway. The fog hung in patches and the harbour looked as if it were on fire, with the shafts of crane-light playing like water hoses on the crawling smoke. In Central she ducked into another basement garage, and he drove straight in after her and parked six bays away, but she didn't notice him.

Remaining in the car, she paused to repair her make-up and he actually saw her working on her chin, powdering the scars. Then she got out and went through the ritual of locking, though a kid with a razor-blade could have cut through the soft top in one easy movement. She was dressed in a silk cape of some kind and a long silk dress, and as she walked toward the stone spiral stair she raised both her hands and carefully lifted her hair, which was gathered at the neck, and laid the pony-tail down the outside of the cape. Getting out after her, he followed her as far as the hotel lobby and turned aside in time to avoid being photographed by a bisexual drove of chattering fashion journalists in satins and bows.

Hanging back in the comparative safety of the corridor, Jerry pieced the scene together. It was a large private party, and Lizzie had joined it from the blind side. The other guests were arriving at the front entrance, where the Rolls-Royces were so thick on the ground that nobody was special. A woman with blue-grey hair presided, doing absolutely nothing but swaying about and speaking gin-sodden French. A prim Chinese public-relations girl with a couple of assistants made up the receiving line, and as the guests filed in, the girl and her cohorts came forward frightfully cordially and asked for names and sometimes invitation cards before consulting a list and saying "Oh, yes, of *course*." The blue-grey woman smiled and growled. The cohorts handed out lapel pins for the men and orchids for the women, then lighted on the next arrivals.

Lizzie Worthington went through this screening woodenly. Jerry gave her a minute to clear, watched her through the double doors marked *"Soirée"* with a Cupid's arrow, then attached himself to the queue. The public-relations girl was bothered by his buckskin boots. His suit was disgusting enough, but it was the boots that bothered her. On her course of training, he decided while she stared at them, she had been taught to place a lot of value on shoes. Millionaires may be tramps from the socks up but a pair of two-hundred-dollar Guccis is a passport not to be missed. She frowned at his press card, then at her guest list, then at his press card again, and once more at his boots, and she threw a lost glance at the blue-grey lush, who kept on smiling and growling. Jerry guessed she was drugged clean out of her mind. Finally the girl put up her own special smile for the marginal consumer and handed him a disc the size of a coffee saucer painted fluorescent pink with "PRESSE" an inch high in white.

"Tonight we are making *everybody* beautiful, Mr. Westerby," she said.

"Have a job with me, sport."

"You like my *parfum*, Mr. Westerby?"

"Sensational," said Jerry.

"It is called Juice of the Vine, Mr. Westerby, one hundred Hong Kong for a little bottle, but tonight Maison Flaubert gives free samples to all our guests. Madame Montifiori . . . oh . . . of *course*, welcome to House of Flaubert. You like my *parfum*, Madame Montifiori?"

A Eurasian girl in a cheongsam held out a tray and whispered, "Flaubert wishes you an exotic night."

"For Christ's sake," Jerry said.

Inside the double doors a second receiving line was manned by three pretty boys flown in from Paris for their charm, and a posse of security men that would have done credit to a President. For a moment he thought they might frisk him, and he knew that if they tried he was going to pull down the temple with him. They eyed Jerry without friendliness, counting him part of the help, but he was light-haired and they let him go.

"The press is in the third row back from the catwalk," said a hermaphrodite blond in a cowboy leather suit, handing him a press kit. "You have no camera, Monsieur?"

"I just do the captions," Jerry said, jamming a thumb over his shoulder. "Spike here does the pictures." He walked into the reception room peering round him, grinning extravagantly, waving at whoever caught his eye.

The pyramid of champagne glasses was six feet tall, with black satin steps so that the waiters could take them from the top. In sunken ice coffins lay magnums awaiting burial. There was a wheelbarrow full of cooked lobsters and a wedding cake of pâté de foie gras, with "Maison Flaubert" done in aspic on the top. Space music was playing and there was even conversation under it, if only the bored drone of the extremely rich. The catwalk stretched from the foot of the long window to the centre of the room. The window faced the harbour but the fog broke the view into patches. The air-conditioning was turned up so that the women could wear their mink without sweating. Most of the men wore dinner-jackets but the young Chinese playboys sported New York-style slacks and black shirts and gold chains. The British taipans stood in one sodden circle with their womenfolk, like bored officers at a garrison get-together.

Feeling a hand on his shoulder, Jerry swung fast, but all he found in front of him was a little Chinese queer called Graham who worked for one of the local gossip rags. Jerry had once helped him out with a story he was trying to sell to the comic. Rows of armchairs faced the catwalk in a rough horseshoe, and Lizzie was sitting in the front between Mr. Arpego and his wife or paramour. Jerry recognised them from Happy Valley. They looked as though they were chaperoning Lizzie for the evening. The Arpegos talked to her, but she seemed barely to hear them. She sat straight and beautiful and she had taken off her cape, and from where Jerry sat she could have been stark naked except for her pearl collar and her pearl earrings. At least she's still intact, he thought. She hasn't rotted or got cholera or had her head shot off. He remembered the line of gold hairs running down her spine as he stood over her that first evening in the lift. Queer Graham sat next to Jerry, and Phoebe Wayfarer sat two along. He knew her only vaguely but gave her a fat wave.

"Gosh. Super. Pheeb. You look terrific. Should be up there on the catwalk, sport, showing a bit of leg."

He thought she was a bit tight, and perhaps she thought he was, though he'd drunk nothing since the plane. He took out a pad and wrote on it, playing the professional, trying to rein himself in. Easy as you go. Don't frighten the game. When he read what he had written, he saw the words "Lizzie Worthington" and nothing else. Chinese Graham read it too, and laughed.

"My new byline," said Jerry, and they laughed together, too loud, so that people in front turned their heads as the lights began to dim. But not Lizzie, though he thought she might have recognised his voice.

Behind them the doors were being closed, and as the lights went lower Jerry had a mind to fall asleep in this soft and kindly chair. The space music gave way to a jungle beat brushed out on a cymbal, till only a single chandelier flickered over the black catwalk, answering the churned and patchy lights of the harbour in the window behind. The drum-beat rose in a slow crescendo from amplifiers everywhere. It went on a long time, just drums very well played, very insistent, till gradually grotesque human shadows became visible against the harbour window. The drum-beats stopped.

In a wracked silence two black girls strode flank against flank down the catwalk, wearing nothing but jewels. Their skulls were shaven and they wore round ivory earrings and diamond collars like the iron rings of slave girls. Their oiled limbs shone with clustered diamonds, pearls, and rubies. They were tall, and beautiful, and lithe, and utterly unexpected, and for a moment they cast over the whole audience the spell of absolute sexuality. The drums recovered and soared, spotlights raced over jewels and limbs. They writhed out of the steaming harbour and advanced on the spectators with the anger of sensuous enslavement. They turned and walked slowly away, challenging and disdaining with their haunches.

Lights came on, there was a crash of nervous applause followed by laughter and drinks. Everyone was talking at once and Jerry was talking loudest: to Miss Lizzie Worthington, the well-known aristocratic society beauty whose mother couldn't even boil an egg, and to the Arpegos who owned Manila and one or two of the out-islands, as Captain Grant of the Jockey Club had once assured him. Jerry was holding his notebook like a headwaiter.

"Lizzie Worthington, *gosh,* all Hong Kong at your feet, Madame, if I may say so. My paper is doing an exclusive on this event, Miss Worth or Worthington, and we're hoping to feature you, your dresses, your fascinating life-style, and your even more fascinating friends. My photographers are bringing up the rear." He bowed to the Arpegos. "Good evening, Madame. Sir. Proud to have you with us, I'm sure. This your first visit to Hong Kong?"

He was doing his big-puppy number, the boyish soul of the party. A waiter brought champagne and he insisted on transferring the glasses to their hands rather than let them help themselves. The Arpegos were much amused by this performance. Craw said they were crooks. Lizzie was staring at him and there was something in her eyes he couldn't make out, something real and appalled, as if she, not Jerry, had just opened the door on Luke.

"Mr. Westerby has already done one story on me, I understand," she said. "I don't think it was ever printed, was it, Mr. Westerby?"

"Who you write for?" Mr. Arpego demanded suddenly. He wasn't smiling any more. He looked dangerous and ugly, and she had clearly reminded him of something he had heard about and didn't like. Something Tiu had warned him of, for instance.

Jerry told him.

"Then go write for them. Leave this lady alone. She don't give interviews. You got work to do, you work somewhere else. You didn't come here to play. Earn your money."

"Couple of questions for *you* then, Mr. Arpego. Just before I go. How can I write you down, sir? As a rude Filipino millionaire? Or only half a millionaire?"

"For God's sake," Lizzie breathed, and by a mercy the lights went out again, the drum-beat began, everyone went back to his corner, and a woman's voice with a French accent began a soft commentary on the loudspeaker. At the back of the catwalk the two black girls were performing long insinuating shadow dances. As the first model appeared, Jerry saw Lizzie stand up ahead of him in the darkness, pull her cape over her shoulders, and walk fast and softly up the aisle past him and toward the doors, head bowed. Jerry went after her. In the lobby she half turned as if to look at him, and it crossed his mind she was expecting him. Her expression was the same and it reflected his own mood. She looked haunted and tired and utterly confused.

"Lizzie!" he called as if he had just sighted an old friend, and ran quickly to her side before she could reach the powder-room door. "Lizzie! My God! It's been years! A lifetime! Super!"

A couple of security guards looked on meekly as he flung his arms round her for the kiss of long friendship. He had slipped his left hand under her cape, and as he bent his laughing face to hers he laid the small revolver against the bare flesh of her back, the barrel just below her nape, and in that way, linked to her with bonds of old affection, led her straight into the street, chatting gaily all the way, and hailed a cab. He hadn't wanted to produce the gun but he couldn't risk having to manhandle her. That's the way it goes, he thought: you come back to tell her you love her and end up by marching her at gunpoint.

She was shivering and furious but he didn't think she was afraid, and he didn't even think she was sorry to be leaving that awful gathering.

"That's all I need," she said as they wound up the hill again, through the fog. "Perfect. Bloody perfect."

She wore a scent that was strange to him, but it smelt a deal better than Juice of the Vine.

Guillam was not bored exactly, but neither was his capacity for concentration infinite, as George's appeared to be. When he wasn't wondering what the devil Jerry Westerby was up to, he found himself basking in the erotic deprival of Molly Meakin or else remembering the Chinese boy with his arms inside out, whining like a half-shot hare after the disappearing car. Murphy's theme was now the island of Po Toi and he was dilating on it remorselessly.

Volcanic, sir, he said.

Hardest rock substance of the whole Hong Kong group, sir, he said.

And the most southerly of the islands, he said.

Seven hundred and ninety feet high, sir; fishermen use it as a navigation point from far out to sea, sir, he said.

Technically not one island but a group of six islands, the other five being barren and treeless and uninhabited.

Fine temple, sir. Great antiquity. Fine wood carvings but little natural water.

"Jesus Christ, Murphy, we're not *buying* the damn place, are we?" Martello expostulated. With action close and London far away, Martello had lost a lot of his gloss, Guillam noticed, and all his Englishness. His tropical suits were honest-to-cornball American, and he needed to talk to people, preferably his own. Guillam suspected that even London was an adventure for him, and Hong Kong was already enemy territory. Whereas under stress Smiley went quite the other way; he became private and rigidly polite.

Po Toi itself has a shrinking population of one hundred and eighty farmers and fishermen, mostly Communist, three living villages and three dead ones, sir, said Murphy. He droned on. Smiley continued to listen intently but Martello impatiently doodled on his pad.

"And *tomorrow,* sir," said Murphy, "tomorrow is the night of Po Toi's annual festival intended to pay homage to Tin Hau, the goddess of the sea, sir."

Martello stopped doodling: "These people really believe that crap?"

"Everybody has a right to his religion, sir."

"They teach you that at training college too, Murphy?" Martello returned to his doodling.

There was an uncomfortable silence before Murphy valiantly took up his pointer and laid the tip on the southern edge of the island's coastline.

"This festival of Tin Hau, sir, is

concentrated in the one main harbour, sir, right here on the south-west point where the ancient temple is situated. Mr. Smiley's informed prediction, sir, has the Ko landing operation taking place *here,* away from the main bay, in a small cove on the east side of the island. By landing on that side of the island, which has *no* habitation, *no* natural access to the sea, at a point in time when the diversion of the island festival in the *main* bay —"

Guillam never heard the ring. He just heard the voice of Martello's other quiet man answering the call: "Yes, Mac," then the squeak of his airport chair as he sat bolt upright, staring at Smiley. "Right, Mac. Sure, Mac. Right now. Yes. Hold it. Right beside me. Hold everything."

Smiley was already standing over him, his hand held out for the phone. Martello was watching Smiley. On the podium Murphy had his back turned while he pointed out further intriguing features of Po Toi, not quite registering the interruption.

"This island is also known to seamen as

Ghost Rock, sir," he explained, in the same dreary voice. "But nobody seems to know why."

Smiley listened briefly then put down the telephone. "Thank you, Murphy," he said courteously. "That was very interesting."

He stood dead still a moment, his fingers to his upper lip in a Pickwickian posture of deliberation. "Yes," he repeated. "Yes, very."

He walked as far as the door then paused again.

"Marty, forgive me, I shall have to leave you for a while. Not above an hour or two, I trust. I shall telephone you in any event."

He reached for the door handle, then turned to Guillam.

"Peter, I think you had better come along too — would you mind? We may need a car and you seem admirably unmoved by the Hong Kong traffic. Did I see Fawn somewhere? Ah, there you are."

On Headland Road the flowers had a

hairy brilliance, like ferns sprayed for Christmas. The pavement was narrow and seldom used, except by amahs to exercise the children, which they did without talking to them, as if they were walking dogs. The Cousins' surveillance van was a deliberately forgettable brown Mercedes lorry, battered-looking, with clay dust on the wings and "H. K. DEVP. & BLDG. SURVEY LTD." sprayed on one side. An old aerial with Chinese streamers trailing from it drooped over the cab, and as the lorry nosed its lugubrious way past the Ko residence — for the second, or was it the fourth time that morning? — nobody gave it a thought. In Headland Road, as everywhere in Hong Kong, somebody is always building.

Stretched inside the lorry on leather bunks fitted for the purpose, the two men watched intently from among a forest of lenses, cameras, and radio-telephone appliances. For them also, their progress past Seven Gates was becoming something of a routine.

"No change?" said the first.

"No change," the second confirmed.

"No change," the first repeated into the radio-telephone, and heard the assuring voice of Murphy at the other end, acknowledging the message.

"Maybe they're waxworks," said the first, still watching. "Maybe we should go give them a prod and see if they holler."

"Maybe we should, at that," said the second.

In all their professional lives, they were agreed, they had never followed anything that kept so still. Ko stood where he always stood, at the end of the rose-arbour, his back to them as he stared out to sea. His little wife sat apart from him, dressed as usual in black, on a white garden chair, and she seemed to be staring at her husband. Only Tiu made any movement. He also was sitting, but to Ko's other side, and he was munching what looked like a doughnut.

Reaching the main road, the lorry lumbered toward Stanley, pursuing for cover reasons its fictional reconnaissance of the region.

20

Liese's Lover

Her apartment was big and unreconciled: a mix of hotel lounge, executive suite, and tart's boudoir. The drawing-room ceiling was raked to a lopsided point like the nave of a subsiding church. The floor changed levels restlessly; the carpet was as thick as grass, and Lizzie and Jerry left shiny footprints where they walked. The enormous windows gave limitless but lonely views, and when she closed the blinds and drew the curtains, the two of them were suddenly in a suburban bungalow with no garden. The amah had gone to her room behind the kitchen, and when she appeared Lizzie sent her back there. She crept out scowling and hissing. "Wait till I tell the master," she was saying.

He put the chains across the front door, and after that he took her with him, steering her from room to room, making her walk a little ahead of him on his left side, open the doors for him and even the cupboards. The bedroom was a television stage-set for a *femme fatale,* with a round, quilted bed and a sunken round bath behind Spanish screens. He looked through the bedside lockers for a small arm because, though Hong Kong is not particularly gun-ridden, people who have lived in Indo-China usually have something. Her dressing-room looked as though she'd emptied one of the smart Scandinavian décor shops in Central by telephone. The dining-room was done in smoked glass, polished chrome and leather, with fake Gainsborough ancestors staring at the empty chairs — all the mummies who couldn't boil eggs, he thought. Black tiger-skin steps led to Ko's den, and here Jerry lingered, staring round, fascinated despite himself, seeing the man in everything, and — for all his rather awful crimes at first remove — his kinship with old Sambo. The king-sized desk with the *bombé* legs and ball-and-claw feet, the Presidential cutlery. The ink-wells, the sheathed paper-knife and scissors, the untouched works of legal reference, the very ones old Sambo trailed around with him: Simons on tax, Charlesworth on company law. The framed testimonials on the wall. The citation for his Order of the British Empire, beginning "Elizabeth the Second by the Grace of God . . ." The medal itself, embalmed in satin like the arms of a dead knight. Group photographs of Chinese elders on the steps of a spirit temple. Victorious racehorses. Lizzie laughing to him. Lizzie in a swim-suit, looking stunning. Lizzie in Paris.

Gently he pulled open the desk drawers and discovered the embossed stationery of a dozen different companies. In the cupboards, empty files, an I.B.M. electric typewriter with no plug on it, an address book with no addresses entered. Lizzie naked from the waist up, glancing round at him over her long back. Lizzie, God help her, in a wedding dress, clutching a posy of gardenias. Ko must have sent her to a bridal parlour for the photograph.

There were no photographs of gunny bags of opium.

The executive sanctuary, thought Jerry, still standing there. Old Sambo had several, he remembered: girls who had flats from him — one even a house — yet saw him only a few times a year. But always this one secret special room, with the desk and the unused telephones and the instant mementoes, a physical corner carved off someone else's life, a shelter from his other shelters.

''Where is he?'' Jerry asked, remembering Luke again.

"Drake?"

"No, Father Christmas."

"You tell me."

He followed her to the bedroom. "Do you often not know?" he asked.

She was pulling off her earrings, dropping them in a jewellery box. Then her clasp, her necklace and bracelets.

"He rings me wherever he is, night or day, we never care. This is the first time he's cut himself off."

"Can you ring him?"

"*Any* bloody time," she said with savage sarcasm. " 'Course I can. Number One Wife and me get on just *great*."

"What about at the office?"

"He's not going to the office."

"What about Tiu?"

"Sod Tiu."

"Why?"

"Because he's a pig," she snapped, pulling open a cupboard.

"He could pass on messages for you."

"If he felt like it, which he doesn't."

"Why not?"

"How the hell should I know?" She hauled out a pullover and some jeans and chucked them on the bed. "Because he resents me. Because he doesn't trust me. Because he doesn't like round-eyes horning in on Big Sir. Get out while I change."

So he wandered into the dressing-room again, keeping his back to her, hearing the rustle of silk and skin.

"I saw Ricardo," he said. "We had a full and frank exchange of views."

He needed very much to hear whether

they had told her. He needed to absolve her from Luke. He listened, then went on:

"Charlie Marshall gave me his address, so I popped up and had a chat with him."

"Great. So now you're family."

"They told me about Mellon. Said you carried dope for him."

She didn't speak so he turned to look at her, and she was sitting on the bed with her head in her hands. In the jeans and pullover she looked about fifteen years old, and half a foot shorter.

"What the hell do you want?" she whispered at last, so quietly she might have been putting the question to herself.

"You," he said. "For keeps."

He didn't know whether she heard because all she did was let out a long breath and whisper "Oh, Jesus" at the end of it.

"Mellon a friend of yours?" she asked finally.

"No."

"Pity. He needs a friend like you."

"Does Arpego know where Ko is?"

She shrugged.

"When did you last hear from him?"

"A week."

"What did he say?"

"He had things to arrange."

"What things?"

"For Christ's sake, stop asking questions! The whole sodding world is asking questions, so just don't join the queue, right?"

He stared at her and her eyes were alight with anger and despair. He opened the balcony door and stepped outside.

I need a brief, he thought bitterly. Sarratt bearleaders, where are you now I need you? It hadn't dawned on him till now that when he cut the cable, he was also dropping the pilot.

The balcony ran along three sides. The fog had temporarily cleared. Behind him hung the Peak, its shoulders festooned in gold lights. Banks of running cloud made changing caverns round the moon. The harbour had dug out all its finery. At its centre an American aircraft carrier, floodlit and dressed overall, basked like a pampered woman amid a cluster of attendant launches. On her deck, a line of helicopters and small fighters reminded him of the air base in Northern Thailand. A column of ocean-going junks drifted past her, headed for Canton.

"Jerry," she called.

She was standing in the open doorway, watching him down a line of tub trees.

"Come on in. I'm hungry," she said.

It was a kitchen where nobody cooked or ate, but it had a Bavarian corner, with pine settles, Chinese-style alpine pictures, and ashtrays saying "Carlsberg." She gave him coffee from an ever-ready percolator, and he noticed how when she was on guard she kept her shoulders forward and her forearms across her body, the way the orphan used to. She was shivering. He thought she had been shivering ever since he laid the gun on her and he wished he hadn't done that, because it was beginning to dawn on him that she was in as bad a state as he was, and perhaps a damn sight worse, and that the mood between them was like two people after a disaster, each in a separate hell. He made her a brandy and soda and the same for himself and sat her in the drawing-room where it was warmer, and he watched her while she hugged herself and drank the brandy, staring at the carpet.

"Music?" he asked.

She shook her head.

"I represent myself," he said. "No connection with any other firm."

She might not have heard.

"I'm free and willing," he said. "It's just that a friend of mine died."

He saw her nod, but only in sympathy; he was sure it rang no bell with her at all.

"The Ko thing is getting very grubby," he said. "It's not going to work out well. They're very rough boys you're mixed up with. I thought maybe you'd like a leg out of it all. That's why I came back. My Galahad act. It's just I don't quite know what's gathering round you. Mellon — all that. Maybe we should unbutton it together and see what's there."

After which not very articulate explanation, the telephone rang. It had one of those throttled croaks designed to spare the nerves.

The telephone was across the room on a

gilded trolley. A pinlight winked on it with each dull note, and the rippled glass shelves picked up the reflection. She glanced at it, then at Jerry, and her face was at once alert with hope. Jumping to his feet, he pushed the trolley over to her and its wheels stammered in the deep pile. The wire uncoiled behind him as he walked, till it was like a child's scribble across the room. She lifted the receiver quickly and said "Worth" in the slightly rude tone women learn when they live alone. He thought of telling her the line was bugged but he didn't know what he was warning her against; he had no position any more, this side or that side. He didn't know what the sides were, but his head was suddenly full of Luke again and the hunter in him was wide awake.

She had the telephone to her ear but she hadn't spoken. Once she said "Yes," as if she were acknowledging instructions, and once she said "No" strongly. Her expression had turned blank, her voice told him nothing. But he sensed obedience and he sensed concealment, and as he did so, the anger lit in him completely and nothing else mattered.

"No," she said to the phone. "I left the party early."

He knelt beside her, trying to listen, but she kept the receiver pressed hard against her.

Why didn't she ask him where he was? Why didn't she ask when she would see him? Whether he was all right? Why he hadn't phoned? Why did she look at Jerry like this, show no relief?

His hand on her cheek, he forced her head round and whispered to the other ear.

"Tell him you *must* see him! You'll come to him. *Anywhere.*"

"Yes," she said again into the phone. "All right. Yes."

"Tell him! Tell him you must see him!"

"I must see you," she said finally. "I'll come to you wherever you are."

The receiver was still in her hand. She made a shrug, asking for instruction, and her eyes were still turned to Jerry — not as her Sir Galahad but as just another part of a hostile world that encircled her.

"I love you!" he whispered. "Say

what you say!"

"I love you," she said shortly, with her eyes closed, and rang off before he could stop her.

"He's coming here," she said. "And damn you."

Jerry was still kneeling beside her. She stood up in order to get clear of him.

"Does he know?" Jerry asked.

"Know what?"

"That I'm here?"

"Perhaps." She lit a cigarette.

"Where is he now?"

"I don't know."

"When will he be here?"

"He said soon."

"Is he alone?"

"He didn't say."

"Does he carry a gun?"

She was across the room from him. Her strained grey eyes still held him in their furious, frightened glare. But Jerry was indifferent to her mood. A feverish urge for action had overcome all other feelings.

"Drake Ko. The nice man who set you up here. Does he carry a gun? Is he going to shoot me? Is Tiu with him? Just questions, that's all.''

''He doesn't wear it in bed, if that's what you mean.''

''Where are you going?''

''I thought you two men would prefer to be left alone.''

Leading her back to the sofa, he sat her facing the double doors at the far end of the room. They were panelled with frosted glass, and on the other side of them lay the hall and the front entrance. He opened them, clearing her line of view to anybody coming in.

''Do you have rules about letting people in, you two?'' She didn't follow his question. ''There's a peep-hole here. Does he insist you check every time before you open?''

''He'll ring on the house phone from downstairs. Then he'll use his door key.''

The front door was laminated hardboard, not solid, but solid enough. Sarratt folklore said, ''If you are taking a lone intruder unawares, don't get behind the door or you'll never get out again.'' For once Jerry was inclined to agree. Yet to keep to the open side was to be a sitting duck for anyone aggressively inclined, and Jerry was by no means sure that Ko was either unaware or alone. He considered going behind the sofa, but if there was to be shooting he didn't want the girl to be in the line of it; he definitely didn't. Her passivity, her lethargic stare did nothing to reassure him. His brandy glass was beside hers on the table, and he put it quietly out of sight behind a vase of plastic orchids. He emptied the ashtray and set an open copy of *Vogue* in front of her on the table.

"You play music when you're alone?"

"Sometimes."

He chose Ellington.

"Too loud?"

"Louder," she said. Suspicious, he turned down the sound, watching her. As he did so, the house phone whistled twice from the hall.

"Take care," he warned and, gun in hand, moved to the open side of the front door, the sitting-duck position, three feet from the arc, close enough to spring forward, far enough to shoot and throw himself, which was what he had in mind as he dropped into a half-crouch. He held the gun in his left hand and nothing in his right, because at that distance he couldn't miss with either hand, whereas if he had to strike he wanted his right hand free. He remembered the way Tiu carried his hands curled, and he warned himself not to get in close. Whatever he did, to do it from a distance. A groin kick but don't follow it in; stay outside those hands.

"You say 'Come on up,' " he told her.

"Come on up," Lizzie repeated into the phone. She rang off and unhooked the chain.

"When he comes in, smile for the camera. Don't shout."

"Go to hell," she said.

From the lift-well, to his sharpened ear, came the clump of a lift arriving and the monotonous "ping" of the bell. He heard footsteps approaching the door, one pair only, steady, and remembered Drake Ko's comic, slightly ape-like gait at Happy Valley, how the knees tipped through the grey flannels. A key slid into the lock, one hand came round the door, and the rest with no apparent forethought followed. By then Jerry had sprung with all his weight, flattening the unresisting body against the wall. A picture of Venice fell, the glass smashed, he slammed the door, all in the same moment that he found a throat and jammed the barrel of the pistol straight into the deep flesh. Then the door was unlocked a second time from outside, very fast, the wind went out of his body, his feet flew upward, a cripplng shock of pain spread from his kidneys and felled him on the thick carpet, a second blow caught him in the groin and made him gasp as he jerked his knees to his chin. Through his streaming eyes he saw the little, furious figure of Fawn the baby-sitter standing over him, shaping for a third strike, and the rigid grin of Sam Collins as he peered calmly over Fawn's shoulder to see what the damage was. And still in the doorway, wearing an expression of grave apprehension as he straightened his collar after Jerry's unprovoked assault on him, the flustered figure of his one-time guide and mentor, Mr. George Smiley, breathlessly calling his leash-dogs to order.

Jerry was able to sit, but only if he leaned forward. He held both hands in front of him, his forearms jammed into his lap. The pain was all over his body, like poison spreading from a central source. The girl watched from the hall doorway. Fawn was lurking, hoping for another excuse to hit him. Sam Collins was at the other end of the room, sitting in a winged armchair with his legs crossed as if he were at home here and the chair his favourite. Smiley had poured Jerry a neat brandy and was stooping over him, poking the glass into his hand.

"What are you doing here, Jerry?" Smiley said. "I don't understand."

"Courting," said Jerry and closed his eyes as a wave of black pain swept over him. "Developed an unscheduled affection for our hostess, here. Sorry about that."

"That was a very dangerous thing to do, Jerry," Smiley objected. "You could have wrecked the entire operation. Suppose I had been Ko. The consequences would have been disastrous.''

''I'll say they would.'' He drank some brandy. ''Luke's dead. Lying in my flat with his head shot off.''

''Who's Luke?'' Smiley asked, forgetting their meeting at Craw's house.

''No one. Just a friend.'' He drank again. ''American journalist. A drunk. No loss to anyone.''

Smiley glanced at Sam Collins, but Sam shrugged. ''Nobody *we* know,'' he said.

''Ring them, all the same,'' said Smiley.

Sam picked up the mobile telephone and walked out of the room with it because he knew the layout.

''Put the burn on her, have you?'' Jerry said, with a nod of his head toward Lizzie. ''About the only thing left in the book that hasn't been done to her, I should think.'' He called over to her. ''How are you doing there, sport? Sorry about the tussle. Didn't break anything, did we?''

''No,'' she said.

''Put the bite on you about your wicked past, did they? Stick and carrot? Promised to wipe the slate clean? Silly girl, Lizzie. Not allowed a past in this game. Can't have a future either. *Verboten.*"

He turned back to Smiley. "That's all it was, George. No philosophy to it. Old Lizzie got under my skin."

Tilting back his head, he studied Smiley's face through half-closed eyes. And with the clarity which pain sometimes brings, he felt somehow that by his action he had put Smiley's own existence under threat.

"Don't worry," he said gently. "Won't happen to you, that's for sure."

"Jerry," said Smiley.

"Yes, sir," said Jerry and made a show of sitting to attention.

"Jerry, you don't understand what's going on. How much you could upset things. Billions of dollars and thousands of men could not obtain a part of what we stand to gain from this one operation. A war general would laugh himself silly at the thought of such a tiny sacrifice for such an enormous dividend."

"Don't ask *me* to get you off the hook, old boy," Jerry said, looking up into his face again. "You're the owl, remember? Not me."

Sam Collins returned. Smiley glanced at him in question.

"He's not one of theirs either," said Sam.

"They were aiming for me," said Jerry. "They got Lukie instead. He's a big bloke. Or was."

"And he's in your flat?" Smiley asked. "Dead. Shot. And in your flat?"

"Been there some while."

Smiley to Collins: "We shall have to brush over the traces, Sam. We can't risk a scandal."

"I'll get back to them now," Collins said.

"And find out about planes," Smiley called after him. "Two first-class seats."

Collins nodded.

"Don't like that fellow one bit," Jerry confessed. "Never did. Must be his moustache." He shoved a thumb toward Lizzie. "What's she got that's so hot for you all, anyway, George? Ko doesn't whisper his inmost secrets to her. She's a round-eye." He turned to Lizzie. "Does he?"

She shook her head.

"If he did, she wouldn't remember," he went on. "She's thick as hell about those things. She's probably never even heard of Nelson." He called to her again. "You. Who's Nelson? Come on, who is he? Ko's little dead son, isn't he? That's right. Named his boat after him, didn't he? And his gee-gee." He turned back to Smiley. "See? Thick. Leave her out of it, that's my advice."

Collins had returned with a note of flight times. Smiley read it, frowning through his spectacles. "We shall have to send you home at once, Jerry," he said. "Guillam's waiting downstairs with a car. Fawn will go along as well."

"I'd just like to be sick again if you don't mind."

Reaching upward, Jerry took hold of Smiley's arm for support, and at once Fawn sprang forward, but Jerry shot out a warning finger at him as Smiley ordered him back.

"You keep your distance, you poisonous little leprechaun," Jerry advised. "You're allowed one bite and that's all.

The next one won't be so easy.''

He moved in a crouch, trailing his feet slowly, hands latched over his groin. Reaching the girl, he stopped in front of her.

''Did they have powwows up here, Ko and his lovelies? Ko bring his boy-friends up here for a natter, did he?''

''Sometimes.''

''And you helped with the mikes, did you, like the good little housewife? Let the sound boys in, tended the lamp? I bet you did.''

She nodded.

''Still not enough,'' he objected as he hobbled to the bathroom. ''Still doesn't answer my question. Must be more to it than that. *Far* more.''

In the bathroom he held his face under cold water, drank some, and immediately vomited. On the way back, he looked for the girl again. She was in the drawing-room, and in the way that people under stress look for trivial things to do, she was sorting the gramophone records, putting each in its proper sleeve. In a distant corner, Smiley and Collins were quietly conferring. Closer at hand Fawn was waiting at the door.

"Bye, sport," he said to her. Putting his hand on her shoulder, he drew her round till her grey eyes looked straight at him.

"Goodbye," she said and kissed him, not in passion exactly, but at least with more deliberation than the waiters got.

"I was a sort of accessory before the fact," he explained. "I'm sorry about that. I'm not sorry about anything else. You'd better look after that sod Ko too. Because if they don't manage to kill him, I may."

He touched the lines on her chin, then shuffled toward the door where Fawn stood, and turned round to take his leave of Smiley, who was alone again; Collins had been sent off to telephone. Smiley stood as Jerry remembered him best, his short arms slightly lifted from his sides, his head back a little, his expression at once apologetic and enquiring, as if he'd just left his umbrella on the underground. The girl had turned away from both of them and was still sorting the records.

"Love to Ann, then," Jerry said.

"Thank you."

"You're wrong, sport. Don't know how, don't know why, but you're wrong. Still, too late for that, I suppose." He felt sick again and his head was shrieking from the pains in his body. "You come any nearer than that," he said to Fawn, "and I will definitely break your bloody neck, you understand?" He turned back to Smiley, who stood in the same posture and gave no sign of having heard.

"Season of the year to you, then," said Jerry.

With a last nod, but none to the girl, Jerry limped into the corridor, Fawn following. Waiting for the lift, he saw the elegant American standing at his open doorway, watching his departure.

"Ah, yeah, I forgot about you," he called very loudly. "You're running the bug on her flat, aren't you? The Brits blackmail her and the Cousins bug her — lucky girl gets it all ways."

The American vanished, closing the door quickly after him. The lift came and Fawn shoved him in.

"Don't do that," Jerry warned him.

"This gentleman's name is Fawn," he told the other occupants of the lift in a very loud voice. They mostly wore dinner-jackets and sequinned dresses. "He's a member of the British Secret Service and he's just kicked me in the balls. The Russians are coming," he added, to their doughy, indifferent faces. "They're going to take away all your bloody money."

"Drunk," said Fawn in disgust.

In the lobby Lawrence the porter watched with keen interest. In the forecourt a Peugeot saloon waited, blue. Peter Guillam was sitting in the driving seat.

"Get in," he snapped.

The passenger door was locked. He climbed into the back, Fawn after him.

"What the hell do you think you're up to?" Guillam demanded through clenched teeth. "Since when did half-arsed London Occasionals cut anchor in mid-operation?"

"Keep clear," Jerry warned Fawn. "Just the hint of a frown from you right now is enough to get me going. I mean that. I warn you. Official."

The ground fog had returned, rolling over the bonnet. The passing city offered itself like the framed glimpses of a junk yard: a painted sign, a shop-window, strands of cable strung across a neon sign, a clump of suffocated foliage; the inevitable building site, floodlit. In the mirror Jerry saw a black Mercedes following, male passenger, male driver.

"Cousins bringing up the tail," he announced.

A spasm of pain in the abdomen almost blacked him out, and for a moment he actually thought Fawn had hit him again, but it was only an after-effect of the first time. In Central he made Guillam pull up and was sick in the gutter in full public view, leaning his head through the window while Fawn crouched tensely over him. Behind them the Mercedes stopped too.

"Nothing like a spot of pain," he exclaimed, settling in the car again, "for getting the old brain out of moth-balls once in a while. Eh, Peter?"

Guillam made an obscene answer.

You don't understand what's going on, Smiley had said. *How much you could upset things. Billions of dollars and thousands of men could not obtain a part of what we stand to gain . . .*

How? he kept asking himself. Gain *what?* His knowledge of Nelson's position inside Chinese affairs was sketchy. Craw had told him only the minimum he needed to know: *Nelson has access to the Crown jewels of Peking, Your Grace. Whoever gets his hooks on Nelson has earned a lifetime's merit for himself and his noble house.*

They were skirting the harbour, heading for the tunnel. From sea-level the American aircraft carrier looked strangely small against the merry backdrop of Kowloon.

"How's Drake getting him out, by the way?" he asked Guillam chattily. "Not trying to fly him again, *that's* for sure. Ricardo put the lid on that one for good, didn't he?"

"Suction," Guillam snapped — which was very silly of him, thought Jerry jubilantly; he should have kept his mouth shut.

"Swimming?" Jerry asked. "Nelson on the Mirs Bay ticket. *That's* not Drake's way, is it? Nelson's too old for that one, anyway. Freeze to death, even if the sharks didn't get his whatnots. How about the pig train, come out with the grunters? Sorry you've got to miss the big moment, sport, all on account of me."

"So am I, as a matter of fact. I'd like to kick your teeth in."

Inside Jerry's brain, the sweet music of rejoicing sounded. It's true! he told himself. That's what happening! Drake's bringing Nelson out and they're all queueing up for the finish!

Behind Guillam's lapse — just one word, but in Sarratt terms totally unforgivable, indivisibly wrong — there lay nevertheless a revelation as dazzling as anything which Jerry was presently enduring, and in some respects vastly more bitter. If anything mitigates the crime of indiscretion, and in Sarratt terms nothing does, then Guillam's experiences of the last hour — half of it spent driving Smiley frantically through rush-hour traffic and half of it waiting, in desperate indecision, in the car outside Star Heights — would surely qualify. Everything he had feared in London, the most Gothic of his apprehensions regarding the Enderby-Martello connection, and the supporting rôles of Lacon and Sam Collins, had in these sixty minutes been proved to him beyond all reasonable doubt as right and true and justified — and if anything somewhat understated.

They had driven first to Bowen Road in the Midlevels, to an apartment block so blank and featureless and large that even those who lived there must have had to look twice at the number before they were sure they were entering the right one. Smiley pressed a bell marked "Mellon," and, idiot that he was, Guillam asked "Who's Mellon?" at the same moment he remembered that it was Sam Collins's work name. Then he did a double take and asked himself — but not Smiley; they were in the lift by now — what maniac, after Haydon's ravages, could conceivably award himself the same work name which he had used before the fall? Then Collins opened the door to them, wearing his Thai silk dressing-gown, a brown cigarette jammed into a holder, and his washable non-iron smile, and the next thing was they were grouped in a parquet drawing-room with bamboo chairs and Sam had switched two transistor radios to different programmes, one voice, the other music, to provide rudimentary anti-bug security while they talked. Sam listened, ignoring Guillam entirely, then promptly phoned Martello direct — Sam had a *direct line* to him, please note, no dialling, nothing; a straight land-line, apparently — to ask in veiled language how things stood with chummy. Chummy — Guillam learned later — being gambling slang for a mug. Martello replied that the surveillance van had just reported in. Chummy and Tiu were presently sitting in Causeway Bay aboard the *Admiral Nelson,* said the watchers, and the directional mikes (as usual) were picking up so much bounce from the water that the transcribers would need days, if not weeks, to clean off the extraneous sound and find out whether the two men had ever said anything interesting. Meanwhile they had dropped one man at the quayside as a static post, with orders to advise Martello immediately should the boat weigh anchor or either of the two quarries disembark.

"Then we must go there at once," said Smiley, so they piled back into the car, and while Guillam drove the short distance to Star Heights, seething and listening impotently to their terse conversation, he became with every moment more convinced that he was looking at a spider's web, and that only George Smiley, obsessed by the promise of the case and the image of Karla, was myopic enough, and trusting enough — and, in his own paradoxical way, innocent enough — to bumble straight into the middle of it.

George's age, thought Guillam. Enderby's political ambitions, his fondness for the hawkish, pro-American stance — not to mention the crate of champagne and his outrageous courtship of the fifth floor. Lacon's tepid support of

Smiley, while he secretly cast around for a successor. Martello's stopover in Langley. Enderby's attempt *only days ago* to prise Smiley away from the case and hand it to Martello on a plate. And now, most eloquent and ominous of all, the reappearance of Sam Collins as the joker in the pack with a private line to Martello! And Martello, heaven help us, acting dumb about where George got his information from — the direct line notwithstanding.

To Guillam all these threads added up to one thing only, and he could not wait to take Smiley aside and, by any means at his command, deflect him sufficiently from the operation, just for one moment, for him to see where he was heading. To tell him about the letter. About Sam's visit to Lacon and Enderby in Whitehall.

Instead of which? He was to return to England. Why was he to return to England? Because a genial thick-skulled hack named Westerby had had the gall to slip the leash.

Even without his crying awareness of impending disaster, the disappointment to

Guillam would have been scarcely supportable. He had endured a great deal for this moment. Disgrace and exile to Brixton under Haydon, poodling for old George instead of getting back to the field, putting up with George's obsessive secretiveness, which Guillam privately considered both humiliating and self-defeating — but at least it had been a journey with a destination, till Jerry bloody Westerby, of all people, had robbed him even of that. But to return to London knowing that, for the next twenty-two hours at least, he was leaving Smiley and the Circus to a bunch of wolves, without even the chance to warn him — to Guillam it was the crowning cruelty of a frustrated career, and if blaming Jerry helped, then damn him, he would blame Jerry or anybody else.

"Send Fawn!"

"Fawn's not a gentleman," Smiley would have replied — or words that meant the same.

You can say *that* again too, thought Guillam, remembering the broken arms.

Jerry was equally conscious of abandoning someone to the wolves, even if it was Lizzie Worthington rather than George Smiley. As he gazed through the rear window of the car, it seemed to him that the very world that he was moving through had also been abandoned. The street markets were deserted, the pavements, even the doorways. Above them the Peak loomed fitfully, its crocodile spine daubed by a ragged moon.

It's the Colony's last day, he decided: Peking has made its proverbial telephone call. "Get out, party over." The last hotel was closing; he saw the empty Rolls-Royces lying like scrap around the harbour, and the last blue-rinse round-eye matron, laden with her tax-free furs and jewellery, tottering up the gangway of the last cruise ship; the last China-watcher frantically feeding his last miscalculations into the shredder; the looted shops, the empty city waiting like a carcass for the hordes. For a moment it was all one vanishing world; here, Phnom Penh, Saigon, London — a world on loan, with the creditors standing at the door, and Jerry himself, in some unfathomable way, a part of the debt that was owed.

I've always been grateful to this service, that it gave me a chance to pay. Is that how you *feel?*

Yes, George, he thought. Put the words into my mouth, old boy. That's *exactly* how I feel, sport. But perhaps not quite in the sense *you* mean it, however. He saw Frost's cheerful, fond little face as they drank and fooled. He saw it the second time, locked in that awful scream. He felt Luke's friendly hand upon his shoulder and saw the same hand lying on the floor, flung back over his head to catch a ball that would never come, and he thought, Trouble is, sport, the paying is actually done by the other poor sods.

Like Lizzie, for instance.

He'd mention that to George one day, if they ever, over a jar, should get back to that sticky little matter of just why we climb the mountain. He'd make a point there — nothing aggressive, not rocking the boat, you understand, sport — about the selfless and devoted way in which we sacrifice other people, such as Luke and

Frost and Lizzie. George would have a perfectly good answer, of course. Reasonable. Measured. Apologetic. George saw the bigger picture. Understood the imperatives. Of course he did. He was an owl.

The harbour tunnel was approaching and he was thinking of her shivering last kiss, and remembering the drive to the mortuary all at the same time, because the scaffold of a new building rose ahead of them out of the fog and, like the scaffold on the way to the mortuary, it was floodlit and glistening coolies were swarming over it in yellow helmets.

Tiu doesn't like her either, he thought. Doesn't like round-eyes who spill the beans on Big Sir.

Forcing his mind in other directions, he tried to imagine what they would do with Nelson: stateless, homeless, a fish to be devoured or thrown back into the sea at will. Jerry had seen a few of those fish before: he had been present for their capture; at their swift interrogation. He had led more than one of them back across the border they had so recently crossed, for hasty *recycling,* as the Sarratt jargon had it — "quick before they notice he has left home." And if they didn't put him back? If they kept him, this great prize they all so coveted? Then after the years of his debriefing — two, three even; he had heard some ran for five — Nelson would become one more Wandering Jew of the spy-trade, to be hidden, and moved again, and hidden, to be loved not even by those to whom he had betrayed his trust.

And what will Drake do with Lizzie, he wondered, while that little drama unfolds? Which particular scrap-heap is she headed for this time?

They were at the mouth of the tunnel and they had slowed almost to a halt. The Mercedes lay right behind them. Jerry let his head fall forward. He put both hands over his groin while he rocked himself and grunted in pain. From an improvised police box, like a sentry post, a Chinese constable watched curiously.

"If he comes over to us, tell him we've got a drunk on our hands," Guillam snapped. "Show him the sick on the floor."

They crawled into the tunnel. Two lanes of north-bound traffic were bunched nose to bumper by the bad weather. Guillam had taken the right-hand stream. The Mercedes drew up beside them on their left. In the mirror, through half-closed eyes, Jerry saw a brown lorry grind down the hill after them.

"Give me some change," Guillam said. "I'll need change as I come out."

Fawn delved in his pockets, but using one hand only.

The tunnel pounded to the roar of engines. A hooting match started. Others began joining in. To the encroaching fog was added the stench of exhaust fumes. Fawn closed his window. The din rose and echoed till the car trembled to it.

Jerry put his hands to his ears. "Sorry, sport. Going to bring up again, I'm afraid."

But this time he leaned toward Fawn, who, with a muttered "Filthy bastard," started hastily to wind his window down again, until Jerry's head crashed into the lower part of his face and Jerry's elbow hacked down in his groin. For Guillam, caught between driving and defending himself, Jerry had one pounding chop on the point where the shoulder socket meets the collar-bone. He started the strike with the arm quite relaxed, converting the speed into power at the last possible moment. The impact made Guillam scream "Christ!" and lifted him straight out of his seat as the car veered to the right.

Fawn had an arm round Jerry's neck and with his other hand he was trying to press Jerry's head over it, which would definitely have killed him. But there is a blow they teach at Sarratt for cramped spaces that is called "the tiger's claw" and is delivered by driving the heel of the hand upwards into the opponent's windpipe, keeping the arm crooked and the fingers pressed back for tension. Jerry did that now, and Fawn's head hit the back window so hard that the safety glass starred. In the Mercedes the two Americans went on looking ahead of them, as if they were driving to a state funeral. He thought of squeezing Fawn's windpipe with his finger and thumb but it didn't seem necessary. Recovering his gun from Fawn's waistband, Jerry opened the right-hand door. Guillam made one desperate dive for him, ripping the sleeve of his faithful but very old suit to the elbow. Jerry swung the gun onto his arm and saw his face contort with pain. Fawn got a leg out, but Jerry slammed the door on it and heard him shout "Bastard!" again, and after that he just kept running back toward town, against the stream.

Bounding and weaving between the land-locked cars, he pelted out of the tunnel and up the hill until he reached the little sentry hut. He thought he heard Guillam yelling. He thought he heard a shot, but it could have been a car backfiring. His groin was hurting amazingly, but he seemed to run faster under the impetus of the pain. A policeman on the curb shouted at him, another held out his arms, but Jerry brushed them aside, and they gave him the final indulgence of the round-eye. He ran until he found a cab. The driver spoke no English so he had to point the way. "That's it, sport. Up there. Left, you bloody idiot. That's it —" until they reached her block.

He didn't know whether Smiley and Collins were still there, or whether Ko had turned up, perhaps with Tiu, but there was very little time to play games finding out. He didn't ring the bell because he knew the mikes would pick it up. Instead he fished a card from his wallet, scribbled on it, shoved it through the letter-box, and waited in a crouch, shivering and sweating and panting like a dray-horse while he listened for her tread and nursed his groin. He waited an age, and finally the door opened and she stood there staring at him while he tried to get upright.

"Christ, it's Galahad," she muttered. She wore no make-up and Ricardo's claw marks were deep and red. She wasn't crying; he didn't think she did that, but her face looked older than the rest of her. To talk, he drew her into the corridor and she didn't resist. He showed her the door leading to the fire steps.

"Meet me the other side of it in five seconds flat, hear me? *Don't* telephone anybody, *don't* make a clatter leaving, and *don't* ask any bloody silly questions. Bring some warm clothes. Now do it, sport. Don't dither. *Please.*"

She looked at him, at his torn sleeve, and sweat-stained jacket; at his mop of forelock hanging over one eye.

"It's me or nothing," he said. "And believe me, it's a big nothing."

She walked back to her flat alone, leaving the door ajar. But she came out much faster, and for safety's sake she didn't even close the door. On the fire stairs he led the way. She carried a shoulder-bag and wore a leather coat. She had brought a cardigan for him to replace the torn jacket — he supposed Drake's, because it was miles too small, but he managed to squeeze into it. He emptied his jacket pockets into her bag and chucked the jacket down the rubbish chute.

She was so quiet following him that he twice looked back to make sure she was still there. Reaching the ground floor, he peered through the window and drew back in time to see the Rocker in person, accompanied by a heavy subordinate, approach the porter in his kiosk and show him his police pass. They followed the stair as far as the car-park, and she said, "Let's take the red canoe."

"Don't be bloody stupid, we left it in town."

Shaking his head, he led her past the cars into a squalid open-air compound full of refuse and building junk, like the backyard at the Circus. From here, between walls of weeping concrete, a giddy stairway fell toward the town, overhung by black branches and cut into sections by the winding road. The jarring of the downward steps hurt his groin a lot. The first time they reached the road, Jerry took her straight across it. The second time, alerted by the blood-red flash of an alarm light in the distance, he hauled her into the trees to avoid the beam of a police car whining down the hill at speed. At the underpass they found a *pak-pai* and Jerry gave the address.

"Where the hell's that?" she asked.

"Somewhere you don't have to register," said Jerry. "Just shut up and let me be masterful, will you? How much money have you got with you?''

She opened her bag and counted from a fat wallet. ''I won it off Tiu at mah-jong,'' she said, and for some reason he sensed she was romancing.

The driver dropped them at the end of the alley and they walked the short distance to the low gateway. The house had no lights, but as they approached the front door it opened and another couple flitted past them out of the darkness. They entered the hall and the door closed behind them, and they followed a hand-borne pin-light through a short maze of brick walls until they reached a smart interior lobby in which piped music played. On the serpentine sofa in the centre sat a trim Chinese lady with a pencil and a notebook on her lap, to all the world a model chatelaine. She saw Jerry and smiled; she saw Lizzie and her smle broadened.

''For the whole night,'' said Jerry.

''Of course,'' she replied.

They followed her upstairs to a small corridor. The open doors gave glimpses of silk counterpanes, low lights, mirrors. The woman was murmuring prices in Jerry's ear. Jerry chose the least suggestive, declined the offer of a second girl to make up the numbers, gave her money, and ordered a bottle of Rémy Martin. Lizzie followed him in, chucked her shoulder-bag on the bed, and, while the door was still open, broke into a taut laugh of relief.

"Lizzie Worthington," she announced, "this is where they said you'd end up, you brazen bitch, and blow me if they weren't right!"

There was a chaise longue and Jerry lay on it, staring at the ceiling, feet crossed, the brandy glass in his hand. Lizzie took the bed and for a time neither spoke. The place was very still. Occasionally, from the floor above, they heard a cry of pleasure or muffled laughter, once of protest. She went to the window and peered out.

"What's out there?" he asked.

"Bloody brick wall, about thirty cats, stacks of empties."

"Foggy?"

"Vile."

She sauntered to the bathroom, poked around, came out again.

"Sport," said Jerry quietly.

She paused, suddenly wary.

"Are you sober and of sound judgment?"

"Why?"

"I want you to tell me everything you told them. When you've done that, I want you to tell me everything they asked you, whether you could answer it or not. And when you've done that, we'll try to take a little thing called a back-bearing and work out where those bastards all are in the scheme of the universe."

"It's a replay," she said finally.

"What of?"

"I don't know: it's all to be exactly the way it happened before."

"So what happened before?"

"Whatever it was," she said wearily, "it's going to happen again."

21

Nelson

It was one in the morning. She had bathed. She came out of the bathroom wearing a white wrap and no shoes and her hair in a towel.

"They've even got those bits of paper stretched across the loo," she said. "And tooth-mugs in cellophane bags."

She dozed on the bed and he on the sofa, and once she said, "I'd like to, but it doesn't work," and he replied that after being kicked where Fawn had kicked him the libido tended to be a bit quiescent anyway. She told him about her schoolmaster — Mr. Bloody Worthington, she called him — and "her one shot at going straight," and about the child she had borne him out of politeness. She talked about her terrible parents, and about Ricardo and what a sod he was, and how she had loved him, and how a girl in the Constellation bar had advised her to poison him with laburnum, so one day after he had beaten her half to death she put a "damn great dose in his coffee." But perhaps she hadn't got the right stuff, she said, because all that happened was that he was sick for days and "the one thing worse than Ricardo healthy was Ricardo at death's door." How another time she actually got a knife into him while he was in the bath, but all he did was stick a bit of plaster over it and swipe her again.

How when Ricardo did his disappearing act she and Charlie Marshall refused to accept that he was dead, and mounted a "Ricardo Lives!" campaign as they called it, and how Charlie went and badgered his old man, all just as he had described to Jerry. And how Lizzie packed up her rucksack and went down to Bangkok, where she barged straight into the China Airsea suite at the Erawan, intending to beard Tiu, and found herself face to face with Ko instead, having met him only once before, very briefly — at a bun-fight in Hong Kong given by one Sally Cale, an old bull-dyke in the antique trade who pushed heroin on the side. And how that was quite a scene she played, beginning with Ko's sharp instruction to get out, and ending with "nature taking her course," as she put it cheerfully: "Another step on Lizzie Worthington's unswerving road to perdition." So that slowly and deviously, with Charlie Marshall's old man pulling, "and Lizzie pushing, as you might say," they put together a very Chinese contract, to which the main signatories were Ko and Charlie's old man, and the commodities to be transacted were, one, Ricardo and, two, his recently retired life partner, Lizzie.

In which said contract, Jerry learned with no particular surprise, both she and Ricardo gratefully acquiesced.

"You should have let him rot," said Jerry, remembering the twin rings on his right hand, and the Ford car blown to bits.

"But Lizzie hadn't seen it that way at all, and she didn't now. "He was one of us," she said. "Although he was a sod."

But having bought his life, she felt free of him.

"Chinese arrange marriages every day. So why shouldn't Drake and Liese?"

What was all the "Liese" stuff? Jerry asked. Why Liese instead of Lizzie?

She didn't know. Something Drake didn't talk about, she said. There had once been a Liese in his life, he told her, and his fortune-teller had promised him that one day he would get another, and he reckoned Lizzie was near enough, so they gave it a shove and called it Liese and while she was about it she pared her surname to plain Worth.

"Blond bird," she said absently.

The name-change had a practical purpose, too, she said. Having chosen a new name for her, Ko took the trouble to have the local police record of her old one destroyed. "Till that sod Mellon marches in and says he'll get them to rewrite it, with a special mention about me carrying his bloody heroin," she said.

Which brought them back to where they were now. And why.

To Jerry, their sleepy wanderings occasionally had the calm of after-love. He lay on the divan, wide awake, but Lizzie talked between dozes, taking up her story dreamily where she had left it when she fell asleep, and he knew that near enough she was telling him the truth, because it made nothing of her that he did not already know, and understand. He realised also that with time Ko had become another anchor for her, somewhat as the schoolmaster had. He gave her the authority from which to survey her odyssey.

"Drake never broke a promise in his life," she said once, as she rolled over and sank back into a fitful sleep. Jerry remembered the orphan: just never lie to me.

Hours, lifetimes later, she was woken by a squawk of ecstasy next door.

"Christ," she declared appreciatively, "she *really* hit the moon." The squawk repeated itself. She changed her mind. "No go," she said disapprovingly. "She's faking it." Silence. "You awake?" she asked.

"Yes."

"What are you going to do?"

"Tomorrow?"

"Yes."

"I don't know," he said.

"Join the club," she whispered, and seemed to fall asleep again.

I need that Sarratt brief again, he thought. Very badly I need it. Put in a limbo call to Craw, he thought. Ask dear old George for a spot of that philosophical advice he's taken to doling out these days. He must be around. Somewhere.

Smiley was around, but at that moment he could not have given Jerry any help at all. He would have traded all his knowledge for a little understanding. The isolation ward had no night-time, so they lay or lounged under the punctured daylight of the ceiling, the three Cousins and Sam on one side of the room, Smiley and Guillam on the other, and Fawn striding up and down the line of the cinema seats, looking caged and furious and squeezing what appeared to be a squash-ball in each fist. His lips were black and swollen and one eye was shut. A clot of blood under his nose refused to go away. Guillam had his right arm strapped to his shoulder and his eyes were on Smiley all the while. But so were the eyes of everyone — or everyone but Fawn. A phone rang, but it was the communications room upstairs saying Bangkok had reported Jerry traced for certain as far as Vientiane.

"Tell them the trail's cold, Murphy," Martello ordered, his eyes still on Smiley. "Tell them any damn thing. Just get them off our backs. Right, George?"

Smiley nodded.

"Right," said Guillam firmly, speaking for him.

"The trail's cold, honey," Murphy echoed into the phone. The "honey" came as a surprise. Murphy had not till now shown such signs of human tenderness. "You want to make a signal or do I have to do it for you? We're not interested, right? Kill it."

He rang off.

"Rockhurst has found her car," Guillam said for the second time, while

Smiley still stared ahead of him. "In an underground car-park in Central. There is a hire-car down there too. Westerby rented it. Today. In his work name. George?"

Smiley gave a nod so slight it might have been no more than an attack of sleepiness he had staved away.

"At least he's doing something, George," said Martello pointedly down the room from his own small caucus of Collins and the quiet men. "Some people would say, when you have a rogue elephant, best thing to do is go out there and shoot him."

"You have to find him first," snapped Guillam, whose nerves were at breaking-point.

"I'm not even sure George wants to do that, Peter," Martello said, in a reprise of his avuncular style. "I think George may be lifting his eye from the ball a little on this, to the grave peril of our common enterprise."

"What do you want George to do?" Guillam rejoined tartly. "Walk the streets till he finds him? Have Rockhurst circulate his name and description, so that every journalist in town knows there's a man-hunt for him?''

At Guillam's side Smiley remained hunched and inert like an old man.

''Westerby's a professional,'' Guillam insisted. ''He's not a natural, but he's good. He can lie up for months in a town like this and Rockhurst wouldn't get a scent of him.''

''Not even with the girl in tow?'' said Murphy.

His strapped arm notwithstanding, Guillam stooped to Smiley: ''It's your operation,'' he whispered urgently. ''If you say we've got to wait, we'll wait. Just give the order. All these people want is an excuse to take over. Anything but a vacuum. Anything.''

Prowling the line of the cinema chairs, Fawn gave vent to a sarcastic murmur: ''Talk, talk, talk. That's all they can do.''

Martello tried again: ''George. Is this island British or is it not? You guys can shake this town out any time.'' He pointed to a windowless wall. ''We have a man out there — your man — who seems bent on running amok. Nelson Ko is the biggest catch you or I are ever likely to land. The biggest of my career, and — I will stake my wife, my grandmother, and the deeds of my plantation — the biggest even of yours.''

''No takers,'' said Sam Collins, the gambler, through his grin.

Martello stuck to his guns: ''Are we going to let him rob us of the prize, George, sit here passively asking one another how it came about that Jesus Christ was born on Christmas Day and not on December twenty-sixth or twenty-seventh?''

Smiley peered at Martello at last, then up at Guillam, who stood stiffly at his side, tipping back his shoulders to support the sling, and finally he looked downward at his own, locked, conflicting hands, and for a period quite meaningless in time he studied himself in his mind, and reviewed his quest for Karla, whom Ann called his ''black Grail.'' He thought of Ann and her repeated betrayals of him in the name of her own Grail, which she called love. He recalled how against his better judgment he had tried to share her faith and, like a true believer, renew it each day, despite her anarchic interpretations of its meaning. He thought of Haydon, steered at Ann by Karla. He thought of Jerry and the girl, and he thought of Peter Worthington, her husband, and the dog-like look of kinship which Worthington had bestowed on him when he called to interview him in the terrace house in Islington: "You and I are the ones they leave behind," ran the message.

He thought of Jerry's other tentative loves along his untidy trail, the half-paid bills the Circus had picked up for him, and it would have been handy to lump Lizzie in with them as just one more, but he couldn't do that. He was not Sam Collins, and he had not the smallest doubt that at this moment Jerry's feeling for the girl was a cause Ann would warmly have espoused. But he was not Ann either. For a cruel moment nevertheless, as he sat still locked in indecision, he did honestly wonder whether Ann was right and his striving had become nothing other than a private journey among the beasts and villains of his own insufficiency, in which he ruthlessly involved simplistic minds like Jerry's.

You're wrong, sport. Don't know how, don't know why, but you're wrong.

The fact that I am wrong, Smiley had once replied to Ann, in the midstream of one of their endless arguments, *does not make you right.*

He heard Martello again, speaking in present time: "George, we have people waiting with *open arms* for what we can give them. What Nelson can."

A phone was ringing. Murphy took the call and relayed the message to the silent room: "Land-line from the aircraft carrier, sir. Navy int. has the junks dead on schedule, sir. South wind favourable and good fishing along the way. Sir, I don't even think Nelson's riding with them. I don't see why he should."

The focus shifted abruptly to Murphy, who had never before been heard to express an opinion.

"What the hell's *that,* Murphy?" Martello demanded quite astonished.

"You been to the fortune-teller too, son?"

"Sir, I was down on the carrier this morning and those people have a lot of data. They can't figure why anybody who lives in Shanghai would ever want to exit out of Swatow. They would do it all different, sir. They would fly or train to Canton, then take the bus maybe to Waichow. They say that's a lot safer, sir."

"These are Nelson's people," Smiley said as the heads swung sharply back on him. "They're his clan. He would rather be at sea with them, even if he's at risk. He trusts them." He turned to Guillam. "We'll do this," he said. "Tell Rockhurst to distribute a description of Westerby and the girl together. You say he hired the car under his work name? Used his escape papers?"

"Yes."

"Worrell?"

"Yes."

"The police are looking for a Mr. and Mrs. Worrell then, British. No photographs, and make sure the descriptions are vague enough not to arouse suspicion. Marty."

Martello was all attentiveness.

"Is Ko still on his boat?" Smiley asked.

"Nestled right in there with Tiu, George."

"It's just possible Westerby may try to reach him. You have a static post at the quayside. Put more men down there."

"What are they looking for?"

"Trouble. The same goes for surveillance on his house. Tell me —" He sank into his thoughts a moment, but Guillam need not have worried. "Tell me, can you simulate a fault on Ko's home telephone line?"

Martello glanced at Murphy.

"Sir, we don't have the apparatus handy," Murphy said, "but I guess we could. . . ."

"Then cut it," Smiley said simply. "Cut the whole cable if necessary. Try and do it near some road-works."

Having dispensed his orders, Martello came lightly across the room and sat himself at Smiley's side.

"Ah, George, about tomorrow, now. Do you think we might, ah, put a little hardware on stand-by as well?" From the desk where he was telephoning Rockhurst, Guillam watched the dialogue most intently. From across the room so did Sam Collins. "Just seems there's no telling what your man Westerby might do, George. We have to be prepared for all emergencies, right?"

"By all means stand anything by. But for the time being, if you don't mind, we'll leave the interception plans as they are. And the competence with me."

"Sure, George. Sure," said Martello fulsomely, and with the same church-like reverence tiptoed back to his own camp.

"What did he want?" Guillam demanded in a low voice, crouching at Smiley's side. "What's he trying to get you to agree to?"

"I will not have it, Peter," Smiley warned, also under his breath. He was suddenly very angry. "I shall not hear you again. I shall not tolerate your Byzantine notions of a palace plot. These people are our hosts and our Allies. We have a written agreement with them. We have quite enough to worry about already without grotesque and — I may tell you honestly — paranoid fancies. Now please —''

''I tell *you!*'' Guillam began, but Smiley closed him down.

''I want you to get hold of Craw. Call on him, if necessary. Perhaps the journey would do you good. Tell him Westerby's on the rampage. He's to let us know at once if he has word of him. He'll know what to do.''

Still walking the line of seats, Fawn watched Guillam leave, while his fists continued restlessly kneading whatever was inside them.

In Jerry's world it was also three in the morning, and the madame had found him a razor, but no fresh shirt. He had shaved and cleaned himself up as best he could, but his body still ached from head to toe. He stood over Lizzie where she lay on the bed and promised to be back in a couple of hours, but he doubted whether she even heard him. *The more papers which are printing pretty girls in preference to politics today,* he remembered Ko saying, *the more chance we get of a damn sight better world.*

He took *pak-pais,* knowing they were less under the thumb of the police. Otherwise he walked, and the walking helped his body and his mystical process of decision-taking, because back there on the divan it had suddenly become impossible. He needed to move in order to find direction. He was heading for Deep Water Bay, and he knew he was entering badland. Now that he was on the loose, they would be on to that launch like leeches. He wondered who they had, what they were using. If it was the Cousins, he would look for too much hardware, and overmanning.

Rain was coming on and he feared it would clear the fog. Above him the moon was already partly free, and as he padded silently down the hill he could make out by its pale light the nearest stockbroker junks groaning and tugging at their moorings. A south-east wind, he noticed, and rising. If it's a static observation post, they'll go for height, he thought, and sure enough there on the promontory to his right he saw a battered-looking

Mercedes van tucked between the trees, and the aerial with its Chinese streamers.

He waited, watching the fog roll, till a car came down the hill with its lights full on, and as soon as it was past him he darted across the road, knowing that not all the hardware in the world would enable them to see him behind the advancing headlights. At the water's level the visibility was down to zero, and he had to grope in order to pick out the rickety wooden causeway he remembered from his previous reconnaissance. Then he found what he was looking for. The same toothless old woman sat in her sampan, grinning up at him through the fog.

"Ko," he whispered. *"Admiral Nelson.* Ko?"

The echo of her cackle bounded away across the water. "Po Toi!" she shouted. "Tin Hau! Po Toi!"

"Today?"

"Today!"

"Tomorrow?"

"Tomollow!"

He tossed her a couple of dollars and

her laughter followed him as he crept away.

I'm right, Lizzie's right, *we're* right, he thought. He's going to the festival. He hoped to God Lizzie was staying put. If she woke up, he wouldnt put it past her to wander.

He walked, trying to stamp away the aching in his groin and back. Take it stage by stage, he thought. Nothing big. Just play it as it comes. The fog was like a corridor leading to different rooms. Once he met an invalid car crawling along the curb as its owner exercised his dog. Once he saw two old men in undervests performing their morning exercises. In a public garden small children stared at him from a rhododendron bush they seemed to have made their home, for their clothes were draped over the branches and they were as naked as the refugee kids in Phnom Penh.

She was sitting up waiting for him when he returned, and she looked terrible.

"Don't do that again," she warned, and shoved her arm through his as they set out to find some breakfast and a boat. "Don't ever bloody walk out on me without waving."

Hong Kong at first possessed no boats at all that day. Jerry would not contemplate the big out-island ferries which took the trippers. He knew the Rocker would have them sewn up. He refused to go down to the bays and make conspicuous enquiries. When he telephoned the listed water-taxi firms, whatever they had was either rented or too small for the voyage. Then he remembered Luigi Tan, the fixer, who was a myth at the Foreign Correspondents' Club; Luigi could get you anything from a Korean dance troupe to a cut-price air ticket faster than any fixer in town. They took a taxi to the other side of Wanchai, where Luigi had his lair, then walked. It was eight in the morning but the hot fog had not lifted. The unlit signs sprawled over the narrow lanes like spent fireworks: "Happy Boy," "Lucky Place," "Americana." The crowded food-stalls added their warm smells to the reek of petrol fumes and soot. Through splits in the wall they sometimes glimpsed a canal. "Anyone tell you where to find me," Luigi Tan liked to say. "Ask for the big guy with one leg."

They found him behind the counter of his shop, just tall enough to look over it, a tiny, darting half-Portuguese who had once earned a living Chinese-boxing in the grimy booths of Macao. The front of the shop was six feet wide. His wares were new motor-bikes and relics of the old China service, which he called antiques: daguerreo-types of hatted ladies in tortoise-shell frames, a battered travelling box, an opium clipper's log.

Luigi knew Jerry already but he liked Lizzie much better, and insisted that she go ahead so that he could study her hind quarters while he ushered them under a washing line to an outhouse marked "Private," with three chairs and a telephone on the floor. Crouching till he was rolled into a neat ball, Luigi talked Chinese to the telephone and English to Lizzie. He was a grandfather, he said, but virile, and had four sons, all good. Even Number Four son was off his hands. All good drivers, good workers, and good husbands. Also, he said to Lizzie, he had a Mercedes complete with stereo.

"Maybe I take you ride in it one day," he said.

Jerry wondered whether she realised that he was proposing marriage, or perhaps something slightly less.

And yes, Luigi thought he had a boat as well.

After two phone calls he knew he had a boat, which he only ever lent to friends, at a nominal cost. He gave Lizzie his credit-card case to count the number of cards, then his wallet to admire the family snaps, one of which showed a lobster caught by Number Four son on the day of his recent wedding, though the son was not visible.

"Po Toi bad place," said Luigi Tan to Lizzie, still on the telephone. "Very dirty place. Rough sea, lousy festival, bad food. Why you want to go there?"

For Tin Hau of course, Jerry said patiently, answering for her. For the famous temple and the festival.

Luigi Tan preferred to speak to Lizzie.

"You go Lantau," he advised. "Lantau

good island. Nice food, good fish, nice people. I tell them you go Lantau, eat at Charlie's. Charlie my friend."

"Po Toi," said Jerry firmly.

"Po Toi hell of a lot of cash."

"We've got a hell of a lot of cash," said Lizzie with a lovely smile, and Luigi looked at her again, contemplatively, the long up-and-down look.

"Maybe I come with you," he said to her.

"No," said Jerry.

Luigi drove them to Causeway Bay and rode with them on the sampan. The boat was a fourteen-foot power boat, common as driftwood, but Jerry reckoned she was sound and Luigi said she had a deep keel. A boy lounged on the stern, trailing one foot in the water.

"My nephew," said Luigi, ruffling the boy's hair proudly. "He got mother in Lantau. He take you Lantau, eat Charlie's place, give you good time. You pay me later."

"Old Boy," said Jerry patiently. "Sport. We don't want Lantau. We want Po Toi. Only Po Toi. Po Toi or nothing.

Drop us there and go."

"Po Toi bad weather, bad festival. Bad place. Too near China. Lot of Commies."

"Po Toi or nothing," Jerry said.

"Boat too small," said Luigi with a frightful loss of face, and it took all Lizzie's charm to build him up again.

For another hour the boys primed the boat, and all Jerry and Lizzie could do was sit in the half-cabin keeping out of sight and sip judicious shots of Rémy Martin. Periodically one or the other of them sank into a private reverie. When Lizzie did this, she hugged herself and rocked slowly on her haunches, head down. Whereas Jerry yanked at his forelock, and once he yanked so hard she touched his arm to stop him, and he laughed.

Almost carelessly they pulled away from the harbour.

"Stay out of sight," Jerry ordered and for safety's sake put his arm round her to keep her in the meagre shelter of the open cabin.

The American aircraft carrier had stripped off her ornamental garb and lay grey and menacing, like an unsheathed knife, above the water. At first they had nothing but the same sticky calm. On the shore, shelves of fog pressed on the grey high-rises, and brown smoke columns slid into a white expressionless sky. On the flat water their boat felt high as a balloon. But as they slipped the shelter and headed east, the waves slapped her sides hard enough to wind her, the bow pitched and cracked, and they had to brace themselves to keep upright. With the little bow lifting and tugging like a bad horse, they tumbled past cranes and godowns and factories and the stumps of quarried hillsides.

They were running straight into the wind and spray was flying on all sides. The coxswain at the wheel was laughing and crowing to his mate, and Jerry supposed it was the mad round-eyes they were laughing at, who chose to do their courting in a pitching tub. A giant tanker passed them, not seeming to move, brown junks running in her wake. From the dockyards, where a freighter was laid to, the white flashes of the welders' lamps signalled to them across the water.

The boys' laughter eased and they began to talk sensibly because they were at sea. Looking back between the swaying walls of transport ships, Jerry saw the Island drawing slowly away from him, cut like a table mountain by the cloud. Once more Hong Kong was ceasing to exist.

They passed another headland. As the sea roughened, the pitching steadied and the cloud above them dropped until its base was only a few feet above their mast, and for a while they stayed in this lower, unreal world, advancing under cover of its protective blanket. The fog ended suddenly and left them in dancing sunlight. Southward, on hills of violent lushness, an orange navigation lamp winked at them through the clear air.

"What do we do now?" she asked softly, looking through the porthole.

"Smile and pray," said Jerry.

A pilot's launch was pulling alongside and for a moment he definitely expected to see the hideous face of the Rocker glowering down on him, but the crew ignored them entirely.

"Who are they?" she whispered. "What do you think?"

"It's routine," said Jerry. "It's meaningless."

The launch veered away. That's it, thought Jerry, with no particular feeling; they've spotted us.

"You sure it was just routine?" she asked.

"Hundreds of boats go to the festival," he said.

The boat bucked violently and kept bucking. Great seaworthiness, he thought, hanging on to Lizzie. Great keel. If this goes on, we won't have anything to decide. The sea will do it for us. It was one of those trips where if you made it, nobody noticed, and if you didn't, they'd say you threw your life away. The east wind could swirl right round on itself at any moment, he thought. In the season between moonsoons, nothing was ever sure. He listened anxiously to the erratic galloping of the engine. If it gives up, we'll finish on the rocks.

Suddenly his nightmares multiplied unreasonably. The butane, he thought;

Christ, the butane! While the boys were preparing the boat, he had glimpsed two cylinders stowed in the front hold beside the water tanks, presumably for cooking Luigi's lobsters. Fool that he was, he had made nothing of them till now. He worked it out. Butane is heavier than air. All cylinders leak. It's just a question of degree. With this sea pounding the bows, they leak faster, and the escaped gas will now be lying in the bilge about two feet from the spark of the engine, with a nice blend of oxygen to assist combustion.

Lizzie had slipped from his grasp and stood astern. The sea was suddenly crowded. Out of nowhere, a fleet of fishing junks had gathered, and she was gazing at them earnestly. Grabbing her arm, he hauled her back to the cover of the cabin.

"Where do you think you are?" he shouted. "Bloody Cowes?"

She studied him a moment, then gently kissed him, then kissed him again.

"You calm down," she warned. She kissed him a third time, muttered "*Yes,*" as if her expectations had been fulfilled, then sat quiet for a while, looking at the deck but keeping hold of his hand.

Jerry reckoned they were making five knots into the wind. A small plane zoomed overhead. Holding her out of sight, he looked up sharply, but was too late to read the markings.

And good morning to *you*, he thought.

They were rounding the last point, tossing and groaning in the spray. Once, the propellers lifted clean out of the water with a roar. As they hit the sea again, the engine faltered, choked, but decided to stay alive. Touching Lizzie's shoulder, Jerry pointed ahead of them to where the bare, steep island of Po Toi loomed like a cut-out against the cloud-torn sky: two peaks, sheer from the water, the larger to the south, and a saddle between.

The sea had turned iron blue and the wind ripped over it, slapping the breath from their mouths and hurling spray at them like hail. On the port bow lay Beaufort Island: a lighthouse, a jetty, no inhabitants. The wind dropped as though it had never been. Not a breeze greeted them as they entered the unruffled water of the island's lee. The sun's heat was direct and harsh. Ahead of them, perhaps a mile, lay the mouth of Po Toi's main bay, and behind it the low brown ghosts of China's islands.

Soon they could make out a whole untidy fleet of junks and cruise boats jamming the bay. The first jingle of drums and cymbals and unco-ordinated chanting floated to them across the water. On the hill behind lay the shanty village, its tin roofs twinkling, and on its own small headland stood one solid building, the temple of Tin Hau, with a bamboo scaffold lashed round it in a rudimentary grandstand, and a large crowd with a pall of smoke hanging over it and dabs of gold between.

"Which side was it?" he asked her.

"I don't know. We climbed to a house and walked from there."

Each time he spoke to her, he looked at her, but now she avoided his gaze. Tapping the coxswain on the shoulder, he pointed the course he wanted him to take. The boy at once began protesting.

Squaring to him, Jerry showed him a bunch of money, pretty well all he had left. With an ill grace the boy swung across the mouth of the harbour, weaving between the boats toward a small granite headland where a tumbledown jetty offered a risky landing. The din of the festival was much louder. They could smell charcoal and suckling pig, and hear concerted bursts of laughter, but for the time being the crowd was out of sight to them, as they were to the crowd.

"Here!" Jerry yelled. "Put in here. Now! *Now!*"

The jetty leaned drunkenly as they clambered onto it. They had not even reached land before their boat had turned for home. Nobody said goodbye. They climbed up the rock hand in hand and walked straight into a money game that was being watched by a large and laughing crowd. At the centre stood a clownish old man with a bag of coins, and he was throwing them down the rock one by one while barefooted boys hurled themselves after them, pushing each other almost to the cliff-edge in their zeal.

"They took a boat," Guillam said. "Rockhurst has interviewed the proprietor. The proprietor is a friend of Westerby's and yes it was Westerby and a beautiful girl, and they wanted to go to Po Toi for Tin Hau."

"And how did Rockhurst play that?" Smiley asked.

"Said in that case it wasn't the couple he was looking for. Bowed out. Disappointed. The harbour police have also belatedly reported sighting it on course for the festival."

"Want us to put up a spotter plane, George?" Martello asked nervously. "Navy int. have all sorts standing by."

Murphy had a bright suggestion: "Why don't we just go right in with choppers and scoop Nelson off that end junk?" he demanded.

"Murphy, shut up," Martello said.

"They're making for the island," Smiley said firmly. "We know they are. I don't think we need air cover to prove it."

Martello was not satisfied. "Then maybe we should send a couple of people out to that island, George. Maybe we ought to do a little interfering, finally.''

Fawn was standing stock-still. Even his fists had stopped working.

"No," said Smiley.

At Martello's side Sam Collins grinned a little thinly.

"Any reason?" Martello asked.

"Right up to the last minute, Ko has one sanction. He can signal his brother not to come ashore," Smiley said. "The merest hint of a disturbance on the island could persuade him to do that."

Martello gave a nervous, angry sigh. He had put aside the pipe he sometimes smoked and was drawing heavily on Sam's supply of brown cigarettes, which seemed to be endless.

"George, what does this man *want?*" he demanded in exasperation. "Is this a blackmail thing now, a disruption? I don't see a category here." A dreadful thought struck him. His voice dropped and he pointed with the full length of his arm across the room. "Now just don't tell me we got one of these *new* ones on our hands, for Christ's sakes! Don't tell me he's one of those cold-war converts with a middle-aged mission to wash his soul in public. Because if he is, and if we are going to read this guy's frank life story in the *Washington Post* next week, George, I personally am going to put the whole Fifth Fleet on that island, if that's what it takes to hold him down." He turned to Murphy. "I have contingencies, right?"

"Right."

"George, I want a landing party on stand-by. You guys can come aboard or stay home. Please yourselves."

Smiley stared at Martello, then at Guillam, with his strapped and useless arm, then at Fawn, who was poised like a diver at the end of a spring-board, eyes half closed and heels together, while he lifted himself slowly up and down on his toes.

"Fawn and Collins," Smiley said at last.

"You two boys take them to the aircraft carrier and hand them right over to the people there. Murphy comes back."

A smoke cloud marked the place where

Collins had been sitting. Where Fawn had stood, two squash-balls slowly rolled a distance before coming to a halt.

"God help us all," somebody murmured fervently. It was Guillam, but Smiley ignored him.

The lion was three men long and the crowd was laughing because it nipped at them and because self-appointed picadors were prodding it with sticks while it lolloped in dance steps down the narrow path, to the clatter of the drums and cymbals. Reaching the headland, the procession slowly turned itself and started to retrace its steps, and at this point Jerry drew Lizzie quickly into the middle of it, bending low in order to make less of his height. At first the track was mud and full of puddles, but soon the dance was leading them past the temple and down concrete steps toward a sand beach where the suckling pigs were being roasted.

"Which way?" he asked her.

She led him quickly left, out of the dance, along the back of a shanty village and over a wooden bridge across an inlet. They climbed along a fringe of cypress trees, Lizzie leading, until they were alone again, standing over the perfect horseshoe bay, looking down on Ko's *Admiral Nelson* where she lay at the very centre point, like a grand lady among the hundreds of pleasure boats and junks around her. There was nobody visible on deck, not even crew. A clutch of grey police boats, five or six of them, was anchored farther out to sea.

And why not, thought Jerry, since this was a festival?

She had let go his hand, and when he turned to her, she was still staring at Ko's launch and he saw the shadow of confusion in her face.

"Is this really the way he brought you?" he asked.

It was the way, she said; and turned to him, to look; to comfirm or weigh things in her mind. Then with her forefinger she gravely traced his lips as if examining the point where she had kissed them. "Jesus," she said, and as gravely shook her head.

They started climbing again. Glancing up, Jerry saw the brown island peak deceptively near, and on the hillside groups of rice terraces gone to ruin. They entered a small village populated by nothing but surly dogs, and the bay vanished from sight. The schoolhouse was open and empty. Through the doorway they saw charts of fighting aircraft. Washing jars stood on the step. Cupping her hands, Lizzie rinsed her face. The huts were slung with wire and brick to anchor them against typhoons. The path turned to sand and the going grew harder.

"Still right?" he asked.

"It's just *up,*" she said, as if she were sick of telling him. "It's just *up,* and then the *house,* and bingo. I mean Christ, what do you think I am, a bloody nitwit?"

"I didn't say a thing," said Jerry. He put his arm round her and she pressed in to him, giving herself exactly as she had done on the dance floor.

They heard a blare of music from the temple as somebody tested the loudspeakers, and after it the wail of a slow tune. The bay was in view again. A crowd had gathered on the shore. Jerry saw more puffs of smoke and, in the windless heat of this side of the island, caught a whiff of joss. The water was blue and clear and calm. Round it, white lights burned on poles. The Ko launch had not stirred, nor had the police.

"See him?" he asked.

She stood apart from him. She was studying the crowd. She shook her head. "Probably having a kip after lunch," she said.

The beating of the sun was ferocious. When they entered the shadow of the hillside it was like a sudden dusk, and when they reached the sunlight it stung their faces like the heat of a close fire. The air was alive with dragonflies, the hillside strewn with big boulders, but where bushes grew they wound and straggled, producing rich trumpets, red and white and yellow. Old picnic cans lay in profusion.

"And that's the house?"

"I told you," she said.

It was a ruin: a broken villa with gaping walls and a view. It had been built with some grandeur above a dried-up stream and was reached by a concrete foot-bridge. The mud stank and hummed with insects. Between palms and bracken the remains of a verandah gave a vast prospect of the sea and of the bay. As they crossed the foot-bridge, he took her arm.

"So let's play it from here," he said. "No interrogations. Just tell."

"We walked up here. Like I said. Me, Drake, and bloody Tiu. The boys brought a basket and the booze. I said 'Where are we going?' and he said 'Picnic.' Tiu didn't want me but Drake said I could come. 'You *hate* walking,' I said. 'I've never even seen you even cross a *road* before!' 'Today we walk,' he says, doing his Captain of Industry act. So I tag along and shut up."

A thick cloud was already obscuring the peak above them and rolling slowly down the hill. The sun had vanished. In moments the cloud reached them and they were alone at the world's end, unable to see even their feet. They groped their way into the house. She sat apart from him on a roof beam. Chinese slogans were daubed

1111

in red paint down the door pillars. The floor was littered with picnic refuse and long twists of lining paper.

"He tells the boys to hop it, so they hop it," she went on. "Him and Tiu have a long earnest natter in whatever they're speaking this week, and half-way through lunch he breaks into English and tells me Po Toi's *his* island. It's where he first landed when he left China. The boat people dumped him here. 'My people,' he calls them. That's why he comes to the festival every year and that's why he gives money to the temple, and that's why we've sweated up the bloody hill for a picnic. Then they go back into Chinese and I get the feeling Tiu is tearing him off a strip for talking too much, but Drake's all excited and little-boy and he won't listen. Then they go on up."

"*Up?*"

"Up to the top. 'Old ways are the best,' he says to me. 'We shall stick to what is proven.' Then his Baptist bit — 'Hold fast to that which is good, Liese. That is what God likes.' "

Jerry glanced into the fog-bank above

him, and he could have sworn he heard the crackle of a small plane, but at that moment he didn't mind too much whether it was there or not, because he had the two things he most badly needed. He had the girl with him, and he had the information: for now he finally understood exactly what she had been worth to Smiley and Sam Collins, and how she had unconsciously betrayed to them the vital clue to Ko's intentions.

"So they went on to the top. Did you go with them?"

"No."

"Did you see where they went?"

"To the top. I told you."

"Then what?"

"They looked down the other side. Talked. Pointed. More talk, more pointing. Then down they come again and Drake's even more excited, the way he gets when he's brought off a big deal and Number One's not there to disapprove. Tiu looks dead solemn, and that's the way he gets when Drake acts fond of me. Drake wants to stay and have a couple of brandies, so Tiu goes back to Hong Kong in a huff. Drake gets amorous and decides we'll spend the night on the boat and go home in the morning, so that's what we do.''

"Where does he moor the boat? Here? In the bay?''

"No.''

"Where?''

"Off Lantau.''

"You went straight there, did you?''

She shook her head. "We did a round of the island.''

"This island?''

"There was a place he wanted to look at in the dark. A bit of coast round the other side. The boys had to shine the lamps on it. 'That's where I land in 'fifty-one,' he says. 'The boat people were frightened to put in to the main harbour. They were frightened of police and ghosts and pirates and customs men. They say the islanders will cut their throats.' ''

"And in the night?'' said Jerry. "While you were moored off Lantau?''

"He told me he had a brother and loved him.''

"That was the first time he told you?''

She nodded.

"He tell you where the brother was?"

"No."

"But you knew?"

This time she didn't even nod.

From below, the clatter of the festival rose through the cloud. He lifted her gently to her feet.

"Bloody questions," she muttered.

"They're nearly over," he promised. He kissed her and she let him, but did not otherwise take part.

"Let's go up there and take a look," he said.

Ten minutes more and the sunlight returned and blue sky opened above them. With Lizzie leading, they scrambled quickly over several false peaks toward the saddle. The sounds from the bay stopped and the colder air filled with screaming, wheeling gulls. They approached the crest, the path widened, they walked side by side. A few steps more and the wind hit them with a force that made them gasp and reel back. They were at the knife-edge, looking down into an abyss. At their very feet the cliff fell vertical to a boiling sea, and the foam smothered the headlands. Dumpling clouds were blowing from the east and behind them the sky was black. Two hundred metres down lay an inlet which the breakers did not cover. Fifty yards out from it, a shoal of rock checked the sea's force, and the spume washed it in white rings.

"That it?" he yelled above the wind. "He landed there? That bit of coast?"

"Yes."

"Shone the lights on it?"

"Yes."

Leaving her where she stood, he moved slowly up the knife-edge, crouching almost double while the wind rushed over his ears and covered his face in a sticky salt sweat and his stomach screamed in pain from what he supposed was a punctured gut or internal bleeding or both. At the inmost point before the cliff cut back into the sea, he looked down once more, and now he thought he could just make out a skimpy path, sometimes no more than a seam of rock or a ridge of rough grass, ekeing its way cautiously toward the inlet. There was no sand in the inlet but some of the rocks looked dry. Returning to her, he led her away from the knife-edge. The wind dropped and they heard the din of the festival again, much louder than before. The snap of firecrackers made a toy war.

"It's his brother Nelson," he explained. "In case you hadn't gathered. Ko's bringing him out of China. Tonight's the night. Trouble is, he's a much sought-after character. Lot of people would like a chat with him. That's where Mellon came in." He took a breath. "My view is that you should get the hell out of here. How do you see that? Drake's not going to want you around, that's for sure."

"Is he going to want you?" she asked.

"I think what you should do, you should go back to the harbour. Are you listening?"

She managed "Of course I am."

"You look for a nice friendly-looking round-eye family. Choose the woman, for once, not the bloke. Tell her you've had a row with your boy-friend and can they take you home in their boat? If they'll have you, stay the night with them; otherwise go to a hotel. Spin them one of your stories. Christ, that's no problem, is it?''

A police helicopter pattered overhead in a long curve, presumably to observe the festival. Instinctively he grabbed her shoulders and drew her back to the rock.

''Remember the second place we went — the big-band sound — the bar?'' He was still holding her.

She said, ''Yes.''

''I'll pick you up there tomorrow night.''

''I don't know,'' she said.

''Be there at seven. At seven, got it?''

She pushed him gently away from her, as if she were determined to stand alone.

''Tell him I kept faith,'' she said. ''It's what he cares about most. I stuck to the deal. If you see him, tell him, 'Liese stuck to the deal.' ''

''Sure.''

''Not *sure. Yes.* Tell him. He did everything he promised. He said he'd look after me. He did. He said he'd let Ric go. He did that, too. He always stuck to a deal.''

She was looking down. He raised her head, holding it with both his hands, but she insisted on going on.

"And tell him — and tell him — tell him they made it impossible. They fenced me in."

"Be there from seven on," he said. "Even if I'm a bit late. Now come on, that's not too difficult, is it? You don't need a university degree to hoist that aboard." He was gentling her, battling for a smile, striving for a last complicity before they separated.

She wanted to say something but it didn't work. She took a few steps, turned and looked back at him, and he waved — one big flap of the arm. She took a few more and kept going till she was below the line of the hill, but he did hear her shout "Seven, then," or thought he did. Having watched her out of sight, Jerry returned to the knife-edge, where he sat down for a bit of a breather before the Tarzan stuff. A snatch of John Donne came back to him, one of the few things he had picked up at school, though somehow he never got quotations completely right:

On a huge hill
Cragged and steep, Truth stands,
   and he that will
Reach her, about must, and
   about must go.

Or something.

For an hour, deep in thought — two hours — he lay in the lee of the rock and watched the daylight turn to dusk over the Chinese islands a few miles into the sea. Then he pulled off his bucksin boots and re-threaded the laces in a herring-bone, the way he used to thread them for his cricket boots. Then he put them on again and tied them as tight as they would go. It could be Tuscany again, he thought, and the five hills which he used to look at from the hornet field. Except that this time he wasn't proposing to walk out on anyone. Not the girl. Not Luke. Not himself. Even if it took a lot of footwork.

"Navy int. has the junk-fleet making around six knots and dead on course," Murphy announced. "Quit the beds right on one one hundred, just like they were following our projection.''

From somewhere he had scrounged a set of bakelite toy boats which he could fix to the chart. Standing, he pointed them proudly in a single column at Po Toi island.

Murphy had returned but his colleague had stayed with Sam Collins and Fawn, so they were four.

''And Rockhurst has found the girl,'' said Guillam quietly, putting down the other phone. His shoulder was acting up and he was extremely pale.

''Where?'' said Smiley.

Still at the chart, Murphy turned.

At his desk, where he was keeping a log of events, Martello put down his pen.

''Picked her up at Aberdeen harbour as she landed,'' Guillam went on. ''She'd cadged a lift back from Po Toi with a clerk and his wife from the Hong Kong & Shanghai Bank.''

''So what's the story?'' Martello demanded before Smiley could speak. ''Where's Westerby?''

''She doesn't know,'' said Guillam.

"Ah, come on!" Martello protested.

"She says they had a row and left in different boats. Rockhurst says give him another hour with her."

Smiley spoke. "And Ko?" he asked. "Where's he?"

"His launch is still in Po Toi harbour," Guillam replied. "Most of the other boats have already left. But Ko's is where it was this morning. Sitting pretty, Rockhurst says, and everyone below."

Smiley peered at the sea chart, then at Guillam, then at the map of Po Toi.

"If she told Westerby what she told Collins," he said, "then he's stayed on the island."

"With what in mind?" Martello demanded very loud. "George, for what purpose is *that* man remaining on *that* island?"

An age went by for all of them.

"He's waiting," Smiley said.

"For *what,* may I enquire?" Martello persisted in the same determined tone.

Nobody saw Smiley's face. It had found its own bit of shadow. They saw his shoulders hunch, they saw his hand rise to his spectacles as if to remove them, they saw it fall back empty in defeat onto the rosewood table.

"Whatever we do, we must let Nelson land," he said firmly.

"And whatever *do* we do?" Martello demanded, getting up and coming round the table. "Westerby's not *here,* George. He never entered the Colony. He can leave by the same damn route!"

"Please don't shout at me," Smiley said.

Martello ignored him. "Which is it going to be, that's all? The conspiracy or the fuck-up?"

Guillam was standing his height, barring the way, and for an extraordinary moment it seemed possible that, broken shoulder notwithstanding, he proposed physically to restrain Martello from coming any closer to where Smiley sat.

"Peter," Smiley said quietly. "I see there's a telphone behind you. Perhaps you'd be good enough to pass it to me."

With the full moon, the wind had dropped and the sea settled. Jerry had not descended all the way to the inlet but made a last camp thirty feet above it, in the cover of a shrub, where he had protection. His hands and knees were cut, and a branch had grazed his cheek, but he felt good: hungry and alert. In the sweat and danger of the scramble he had forgotten his pain. The inlet was larger than he had imagined when he looked down on it from higher up, and the granite cliffs at sea-level were pierced with caves. He was trying to guess Ko's plan. He had been trying all day. What Ko had to do he would do from the sea, because he was not capable of the nightmarish climb down the cliff. Jerry had wondered at first whether Ko might try to intercept Nelson before he landed, but could see no safe way for Nelson to slip the fleet and make a sea-meeting with his brother.

The sky darkened, the stars came, and the path of the moon grew brighter. And Westerby? he thought. What does A do now? A was one hell of a long way from the syndicate solutions of Sarratt, *that* was for sure.

Ko would also be a fool to attempt to

bring his launch to this side of the island, he decided. She was unwieldly and drew too much water to come inshore on a windward coast. A small boat was better, and a sampan or a rubber dinghy best. Clambering down the cliff till his boots hit pebbles, Jerry huddled against the rock, watching the breakers thump and the sparks of phosphorus riding with the spume.

She'll be back by now, he thought. With any luck, she's talked her way into someone's house and is charming the kids and wrapping herself round a cup of Bovril. "Tell him I kept faith," she said.

The moon lifted and still Jerry waited, training his eyes on the darkest spots in an effort to improve his vision. Then, over the clatter of the sea, he could have sworn he heard the awkward slap of water on a wooden hull and the short grumble of an engine switched on and off again. He saw no light. Edging his way along the shadowed rock, he crept as close to the water's edge as he dared and once more crouched, waiting. As a wave of surf soaked him to the thighs, he saw what he was waiting for: against the moon path, not twenty yards from him, the arched cabin and curled prow of a single sampan rocking on its anchor. He heard a splash and a muffled order, and as he sank as low as the slope allowed, he picked out the unmistakable shape of Drake Ko, in his Anglo-French beret, wading cautiously ashore, followed by Tiu carrying an M-16 across both arms. So there you are, thought Jerry. End of the long trail. Luke's killer, Frostie's killer — whether by proxy or in the flesh is immaterial — Lizzie's lover, Nelson's father, Nelson's brother. Welcome to the man who never broke a deal in his life.

Ko also had a burden but it was less ferocious, and Jerry knew long before he made it out that it was a lamp and a power pack, pretty much like those he had used in the Circus water games on the Helford Estuary, except that the Circus favoured ultraviolet, and shoddy wire-framed spectacles which were useless in rain or spray.

Reaching the beach, the two men made their way over the shingle until they reached the highest point; then, like Jerry, they merged against the black rock. He reckoned they were sixty feet from him. He heard a grunt and saw the flame of a cigarette lighter, then the red glow of two cigarettes followed by the murmur of Chinese voices. Wouldn't mind one myself, thought Jerry. Stooping, he spread out one large hand and began loading it with pebbles until it was full, then padded as stealthily as he could manage along the base of the rock toward the two red embers. By his calculation he was eight paces from them. He had the pistol in his left hand and the pebbles in his right, and he was listening to the clump of the waves, how they gathered, tottered, and fell, and he was thinking that it was going to be a lot easier to have a chat with Drake once Tiu was out of the way.

Very slowly, in the classic posture of the outfielder, he leaned back, raised his left elbow in front of him, and crooked his right arm behind him, prepared for a throw at full stretch. A wave fell, he heard the shuffle of the undertow, the grumble as another gathered. Still he waited, right arm back, palm sweating as he clasped the pebbles. Then as the wave reached its height he hurled the pebbles high up the cliff, using all his strength, before ducking to a crouch, gaze fixed upon the embers of the two cigarettes. He waited, then heard the pebbles patter against the rock above him and the hailstorm gather as they tumbled down. In the next instant he heard Tiu's short curse and saw one red ember fly into the air as he leapt to his feet, M-16 in hand, barrel lifted to the cliff and his back to Jerry. Ko was scrambling for cover.

First Jerry hit Tiu very hard with the pistol, taking care to keep his fingers inside the guard. Then he hit him again with his closed right hand, a two-knuckle strike at full force, "with the fist turned down and turning," as they say at Sarratt, and a lot of follow-through at the end. As Tiu went down, Jerry caught his cheekbone with the whole weight of his swinging right boot and heard the snap of his closing jaw. And as he stooped to pick up the M-16 he smashed the butt of it into

Tiu's kidneys, thinking angrily of both Luke and Frost, but also of the cheap crack Tiu had made about Lizzie not rating more than the journey from Kowloon-side to Hong Kong-side. Greetings from the horse-writer, he thought. Then he looked toward Ko, who, having stepped forward, was still no more than a black shape against the sea: a crooked silhouette with piecrust ears sticking out below the line of his odd beret. A strong wind had risen again, or perhaps Jerry was only now aware of it. It rattled in the rocks behind them and made Ko's broad trousers billow.

"That Mr. Westerby, the English newsman?" he enquired, in precisely the deep, harsh tones he had used at Happy Valley.

"The same," said Jerry.

"You're a very political man, Mr. Westerby. What the hell do you want here?"

Jerry was recovering his breath, and for a moment he didn't feel quite ready to answer.

"Mr. Ricardo tells my people it is your

aim to blackmail me. Is money your aim, Mr. Westerby?''

''Message from your girl,'' Jerry said, feeling he should discharge that promise first. ''She says she keeps faith. She's on your side.''

''I don't have a side, Mr. Westerby. I'm an army of one. What do you want? Mr. Marshall tells my people you are some kind of hero. Heroes are very political persons, Mr. Westerby. I don't care for heroes.''

''I came to warn you. They want Nelson. You mustn't take him back to Hong Kong. They've got him all sewn up. They've got plans that will last him the rest of his life. And you as well. They're queueing up for both of you.''

''What do you *want,* Mr. Westerby?''

''A deal.''

''Nobody wants a deal. They want a commodity. The deal obtains for them the commodity. What do you want?'' Ko repeated, raising his voice in command. ''Tell me, please.''

''You bought yourself the girl with Ricardo's life,'' said Jerry. ''I thought I might buy her back with Nelson's. I'll speak to them for you. I know what they want. They'll settle."

That's the last foot in the last door for me, he thought, forever and a day.

"A *political* settlement, Mr. Westerby? With *your* people? I made many political settlements with them. They told me God loved children. Did you ever notice God love an Asian child, Mr. Westerby? They told me God was a *kwailo* and his mother had yellow hair. They told me God was a peaceful man, but I read once that there have never been so many civil wars as in the kingdom of Christ. They told me —"

"Your brother's right behind you, Mr. Ko."

Ko swung round. On their left, heading from the east, a dozen or more junks in full sail trembled southward across the moon path in ragged column, lights prickling in the water. Dropping to his knees, Ko began frantically groping for the lamp. Jerry found the tripod, wrenched it open; Ko stood the lamp on it, but his hands were shaking wildly and Jerry had to help him. Jerry seized the wires, struck a match, and clipped the cables to the terminals. They were staring out to sea, side by side. Ko flashed the lamp once, then again, first red then green.

"Wait," Jerry said softly. "You're too soon. Go easy or you'll muck it all up."

Moving him gently aside, Jerry bent to the eyepiece and scanned the line of boats: "Which one?"

"The last," said Ko.

Holding the last junk in view, though it was still only a shadow, Jerry signalled again, one red, one green, and a moment later heard Ko let out a cry of joy as an answering flicker darted back across the water.

"Can he fix on that?" said Jerry.

"Sure," said Ko, still looking out to sea. "Sure. He will fix on that."

"Then leave it alone. Don't do any more."

Ko turned to him, and Jerry saw the excitement in his face, and felt his dependence.

"Mr. Westerby, I am advising you sincerely: if you have played a trick on me for my brother Nelson, your Christian Baptist hell will be a very comfortable place by comparison with what my people do to you. But if you help me I give you everything. That is my contract and I never broke a contract in my life. My brother also made certain contracts." He looked out to sea. "I am pleased to advise you that he has seen the error of his ways."

The forward junks were out of sight. Only the tail-enders remained. From far away Jerry fancied he heard the uneven rumble of an engine, but he knew his mind was all over the place and it could have been the tumble of the waves. The moon passed behind the peak and the shadow of the mountain fell like a black knife-point onto the sea, leaving the far fields silver. Stooped to the lamp, Ko gave another cry of pleasure.

"Here! Here! Take a look, Mr. Westerby."

Through the eyepiece Jerry made out a single phantom junk, unlit except for three pale lamps, two green ones on the mast and a red one to starboard, making its way toward them. It passed from the silver into the blackness and he lost it. From behind him, he heard a groan from Tiu. Ignoring it, Ko remained stooped to the eyepiece, one arm held wide like a Victorian photographer while he began calling softly in Chinese. Running up the shingle, Jerry pulled the pistol from Tiu's belt, picked up the M-16 again, and, taking both to the sea's edge, chucked them in. Ko was preparing to repeat the signal but mercifully he couldn't find the button and Jerry was in time to stop him.

Once more Jerry thought he heard the rumble, not of one engine but two. Running out onto the headland, he peered anxiously north and south in search of a patrol boat, but again he saw nothing and again he blamed the surf and his strained imagination. The junk was nearer, beating in toward the island, her brown batwing sail suddenly tall and terribly conspicuous against the sky. Ko had run to the water's edge and was waving and yelling across the sea.

"Keep your voice down!" Jerry whispered from beside him.

But Jerry had become an irrelevance: Drake Ko's whole life was for Nelson. From the shelter of the near headland, the sampan tottered alongside the rocking junk. The moon came out of hiding, and for a moment Jerry forgot his anxiety as a little grey-clad figure, small and sturdy, in stature Drake's antithesis, in a kapok coat and bulging proletarian cap, lowered himself over the side and leapt for the waiting arms of the sampan's crew. Drake Ko gave another cry; the junk filled its sails and slid behind the headland till only the green lights on its masthead remained visible above the rocks, and then they too vanished. The sampan was making for the beach, and Jerry could see Nelson's stocky frame as he stood on the bow waving with both hands and Drake Ko in his beret wild on the beach, dancing like a madman, waving back.

The throb of engines grew steadily louder, but still Jerry couldn't place them. The sea was empty, and when he looked upwards he saw only the hammerhead cliff and its peak black against the stars. The brothers met and embraced and stayed locked in each other's arms, not moving.

In a burst of realisation Jerry seized hold of both of them, began pummelling them, and cried out for all his life, "Get back in the boat! Hurry!"

They saw no one but each other. Running back to the water's edge, Jerry grabbed the sampan's prow and held it, still calling to them as he saw the sky behind the peak turn yellow, then quickly brighten as the throb of the engines swelled to a roar and three blinding searchlights burst on them from blackened helicopters. The rocks danced to the whirl of landing lights, the sea furrowed, pebbles bounced and flew around in storms. For a fraction of a second Jerry saw Drake Ko's face turn to him beseeching help, as if too late he had recognised where help lay. He mouthed something but the din drowned it.

Jerry hurled himself forward, not for Nelson's sake, still less for Drake's; but for what linked them, and for what linked him to Lizzie. But long before he reached them a dark swarm closed on the two men, tore them apart, and bundled the baggy shape of Nelson into the hold of one of the helicopters. In the mayhem Jerry had drawn his gun and held it in his hand. He was screaming, though he could not hear himself above the hurricanes of war. The helicopter was lifting. A single figure remained in the open doorway, looking down, and perhaps it was Fawn, for he looked dark and mad. Then an orange flash broke from in front of him, then a second and a third, and after that Jerry wasn't calling any more. In fury he threw up his hands, his mouth still open, his face still silently imploring. Then he fell and lay there. Soon there was once more no sound but the surf flopping on the beach and Drake Ko's hopeless, choking grief against the victorious armadas of the West, which had stolen his brother and left their hard-pressed soldier dead at his feet.

22

Born Again

In the Circus a mood of wild triumph broke out when the grand news came through from the Cousins. Nelson landed, Nelson bagged! Not a hair of his head injured! For two days there was speculation about medals, knighthoods, and promotions. They must do *something* for George at last, they *must!* Not so, said Connie shrewdly from the touch-line. They would never forgive him for raking up Bill Haydon.

The euphoria was followed by certain perplexing rumours. Connie and Doc di Salis, for instance, who were eagerly ensconced in the Maresfield safe house, now dubbed the Dolphinarium, waited a full week for their body to arrive, and waited in vain. So did the interpreters, transcribers, inquisitors, baby-sitters, and allied trades who made up the rest of the reception and interrogation unit there.

The match was rained off, said the housekeepers. Another date would be fixed. Stand by, they said. But quite soon a source at the local estate agent in the neighbouring town of Uckfield revealed that the housekeepers were trying to renege on the lease. Sure enough, after another week the team was stood down "pending policy decisions." It was never reassembled.

Next, word filtered out that Enderby and Martello jointly — the combination even then seemed odd — were chairing an Anglo-American processing committee. It would meet alternately in Washington and London and have responsibility for simultaneous distribution of the Dolphin product, code-name Whitebait, on either side of the Atlantic.

Quite incidentally it emerged that Nelson was somewhere in the United States, in an armed compound already prepared for him in Philadelphia. The explanation was even slower in coming. It was *felt* — presumably *by* somebody, but feelings are hard to trace among so many corridors — that Nelson would be safer there. Physically safer. Think of the Russians. Think of the Chinese. Also, the housekeepers insisted, the Cousins' processing and evaluation units were more of a scale to handle the unprecedented take that was expected. Also, they said, the Cousins could afford the cost. *Also·* —

"Also gammon and spinach!" Connie stormed when she heard the news.

She and di Salis waited moodily to be invited to join the Cousins' team. Connie even got herself the injections to be ready, but no call came.

More explanations. The Cousins had a new man at Harvard, the housekeepers said, when Connie sailed in on them in her wheelchair.

"Who?" she demanded in a fury.

A professor somebody, young, a Moscow-gazer. He had made a *life specialty* of the dark side of Moscow Centre, they said, and had recently published a paper for private distribution only, but based on Company archives, in which he had referred to the "mole principle" and even in veiled terms to Karla's private army.

"Of course he did, the maggot!" she blurted at them, through her bitter tears of frustration. "And he hogged it all from Connie's blasted reports, didn't he? Culpepper, that's his name, and he knows as much about Karla as my left toe!"

The housekeepers were unmoved however by thoughts of Connie's toe. It was Culpepper, not Sachs, who had the new committee's vote.

"Wait till George gets back!" Connie warned them. The threat left them strangely unaffected.

Di Salis fared no better. China-watchers were two a penny in Langley, he was told. A glut on the market, old boy. Sorry, but Enderby's orders, said the housekeepers.

"Enderby's?" di Salis echoed.

The committee's, they said vaguely. It was a joint decision.

So di Salis took his cause to Lacon, who liked to think of himself as a poor man's ombudsman in such matters, and Lacon in turn took di Salis to luncheon, at which they split the bill down the middle because Lacon did not hold with civil servants treating one another at the taxpayers' expense.

"How do you all *feel* about Enderby, by the by?" he asked at some point in the meal, interrupting di Salis's plaintive monologue about his familiarity with the Chiu Chow and Hakka dialects. *Feeling* was playing a large part just at the moment. "Does he go down well over there? I'd have thought you liked his way of seeing things. Isn't he rather sound, wouldn't you say?"

"Sound" in the Whitehall vocabulary in those days meant hawkish.

Rushing back to the Circus, di Salis duly reported this amazing question to Connie Sachs — as Lacon of course wished him to — and Connie was thereafter seen little. She spent her time quietly "packing her trunk," as she called it: that is to say, preparing her Moscow Centre archive for posterity. There was a new young burrower she favoured, a goatish but obliging youth called Doolittle. She made this Doolittle sit at her feet while she gave him of her wisdom.

"The old order's hoofing it," she warned whoever would listen. "That twerp Enderby is oiling through the back door. It's a pogrom."

They treated her at first with much the same derision that Noah had to put up with when he started building his ark. No slouch at tradecraft still, Connie meanwhile secretly took Molly Meakin aside and persuaded her to put in a letter of resignation. "Tell the housekeepers you're looking for something more fulfilling, dear," she advised, with much winking and pinching. "They'll give you a rise at the very least."

Molly had fears of being taken at her word, but Connie knew the game too well. So she wrote her letter and was at once ordered to stay behind after hours. Certain changes were in the air, the housekeepers told her in great confidence. There was a move to create a younger and more vigorous service, with closer links to Whitehall. Molly solemnly promised to reconsider her decision, and

Connie Sachs resumed her packing with fresh determination.

Then where *was* George Smiley all this while? In the Far East? No, in Washington! Nonsense! He was back home and skulking down in the country somewhere — Cornwall was his favourite — taking a well-earned rest and mending his fences with Ann!

Then one of the housekeepers let slip that George might be "suffering from a spot of strain," and his phrase struck a chill everywhere, for even the dimmest little gnome in Banking Section knew that strain, like old age, was a disease for which there was only one known remedy, and it did not entail recovery.

Guillam came back eventually, but only to sweep Molly off on leave, and he refused to say anything at all. Those who saw him on his swift passage through the fifth floor said he looked shot-about, and obviously in need of a break. Also he seemed to have had an accident to his collar-bone; his right shoulder was all strapped up. From the housekeepers it became known that he had spent a couple of days in the care of the Circus leech at his private clinic in Manchester Square. But still there was no Smiley, and the housekeepers showed only a steely bonhomie when asked when he would return. The housekeepers in these cases become the Star Chamber, feared but needed. Unobtrusively Karla's portrait disappeared, the wits said for cleaning.

What was odd, and in a way rather terrible, was that none of them thought to drop in on the little house in Bywater Street and simply ring the doorbell. If they had done so they would have found Smiley there, most likely in his dressing-gown, either clearing up plates or preparing food he didn't eat. Sometimes, usually at dusk, he took himself for a solitary walk in the park and peered at people as if he half recognised them, so that they peered in return, and then looked down. Or he would go and sit himself in one of the cheaper cafés in the King's Road, taking a book for company and sweet tea for refreshment — for he had abandoned his good intentions about saccharin for his waistline. They would have noticed that he spent a deal of time looking at his hands, and polishing his spectacles on his tie, or re-reading the letter Ann had left for him, which was very long, but only because of repetitions.

Lacon called on him and so did Enderby, and once Martello came along with them, dressed in his London character again; for everyone agreed, and none with greater sincerity than Smiley, that in the interest of the service the hand-over should be as smooth and painless as possible. Smiley made certain requests regarding staff and these were carefully noted by Lacon, who let him understand that toward the Circus — if toward no one else — Treasury was at present in a spending mood. In the secret world at least, sterling was on the up. It was not merely the success of the Dolphin affair which accounted for this change of heart, Lacon said. The American enthusiasm for Enderby's appointment had been overwhelming. It had been felt even at the highest diplomatic levels. ''Spontaneous applause'' was how

Lacon described it.

"Saul really knows how to talk to them," he said.

"Oh, does he. Ah, good. Well, good," Smiley said and bucked his head in approval, as the deaf do.

Even when Enderby confided to Smiley that he proposed to appoint Sam Collins as his head of operations, Smiley showed nothing but courtesy toward the suggestion. Sam was a hustler, Enderby explained, and hustlers were what Langley liked these days.

"Ah, yes. No doubt," said Smiley.

The two men agreed that Roddy Martindale, though he had bags of entertainment value, was *not* cut out for the game. Old Roddy really was *too* queer, said Enderby, and the Minister was scared stiff of him. Nor did he exactly go down swimmingly with the Americans, even the ones that happened to be that way themselves. Also, Enderby was a bit chary of taking in any more Etonians. Gave the wrong impression.

A week later the housekeepers reopened Sam's old room on the fifth floor and removed the furniture. Collins's ghost laid for good, said certain unwise voices with relish. Then on the Monday an ornate desk arrived, with a red leather top, and several fake hunting prints from the walls of Sam's club, which was in the process of being taken over by one of the larger gambling syndicates, to the satisfaction of all parties.

Little Fawn was not seen again. Not even when several of the more muscular London outstations were revived, including the Brixton scalp-hunters, to whom he had formerly belonged, and the Acton lamplighters under Toby Esterhase. But he was not missed either. Like Sam Collins somehow, he had stalked the story without ever quite belonging to it; but unlike Sam, he stayed in the thickets when it ended, and never reappeared.

To Sam Collins, on his first day back in harness, fell the task of breaking the sad news of Jerry's death. He did it in the rumpus room, just a small, unaffected speech, and everyone agreed he did it well. They had not thought he had it in him.

"For fifth-floor ears only," he told them. His audience was stunned, then proud. Connie wept and tried to claim Jerry as another of Karla's victims, but she was held back in this for want of information about who or what had killed him. It was operational, went the word, and it was noble.

Back in Hong Kong, the Foreign Correspondents' Club showed much initial concern for its missing children Luke and Westerby. Thanks to heavy lobbying by its members, a full-scale confidential enquiry was set up, under the chairmanship of the vigilant Superintendent Rockhurst, to solve the double riddle of their disappearance. The authorities promised full publication of all findings, and the United States Consul General offered five thousand dollars of his own money to anyone coming forward with helpful information. As a gesture to local feeling he included Jerry Westerby's name in the offer.

The two became known as "the missing newsmen," and suggestions of a disgraceful attachment between them were rampant. Luke's bureau matched the five-thousand-dollar figure, and the dwarf, though he was inconsolable, entered a strong bid to have the moneys paid to him. It was he, after all, working on both fronts at once, who had learned from Deathwish that the Cloudview Road apartment, which Luke had last used, had been redecorated from floor to ceiling before the Rocker's sharp-eyed investigators got round to visiting it. Who ordered this? Who paid? Nobody knew. It was the dwarf also who collected first-hand reports that Jerry had been seen at Kai Tak airport interviewing Japanese package tourists. But the Rockers' committee of enquiry was obliged to reject these reports. The Japanese concerned were "willing but unreliable witnesses," they said, when it came to identifying a round-eye who sprang at them after a long journey.

As to Luke — well, the way he had been going, they said, he was heading for some kind of breakdown anyway. The knowing spoke of amnesia brought on by alcohol and fast living. After a while even the best stories grow cold. Rumours went out that the two men had been seen hunting together during the Hué collapse — or was it Danang? — and drinking together in Saigon. Another had them sitting side by side on the waterfront at Manila.

"Holding hands?" the dwarf asked.

"Worse" was the reply.

The Rocker's name was also in wide circulation, thanks to his success in a recent spectacular narcotics trial mounted with the help of the American Drug Enforcement Administration. Several Chinese and a glamorous English adventuress, a heroin carrier, were featured, and though as usual the Mr. Big was never brought to justice, it was said the Rocker came within an ace of nailing him. "Our tough but honest trouble-shooter," wrote the *South China Morning Post* in an editorial praising his astuteness. "Hong Kong could do with more like him."

For other distractions the Club could turn to the dramatic reopening of High Haven behind a twenty-foot floodlit wire perimeter patrolled by guard dogs. But there were no free lunches any more and the joke soon faded.

As to old Craw, for months he was not seen and not spoken of. Till one night he appeared, looking much aged and soberly dressed, and sat in his former corner gazing into space. A few were still left who recognised him. The Canadian cowboy suggested a rubber of Shanghai bowling, but he declined. Then a strange thing happened. An argument broke out concerning a silly point of Club protocol. Nothing serious at all: whether some item of tradition about signing chits was still useful to the Club's running. As trifling as that. But for some reason it made the old fellow absolutely furious. Rising to his feet, he stomped toward the lifts, tears pouring down his face, while he hurled one insult after another at them.

"Don't change anything," he advised them, shaking his stick in fury. "The old order changeth *not,* let it all run on. You won't stop the wheel — not together, not divided — you snivelling, arse-licking novices! You're a bunch of suicidal tits to try!''

Past it, they agreed, as the doors closed on him. Poor fellow. Embarrassing.

Was there really a conspiracy against Smiley, of the scale that Guillam supposed? If so, how was it affected by Westerby's own maverick intervention? No information is available and even those who trust each other well are not disposed to discuss the question. Certainly there was a secret understanding between Enderby and Martello, that the Cousins should have first bite of Nelson — as well as joint credit for procuring him — against their championship of Enderby for chief. Certainly Lacon and Collins, in their vastly different spheres, were party to it. But at what point they proposed to seize Nelson for themselves and by what means — for instance, the more conventional recourse of a concerted *démarche* at ministerial level in London — will probably never be known. But there can be no doubt, as it turned out, that Westerby was a blessing in disguise.

He gave them the excuse they were looking for.

And did Smiley *know* of the conspiracy, deep down? Was he aware of it, and did he secretly even welcome the solution? Peter Guillam, who has since had two good years in exile in Brixton to consider his opinion, insists that the answer to both questions is a firm *yes*. There is a letter Goerge wrote to Ann Smiley — he says — in the heat of the crisis, presumably in one of the long waiting periods in the isolation ward. Guillam leans heavily on it for his theory. Ann showed it to him when he called on her in Wiltshire, in the hope of bringing about a reconciliation, and though the mission failed, she produced it from her handbag in the course of their talk. Guillam memorised a part, he claims, and wrote it down as soon as he got back to the car. Certainly the style flies a lot higher than anything Guillam would aspire to for himself:

I honestly do wonder, without wishing to be morbid, how I reached this present pass. So far as I can ever remember of my youth, I chose the secret road because it seemed to lead straightest and furthest toward my country's goal. The enemy in those days was someone we could point at and read about in the papers. Today, all I know is that I have learned to interpret the whole of life in terms of conspiracy. That is the sword I have lived by, and as I look round me now I see it is the sword I shall die by as well. These people terrify me, but I am one of them. If they stab me in the back, then at least that is the judgment of my peers.

As Guillam points out, the letter was essentially from Smiley's blue period.

These days, he says, the old boy is much more himself. Occasionally he and Ann have lunches, and Guillam personally is convinced that they will simply get together one day and that will be that. But George never mentions Westerby. And nor does Guillam, for George's sake.